CW01209542

DRAGON BLOOD SERIES

OATHS

BOOK EIGHT

LINDSAY BUROKER

Oaths

by Lindsay Buroker

Copyright © Lindsay Buroker 2018
Cover and Formatting: Deranged Doctor Design

No part of this book may be reproduced, scanned, or distributed in any printed or electronic form without permission. Please do not participate in or encourage piracy of copyrighted materials in violation of the author's rights. Thank you for respecting the hard work of this author.

This is a work of fiction. Names, characters, places, and incidents either are the product of the author's imagination or are used fictitiously, and any resemblance to locales, events, business establishments, or actual persons—living or dead—is entirely coincidental.

Author's Notes

When I wrote *Soulblade* a couple of years ago, I thought I was done with the Dragon Blood series. Oh, a comment from a beta reader enticed me to write *Shattered Past* (Therrik and Lilah's story), but I didn't have any plans to continue on with Ridge, Sardelle, and the gang. Though Bhrava Saruth informed me that it was quite rude of me to stop writing about *him* (or is that *Him?*), considering he had come into the story so late in the game.

I wandered off to try my hand at space opera (the Fallen Empire series) and wrote some scifi romance under my pen name, Ruby Lionsdrake. It wasn't until I was listening to the Dragon Blood books on audio (thanks to Podium Publishing for putting all the books out that way) that I remembered how much I enjoyed the world and the characters.

I don't know about other authors, but I don't re-read my own books very often, and I can't remember what prompted me to start listening to the series, but whatever it was, it got me excited to return and see if King Angulus forgave Ridge for dropping a sorceress in his castle and what kind of wedding Ridge and Sardelle would have. And if the dragon "god" Bhrava Saruth would get the temple that his divine self deserved. And of course, I would check in on Cas and Tolemek and many of the other characters...

The only problem with a Book 8, or any later book in a series, is that the only people who will pick it up are fans of the first seven books. And since nobody was expecting a new book, I didn't know how many people would spot it. I decided to write another series before this one, something that would serve as another entry point into my Dragon Blood world and that would, I hoped, renew interest in the original books. Thus, the five-book Heritage of Power series was born. It takes place three years after the original books, so you don't need to have read it before reading *Oaths*, but you may want to check it out afterward. (As I write this, it's exclusive in one store, but it'll be everywhere by the end of 2018.)

What you definitely *should* read before *Oaths* are "The Fowl Proposal" bonus scenes. I originally posted them on my website a couple of years ago, but they're out as a free ebook in all the stores now. As you might guess from the title, they cover Ridge and Sardelle's proposal.

You may also wish to read *Shattered Past* if you haven't yet. That's a bit of a side story that focuses on Therrik and the new lady in his life (Professor Lilah Zirkander — yes, she's related to the famous pilot, and no, she won't get him to sign anything for you). It's not necessary to read before *Oaths*, but you may be wondering about their relationship, otherwise. They both poke their noses into *Oaths*, Lilah to lend Sardelle some support with dress shopping and Therrik to insult Ridge (what else?).

Also, I've included the short story "Crazy Canyon" at the end of this book. It, too, originally appeared on my website, and I know folks wanted it in a book somewhere for their convenience, so I've added it to this one. It takes place shortly before *Oaths*, so if you're a fan of reading in chronological order, you may want to jump to the end for that before starting on the novel. That said, it's just a fun little side story and doesn't have much to do with *Oaths*.

There, I think that's all you need to know before jumping into this one. While I'm chatting you up, let me also take a moment to thank my editor, Shelley Holloway, for sticking with me for all the books I've mentioned here, the entire Dragon Blood and Heritage of Power series. Also, thank you to my beta readers Sarah Engelke, Cindy Wilkinson, and Rue Silver. They've also stuck with me over the years. I know none of us expected *Balanced on the Blade's Edge*, a little fantasy romance that was supposed to be a stand-alone novel, not the start of a series, to lead into all these stories. Also, a big thank you to the sharp-eyed typo hunters who have been reading the stories early to help me catch most of those pesky slips that get past the rest of us.

Lastly, thank you for picking up *Oaths* and following along with these series. Many of you have emailed and let me know how much you enjoy spending time with my quirky characters. As a rather quirky soul myself, that means a lot to me. Thanks!

Prologue

AS STEAM CARRIAGES AND HORSE-DRAWN wagons filled the busy street behind him, Lieutenant Farris "Pimples" Averstash gazed through the window of a stationery shop at the handsome leather-bound writing journals on display. He would have loved one with blank pages for the houses he enjoyed designing when he wasn't busy flying—and sometimes when he was. Lately, he had been sketching larger houses with rooms for children—and princesses and their retinues.

Did Zia have a retinue? Just because she was the youngest of the Cofah emperor's children and he'd first run into her alone in the middle of an alligator-filled swamp didn't mean she didn't typically travel with an entourage.

"You're not going to buy them a *book*, are you?"

Lieutenant Duck walked up to peer—or was that a sneer?—through the window. They had only been on this quest for fifteen minutes, and Farris already regretted inviting one of his male Wolf Squadron colleagues along to help him shop. He should have asked a woman. Women *liked* to shop, and they knew all about weddings and what made appropriate gifts for brides and grooms.

He should have brought Lieutenant Ahn. No, wait. She wasn't very womanly. She would likely give the bride and groom a sniper rifle. He should have brought Captain Blazer. No, she was even less womanly. Seven gods, Farris needed to make the acquaintance of more womanly women. Like Zia. She was beautiful and smart and... Why did she have to be an ocean and a continent away?

"Farris?" Duck poked him. "No books. That's boring."

"Sardelle is a historian. She may enjoy a journal to record her musings in."

"But what about General Zirkander? I don't think he muses."

"He must do some musing out in that duck blind he converted into his private sanctuary. There are shelves in it with books and magazines on them."

"I think he just goes out there to hide from the magic lessons going on inside the house. And the shape-shifted dragons strolling through the kitchen and stealing his cheese like foxes slipping into the henhouse." Duck shook his head. "If you'd told me a year ago that I would say sentences like that, I would have fallen over laughing. Or I would have run and hidden at the notion of magic existing in the world."

"It has been an eventful year."

Reluctantly, Farris stepped back from the window. Though the journals appealed to *him*, he supposed one should buy gifts appropriate to the individuals receiving them. But Sardelle and Zirkander were such different people. Farris didn't know what exactly had brought them together. He also didn't know what kinds of items would be useful to them after they married. They already lived together. Was there anything for the house that they might need? Something practical? Were wedding gifts supposed to be practical? Or frivolous and fun?

He should have asked someone. He had never been invited to a wedding before. He was thankful he'd been told his Iskandian army dress uniform was suitable attire because he didn't own any fancy civilian clothing.

Duck grabbed his arm and pointed across the street. *"That's the shop."*

"Enh?"

Farris allowed himself to be dragged across the busy street, doing his best to dodge fresh piles of horse droppings. He would be glad when steam vehicles completely replaced horse-drawn wagons and carriages. Especially here in the capital where the ocean breezes blew away the smoke from the stacks.

"This." Duck stopped in front of a shop with all manner of clockwork children's toys on display in the window. Several of

them trundled around on stubby legs, while wheels or treads propelled others. A fuzzy ball rolled around in circles, seemingly of its own accord. "No, *that*."

Duck grinned at Farris, his eyes gleaming as he pointed at a bronze, dog-shaped toy with iron rivets. It walked several steps in a line, then turned and walked back. At the end of its circuit, it lifted a back leg.

"Is that dog peeing?" Farris asked, prepared to drop his face in his hand.

"Well, I don't see any actual liquid. That's good. That would be messy. Oh, look. I think you can add on that little lamppost over there. For versi— verisimi— to make it more lifelike."

Farris finally did drop his face in his hand. "Verisimilitude. Did you not take any classes unrelated to fliers at that little Eastern Iskandian university you attended?"

"Not when I could help it. You know I didn't learn to read until I was eighteen. You should be pleased I can tell the lamppost is half off with the purchase of the dog." Duck pointed at a sign in the window. "I'm going in."

"*No*." Farris grabbed his arm. "Think of Sardelle, man. She doesn't want a peeing dog toy."

"How can you be sure?"

"Her sword told me."

Duck squinted at him.

Actually, from the handful of times Jaxi, Sardelle's soulblade, had spoken into his mind, Farris suspected she would cackle with delight at the atrocious gift. Well, maybe not. He'd heard that Jaxi had forbidden Sardelle to lay her scabbard on the bullet-riddled couch made from flier parts that the squadron had gotten the general as a housewarming gift.

"Why don't you get something a little classier?" Farris suggested, lowering his hand. "You should be feeling flush with cash, given that you won the hangar betting pool about the wedding date."

He was hoping for better luck with the baby pool. The wedding one had been put together at the last minute when General Zirkander had started asking people for advice on proposals. All the prime dates had been chosen by the time Farris had gotten in on it.

"Nah, nobody guessed the exact date. I'm one of three people who guessed a day in the first week of fall. There's going to be a tie-breaker to see who gets the money."

"Oh? How will that work?"

"Whichever one of us guesses the correct number of dragons that will appear at the wedding wins. That means nobody gets the payout until the day after the wedding. So, I'm not any more flush with money than a bear is flush with fat at the end of its winter's nap."

"Flush with fat?" Farris curled a lip. He definitely should have found a woman to bring with him.

"It's an expression."

"I doubt it. How many dragons did you say would come?"

"One. I figured Bhrava Saruth and General Zirkander are close buddies." Duck clasped his hands together in front of him, fingers intertwined. "He'll definitely invite the dragon. He might even ask Bhrava Saruth to be one of his two kin watchers."

"Uh, considering that job involves leering at the bride and saying whether she looks healthy and hale and capable of birthing babies, I doubt Zirkander will ask a dragon. Especially not *that* dragon. He's randy."

"Hm, that is true. I do hope I'm right about the guess though. Usually, I'm about as lucky as a wolf with a thorn in his paw. I never win anything. It would be great to break that streak."

"What were the other guesses?" Farris asked. "We don't have that many dragon allies."

"Colonel Coyote said two. Captain Kaika said three. Which is alarming."

"We don't have three dragon allies."

"That's why it's alarming." Duck looked toward the cloudy sky, perhaps remembering their battle with dragons from earlier in the summer. Fortunately, there hadn't been any more attacks since they had sent those Cofah dragons fleeing. "I've been enjoying the last few trouble-free months."

Yes, the capital had been quiet—almost boringly so—since the Cofah emperor had officially disappeared from the world.

Farris had been on the team responsible for the kidnapping, but he had no idea what King Angulus had done with the prisoner after they'd gotten him back to Iskandian soil. There had been talk of a forced exile, but as a lieutenant, Farris wasn't told much of what happened behind the scenes. For all he knew, the emperor could have been made to disappear forever.

"Uh," Duck said, his gaze still skyward.

"What is it?" Farris looked up. He supposed it was silly to hope for an air pirate attack that would need to be fended off. Sardelle and General Zirkander would likely appreciate it if nothing eventful happened until *after* they were happily married.

Of course, if the city-wide alarm went off now, and all Wolf Squadron pilots were called to the hangar, that would keep Duck from buying that clockwork dog. *That*, at least, should please the couple.

"Trouble," Duck said.

A gold dragon flew into sight, heading in the direction of the army fort.

"I think that's Bhrava Saruth," Farris said.

"That doesn't necessarily negate my statement."

As far as Farris knew, the dragon hadn't been seen in the capital for a while. His return could indeed herald trouble. But maybe he'd simply returned for a visit and to cadge tarts from the Zirkander household.

"Guess we'll find out soon."

Chapter 1

General Ridgewalker Zirkander had a thousand things to do before his wedding, so he hoped the citadel would be quiet and he could work without any interruptions. Sardelle and his mother were handling most of the preparations for the event itself, so they weren't cluttering up his to-do list, but he was in the process of redoing the curriculum at the flight academy, as well as assigning pilots to a new squadron he'd gotten permission to form. Rather than being based out of a city, the squadron would be intended from the start to be itinerant and ready to fly around the continent at a moment's notice. Ridge didn't believe that just because the Cofah had misplaced their emperor they would truly cease to be a threat in the foreseeable future.

His office door banged open, and a young man with golden locks, sandals, and a loose tunic—or was that a dress?—strolled in without knocking. Perhaps because he was usually a dragon, and dragons didn't knock. Presumably, dragons didn't have doors of their own. Just caves or dens. Whatever they were called.

"We call them *lairs*," Bhrava Saruth said, his deep emerald-green eyes locking on to Ridge's. "But such dwellings tend toward dampness. Mildew. Mold." He crinkled his nose. "They're not at all befitting a god such as myself. Which is why I must have a temple, as you know, mate of my high priestess. We have had this conversation many times. I *need* a temple."

Those green eyes held an allure that made it hard to look away. And hard to deny the dragon anything he wished.

"It is not only for my own pleasure that I ask this, Ridgewalker." Bhrava Saruth pressed a hand to his chest, loose bracelets jangling on his wrist. "I have been traveling all around Iskandoth and have obtained thirteen more worshippers. Having a temple here in this most central of human cities will be ideal since many of them live on this coast. With a temple, my worshippers can easily find me and have a place where I can attend their needs and bless them. I have already constructed a *hysrinthiea-narsh*."

"Of course," Ridge said, having no idea what the mouthful of letters meant. "I hear every temple needs one."

"It does! The device will allow me to know when one of my worshippers has arrived, touched my throne, and needs my assistance."

"You're planning to have a throne?"

"For when I am in human form." Bhrava Saruth used his hand to gesture up and down his body. Ridge tried not to pay attention to how much leg was on display. It was summer, after all. Maybe this was the dragon version of shorts. Airy shorts that swayed when he moved. "I must be comfortable when delivering my blessings."

"Will it be bigger than King Angulus's throne?"

"It must be sufficient to contain my magnificent form."

"I'll take that as a yes."

Ridge shifted aside a few folders to make room on his desk, then grabbed a rolled-up map and several preliminary blueprints that were leaning against his filing cabinet.

"You can see that I am fully prepared to be accessible to my followers and a good god," Bhrava Saruth said. "All I need is my temple. Which you *have* agreed to help construct. I would have simply constructed it myself, but you and your king have not yet granted land suitable for the project."

"I know, I know. I promised to help you build your temple."

Ridge still wondered how he had ever allowed himself to be talked into that. Most likely, he had made the mistake of looking the dragon in the eyes when he was radiating that aura of his, an aura that made obeying him seem like the most natural thing in the world. But Bhrava Saruth had helped fight off enemy dragons on numerous occasions, and he'd also helped Sardelle find Ridge when he'd been without his memory and in the hands of that enemy sorceress.

Ridge sighed to himself. No, even if the powerful dragon's aura had influenced him somewhat, he, the city, and the country owed Bhrava Saruth a few favors. This was a small price to pay for the help he'd provided.

"With that in mind," Ridge said, "I went to the tax office and got some maps of the king's lands. I don't think we're going to convince any private individuals to give up property for your temple, though I was tempted to point out to the king that Therrik's family estate isn't that far outside the city. It sounds like you would prefer to be as close to the capital as possible."

"Oh yes. It would be most convenient for my worshippers if my temple were located near your harbor and also near the disembarkation point for your rolling boxes."

"The train station?" Ridge spread the maps. "It'll be a challenge to build close to that, since that's all private land, but I've circled a couple of potential spots. This is Crazy Canyon, about twenty miles north of the city. It's quite breathtaking, especially when you're zipping around the rock pillars and under the arches at top speed."

"I remember it. I took you and my high priestess there for your mating ritual."

"Uh, that was the proposal." Ridge smiled, fondly remembering how he and Sardelle had ended up atop that arch with a blanket, picnic basket, his promise necklace, and her *referatu* cuff that she had made for him.

"Did you not mate afterward?"

"Yes, but you weren't supposed to stay and watch."

"As I recall, there was some concern that you would, due to your vigorous copulation, roll off the edge of the arch and possibly need saving with magic."

Ridge could have sworn he was far too old to be embarrassed by anything, but having his copulation concerns echoed back to him by a member of another species seemed grounds for discomfiture.

"Jaxi was going to handle that, but back to the map, eh?"

"Indeed. Crazy Canyon is far too distant a location for my temple. And it's in a canyon. It would not be visible from your highway or the sea. How would people admire its magnificence?"

"I thought you might like a private location. For the comfort of your followers." Ridge wondered how many "worshippers" the dragon was up to but decided he didn't want to ask. It was bad enough Bhrava Saruth counted *him* among his devotees, no matter how many times Ridge had tried to suggest they should just be friends. The fact that he had been rubbing his wooden dragon figurine for luck for years had cinched it for Bhrava Saruth, who was convinced the charm represented him. "How about a serene location in the Trenchwood Forest?" He used his finger to point at a circled location while covering the nearby small print that said Mirinath Mudslides.

Bhrava Saruth gently pushed his finger aside. "It sounds remote and inhospitable."

"It's less than fifteen miles from the city." Ridge figured his odds of getting Angulus to agree to give up royal land for this endeavor would be better the farther away that land was from his castle.

"What is this circle here?" Bhrava Saruth pointed at the last spot. "It appears quite near your harbor and within walking distance of the city walls, although these cliffs may be difficult to navigate for those who can't fly. I can, of course, levitate my worshippers down to that small island. That is the location, yes? Not something underwater, I presume? It would take powerful magic to make an underwater location hospitable for humans."

"I was thinking of the island, yes." Ridge's mind boggled at the notion that magic could make an underwater location hospitable to anything except creatures with tentacles and fins. "It's protected by this inlet with cliffs all around. It might not be as visible as you'd hoped, but it will be private and secluded while being in convenient proximity to the city."

Ridge thought Angulus might be convinced to give up that island. He'd flown over it countless times and knew it was nothing but rocks and sea lion droppings.

Bhrava Saruth's blond eyebrows rose. "Sea lion excrement? Really, Ridgewalker."

"I'm sure it can be cleaned before the temple construction begins. Here are a few sketches I asked a local architect to come up with." He'd *paid* a local architect to come up with them. Despite his attempts to persuade the woman that working for a dragon god was its own reward, he'd ended up with an invoice for this side job. At least she had been willing to accept his offer of free beer at his buddy Towee's tavern as part of the payment. Still, these were only preliminary drawings. It was a good thing he'd accepted that promotion earlier in the summer.

"Hm." Bhrava Saruth touched a finger to his chin and eyed the offerings as Ridge spread them out.

"They *all* have room for the statue of yourself that you requested."

"And a throne?"

"I didn't know to mention a throne, but I assume furnishings will fit inside. The architect made them large enough for you to go in whether you're in human or dragon form."

"Oh excellent. And thoughtful. I like that one there, with the open front and back and the marble columns. Yes, very majestic. Ridgewalker, this is wonderful. I feared you would not take on this task for me, but you truly are a wonderful and devoted worshipper."

Bhrava Saruth grinned, his shaggy bangs hanging in his eyes, and stepped around the desk with his arms spread. By the time Ridge realized a hug was imminent, enthusiastic arms wrapped around him.

"I'm glad you're appreciative, but this isn't necessary," Ridge said. "Especially when you're wearing a dress."

Bhrava Saruth stepped back. "It's a *kryka*. A flow-wrap. They're very popular among the clansmen that live on the southern side of your continent."

"I'm sure it effectively aerates everything." Ridge stepped out of the dragon's embrace and rolled up the map and blueprints. "I'll take these to the king tomorrow and see if he'll approve the donation of his island for one of them."

The other thing he'd been thinking about asking the king came into his mind, and his stomach did a nervous flip. He would have to do it soon if he was going to do it. He'd already asked General Ort to stand at his side in the wedding as one of his kin watchers. If the event had taken place several years ago, he would have asked his old friend Mox to serve as the second kin watcher. Or maybe Digger or Major Antar. But those colleagues had all been lost in the line of duty in the last five or six years. It was distressing to think of all the fellow officers he'd outlived, some of whom had been very good friends.

He knew many of the younger men in Wolf Squadron would be happy to fill in, but he thought of what Sardelle would like. He knew she considered Angulus a friend—one of the first she'd made in this time period—and would be honored to have him at the wedding in some capacity or another. Maybe Ridge should simply ask him as a guest. They had already filled out an invitation for him, one he hadn't yet delivered. He admitted that he'd like to be able to consider Angulus a friend, and vice versa, especially since they worked together more often now that Ridge was in charge of the flier battalion. Maybe asking him to stand as kin watcher at the wedding would show Angulus that Ridge appreciated him as a king and a leader of the nation. He knew his flippant remarks didn't always convey that.

"Your king would be foolish not to approve this use for his land," Bhrava Saruth said. "Surely, having a dragon god's temple located near his city would bring many people to visit. This would help your economy, would it not? Yes, your king should be very grateful that I wish to reside here and be accessible to my worshippers."

"I'm sure he thanks the gods every night."

"He could simply thank me."

"Do other dragons find your arrogance appealing?" Ridge shook his head and walked toward the door.

"Other dragons are stuffy and humorless. Who would wish to spend time with them to find out *what* they think?"

"We may be in agreement there."

Ridge escorted his guest to the door, mentioning that there were freshly baked dragon horn cookies at the house. He felt guilty foisting Bhrava Saruth off on Sardelle, but he had work to finish and a request to rehearse. Assuming he got up the courage to do it. Why was asking the king to stand at his side in his wedding far more daunting than facing enemy soldiers, pirates, or even dragons?

* * *

"Do you need your pokey doohickey yet?"

Tolemek cocked an eyebrow at Cas as he carefully stirred the gooey green compound gurgling in a ceramic crucible over his Micon Burner. She had stopped by to visit him in the lab on her way home from work, which brightened his evening tremendously, especially since it would be a couple more hours before he could break away from his current project.

"It's called a volumetric pipet," he said.

"Imagine my embarrassment at not knowing that."

"In a gathering of scientists, you would be ridiculed."

"Even if I was carrying my Mark 500?"

"Ah, perhaps not." Tolemek doubted many academics would mock someone who toted a sniper rifle around more comfortably than other women carried purses. "They would be too scared to ridicule you then." He smiled, came around to Cas's side of the table, and draped an arm around her shoulders. "Fortunately, *I'm* not so easily scared."

"Not at all?" She returned his smile, but hers held a hint of mischievousness, and she promptly poked him in the stomach with the pipet.

"Certainly not. I have means of defending myself." He grabbed a pencil and brandished it fiercely, and they engaged in a lively fencing match.

When they broke apart, he was tempted to give her a kiss, but he stank of chemicals and was wearing rubber gloves. He would probably get something else poked if he tried.

But she surprised him by rising onto her tiptoes and kissing him. It warmed his heart, and he was tempted to finish up his project early for the night. Especially since he'd forgotten to turn on the vent fan, and it was starting to stink.

Cas must have thought so, too, because she broke the kiss and cocked an eyebrow toward the steaming concoction. "What are you making? It smells like burning rubber."

"It's an experimental explosive that will have a malleable body, not dissimilar to putty, with a slight adhesive integrated into it, so it can be adhered to walls and other vertical surfaces. I haven't started working on a detonator yet, but Captain Kaika did give me some ideas." Tolemek pointed to an open notebook with sketches in it.

Cas crinkled her nose. "I thought you'd shifted away from using your power and knowledge to create weapons and had started making medical and healing goos that *help* people."

It amused Tolemek somewhat that Cas preferred it when he worked on innocuous substances when she was herself so deadly, both with her sniper rifle and with her flier's machine guns. Not that she'd ever suggested she enjoyed killing people. She was just efficient at it, like her assassin father, Ahnsung.

But Cas knew Tolemek's past as well as any and that he deeply regretted that one of his creations had been used to kill hundreds of innocent people. He knew her concern was as much for his soul as for the people the Iskandian army might kill with the formulas he invented.

"Captain Kaika informs me that explosives are tools, not weapons," Tolemek said.

Kaika had been with King Angulus when Tolemek had been called to the castle for the meeting where they had discussed the possibility of inventing something like this. Tolemek wouldn't be surprised to learn that it had originally been Kaika's idea, and that Angulus had commissioned it, at least in part, to make her happy. He had been late to realize it, but they had been a romantic couple for many months. An unlikely pairing, he thought, but then, who would have thought he, a former Cofah military officer and alchemist pirate, would fall in love with an Iskandian fighter pilot?

"Captain Kaika has blown up a lot of airships and *people* with her tools," Cas said.

"She does seem adept at that. The king also ordered more healing salves and burn ointments from me, in addition to a lubricant that I came up with by accident that's proving useful for maintaining steam vehicles. I can't complain about a lack of work. In addition, I'm receiving a lot of orders for my personal grooming products."

"The pimple cream?" Cas smiled again.

Tolemek liked seeing those smiles and was pleased there had been more of them lately. She seemed to have recovered, at least in part, from her accidental role in killing one of her fellow pilots that spring, but she still tended toward the grave. Even when she delivered jokes, her tone was so deadpan that Tolemek wasn't always sure they *were* jokes.

"Pore Cleansing Tincture Number Two is indeed proving effective."

"So I've heard from Lieutenant Pimples. We may have to give him a new nickname soon."

"I am surprised how quickly the word has gotten out among students and young soldiers. It's resulted in a great many orders. I'm actually falling behind in production, and it's not leaving me much time for inventing new substances, which is, as you know, my passion. Even if it's not in and of itself profitable. I wouldn't have made the time to work on this for anyone else but the king." Tolemek waved at the compound as he stirred it. "I've been thinking of taking on an assistant. I don't suppose you're interested in resigning your commission and coming to work for me."

"Stirring your goos?"

"Bottling them. Creating labels, taking orders, cleaning up around the shop."

Her nose crinkled again.

"Don't tell me you don't have to clean things at work now. I used to have to buff floors, scrub latrines, and clip grass in the Cofah army. I haven't observed that the Iskandian military is much different."

"Yes, but we get to *fly* after we clean things. Maybe Tylie would like to help out and earn some extra money."

"She's starting some formal schooling in town this fall in addition to the studies she's doing with Sardelle. What should have been a typical Cofah education for her was interrupted by the years she spent in that asylum. I *do* have her do a few duties from time to time, so she can earn a little money." Tolemek turned and pulled a label off a stack on the shelves behind him. "She came up with the artwork for this."

Cas came around to his side of the table to examine the image, a waterfall flowing from the snow-capped Ice Blades and into a pristine forest pool. At the bottom read *Pore Cleansing Tincture Number 2*.

"That is certainly the most beautiful pimple cream label I've ever seen," Cas said.

"You have an aversion to using the proper names for my formulas, don't you?"

She smiled again. "I told you I would use the proper names when you started giving them more interesting and creative names."

"Being clear is better than being creative."

"Uh huh. Put marketing director on your list of people to hire."

"Sales are exploding. I hardly think I need marketing help."

"I suppose it helps you that the only competition out there sears off your skin and facial hair more than it removes pimples."

"You know this from experience?" Tolemek had never known Cas to have anything except clear skin, assuming one didn't count the freckles scattered across her nose and cheeks.

"One summer at camp, the boys I competed with at marksmanship competitions were teasing me for having targets on my face."

"I presume you got your revenge by out-shooting them."

"I did do that. I also decided it would be a good idea to sneak into the boys' tent and pour honey in the boots of the ringleader. In the hope that a bear would come visit him in the middle of the night."

"Did it work?" Tolemek wouldn't have guessed that his mature pilot would have played such pranks, even in her teenage years.

"Not exactly. I didn't realize one of the instructors was also sleeping in that tent. He was the one who was most startled by a bear pushing its way in. He ran out screaming, tripped, and rolled down a hill and broke his arm. Nobody knew who'd put the honey in the tent, but I felt too guilty to stew more than two hours before running to the lead instructor and confessing everything. This led to a stern letter being sent to my father and a long lecture when I got home, during which he informed me that it didn't matter what buffoons thought of me and that I should be above returning insults with insults. Or insults with pranks."

"And so you have been ever since?" Tolemek hadn't adored his own father, especially after he'd stuck Tylie in that sanitarium, but he thought having the humorless Ahnsung as a father might have been even worse.

"I suppose." Cas handed the label back to him. "Are you coming home for dinner? I can pick up something from the Dakrovian deli on the way."

Home. Hearing her use the word to refer to the small house they had rented warmed his heart. They had been living together for most of the summer, and he still found the domestic quaintness appealing. He hadn't realized how much he could enjoy something as simple as sharing a home with another person. Flying around on airships full of scruffy pirates hadn't filled him with a sense of domestic bliss.

Lately, he'd caught himself wondering what it would be like to have children tramping around the place and kicking balls around in the garden out back. He hadn't broached the subject with Cas. They hadn't even truly broached the subject of marriage. He knew that she liked her career and wouldn't likely give it up to stay home and raise children, so he had been hesitant to speak of it.

"Tolemek? Are you stuck debating the merits of sliced beef versus traditional Dakrovian alligator steaks?"

"Sorry, no. The deli is a good idea. Maybe once I get an assistant, I can leave earlier a couple of days a week and attempt to cook us a meal myself." He was somewhat amused that neither of them ever prepared the meals they shared. When she'd been growing up, her father had kept a maid, a cook, and a butler, and

Cas had said he'd deemed it more important to teach her to use weapons than measuring cups. "My mother showed me some of the basics long ago," he added. "She promised that knowing how to prepare meals would endear me to women."

"Well, I've had your sandwiches."

One of which had been tainted with a truth serum he'd concocted. They both grimaced, and he was sure they were sharing the memory.

"*I* didn't make that one," he said. "My captain did. But perhaps a hearty and robust Ergrotton spicy stew would be more palatable. I just need a day off since it takes a long time to cook."

He vowed to *take* a day off sometime. Funny how he worked longer hours now that he worked for himself than he had back in his army days.

"I'll look forward to it then." Cas tilted her head toward the door. "I'll leave you to your work. Don't blow yourself up. And don't let me catch you obliviously breathing in noxious fumes again, either. I hear that's a practice that can wither a man's gonads."

"My gonads are as hearty and robust as my Ergrotton stew."

She gave him a weird look, and he decided that hadn't been the best analogy.

"I simply meant to say that should the need to sire children ever come up, my lower regions will be healthy and up to the task."

"I guess that's good to know."

"The knowledge makes *me* comfortable." Granted, he wouldn't truly know if everything was up to the task of creating children until they tried. *If* they tried. This wasn't quite how he'd meant to broach the subject, but maybe it would be good to know if she would ever be open to it. "In case, you—er, *we* ever decide to have children."

Her nose scrunched up. She had a decidedly expressive nose. Unfortunately, he wasn't positive what it was expressing this time. Distaste for the idea? Doubtfulness that they'd find time for raising children? Dubiousness in regard to his fertility after breathing so many fumes?

"I hadn't planned to have children," Cas said.

"Ever? Or just not for a while?"

He could understand her not being ready, as she was several years younger than he, even if she often *was* the more mature one in their relationship, but he struggled to imagine never wanting them. If one found a life mate, wasn't it normal to eventually have children? To co-mingle their genetic material to create a being born of both of them?

"Ever. Sorry, Tolemek, but I don't have any motherly instincts. I don't know what to do when kids talk to me, and hearing a baby cry makes me want to run the other way, instead of hurrying over to soothe it."

"Ah."

He didn't know what else to say. He hadn't expected her to shut down the idea entirely.

"Do *you* want children?" Cas asked, a hint of wariness entering her eyes.

"I know it may sound odd, given the pirate career I was engaged in when we met—the distinctly womanless pirate career—but when I was a younger man, I always imagined myself having children one day. Tanglewood made me stop thinking about that, about deserving any kind of happiness in life." He shrugged a shoulder. "But now that we're—we've been living together for a while, those parental stirrings have returned, I admit."

"Oh."

Tolemek didn't like the flatness of her tone. She didn't sound disappointed—not exactly—but she did sound like she had no idea what to say.

"We don't have to talk about it now." Tolemek, realizing he hadn't been paying enough attention to his concoction, hurried to stir it and scrape the sides of the crucible. He hadn't yet added the full amount of the explosive element that would complete the compound, but he had layered in some. He didn't need it to overheat and blow up in his lab. Or blow *up* his lab.

"All right," Cas said slowly, "but I need you to know that I don't plan to change my mind in the future. As much as I hate to admit it, I seem to be my father's child in a lot of ways. I think

I was born without *that* part of me that could want to raise children."

Tolemek stopped himself from saying that she might feel differently one day, that maybe things would change for her as she grew older. He didn't want to try to talk her into something as major as having children. He just... found it disappointing to learn it might never happen.

"Sorry," she said again.

Her expression grew bleak, and he wished he'd said something instead of frowning at his work table in silence.

"You don't have to feel sorry," he said. "It's not a thing you're supposed to apologize about. I just didn't know what to say."

"Would you be able to stay with someone who doesn't want children?" she asked quietly.

Would he? He couldn't imagine ending their relationship over this, not when he'd just been thinking about how much he was enjoying living with her, but that was today. Would he feel the same way in a year? Five years? By then, Zirkander and the other men he'd come to know since arriving in Iskandia would no doubt be having children of their own.

"I see," Cas said, maybe seeing too much when he didn't answer right away.

"Cas, I'm just thinking. I didn't mean to imply anything."

"Well, not giving me a firm *yes* to that question *does* imply things. Whether you meant to or not." Her face was masked now, impossible to read, but he thought he read hurt in her tone.

She turned and strode for the door.

"Cas, wait."

Tolemek jogged around the counter, but she disappeared into the hallway without looking back. He caught his hip on the corner of the table as the door shut. The crucible rattled ominously on the burner. He lunged back, steadying it, but only for a second. He hurried back around the table and ran after Cas.

But when he opened the door, she'd already disappeared from the hallway. He didn't even hear her steps on the stairs. Seven gods, had she sprinted away at top speed?

He leaned his head against the doorjamb. Why had he chosen that moment to bring up children? And why had he hesitated when she'd asked about their future together? He hadn't wanted to lie, but he wished he'd managed to say something that wouldn't imply he might leave her someday. He wished—

A soft clink came from the stairwell, and he lifted his head.

Maybe Cas was coming back to give him a second chance to explain himself. But what had she been wearing that would have clinked?

A bronze ball arched through the air, coming from the stairs. It clanked as it bounced on the floorboards and headed in his direction.

His first thought was that one of the inventors in the shared laboratory building had built something that he was testing out. His second thought was that someone was throwing a weapon, a weapon meant for him.

Given his past and all the people who would like to see him dead, that was too real a possibility to ignore. He jumped back into his lab and flung the door shut.

Half-expecting to hear the thunderous boom of an explosion, he ran for his desk. Ever since that unstable Colonel Therrik had barged in and attacked him, Tolemek kept a firearm in his lab.

Before he reached it, a noisy hiss came from the hallway. He lunged for the drawer, yanking it open. As he drew the pistol, the scent of rotten eggs reached his nose. Green smoke curled into the room from under the door.

Tolemek resisted the urge to curse—that would require air. Instead, he held his breath and ran toward a cabinet that held filtering masks. On the way, he flicked on a hood vent over a workstation, hoping it would draw the smoke up and out.

The door banged open, and men in wildly colored masks and fringed hoods rushed in. Despite the goofy headwear, they carried guns.

Tolemek fired at the doorway as he lunged behind the cabinet he'd wanted to open. Someone swore, his voice muffled by his mask. Tolemek didn't recognize the language. What the hells was going on?

Guns fired, bullets thudding into the back wall, and he was glad he'd taken cover. But what now? He couldn't hold his breath indefinitely, and he couldn't get into the cabinet with the masks while people were shooting at it.

He leaned out to fire but spotted the barrels of four pistols pointing at him and jerked back. The invaders fired again. Glass beakers shattered, the shards clattering to the floor.

Tolemek patted himself down, looking for inspiration, but he didn't have any of his compounds on him. Now he wished he had gone for his vials of knockout liquid instead of the gun.

He eyed his steaming compound on the burner ten feet away. It might as well have been ten miles away.

Someone barked something in the foreign language. Tolemek guessed it was the equivalent of, "Get him."

With his lungs burning, he had to try something. He feared these people wanted him dead, not simply to question or capture him.

He crouched low, careful not to reveal any part of his body, then stuck his pistol out and fired twice. As his enemies were—he hoped—jumping for cover, he sprang from behind the cabinet. Staying low, he ran two steps and dove behind the work table.

Pistols fired, bullets shattering floor tiles as they skipped off them. Something burned the bottom of Tolemek's foot. Had one gouged a hole in the sole of his shoe?

He yanked his legs in close. His lungs ached for air and felt like they would soon explode, but he dared not inhale. The green smoke fogged the entire lab now, the fan not able to combat it fast enough.

He reached for the crucible, but something smacked against his hand. At first, he thought the crucible had fallen against him and that the explosive putty would pour out onto his head.

Horrified, he jerked his hand away and scrambled backward. Something with the feel and texture of a spider web had wrapped around his fingers. Confused, he scrambled back farther, dropping his pistol and trying to tear the substance off. As soon as he touched it, he realized his mistake and cursed inwardly.

Idiot. The stuff was so sticky that his fingers were now stuck to the back of the opposite hand. He couldn't pick up the pistol again.

Not that he could have found it anyway. Blackness was creeping into his vision from the lack of oxygen to his brain. He bumped his shoulders against the counters behind him, and his held breath escaped. His instincts overrode his brain, and he sucked in air.

A figure in tan clothing appeared, stepping around the corner of the work table. The hooded man glanced at the crucible still smoldering. Tolemek hoped vainly that the unattended burner would overheat the substance inside and that it would blow up. It might be worth taking out his lab if the explosion would take out all of these… whoever they were.

The figure strode forward. Tolemek tried to leap to his feet, certain he was about to be shot.

But his legs had grown rubbery, and he stumbled, crashing back to the floor. Whatever that smoke was, it was already affecting him. Damn it.

"Cas!" he tried to yell, but it came out as a raspy croak.

The man held a pistol toward Tolemek's face. But he didn't shoot. He jerked his chin toward Tolemek as he said something in his language. Two more men rushed forward, the green smoke swirling about them, and Tolemek realized they had to have filters in their flamboyant masks. Unless some magic protected them.

The men stretched a net between them.

Tolemek, his limbs no longer responding to his mental commands, could only stare as it descended atop him. The last thing he was aware of was being trussed up like a chicken and lifted between two men. Then the world went black.

Chapter 2

"Am I doing it right, Sardelle?" Tylie asked.

"Hm?" Sardelle looked up from the newspaper she had been perusing with increasing distress. Lovely late summer sunlight slanted into the backyard, already warming the morning air while she sat at the picnic table, drinking her spiced orange tea. Tylie practiced her burgeoning levitation skills nearby while Spots the cat sniffed around the house for mice. It should have been a relaxing and pleasant start to the day, but the Society page assured it was not.

"I floated the rock back and forth over Phel twice without him noticing," Tylie said.

I noticed. I was simply indifferent to it. Phelistoth lay stretched out on the lawn, taking up most of the backyard. The sun gleamed on his scaled silver side as the tip of his tail occasionally flapped in the grass. He looked like a cat in a sunbeam. A very large dragon-shaped cat. *You need not stick your hand out or make any gesture when you draw upon your power, Tylie. It is a mental skill. There is no need to add human flair.*

"I like flair." Tylie smiled, not appearing chagrined by the dragon's correction, though she did lower her arm.

"In my opinion, if you didn't drop the rock on your large, scaled friend, you're doing it right," Sardelle said, also smiling, though her gaze inevitably went back to the newspaper.

As if I would have allowed that to happen, Phelistoth spoke into their minds with something akin to a haughty sniff.

I don't know why you're worrying about that silly newspaper article, Jaxi said to Sardelle, apparently observing her reading from the rack where she and Wreltad, Tylie's new soulblade, hung in the living room.

Indeed, Wreltad put in. *Ridge is certainly not worried about what your city's journalists report about him.*

I'm so glad the two of you can effectively spy on me from inside the house. Sardelle glowered, the gesture more for the paper than for the soulblades, though she did feel out of sorts in general this morning.

Spying? Wreltad asked. *We are simply observing what goes on around the house. I must oversee Tylie's training to ensure it progresses adequately.*

And I can't possibly be spying, Jaxi said. *You're my handler. We're linked. There are no secrets between us. Besides, reading that newspaper was more interesting than staring at this junkyard of a couch. I still can't believe you thought this room would be a good place to hang me.*

You don't have eyes. What does it matter?

I have senses, Sardelle. Goodness.

Sardelle pushed the newspaper away, unable to read any more of the drivel. This was the fourth time the same journalist had gathered so-called evidence and reported that she was using her "witchy" powers to *force* the capital's most eligible bachelor to marry her.

What evidence she had, Sardelle couldn't imagine. The female journalist certainly had never come out to speak with her. Though the woman had, Ridge had mentioned the week earlier, caught him walking out of the army fort and thrown all manner of questions at him. She'd even had the audacity to pull out some feather-covered travesty of a "magic detector" that could supposedly tell if a person was possessed by a spirit or under the influence of a sorcerer.

Sardelle didn't need to see the device to know it was a sham. She could imagine the journalist hovering all around Ridge, using the detector as an excuse to touch him. Maybe squeeze him a few times through his uniform. Sardelle gritted her teeth.

That's not *what happened,* Jaxi said dryly. *Don't you share memories with your soul snozzle?*

I'm sure it's what she wanted *to happen.*

Nonetheless, Ridge foisted the woman onto the privates at the gate, telling them to hold her until they could find someone to perform a thorough inspection of the so-called magic detector. He said he might be mistaken, but he believed he'd seen something similar in Cofahre and worried the device might be delivering information back to the empire unbeknownst to the journalist. Then he strode away, leaving the poor young privates flummoxed, one holding the detector between two fingers and at arm's length, and the other uncertainly holding the woman's arm and saying she would have to stay with them until their superiors arrived to speak with her.

I know, Jaxi. He did tell me the story. And I do love him for being so...

Mendacious?

He only lied to protect me. And to escape the woman's clutches. I love him for that.

And he loves you, probably because of me and the way my calming influence improves you as a person.

Sardelle snorted.

So why are you worried about the newspapers? The king has your back, Ridge has your back, and most important, I have your back. Had I been there, I would have incinerated that ludicrous device. And possibly the woman's hair as well.

I just thought we were past all these silly newspaper stories. *Silly? Annoying was the word Sardelle should have used. Last spring, when you and I helped the army destroy that floating Cofah fortress, Angulus publicly announced that I was an ally to Iskandia and that anyone who attempted to do me harm would be dealt with firmly.*

Technically, the newspaper journalists aren't harming you, Jaxi pointed out.

They're harming my reputation. Nobody is going to want to come to me for healing, or, if they have dragon blood themselves, for tutelage. Sardelle was up to four young students now, in addition to Tylie, but the new ones were all of school age, and only came out to study magic a few evenings a week. So far, their parents hadn't expressed any concerns about the scandalous stories, at least not to Sardelle, but she did worry it could become a factor. *And besides, Jaxi, it's just so infuriating. I may spit.*

Unlikely. There are witnesses, and you're far more ladylike than that.

Sardelle looked around the yard, not particularly worried about the witnesses present. Phelistoth's eyes were closed, and she was fairly certain that deep breathing signaled sleeping, if not the dragon equivalent of snoring. Tylie, barefoot and in a paint-spattered dress, had her tongue stuck in the corner of her mouth while she focused on floating the smooth rock back and forth over Phelistoth. Sardelle doubted either of them would judge her for unladylike actions, such as crinkling the newspaper into a ball and kicking it into the nearby pond.

I, being less ladylike, would spit on your behalf, Jaxi offered. *If I had saliva.*

You're a good friend.

Naturally. Which is why my sword rack should overlook flowers or a serenity garden, not a couch made from bullet-riddled flier parts. With puke-colored cushions.

We don't have a serenity garden. And a dragon trampled the flowers in the front yard again.

Those dragons are heavier than they look. Jaxi made a throat-clearing noise in Sardelle's mind, a surprisingly diffident one. *Are you perhaps letting this newspaper drama affect you more than usual because you're in an... altered state?*

An altered state?

Yes, you haven't spoken about it to me yet, but since we're bonded, I am of course aware of things you haven't told others yet. Including Ridge. Those last two words seemed to hold a hint of reproof.

Sardelle propped her elbow on the table and rested her forehead in her hand.

You're not distressed about it, are you? Jaxi asked. *Now that you're paired—and planning to permanently pair—with a man you love and who loves you, this seems like a natural thing to happen. Not that I would have approved of it if you'd asked me. Babies are messy. Loud. Smelly. Loud. Demanding. And loud.*

Afraid the noise will make it difficult for you to relax and admire the view in the living room?

Now you're just mocking me.

Sardelle lowered a hand to her belly, aware of the tiny life that had started growing inside of her womb. She guessed it to be six or seven weeks along and to have been conceived around the time she had proposed to Ridge—and vice versa. Perhaps it had even been that night. She'd been somewhat distracted by the fact that they'd been celebrating their proposal atop a thousand-foot-high stone arch in Crazy Canyon—his dream location for such an event, one she'd gone along with even though dinner at a nice restaurant in town would have suited her fine.

Jaxi had been there, willing to lend magical levitation assistance if she or Ridge rolled off the blanket spread on the flat spot at the top of the arch, but Sardelle had been somewhat concerned about the height and hadn't been focused on keeping certain things from taking root afterward. And because she'd told Ridge months earlier that she could do that with her magical powers and that there was no need for them to use contraceptives, they hadn't been. It had been several days before she'd realized her post-coital sweep hadn't been as thorough as it should have been. At that point, she'd considered whether or not to let the process continue, but not for long. Even though it had been very early, she hadn't been able to imagine ending the life they had created.

She just hadn't figured out how or when to tell Ridge. The last time they had discussed children, he'd been startled and even alarmed by the idea of himself as a father, claiming his reckless past meant he wasn't a fit role model. She thought she had been on the verge of talking him out of that, promising that it only mattered what he did after the baby was born, not what kind of man he'd been ten or twenty years earlier, but then they'd battled Morishtomaric, and Ridge had been captured by that sorceress. Sardelle and Ridge hadn't spoken about children since then, and she worried about what his reaction would be. Would he truly welcome such a drastic change to his life? Especially now, when he was still settling in to his new duties and responsibilities as general, and they weren't positive that peaceful times lay on the horizon?

Give him a chance, Sardelle, Jaxi suggested. *Even if he's taken aback at first, I believe he'll be delighted in the long run. He's a good man. I wouldn't have allowed you to fall in love with him otherwise.*

You wouldn't have allowed it? I believe you were buried under thousands of tons of mountain when I was first falling for him.

I could have asserted my influence if necessary.

I—

A shriek came from the side of the house, and Sardelle almost pitched off the picnic bench. She jumped up, whirling in that direction as she stretched out with her senses.

Uh oh.

Ridge's mother, Fern, a woman who believed in neither magic nor dragons, stood on the pathway at the side of the house, a basket of vegetables gripped in one hand and folders clutched against her chest with the other as she gaped at Phelistoth. Tylie lost her concentration, her rock thumping to the ground, and she stared at Fern. Phelistoth lifted one eyelid for a few seconds, then closed it again, indifferent to human cries of alarm.

"Fern." Sardelle rushed toward her as she groped for words to explain.

For months, she had worried that Fern would learn she was a sorceress—and that magic existed—from reading the newspapers or hearing of Sardelle's exploits in one of the battles to defend the city. She'd never imagined that Fern would simply walk into the yard and spot Tylie floating rocks around. Or had she seen that? Maybe Fern had been focused on Phelistoth. An admittedly alarming sight to a woman who didn't believe in dragons.

The folders slipped unnoticed from Fern's arms as she continued to gawk at him.

"Are you all right?" Sardelle asked when she reached Fern's side. It relieved her when Fern didn't jerk away from her—though maybe that was because she was too stunned to notice Sardelle.

Jaxi, why didn't you warn me she was coming? she asked telepathically as she bent to pick up Fern's folders and take the basket of vegetables from her. They looked to be fresh from her garden.

Jaxi offered the mental equivalent of a shrug. *Because I wasn't paying attention. Just like you.*

Sardelle thought about asking Phelistoth the same question, but it was clear he was enjoying the sun, like a fat iguana on a warm boulder, and cared nothing about who wandered onto the property.

"Fern?" Sardelle asked. "That is Phelistoth, one of the two dragon allies that Iskandia currently claims." She thought about also introducing Fern to Phelistoth but doubted he would care.

Good guess, Jaxi said.

"I... I..." Fern closed her mouth and swallowed before she managed to get more out. "I've heard the stories, of course, and read the accountings in the newspapers, but the newspapers have been so ridiculous of late..." Fern glanced at Sardelle, and Sardelle winced, certain she'd seen the sorcery accusations. "I just didn't truly believe there were such things as dragons, now or ever, to be honest. I thought they were just stories. Mythological tales from long ago."

Aren't there dragon bones in the museum in the city? Jaxi asked. *Maybe she hasn't been.*

Not a very worldly woman, is she? Especially considering Rock Cheetah is an explorer.

I don't think Moe *is home very often to chat with her about his explorations,* Sardelle replied, using Ridge's father's true name rather than the silly moniker he'd given himself.

"I saw him blink," Fern said, still staring at Phelistoth.

"Yes, he's real," Sardelle said. "He's usually more animated."

"What is he doing *here*?" Fern lowered her voice. "Are we in danger?"

"We shouldn't be. As I said, he's one of our allies. Do you want to go inside? Or I can get you some tea, and we can have it at the picnic table?" Sardelle started to wave to it, then caught herself. The newspaper was still open to *that* page. If Fern hadn't yet seen the latest issue, Sardelle didn't want to point her to it or do anything to remind her about magic. For the moment, she seemed only to have realized that there was a dragon sunning himself in the yard, not that Tylie had been levitating rocks.

"Inside," Fern said firmly, her eyes still wide.

"Yes, let's get that tea." Sardelle smiled, attempting to radiate serenity, though that emotion was fleeting this morning.

"Shall I keep practicing, Sardelle?" Tylie asked as Sardelle led Fern to the back door.

Fern tilted her head, no doubt wondering what she could be practicing while standing barefoot in the yard next to a snoozing dragon.

"If you wish." Sardelle silently added, *If you need a break, perhaps you and Phelistoth could go for a ride. Ridge's mother isn't used to seeing dragons, and his presence is... large.*

But he's not at all fearsome right now. He's enjoying his nap.

Not sure if those two would end up leaving or not, Sardelle directed Fern through the kitchen and into the living room, to a spot where she wouldn't be able to see through a window to the backyard. Assuming the vegetables were for her and Ridge, she set them on the kitchen table before joining her.

Fern, still looking dazed, started to sit on one of the fuzzy green cushions Jaxi had recently maligned. Fern caught herself halfway down, pursed her lips, and stepped over to one of the more sedately—and, Sardelle liked to think, tastefully—upholstered armchairs.

"I'll get that tea," Sardelle said, after returning Fern's folders to her. "There are some biscuits and jam, too, if you'd like. Are these vegetables for us? They look wonderful. Thank you."

"Yes," Fern managed. "Ah, just the tea will be fine, dear. Thank you."

"What brought you over here?" Sardelle asked from the kitchen, selecting a cup for her and pouring some of the spiced orange tea.

"Wedding planning. There's so much to do and so little time. I'm still not certain why you two decided on such an early date, but I suppose winter is on its way, and nobody wants to freeze while watching the bride and groom be blessed by the priest. Uhm, that dragon won't be there, will he? I've been working on a seating chart, and I just don't see how it could fit. It wasn't anticipated."

"I believe Ridge invited *him*," Sardelle said, emphasizing the pronoun slightly, hoping Fern would pick up on it without needing to be corrected. "I don't believe Phelistoth has accepted the invitation, but if he does come, we'll ask him to change into his human form."

"Human form," Fern mouthed, that stunned and slightly wild look returning to her eyes.

Sardelle walked in with a tray containing tea cups and a sugar bowl. "Yes, you've seen him in the house when you've visited before, I believe. A young man with silver hair. And the other dragon, Bhrava Saruth, is sometimes here too. He has shaggy blond hair that hangs into his eyes."

Sardelle had wondered from time to time what Fern thought of their peculiar house guests, but she lived fifteen miles away, so she didn't come down to visit that often. Especially not unannounced. If she did, Sardelle would have been more careful about what went on in the backyard. And who napped there.

"Dragons are magical beings," Sardelle explained into the silence. "They're capable of a variety of things, such as changing shapes."

Fern's mouth parted, but she didn't speak.

Sardelle decided this wasn't the time to bring up her own magical capabilities. Though she would have liked to. Hiding what she was had made her uncomfortable from the beginning, when Fern had hugged her and welcomed her into her home—and into her family—with such warmth. That had been before she'd known magic existed. And she *still* didn't know Sardelle was capable of using it.

Ridge never seemed that worried about her finding out, but Sardelle couldn't help but fear Fern's friendliness—and her interest in seeing Sardelle married to her son and the mother of his children—would disappear when she learned the truth. So many Iskandians were terrified by the notion of magic and sorcerers.

But could Sardelle and Ridge truly get married without mentioning that little bit of her background to his mother?

"Tylie will certainly come, as well as Tolemek," Sardelle said, going on in the hope that Fern would recover from her stunned silence, "so it's possible Phelistoth will come. He and Tylie are friends, in a manner of speaking. And it's also possible Bhrava Saruth will come. He is also our friend, of a sort."

Are you not going to admit to being his high priestess? Jaxi asked.

No.

Are you certain you shouldn't? While divulging other background information? I would find it entertaining to see you explain that.

Fern rubbed her face, then accepted the tea cup Sardelle had been holding out for a long minute. "So, I need to add two to my seating chart?"

"It may be wise."

Fern cleared her throat and opened a folder, looking like she'd recovered enough to get to business. Sardelle sat on the other upholstered chair even though it would have been more natural to face her from the couch. It wasn't an uncomfortable couch, just a hideous one, hideous enough that she avoided touching it, except to dust. It was possible that sitting *on* it would be preferable to sitting *across* from it, since one wouldn't be looking at it then... but she couldn't quite bring herself to do so.

"Have you decided on a venue yet?" Fern asked. "Since you're determined to do this first-week-of-fall date, something really should have been booked last winter. I've already checked, and Seagull Island Estate, the Ivy Gardens, and the Blue Hills Castle are booked for the rest of the year. Even the Officers' Club in the army fort is booked. I suppose Ridge might have some sway these days to get things moved around for him, but it's rather unseemly for important people to trample all over the needs of those deemed less important." She paused and sipped from her cup. "I must confess, it's strange to think of my little boy as Important People."

"We're not interested in trampling anyone," Sardelle said, relieved that Fern seemed to have recovered from the Phelistoth sighting. Was it possible she would accept magic—and a sorceress for a daughter-in-law—as easily as the existence of dragons? "We were thinking of having it in the yard right here."

"Here?" Fern's eyebrows flew up. "Overlooking that swamp?"

She flung her hand in the direction of the pond and Ridge's converted duck blind. She looked like she would say more, but the idea distressed her so much that she broke into a coughing fit.

"It's quite lovely for those who enjoy nature," Sardelle said when she finished. "And the mud has finally dried up."

Fern's expression grew horrified as she mouthed, "Mud."

"You've met the ducks. It's really quite serene out there."

"Sardelle, I know you mean well, but Ridge is my only child, and I can't bear the idea of him getting married in a backyard overlooking a swamp. And all those generals and important people that are likely to come—what will they think?"

"I believe most of the people he's invited have been here before for his barbecues. Why, even Angulus came out to the first one he hosted."

"The king!" Fern lurched to her feet, almost spilling her tea as she thunked the cup down on a side table. "Will he be coming?"

"I'm not sure, but we did fill out an invitation for him."

Ridge should have sent it by now, or perhaps delivered it by hand during one of his meetings at the castle. Sardelle would have to check to see if he'd received a response.

"To your swamp? Seven *gods*."

"To the lawn adjacent to the *pond*," Sardelle murmured. "We believe we could seat about a hundred people if they don't mind bumping elbows."

"The grass is brown. And—and *dragon* covered."

Sardelle wasn't sure which of those represented the greater horror. Fern paced back and forth in front of the couch, muttering to herself in distress, her arms jerking about.

And you thought your sorceress status was going to be the main problem today, Jaxi said.

I'm not sure whether to be upset or glad that something else has her distressed. "I believe with a little water siphoned in from the pond, we could get the grass green by the time of the wedding," Sardelle offered.

Very good, Jaxi said. *That will fix all of her objections.*

"And I'm sure we can convince Phelistoth to nap elsewhere that day."

Fern shook her head. "I'll look around for other venues and let you know what I come up with. Perhaps a winter wedding wouldn't be so bad. One would need a dress appropriate to the weather though. A lovely white one to match the possible snow. Or perhaps red to stand out from it. Have you gone dress shopping yet? I was going to offer to make you one. But if you prefer a store-bought one, we could go shopping together. But we need to do it soon. Unless you change the date. If it ends up being a winter wedding, we could add a white fur-trimmed cloak around your shoulders. The trouble is that you can't count on snow here. It so often just rains. A rainy wedding wouldn't appeal to anyone."

Sardelle imagined Fern convincing Ridge to postpone the wedding until after the Winter Solstice festivities. How far along would her pregnancy be then? Would she show?

Maybe you should distract her from dire thoughts of brown grass, dragons, and swamps by making that announcement, Jaxi said.

I can't tell her I'm pregnant before I've told Ridge.

Why not? She's looking forward to babies more than he is.

Sardelle grimaced, reminded that Ridge might not be as delighted about her announcement as his mother would be. And even Fern wasn't a guarantee if she found out about—

"Sardelle," Tylie blurted, running into the kitchen. "Look, I'm doing two rocks at once."

Two large smooth stones floated into the living room ahead of Tylie as Fern turned to look at her—and at them. Sardelle gasped and used her own power to flatten the stones to the floor, but it was too late. Fern stumbled back, hit the couch with the backs of her knees, and pitched onto it, her hand to her chest. She had seen.

Tylie tilted her head in confusion. "Why did you force them down, Sardelle?" She pointed at the rocks. "I thought you'd be pleased with my progress."

"I'm very pleased, but—" Sardelle, staring at the shocked expression on Fern's face, didn't know what to say. Had nobody ever told Tylie that Fern didn't believe in magic and would be shocked to see it in use? Sardelle could have sworn she'd mentioned that at least once.

"What is going on in this house?" Fern cried, her voice almost a shriek. A shriek of panic more than one of outrage.

Sardelle drew upon her power to send soothing energy toward Fern, the way she would to settle a spooked horse.

It didn't work. Fern bolted upright, glancing in all directions, as if to look for the most direct exit. The most direct *escape*.

"I'm practicing my magic studies," Tylie said. "We do that in the mornings. Sardelle teaches me."

Fern's round-eyed stare turned toward Sardelle. "You… teach…?"

Tylie, Sardelle said silently, *please stop talking about magic. Fern doesn't believe—isn't aware that it exists. Or she wasn't.*

Oh, I forgot. I was thinking that was Lilah. Tylie frowned, though she still looked a touch confused, like she couldn't understand why it would matter. *But doesn't she need to know?*

Yes, but this isn't how—

Fern snatched up her folders and hastened for the door. "I need to go. I have a—a thing. An appointment. Yes. I have to go."

She coughed again and dropped two of the folders on the way but didn't stop to pick them up. Fern flung the door open and raced outside, tripping on the step down from the stoop, but recovered and only ran faster toward the horse tied to the hitching post. As she mounted, she dropped another folder. Again, she didn't stop to pick it up. Fern urged the horse out to the road—quickly—and soon rode out of Sardelle's awareness.

"I'm sorry," Tylie whispered, moisture brimming in her eyes as she realized she'd done something wrong. "I've gotten so used to everyone here understanding, and I forgot that magic has to be a secret sometimes, that people don't—I was just so excited that I did two at once. I've never done that before."

Sardelle took a deep breath, suddenly feeling queasy. "It's all right." She walked to Tylie and laid an arm around her shoulders. "You're right. This wasn't how I envisioned telling her, but she needed to find out eventually."

Ridge, she recalled, had suggested they mention it on their tenth wedding anniversary.

Tylie looked toward the folders on the floor. "I didn't… ruin your wedding, did I? Will she still… I remember my grandmother stopped coming to the house and talking to me once she found out I was different. That I could do magic."

Sardelle squeezed her shoulders and groped for something comforting to say, though all she wanted to do was go upstairs, crawl back into bed, and bury her head under a pillow. Providing she didn't get ill first. That feeling of nausea was not pleasant.

It's probably morning sickness, Jaxi said. *You can look forward to all kinds of days like this now that you're pregnant.*

Thank you, Jaxi. You're extremely helpful.

Sardelle would have to talk to Fern, but maybe she should wait a day or two. Let her calm down.

Would Fern return home now? Or would she rush to see Ridge at the fort and ask him if the things the newspapers were printing were true? Now that the dragon stories had been confirmed, she might be more likely to believe those journalists. She might change her mind about going dress shopping with a sorceress daughter-in-law-to-be. She might withdraw her approval of the marriage altogether.

Look on the sunny side. Think how much more relaxed you'll be now that your secrets are out. One of them, at least.

Sardelle looked down at her midsection, feeling far more bleak about her secrets than relaxed.

Chapter 3

THE SUN'S RAYS WARMED CAS'S shoulders as she turned off the street and up the drive toward the modern brick building that held Tolemek's lab. Technically, she was supposed to be at work, but she'd gotten permission from Wolf Squadron's new commander, Colonel Tranq, to come into town to pick up a delivery of healing salve for the flier first-aid kits.

It would give her a chance to check on Tolemek. And to apologize for hurrying away the night before without saying goodbye. She hadn't meant to be judgmental or short with him, but she had been surprised at his admission that he wanted children someday—and stung at the realization that he might not stay with someone for the long-term who *didn't* want them.

He hadn't come home the night before, so Cas had no idea what he was thinking now. She feared she had overreacted and made him feel that he wouldn't be welcome if he *did* come home.

An odd odor met Cas as she stepped into the foyer of the building. Odd odors weren't that unusual an occurrence, since more than a dozen scientists and inventors worked and ran experiments here, but it reminded her of Tolemek's knockout grenades.

She looked toward the reception desk, thinking to ask for a possible explanation, but there was nobody there. That also wasn't that unusual, as the scientists were independent folks and the person hired to manage the building tended to be there infrequently.

As Cas climbed the wooden steps toward the second floor and Tolemek's lab, the scent grew stronger. She paused halfway up, noticing scratches and dents on a few of the stair treads. Had they been there before? She didn't think so. Her father had always trained her to be observant, so she tended to pay attention to such things.

Frowning, she picked up her pace. His door near the end of the hallway stood open. And was that soot on the jamb?

She raced up, her hand on her pistol, though her gut told her that it was too quiet for anything troublesome to be going on now. Whatever had happened, she was too late.

She stopped on the threshold and gaped at the mess inside. Cabinets were overturned, a table had been destroyed, and broken equipment was scattered all over what counters and tabletops remained standing. Far more broken equipment lay on the floor along with shattered glass and puddles of viscous goo. In one corner, the ceiling had collapsed. A vault door in the back, one that held valuable chemicals and components, had been wrenched open. No, it had been *blown* open.

"Tolemek?" Cas called softly, though she didn't think anyone was there. Anyone *alive*.

Her gut twisted as she thought of his past and all the people in the world who would like him dead. What if someone had come to make that a reality?

Pistol in hand, Cas stepped into the lab. Glass crunched under her army boots as she maneuvered around dented and toppled cabinets and metal shelving units that had fallen over—or been *pushed* over. She couldn't tell if someone had done the destruction by hand or if an explosion had caused the entire mess.

She peered behind all the cabinets and all the workstations, terrified that she would find Tolemek's body crumpled there, his eyes open but glazed in death. And if she did, their last conversation would have been a fight. Well, not exactly a fight as neither of them was the type to lose their temper and start shouting matches, but she'd been frosty when she left. And he'd known it.

When she didn't find his body, Cas didn't know how relieved to be. The laboratory and home were the places he spent the majority of his time. If he wasn't here, where was he?

"Kidnapped?" she wondered.

She didn't know who might want him, but she preferred that to the possibility of death. Just because his body wasn't here didn't mean he wasn't dead. His killers could have removed his corpse and thrown it into the harbor.

She shuddered and pushed the thought from her mind as she moved to the destroyed workstation where he had been working the evening before. What remained of it. There was more soot in that area and more destruction. If the burner or crucible he'd been working with remained, she couldn't see them.

Cas ran her finger over some of the soot. Maybe the substance had blown up. Maybe it was even the sole reason for the mess in the lab.

She blinked, wondering if that was possible, if he'd had an accident. Maybe no enemies had barged in on him after all, and he'd gone off somewhere to ask about insurance or repairs.

Her roving gaze snagged on a hole in the wall nearby. A *bullet* hole.

She grimaced and stepped closer to examine it. Yes, a bullet hole; she was certain of it. And there were others.

"Who came after you, Tolemek?" she whispered, walking around the lab again. This time, she looked for clues as to who might have barged in. "And what did they want?"

Her gaze shifted back toward his workstation. She wished she had paid more attention when he'd been telling her about his new project. Was it possible some military organization had heard of it and wanted it for themselves? It had sounded like a weapon—or a tool—that armies might find useful, but was it truly so groundbreaking that it would prompt someone to do this?

When her search didn't reveal anything about the invaders— no food or cigarette wrappers left behind that might have suggested where they had come from—she headed for the door. Maybe digging the spent bullets out of the walls would provide some clues, but she needed to report this first.

But to whom? General Zirkander? Tolemek didn't work for him. Tolemek was essentially an independent contractor, but he worked most directly for the king. Angulus was the one who'd given him the lab and supplied Tolemek with all the modern equipment he needed. Angulus had also given Tolemek the assignment he'd been working on when this had happened.

"Guess it's time to see the king."

Cas nodded to herself and headed out of the building. She hoped the king would deign to see a lowly lieutenant, one who didn't have an appointment. He probably would if he knew she wanted to see him. It would be convincing one of his gatekeepers to tell him that would be a challenge.

"I'm up for it," Cas whispered, worried and determined. She *would* find out what had happened to Tolemek.

* * *

Ridge whistled cheerfully as he strode through the hallways of the castle, two guards accompanying him. They didn't pass anyone else who was whistling, and the guards glanced at him occasionally, and also at each other, maybe wondering if they should ask him to pipe down. Ridge had noticed that people rarely told generals to stuff a sock in it, and the guards, likely former soldiers themselves, did not do so now. At least there was one perk of having accepted the lofty rank. He could whistle as he pleased.

He peeked through open doorways as the guards led him up the stairs to the private suites, half-expecting to stumble across Captain Kaika in here somewhere. She was likely at work, since it *was* a workday, but the idea of seeing her roaming the castle in slippers and a robe made him smirk. Some people were hard to imagine out of uniform without smirking.

"Either of you boys have any construction experience?" Ridge asked his escorts.

"Sir?"

"We're building a residence for Bhrava Saruth." Ridge decided "residence" sounded less pompous than "temple" and had far fewer connotations of delusion. "I'm not sure if the king will approve any funds for it, so it'll likely be a largely volunteer kind of thing. But a memorable project to be a part of."

"Bhrava Saruth... the dragon, sir?"

"Yup. The dragon who's been an ally to Iskandia and helped defend the capital from enemy dragons on several occasions. We might not have survived if not for him."

"Uh, I guess I could help a little."

"Great, want to put your name on this list?" Ridge paused and pulled a pen and folded piece of paper out of his uniform pocket.

The guard gaped, maybe surprised to see that dozens of names already occupied the list. Ridge felt a little silly procuring help for the dragon—it wasn't as if he was Bhrava Saruth's high priestess, er, priest, after all—but the sooner the temple was built, the sooner he would stop pestering Ridge about it.

They paused in the hallway, and the guard wrote his name down.

"Address too," Ridge said. "So my assistant can find you when it's time to round up the helpers."

"Er, I live in the bunkhouse here, sir."

"That'll make it easy then. See if you can recruit some of your guard buddies, will you? There'll be beer. And I'm sure Bhrava Saruth will bless you."

"Bless me, sir? He's not really a god, right?"

"Nah, but whatever he does when he blesses you works. I've healed much more quickly than normal since he wriggled his tail at me. Also, his blessings are supposed to improve fertility." Ridge had no idea if that part was true. Sardelle could apparently wave a hand and ensure no babies resulted from their evenings together, so he didn't know how fertile his... fertileness was right now.

"Uh, I don't need to be fertile at the moment, sir."

"Lisella will be relieved to hear that," the other guard murmured, eliciting a blush from his comrade.

Ridge took the paper back from the first guard—he'd already signed—and turned to the other one. "Have any evenings to spare? Days are still long with lots of light until late in the evening. Plenty of time to build a dragon residence after work."

Judging by the way his mouth twisted, the second guard didn't want to sign up.

"I don't think it's allowed to refuse generals," the first one whispered to him.

"Are you sure? I'm not in the army."

"It doesn't have to be *every* evening," Ridge said. "Maybe just a couple of weekends here and there."

"You said there'd be beer, sir?"

"Absolutely. A fine stout from the Low Dog Brewery."

Ridge resumed whistling as the second guard signed the list.

"What's going on out there?" a familiar stern voice asked.

King Angulus leaned out of the doorway of his office, one of several of his offices in the castle, but the only one attached to his personal suite. Ridge had only been up here once, years ago with General Ort when they had reported late at night about pirates spotted up north along the coast.

"Recruiting, Sire." Ridge lifted one hand to salute while he took his paper and pen back with the other.

"Not for your flier squadrons, I assume." Angulus frowned at the guards, and they did an impressive job of straightening up and arranging their faces in a stern and expressionless manner.

"For the building of the dragon residence you're eager to approve the location and construction of."

Angulus lifted his eyes toward the ceiling—or perhaps the heavens. "I knew there was a reason I was dreading this meeting."

He disappeared back inside, and Ridge followed him into the office, shedding the guards outside. He closed the door behind him.

"Sire, I can't believe this meeting doesn't excite you more than ones with stuffy, self-important bureaucrats. Talking to me must be a delight in comparison."

Angulus gave him a flat look as he walked around the desk to sit down. "Do you know the meaning of the word deferential, Zirkander?"

"I know obsequious is a synonym."

Angulus's look grew flatter.

Ridge, remembering that he wanted to ask him to stand at his side during the wedding, decided he should rein in his lippy streak, at least for today. Perhaps for all days he interacted with him. Ridge wasn't sure why he struggled so to be *deferential* with authority figures, just that it had started early in his life. He distinctly remembered being dragged home by his ear by a teacher when he'd been a boy. On several occasions.

But Angulus was more than an irritated teacher. He was the ruler over all of Iskandia. And he hadn't been that openly pleased with Ridge since the incident with the sorceress. Understandably so, since Ridge had, however inadvertently, flown the woman directly into the castle. Where she'd proceeded to kill numerous government leaders and had *tried* to kill Angulus.

"I miss the days when General Ort accompanied you to meetings and kicked you under the table when you were inappropriate."

"Sorry, Sire. I can be serious."

"Doubtful," Angulus said as Ridge stepped forward with the drawings.

"As you know, I'm here to discuss Bhrava Saruth's temple. Residence. These are plat maps I got from the tax office of some of the royal lands near the city. I figured it would be difficult to get a private party to donate land for the cause, but that you, being eager to keep the dragon nearby so he can help us fight off aerial invaders that come our way, would be willing to sacrifice a few acres."

Eager was perhaps another word he needed to find synonyms for. Ridge doubted Angulus had ever been eager about anything in his life. He'd seen portraits of Prince Angulus painted in his boyhood years, and he'd appeared staid in all of them.

Angulus squinted and peered into Ridge's eyes.

Ridge didn't know what he was looking for—seriousness?— but he gazed back, even though he doubted he was supposed to make eye contact with people from the nobility. There was an old rule about that, if he recalled correctly. One with a ridiculously heinous punishment. Like castration. Or death. Something along those lines.

"Sardelle tells me they're a charming and delightfully lively brown," Ridge said after a few uncomfortable moments.

"What?"

"My eyes. I thought you might have forgotten their color, Sire."

Angulus dropped his face into his palm. Well, at least he'd broken the stare.

"I was trying to tell if you were under the influence of that dragon right now," Angulus said. "Otherwise, you seem an unlikely advocate for this project."

Ridge thought about mentioning that, according to Bhrava Saruth, he'd been the dragon's—dragon *god's*—first worshipper in this era. But that would likely get him more eye rolling.

"I don't think so, Sire. He's helped in numerous battles, battles that a lot of my people survived, specifically because we had him up there with us, fighting alongside our fliers. I'm utterly serious when I say it's worth doing a few favors for him, both because it's appropriate to show him some gratitude and appreciation, and also for more selfish reasons. As I said, we'll surely benefit from him sticking around."

"And coercing our people to worship him like a god?" Angulus grumbled, but he did lean forward to look at the maps.

He hadn't invited Ridge to sit in either of the chairs facing his desk, so Ridge clasped his hands behind his back in a polite parade rest.

"This rocky island is your preferred location?" Angulus asked.

"Not *my* preferred location. I just couldn't sell him on Crazy Canyon or a mud-covered hillside. He's brighter than he lets on."

"Hm. I suppose much of the rock for the structure could be taken from the island itself and the surrounding cliffs."

"Yes, Sire. I'm doing my best to recruit volunteers to help with the construction. I haven't yet visited the masons' guild, but I will. I'm sure you have enough to pay for right now, so I didn't want to ask for funds for this. Just some land that's not being used anyway."

"You have a list of volunteers?" Angulus glanced toward the door, no doubt thinking of the recruiting pitch he'd overheard.

"I do." Ridge pulled out the paper and unfolded it to show him the names. Most of them were soldiers, so far, but he would find the necessary civilian experts. Fortunately, he had a number of army engineers already. "They're excited to assist our scaled ally."

"More likely, they're excited to swill the free beer you're offering."

"I don't think Bhrava Saruth will object to *how* I get the workers there, so long as he gets a residence in the end."

"If I'm going to give away royal land, owned by the crown for generations and generations, to this, then I want to make sure the people assembling the temple aren't drunk."

Ridge arched his eyebrows. "You're willing to do it then? Give up the land?"

Angulus sighed. "Yes. I'm concerned about his claims of being a god and perhaps tricking people into joining his so-called religion, but I can't deny that he's helped us without asking for anything else in return."

"I don't think many people who, ah, follow him truly believe they're joining a real religion or worshipping a real god."

"Cults start that way." Angulus tapped the map. "I want to see the building plans before I approve anything."

"I've already got some preliminary sketches, Sire." Ridge rolled out his other papers on the desk. "They'll have to change and be refined now that a site has been chosen, of course, but Bhrava Saruth liked that one."

Angulus squinted at him for a long moment before looking down. Ridge couldn't read that squint. Too bad Jaxi wasn't here to read the king's mind and relay secrets.

"The columns are as wide as houses."

"Yes, I believe he liked the majesty of them, the openness of the front and the back, and the fact that there would be room for his throne."

Angulus looked up. "His *throne?*"

"Yes, Sire. Are there any rules the architect needs to be aware of? Such as a dragon's throne can't be larger than the king's throne? I suppose we can just call it a large chair if need be."

There was that squint again. "Just get me the final plans before ground is broken. Even though that island is hidden in that inlet, it is along a prominent part of our coastline. I don't want our country to be embarrassed."

Ridge suspected it was Angulus who didn't want to be embarrassed, but he found that perfectly understandable.

"Yes, Sire. I'll get Wralani right on it. She's the architect that sketched those."

"Is she also working for beer?"

"And a ride in one of the fliers. Apparently, she's always wanted to go up in one."

"I almost feel like I should assign you the task of getting fliers built without requiring money, but I fear what kind of equipment we'd get if beer was the payment bartered."

"I do too," Ridge said. "I'm more comfortable bartering for temples I'll never have to live in."

"You don't think he'll expect you to attend him there? As a loyal worshipper?"

"I think he'd be pleased if I simply had tarts delivered."

Angulus smiled faintly. Ridge took that as a positive sign, or at least a sign that he hadn't irritated him too much. Perhaps this was the time to make his request. Or should he apologize first about the sorceress incident? He'd been too chagrined at the time to think of dropping to his knees in abject apology, but maybe he should have.

A knock sounded at the door.

Angulus looked at a clock on a mantel and frowned. "What is it?"

"It's about Deathmaker, Sire," a man called through the door. One of the guards?

Angulus looked at Ridge.

"I haven't seen him in a few days, Sire," Ridge said.

"Come in," Angulus called.

Ridge gaped when Lieutenant Ahn walked in, her chin high and a determined expression on her face. Surprise flashed through her green eyes when she saw Ridge. She recovered and saluted him and the king.

"What's wrong?" Ridge asked, certain something was. Ahn wasn't the type to request an audience with the king on a whim. Or ever.

"Tolemek's missing, and his lab is a mess, sir. An explosion went off, but I think someone might have ransacked it looking for something too." Ahn looked at Angulus. "Sire, I know you're busy, and I apologize for barging in, but I talked to Tolemek last night, and he said he was working on something for you, a malleable explosive."

"Yes." Angulus gripped his chin and studied her, his expression difficult to read.

"I'm afraid his disappearance might have something to do with the project."

Ridge hadn't heard anything about this latest endeavor, but he wouldn't be surprised if Tolemek was involved in creating some new weapon for the king.

Angulus lowered his hand and shook his head. "I don't see why it would. It wasn't anything top secret. It would be an advantageous upgrade to our current line of explosives for demolitions, but it's hard to imagine someone ransacking his lab and kidnapping him over it. Assuming that's what you believe happened?"

Ahn hesitated. "I'm *hoping* he's still alive, Sire. But there were bullet holes in the walls. I'm afraid it's possible he was—" she took a deep breath, "—killed and his body disposed of. But I'd like to operate under the assumption that he's been taken somewhere. Somewhere we can find him."

"Any idea who took him?"

"No, Sire. I didn't do a deep investigation—I'm sure I'm not the most qualified person to do so—but I didn't see any clues when I went in. I was hoping you might have some ideas." Ahn, her fine-featured face bleak, looked at Ridge.

He wished he had some ideas for her. She'd been to the hells and back this last year, and he never would have wanted more trouble for her.

Angulus took a pad of paper out of a drawer. "I can write down a few of the recent projects he's done for me, and I'll get Colonel

Porthlok from intelligence up here. He can have some people look over the lab more thoroughly for clues. I'll send Kaika over there too. You mentioned an explosion. She could probably tell us if it was one of Tolemek's concoctions or something out of a factory."

"I'd like to help too, Sire. Sir." Ahn glanced at Ridge. "If there's anything I can do…"

"I suspect Intelligence is better equipped to handle this than a pilot," Angulus said, his voice far gentler than when he spoke to Ridge. "But I understand Tolemek is a friend of yours. I'll keep you apprised of what we find out."

Ahn looked like she wanted to protest, to insist that she be put on the investigation team, but she must have remembered she was addressing the king. All she said was, "Yes, Sire."

"Dismissed," Angulus said. "Both of you."

Ridge hadn't gotten a chance to broach the topic of the wedding, but with Tolemek missing and Angulus frowning and making notes in his pad, this wasn't the best time.

"Yes, Sire," he and Ahn said and walked out together.

The guards were still out there, plus two more, ones who had accompanied Ahn up. They followed at a discreet distance, letting Ridge and Ahn head out of their own accord.

"Sir," Ahn said quietly, "do you think he'll do enough? I mean, I know he's the king and can do a lot, but I'm worried Tolemek won't be his priority. Even if he was, I don't know if I can just step back and let someone else handle the investigation."

"I can understand why that would be hard," Ridge said, "but you better at least stay out of the lab until Intelligence has had a chance to go over everything. You wouldn't want to disturb evidence. But there's nothing to keep you from looking for clues at home. Does Tee have an office there? Any correspondence he might have gotten that he didn't tell you about? Threats from people who aren't admirers of his past work?" Ridge lifted his eyebrows. He didn't want to bring up Tanglewood or what had been the Cofah equivalent of the incident on their continent, but between those two towns that had been destroyed and all the work Tolemek had done for the Roaming Curse pirates, there were plenty of people who would like to see him dead. Not to mention that he'd betrayed the Roaming Curse itself, leaving countless pirates with a grudge against him.

"He doesn't usually bring work home, but I can check," Ahn said.

"Good. If Kaika gets assigned to this, I'm sure you can bug her for updates too. You better get to work for now. Isn't Wolf Squadron doing its supply and maintenance checks on the fliers today?"

"Yes, sir. I was sent to pick up healing salves."

"Ah. Well, let Tranq know what happened," Ridge said as they exited the castle into the warm noon sun. "And I'll let you know if I hear anything before you do."

Ahn hesitated before saying, "Yes, sir."

That hesitation concerned Ridge. As did that determined look on Ahn's face. He couldn't blame her for wanting to help Tolemek, who was much more than a *friend* to her, but he hoped she wouldn't disappear from work or do anything that could get her in trouble.

Ridge? a voice spoke into his mind.

Jaxi?

Who else speaks telepathically to you?

Sardelle, Bhrava Saruth, and Wreltad. Occasionally Phelistoth if there's no cheese in the house and he wishes me to correct the deficiency.

Well, I should think you would recognize my sage voice at once. Especially since I'm not requesting cheese. I am, however, requesting that you come to your office in the citadel. Sardelle and I are waiting for you.

Ridge paused just outside the castle gate. Ahn continued on without looking back—she appeared to be deep in thought.

More trouble? Ridge wondered if Sardelle and Jaxi had heard about Tolemek already.

Sardelle insists I tell you it's simply a concern and that you don't need to hurry to see us.

Ridge grimaced. Sardelle would call anything short of dragons invading the city a "concern."

I'll be right there.

Chapter 4

STOP PACING, Jaxi said.

I'm not pacing. I'm walking. Sardelle glanced toward the door of Ridge's office for the dozenth time. She couldn't know for certain that Fern would come out here to talk to her son about the morning's events, but Sardelle did expect it. And what would she say if Fern walked in before Ridge did? There was so much to explain, but she had no idea where to start. She just knew she would find it easier with Ridge at her side.

It's called pacing when you're going back and forth in the same spot. There's a dictionary on the shelf. I can look it up if you don't believe me.

That's not necessary. Sardelle stretched out with her senses, brushing past all the other officers in the building and looking for Ridge. She had expected him to be here, tackling stacks of paperwork, but she wasn't surprised he wasn't. For a general, he seemed to run a lot of errands, personally checking on his squadrons and their equipment, and making sure everything at the hangars here and at other bases ran smoothly. He also gave frequent lectures at the flight academy. If one could call them lectures. She'd observed one. He tended to use props and make propeller and machine-gun noises as he demonstrated air-battle techniques. If nothing else, his methods kept the students awake and raptly watching him. She smiled, imagining him one day entertaining their children. Starting with the one she had yet to tell him about...

He's coming, Jaxi said. *I told him you were waiting here, so he's hurrying back from his meeting with the king.*

He was at the castle? Sardelle had told Jaxi not to interrupt him if he was doing something important or to say anything that would worry him. Her news wasn't that important, not compared to whatever had taken Ridge to Angulus's doorstep.

That's what you think. He was asking the king for land to build Bhrava Saruth's temple on. I think his mother's discovery of magic and dragons rates at least as high as that.

Sardelle pursed her lips but didn't reply. She sensed Ridge's approach. He was outside, heading for the front steps of the citadel. She made herself stop walking—she wasn't pacing, damn it—and clasp her hands behind her back as she waited for him.

Voices sounded in the hallway outside as a couple of officers stopped to ask him questions. Sardelle resisted the urge to pace again.

Are you going to tell him about Ridgewalker Junior while you're broaching the subject of dealing with kin? Jaxi asked.

I don't think this is the time for that. I was envisioning a quiet dinner together, a peaceful summer evening where we can chat about light topics without other troubles looming over our heads.

If you wait until there are no troubles, the kid could be ten by the time you tell Ridge about it.

I'd like to think his observational skills would allow him to suss out the secret on his own by then.

The door opened, and Ridge walked in with rolled papers in his hand, smiling broadly when their eyes met. His twinkled with warmth and good cheer, and Sardelle caught herself returning the smile despite her concerns. She did sense a thread of worry in his thoughts and wondered what Jaxi had told him.

"Greetings, my soon-to-be wife," he said, tossing the rolls of paper on the desk as he came forward to hug and kiss her.

It wasn't a chaste kiss, and she was on the verge of putting her arms around him, but someone walking past in the corridor whistled.

Ridge released her and stepped back, his lips quirking into a wry smile. "When I walk in with amorous thoughts in mind, you're supposed to use your magic to blow the door shut behind me."

"I wasn't expecting you to have amorous thoughts. Also, I believe you have hands capable of closing doors."

"Yes, but I'm a general now. I'm not supposed to have to close my own doors."

"No? Perhaps you could have a private stand in the hallway outside whose sole purpose is to open and close the door for you."

He tapped a finger to his jaw. "This suggestion is not without merit."

Sardelle stirred a whisper of air to close the door. She *did* want privacy for this chat.

He glanced over his shoulder, then wriggled his eyebrows at her. "Are *you* having amorous thoughts?"

"I wasn't until you kissed me."

"I'm glad my lips can inspire such thoughts in you." Ridge clasped her hands, his face growing more serious. "Jaxi said something is wrong?"

"I hope she didn't give you the wrong impression. It's nothing dire for the country or the city."

"Is it dire for *us*?"

She hesitated, and the worry she'd sensed within him grew visible in his eyes. "I'm not sure. Your mother came by this morning, and she saw Phelistoth in dragon form."

"Oh? Was he being fearsome?"

"He was sunning himself in the backyard the way Spots does on the windowsill."

"Fearsomely?"

"No, but his size alarmed her. As I'm sure you know, she's somehow managed to continue believing dragons aren't real despite evidence to the contrary."

"I'm sure she'll recover," Ridge said.

"Yes, I took her inside and offered her tea, and she pulled herself together enough to get down to the business of wedding planning. She told me we need to go dress shopping, that we can't have the wedding in a swamp—that's what she's calling the pond—and that she's concerned she hadn't accounted for dragons in her seating chart."

Ridge relaxed, and she realized she needed to get to the part that was troublesome, but he started speaking first.

"I've heard most of those concerns from her before. Dress shopping sounds like a great idea. Oh, will you invite Lilah to go along with you? She accepted a teaching job at the university here and just moved up to the capital. To advance her career, she said, but I'm terrified and horrified that she may just want to be close to *him*."

"Colonel Therrik? Well, they are dating, I understand."

He winced. "That's what I'm worried about. Girls gossip when they shop, right? Can you make sure he's treating her all right? I mean, I know she can take care of herself when it comes to most men, but he's an overpowering personality. And an overpowering *person*."

Sardelle rested her hand on his arm. "I appreciate your protective feelings toward your cousin, but her love life isn't my main concern right now. While I was talking to your mother, Tylie ran in, excitedly demonstrating her ability to levitate rocks. And making it clear I'd instructed her in this skill."

"Ahhh," Ridge said, drawing out the syllable as understanding blossomed on his face. "So, Mom has now seen for herself that magic exists."

"And she knows that I practice it."

"Well, I'm certain she will recover and still want to take you dress shopping."

"I'm less certain. She rushed out the door, stumbling and dropping her folders, and rode off without looking back."

"Only because it must have been a blow to her to learn that dragons and magic exist—all in the same morning."

"Understandably so, but I'm concerned she won't be able to get past the fact that I am a sorceress. You know how the average Iskandian feels about magic. I don't want her to fear me. Or worse, believe those damn newspaper stories about me controlling you. I—" Sardelle's throat was growing tight, and she paused to swallow, trying to rein in her emotions. "I've come to care about her, Ridge, and very much like having her care about me. It meant so much that she welcomed me into the family. You know how much I miss my own family and how much it stings to know they all died centuries ago and won't be at the wedding.

Sometimes, I can push that out of my mind, but it's hard right now, when we've been working on the guest list and invitations, and I'm forced to remember that I can't invite the old friends and kin that I wish could have seen me getting married…"

Her attempt to wrangle her emotions didn't work, and tears formed in her eyes.

"I know." Ridge wrapped his arms around her and pulled her into a hug. She leaned her face against his shoulder as he rested a hand on the back of her head. "I'm sorry there's no way to travel back in time to get your family and bring them here for the wedding."

Sardelle took a few deep breaths, appreciating the hug and the warmth that emanated from him, physically and emotionally. She hadn't come here to weep all over his uniform, so she sniffed a couple of times and tried to pull herself together.

"As far as my mom goes, I'm positive she'll recover and accept you as her daughter-in-law. I've told you before that she'd about given up on me getting married and her having grandchildren."

Ah ha, Jaxi said. *There's your segue into your other announcement.*

Ignoring Jaxi's commentary, Sardelle said, "As I recall, you said she'd be happy if you had babies with a baboon at this point."

"I don't think that's exactly what I said—"

"It's very close."

"—but you're *much* better than a baboon." Ridge leaned back enough to smile and meet her eyes, and she sensed him wanting to make her feel better. "You don't have any fur you have to shave before you can go out dress shopping."

Apparently, he doesn't know all the details of your grooming regimen, Jaxi thought.

There isn't any fur involved, Sardelle replied tartly.

Armpit hair is close to fur.

Gross.

I certainly think so.

"Is Jaxi making comments?" Ridge asked. "My jokes don't usually prompt that weird of an expression from you."

"You know me well. *Us* well." She patted his chest. "I'm relieved she didn't share the conversation with you."

It's not too late, Jaxi said.

Ssh.

"I'll find some time to go up and talk to Mom," Ridge promised. "Is there anything else worrying you that I should know about?" He raised his eyebrows.

There's your baby-announcement prompt again.

Sardelle bit her lip. Maybe this *would* be the time to bring it up.

"Oh, wait." Ridge dropped his arms and stepped back. "I better tell you about Tolemek. Hells, I bet Tylie doesn't know yet either."

"What happened?"

"He's missing. And his lab was ravaged, or so Ahn reported. She said something about an explosion. The king knows and said he'd send Kaika and someone from army intelligence over to look for clues about who did it and where they might have taken Tolemek."

"Jaxi was right," Sardelle said, her shoulders slumping at the news. "There never seem to be any truly untroubled times, do there?"

"Every now and then, there are a couple of peaceful hours in the evenings." Ridge smiled, but it wasn't as broad and cheerful as before. "Maybe you could go over to his lab and look around with your magical senses. Do you think you might see something Kaika and an intelligence officer wouldn't?"

"Not necessarily, not if it happened hours ago, though if magic was used, Jaxi or I might find some indications of it."

"Yes, good. Do you mind going? I'd offer to accompany you, but I have an architect to bribe with beer—" Ridge waved at the papers he'd thrown on the desk, "—and I'm due to inspect a couple of fliers being delivered to the hangar this afternoon. The new models are finally in production."

"Architect?" Despite her concern for Tolemek, Sardelle felt a twinge of curiosity and pushed the topmost rolled paper open.

"For someone's temple, yes."

"Oh, this design is lovely. Reminiscent of the temples and colosseums from the Tvakmar Era. They incorporated columns and arches in their architecture before mathematicians quite understood why arches worked so well to distribute weight. Some of their ruins still stand deep in the Cofah empire."

"That's the design Bhrava Saruth liked," Ridge said. "Because there's a good place for his throne, and it will be visible right when you walk in."

Sardelle snorted and released the paper. "I'll go check out Tolemek's lab. Will you be home tonight?"

"You should know how little sleeping on the couch in here excites me." He waved to the well-used leather sofa. "Aside from Tolemek's disappearance, there's nothing dire going on in the city, though I suppose if I go up to my mother's house, that'll make me late. Unless I take a flier. The army frowns on us using their craft for reasons that aren't work-related, but maybe I can say I'm going to check on the temple's building site if someone asks."

"And that is considered work-related?"

"Bhrava Saruth is *definitely* work."

"I can't argue with that. I'll see you tonight." Sardelle rose on tiptoes to kiss him before heading for the door.

"Don't forget dress shopping," he called after her. "And inviting Lilah. She'll be a good stand-in if my mom needs a few more days to recover. I mean, she doesn't care about art or fashion or buying pretty clothes, but at least she can hold your sword while you try things on."

Sardelle paused with her hand on the doorknob, surprised that dresses were on his mind when Tolemek was missing. "Are you bringing this up again because you want me to prepare for the wedding or because you want me to finagle information out of Lilah about her romance with Therrik?"

"Not about their *romance*. Seven gods, I don't want *any* details on *that*. I just want to make sure he's treating her well. You know, the *opposite* of how he treats me."

"I don't believe Lilah is as lippy to him as you are," she said, releasing the doorknob and turning back around.

"She states her opinions, stands up for herself, and does as she wishes," Ridge said.

"That's not the same as being lippy."

"Maybe not, but Therrik doesn't like people arguing with him. I'm surprised they're even— Doesn't he seem like someone who'd like a sweet docile woman who obeys him a lot?"

"I haven't spent much time contemplating his ideal partner," Sardelle said.

"Neither have I. But still." Ridge frowned and stuffed his hands into his pockets.

"Have I mentioned that it's sweet that you're worried about your cousin? But at the same time, that you should accept that she's a mature adult who can make her own decisions when it comes to the men she dates? Without the guidance of meddling older cousins?"

"So, I'm a sweet meddling pest?"

"That sums it up nicely." She smiled at him and opened the door.

"The serene way you smile makes it seem like that wasn't an insult, but I know better."

Her smile widened as she walked out.

"You're lucky I'm used to being insulted," Ridge called after her, "and that I still want to marry you."

The door had closed, so Sardelle replied telepathically. *I'd be devastated if you didn't.*

Good. I love you.

I love you too. She smiled as she walked out of the citadel, and it wasn't until she was far down the walkway that she realized she still hadn't told him about the baby.

"After I figure out what happened to Tolemek," she murmured. It didn't seem right that she should be planning her wedding and speaking of love when Cas was worried sick about *her* missing love.

* * *

Cas wanted to pace while Captain Kaika and Captain Bitinger poked around in Tolemek's lab, but the intelligence officer had already warned her once not to tramp around and break more glass with her diminutive elephant feet. Whatever that meant. So instead, she lingered in the doorway, examining the lab with only her eyes, and tried not to think about what she would do if they didn't find Tolemek.

It had taken her most of the summer to get used to living with someone else—with him—and she'd barely begun to realize that she liked it, liked having someone to come home to, someone to share breakfast with, and someone to hash out problems with. Someone who cared about her. And someone *she* cared about.

A brown-haired man in a lab coat with goggles perched on his forehead came up the stairs. He turned toward the first door on the right but noticed Cas and heard Kaika and Bitinger discussing residues from explosives.

"What happened in there?" the man asked, coming forward to peer past Cas. He looked to be in his mid-twenties and reminded her of Lieutenant Pimples.

"Tolemek was kidnapped and his lab ransacked."

"Kidnapped? From the middle of the city? That's statistically improbable."

"I don't suppose you were here last night and heard anything?"

He shook his head. "Not me. I just came in to check my gels."

Cas hadn't expected anything else. She and the intelligence captain had already questioned the building's occupants, the three they had managed to round up. From what she'd heard, half the people who worked here only did so part time because they had offices elsewhere or also taught at the university. Nobody had been here the night before, at least nobody that had been by yet. Bitinger's people ought to hunt down the other tenants for questioning. Or the police. Someone must have reported the destroyed lab to them while Cas had been at the castle. When she'd returned with Kaika and Bitinger, two police officers had been walking around the room, breaking more glass and perhaps destroying evidence. The intelligence captain had shooed them away in exasperation.

Kaika left Bitinger, who was peering at things with a magnifying glass, and walked to the door.

Cas lifted her gaze, hoping Kaika had learned something. But she didn't meet Cas's eyes. Instead, she licked her finger and wiped the sooty doorjamb. Some of the soot came away on her skin, and she lifted it to her nose to sniff it. Then she touched it to her tongue.

The scientist blinked. "You shouldn't do that, my lady. Soot is a byproduct of the incomplete burning of carbon-containing materials and may contain numerous carcinogens such as cadmium, chromium, and arsenic."

"Good thing I know a dragon who will bless me then." Kaika rubbed her fingers together. "Did you just call me 'my lady'?"

"Er, yes, my—ma'am. You seem…" He looked her up and down, taking in the army uniform and her six feet in height. His gaze lingered for a moment at her chest, though the uniforms didn't exactly accentuate a woman's breasts.

"Noble?" Kaika asked skeptically.

"Tall enough and strong enough to beat me up." He smiled faintly, as if the idea appealed to him rather than alarming him. "I thought I should try to get on your good side. Are those grenades on your belt?"

"Yes, they are. Nice of you to notice." She patted him on the cheek. "I think your gels are calling you."

"Uhm, right." He headed to his own laboratory but glanced back at her grenades again before disappearing through the doorway.

"Scientists are quirky," Kaika announced.

"I've noticed, ma'am." Cas felt a pang of loss as she thought of her own scientist. But she firmly told herself it was too soon to believe him lost. "Did your soot tasting tell you anything?"

"Not really, but this is telling me a lot." Kaika drew a piece of twisted metal out of her pocket. "It's the safety pin from a Farongi bomb."

"Farongi?" Cas hadn't heard the name but allowed herself a smidgen of hope that Kaika may have found some useful clue.

"*Farongi?*" Bitinger asked from across the lab. "I was getting ready to declare this a Cofah invasion."

"Based on what evidence?" Kaika asked.

"They're our greatest enemy with the most to fear from technological military advancements we make, and since Dr. Targoson was originally one of theirs, they have reasons to resent him defecting."

"So... *no* evidence," Kaika said.

The captain, a reed-thin man in a perfectly pressed uniform and painfully polished boots, frowned. "Why would the *Dakrovians* kidnap Targoson and wreck his lab? They're not even a unified nation. It would have to be a team sent from one of their independent city-states. If you can call them cities." He sniffed. "Few of their jungle population centers have more than twenty or thirty thousand people."

"Nonetheless, this is a Farongi pin."

"Dakrovians?" Cas eyed the pin, thinking of the mission she and Tolemek had gone on to the continent a few months earlier. They had attacked the Cofah there and kidnapped their emperor, but she didn't think her team had done any actual damage to Tildar Dem, the town they had visited. The Dakrovians shouldn't have vengeful thoughts toward Iskandia—or Tolemek.

Kaika nodded. "Most of the continent is technologically behind the times, but there are a few exceptions. In Jlongar Jalak, one of the larger cities near the southern end, there's a renowned weapons manufacturer—Hur Farongi—that supplies rifles for big-game hunters and also makes three types of explosives, at the request of the warring tribes in the area. The safety pins are the same on all three, with a distinct twisted-strand style pull." She held up her find. Her twisted find.

Captain Bitinger came over to look at it.

"Farongi is popular with pirates and mercenaries," he said, "because Jlongar Jalak is easy to get into and out of without dealing with anyone's military. The city has a modest police force, but that's it, and they have a free-trade policy. Anyone can dock there for a fee."

"So, pirates might have done this?"

"Would pirates have kidnapped him?" Kaika asked. "Or just shot him?"

"The people here *did* try to shoot him." Bitinger waved at the bullets in the walls. "And we don't have any proof that they kidnapped Targoson. They may have shot him and removed the body."

Cas didn't like hearing someone else voice the thought she'd had earlier. Not *that* thought.

"I see sensitivity training isn't required in the intelligence units." Kaika frowned at Bitinger and gave Cas a concerned look.

Bitinger's brow furrowed. "Is it required in the elite troops?"

"No, Colonel Therrik would explode if he had to be sensitive."

Cas looked into the hallway, debating how she could find Tolemek if pirates had kidnapped him—she chose to believe that had happened rather than someone shooting him and dumping the body. They could have taken him right out to a sailing ship or an airship, meaning he might already be hundreds of miles from the mainland. She could give chase in her flier, assuming she could get permission to take it out, but where would she start looking? It was a large world. Could Tylie help find him?

Someone new came up the stairs at the end of the hallway. Sardelle.

Cas hadn't expected her, but she lifted a hand in greeting, wondering if her magic might allow her to see something that the two captains had not.

Bitinger shifted his weight, frowning uneasily down the hallway as Sardelle approached. Cas wondered if he recognized her and had a problem with her occupation. Or maybe he'd seen some of those silly newspaper articles of late.

"Afternoon, Sardelle," Kaika drawled. "Come to join the party?"

"Party?" Bitinger asked. "I don't think *I'm* the insensitive one here."

Kaika shooed him away. "Weren't you trying to figure out what was in that vault?"

"Yes, yes. Don't let her come in and trample things." He pointed at Sardelle, then returned to his investigation.

"Good afternoon, Cas, Kaika." Sardelle nodded gravely to them. "Ridge asked me to come help figure out what happened."

"Nothing good," Cas said, sighing. She did appreciate that General Zirkander had sent someone else to help, someone with a different set of skills. That morning, when she had left the castle, she hadn't been certain the king would prioritize Tolemek highly enough and send enough people.

"Are there any clues yet as to who did this?" Sardelle peered past them and into the lab, her eyebrows lifting when she saw the destruction.

Kaika held up the twisted piece of metal.

"That looks like the pin you use to open an anchovy tin," Sardelle said.

"It's the pin you use to *open* a Dakrovian grenade," Kaika said. "It's a good thing Angulus sent me over here. Bitinger would have had us haring off after the Cofah, and you'd have us harassing innocent fishermen."

Sardelle's cheeks grew a little pink. Or maybe they'd been pink when she had come in. Had she run over here? She wasn't breathing heavily, but her skin seemed a little brighter than usual.

"I'll see if I can find anything that might suggest magic was used." Sardelle stepped past Cas and Kaika and into the room. "Tolemek is a capable fighter, even if it isn't his first nature, and he usually has explosives of his own within reach when he's in his own lab. I suspect the numbers were either overwhelming or someone used magic on him."

Cas hadn't considered that, but it was a good point.

Bitinger frowned at Sardelle when glass crunched under her shoes, but he didn't say anything to her. Rather than looking around, she walked in, rested her hand on a work bench and closed her eyes. She wore a dress, a flattering blue with white trim, and her soulblade hung from a braided leather belt, so Cas imagined Jaxi also using magic to search the room.

Bitinger shuddered and looked back at the broken vault. He scraped some residue from the inside and placed it in a test tube.

Once again, Cas resisted the urge to pace. She felt useless here, but what could she do? Before she could hop into her flier, she needed more of a clue than that the kidnappers had visited a Dakrovian weapons maker.

After a long minute of standing with her eyes closed, Sardelle moved toward the area where Tolemek had been working the day before. She rounded the broken table, crouched, and scraped at something on the floor with her fingernail.

Cas watched to see if she would sniff it and lick it.

"This sticky goo is magical." Sardelle stood up, and Cas came into the lab. Whatever Sardelle had scraped up was too small to see from across the room. "There are a lot of things in here with a magical residue to them," Sardelle added, "but I recognize them as Tolemek's work, with *his* magic imbued in them. This has someone else's magic imbued in it."

"I don't suppose you can tell whose," Cas said.

"Nobody I'm familiar with, I don't think. So that rules out Tylie. And Phelistoth and Bhrava Saruth, I suppose, though I don't think a dragon made this."

"What *is* it?" Kaika peered at Sardelle's finger.

"At the microscopic level, it's similar in makeup to a spider web."

"Microscope?" Kaika glanced around the lab, as if looking for a piece of equipment Sardelle had employed.

"Sorry, I didn't mean to imply that I'd used one. As a healer, I'm used to seeing, in a manner of speaking, things at the cellular level."

"Uh, what does that mean?" Kaika looked at Cas.

Cas could only shrug back, vaguely remembering reading about onion cells in a biology book as a student.

"That it's unlikely I would have blamed Tolemek's kidnapping on fishermen." Sardelle rubbed the substance she'd scraped up between her fingers, then had to use force to pull her fingers apart. "It's sticky and bonds quickly. Like a fast-acting glue."

"Does it seem like Dakrovian magic?" Cas doubted the pirates, or whoever was after Tolemek, had originated on that continent, but maybe there was a reason they'd chosen it for their bomb shopping.

"Hm." Sardelle's eyes grew distant. "I believe it does, actually. It seems like the work of a shaman, but there's another element…

a mundane science element in the construction of the matrix. To be honest, it seems like the kind of thing Tolemek would make."

"But you know it's *not* something he made, right?" Kaika asked. "That's what you said."

"It doesn't have his signature embedded in it, no."

"Can I get a sample of that?" Bitinger eyed Sardelle warily as he came over with tweezers and a fresh test tube. He made sure to keep Kaika between him and Sardelle. "I can have the army's science lab analyze it."

A bemused expression crossed Sardelle's face, and Cas expected her to point out that she had just analyzed it. Instead, she stepped to the side and gestured toward the floor. "There's more stuck to that tile down there."

"Ah."

Bitinger walked around Kaika and to Sardelle's side of the broken work table. He looked down at the tile, but hesitated, glancing from her to the floor. Not wanting to get too close to her?

"I don't bite," Sardelle said dryly, though her eyes looked more hurt than amused as she took a couple of steps back.

"Not at all?" Kaika asked. "Doesn't the general find that disappointing?"

Cas didn't expect Sardelle, who always came across as being serene and even regal, to respond to the joke.

However, she arched an eyebrow and said, "I do nibble occasionally."

"Sounds sedate," Kaika said. "Zirkander's tastes are much mellower than I imagined."

Sardelle's cheeks grew pink again.

"Do you imagine him often?" Cas asked, more to deflect Kaika's attention from Sardelle than because she wanted to know.

"Oh, frequently. Or I used to, I should say. Now, I have another robust man to imagine naked and sweaty."

Bitinger cleared his throat. He was down on the floor scraping at the substance with his tweezers.

"Did you want to chime in on the conversation, Captain?" Kaika asked. "What do you prefer? Biting? Nibbling? Full-on gnashing of teeth and howling at the moon in ecstasy?"

Bitinger lurched to his feet, his cheeks far redder than Sardelle's had been, though he lacked her appealing glow.

"I'm done collecting evidence," he said, capping his test tube and backing toward the door. Quickly. "I'll report my findings to my superiors, and, uh, maybe they'll inform you."

He disappeared from view, and the sound of rapid footfalls announced his hasty retreat.

"I bet he doesn't even wrinkle the sheets," Kaika said.

"In the throes of passion?" Cas asked.

"Ever."

"I don't expect his laboratory to find anything more than I did," Sardelle said, "though it's possible an analysis of the non-magical ingredients would be helpful. Still, even if we find out more about the substance, it won't necessarily give us any clues as to where Tolemek is now. Or what his kidnappers wanted. Him? Or something from his lab?" She looked toward the destroyed vault. "Or both?"

"What does he store in there?" Kaika pointed at the vault and looked at Cas.

"I'm not sure exactly. I've seen it open before, but I only know there were a bunch of vials, bottles, small bags, and a few boxes in there. He mentioned that he keeps valuable ingredients in there."

"Extremely valuable?" Kaika asked. "Anything rare that people would have trouble acquiring on their own?"

Cas spread her arms. "I wish I knew."

"While I see it as possible that someone raided his lab for ingredients," Sardelle said, "they wouldn't have needed to take him with them if all they wanted were alchemical goodies."

"Unless he witnessed the theft when he wasn't meant to," Kaika said. "Didn't you say it happened late at night, Ahn?"

Cas nodded. "After I left, at least. That was evening."

"Maybe they stumbled upon him when they hadn't expected him and had to take him with them when they left, to be sure he couldn't identify them to the authorities."

"We're just guessing," Sardelle said.

"Yeah," Kaika said, "that's what you do when you don't have many clues."

"The clues we do have point to this being someone, or a team of someones, who aren't from Iskandia. Which implies they came via boat or aircraft. I think we should begin our search in the harbor and at the commercial dirigible field. Let's find out if any foreign craft were there yesterday or are possibly still there. Also, if any of our local ships, air or water, left the country, last night or today. It would have been harder for kidnappers to board an Iskandian ship while dragging along an unwilling victim—especially one as recognizable as Tolemek—but I'm sure it's possible. Still, looking for ships of suspicious origins seems our best bet."

Cas found herself nodding as Sardelle spoke. This was the best lead she had so far.

"Will you help me check the harbor, Sardelle?" she asked, knowing Sardelle could use her magic to sense inside of a ship without going aboard. If Tolemek was anywhere in the harbor, maybe she would recognize his aura, or whatever it was called, from afar.

Sardelle hesitated, and Cas remembered she was busy planning her wedding and teaching Tylie and who knew what else.

"Yes, of course." Sardelle nodded firmly.

"If you need any assistance with the wedding preparations, I would be happy to help after we find Tolemek," Cas offered, feeling she should offer some of her time since she was asking for Sardelle's.

"Thank you, but that's not necessary." Her tone turned dry. "Unless you want to go dress shopping with me."

"Not looking forward to that, eh?" Kaika smirked. "I know I wouldn't be, not for a floofy wedding dress. Slinky and sexy dresses designed to make men drool are more fun to try on."

"I don't mind the idea of shopping for a dress, floofy or otherwise. It's more that Ridge wants me to take his cousin Lilah along. Which would normally be fine—she and I actually have quite a bit in common—but he wants me to play the role of spy and find out if Lilah and Therrik are getting along well. Ridge doesn't seem to be able to conceive that someone who doesn't appreciate his mouth could be good to a woman."

"Therrik doesn't appreciate a lot," Kaika said, "but he's got this notion of himself as being noble and honorable, so he's all right with women. And Lilah is pretty fearless, from what I observed, and doesn't mind standing up to him. And I think he likes that about her."

"I told Ridge as much. I don't know why he can't go visit her himself if he wants to see how she's doing."

"He's probably afraid he'll run into Therrik at her flat." Kaika grinned. "Naked."

Cas cleared her throat and pointed toward the hallway. "Maybe we should go to the harbor now. Before it gets dark."

"Of course," Sardelle said again and nodded for Cas to lead the way out.

Kaika thumped Sardelle on the shoulder. "Let me know if you need help dress shopping."

The offer surprised Cas—and Sardelle, as well, judging by the startled look she tossed Kaika. Cas wouldn't have guessed Kaika even *owned* a dress. Though she did go on undercover missions. Presumably, she dressed as a lady on some of them, especially in the countries where women rarely wore trousers. And maybe she liked to put on slinky things when she went to that brothel she favored. Had she stopped going there since she started seeing the king? Cas hoped so.

"You're welcome to come," Sardelle said. "And you, too, Cas."

"I just want to see how Lilah's doing," Kaika said.

"Ah, that's right. You were her bodyguard up at the mines earlier this summer."

"Yup, I got to watch that romance blossom." Kaika grinned. "But if you want help picking out a dress, I can do that too. I'm great at finding outfits that make it easy to keep hidden daggers a secret."

"I wasn't planning to take a dagger to my wedding."

"No? Well, surely you're not going without your sword." Kaika pointed at Jaxi's scabbard as they descended the steps.

"That is true," Sardelle said. "Jaxi is not an accessory I can leave behind."

"Should make for an interesting night when you and the general consummate the marriage. And here I thought he'd be bored by the nibbling."

Cas quickened her pace as they left the building, eager to find Tolemek. And also eager to *not* hear about General Zirkander being nibbled.

Chapter 5

RIDGE FELT SILLY TAKING A flier to his mother's house a mere fifteen miles north of the city, but he piloted it out over the coast, telling himself he was looking for sign of Tolemek's kidnappers while he was aloft. Of course, he had no idea if the kidnappers were local or foreign or likely to be airborne or not, but he liked to eye the coastline near the capital now and then, regardless. If there was trouble coming, he wanted to spot it before it spotted him. And what had started with the kidnapping of one man could certainly escalate to more.

Mate of my high priestess! a perky voice sounded in Ridge's mind, the power of the words making him wince.

Good evening, Bhrava Saruth. Ridge twisted his neck and spotted the gold dragon flying up the coast behind him. Anticipating what Bhrava Saruth wanted, Ridge opened with an update on the temple. *It shouldn't be long now. The king asked to see the final drawings, but I believe he's going to approve the use of that island.*

Excellent. Are you going off to engage in battle? Do you need the assistance of a powerful and mighty god?

I'm going to see my mom.

She who hatched you? I have met her before, yes? She wears the colorful clothing and beaded adornments that I like, but she does not believe in dragons.

That's her, but she believes in dragons now. I assume. She tripped over Phelistoth sunning himself in the yard this morning. I understand she found the experience alarming.

I also find it alarming when I trip over Phelistoth. For a silver dragon, he is extremely haughty.

Yes. Ridge spotted the familiar village where his mother lived and turned inland, heading for the field where he'd landed before when his somewhat AWOL squadron had been hiding out at her house.

He will never be a god.
Of that I have no doubt.
Is your intent to familiarize your mother with dragons now that she knows we exist? Bhrava Saruth asked. *Perhaps you should introduce her to me. I am most appealing, far more so than that silver dragon, and an excellent representation of my kind. And I am a god!*

Ridge wondered if Bhrava Saruth ever found it odd to identify as a dragon *and* a god. One would think being a deity and being… anything else would be mutually exclusive.

I'm going to talk to her about magic, Ridge thought. *She didn't believe in that, either, and then she saw Tylie levitating rocks through the house.*

Ridge didn't know why he was explaining all of this to the dragon. Or why Bhrava Saruth was following him.

I can also be of assistance there, mate of my high priestess. I know all there is to know about magic.

That's really not necessary, Ridge thought. *I know how important your time is, how many of your followers seek you out in the evenings.*

This is often true, but the voluptuous lady who was to come worship me tonight did not show up. Can you imagine the audacity? When I used my powers to locate her, I found her rutting with abandon with some grime-covered human male. She forgot all about me.

You were stood up.
Is that what it's called? It's most deplorable.

Yes. Ridge flew low over houses and fields, eliciting a few vocal complaints from horses and cows below, then activated his thrusters. He had to select his spot carefully since what had been a fallow field that spring when he'd used it was now covered in squash vines and fruits. He found a wide path and set down as Bhrava Saruth landed right behind him. His taloned feet touched down without doing damage to the vegetation.

Had I known you intended to travel, Bhrava Saruth said, *I could have given you a ride, so you needn't have brought that clunky flying machine.*

Accustomed to the dragon's opinions on fliers, Ridge didn't bristle at the comment. Much.

"Unless you want all the farmers around here to start screaming and lunging for guns, you may wish to change forms." Ridge climbed out of his cockpit and dropped into the dirt.

"Like this, Ridgewalker?" Bhrava Saruth skipped out of the squash patch, wearing loose cotton trousers, a tunic with a deep V that revealed half his chest, and all manner of beaded bracelets and necklaces clattering as he moved. As he *skipped*. How was it that he attracted so many women in that form? At least he wasn't wearing that weird dress again.

"Yes. You might still alarm the farmers, but I doubt they'll reach for weapons."

Ridge headed toward the highway, wondering how to ditch his tagalong. Though maybe Bhrava Saruth could be useful, in case his mother had retreated to her home and was in a state of denial. The dragon could certainly demonstrate some magic to prove it existed.

And *then* Ridge could shoo him away. Even though he believed his mother would come to accept Sardelle's occupation, he did think they might have to have a serious conversation about it. It was hard to discuss anything seriously with a dragon god along.

"It is a glorious evening," Bhrava Saruth announced. He'd stopped skipping, but he spread his arms toward the clear sky as he walked alongside Ridge.

"Do I have you to thank for that? Because if you can control weather, Sardelle and I would appreciate a sunny day for our wedding."

"No. I am a very powerful god, but I do not attempt to meddle with weather. That can have unforeseen consequences." Bhrava Saruth clapped him on the back. "But I am positive your wedding will be divine."

"Because you'll be there?"

"Indeed so."

"You're in a good mood for someone who was stood up tonight."

"Because I see in your mind that you truly intend to make sure my temple is built. I am most pleased."

"Glad to hear it." Ridge turned down the street that led to his mother's house, remembering that spring when he'd led Sardelle and his rain-soaked team this way. And also remembering how delighted Mom had been when he introduced Sardelle.

A nervous strand of doubt entered his gut as the house came into sight. What if he was wrong and Mom *couldn't* learn to accept Sardelle's occupation? He'd spoken the truth to Sardelle, as he'd believed it, but now that Mom had actually found out, and he had to talk to her about it... it was hard not to have a few tiny doubts.

"I don't suppose you know anything about Tolemek and the people who broke into his lab last night?" Ridge asked Bhrava Saruth, both to distract his mind from the impending talk and also because it would be helpful if the dragon somehow did know. Who knew—maybe his divine self had been flying over the city and noticed it happening.

"Who?"

"Dr. Tolemek Targoson. You've met him a few times at our house."

Bhrava Saruth scratched his jaw. "Has he ever brought me tarts?"

"I don't think so."

"Rubbed my belly as a dragon or a ferret?"

"Not that I know of."

"Then I don't remember him."

Ridge snorted and started to describe Tolemek, but he felt a slight tickle in his mind. Bhrava Saruth rooting through his thoughts?

"Ah, yes," Bhrava Saruth said. "The shaggy-headed brother of Phelistoth's rider. No, I know nothing of him or where he resides. Perhaps if he brought me offerings occasionally, he would be more in my awareness."

"I'll tell him to change his ways and start sending baked goods as soon as I see him again."

"Excellent."

So much for divine notice.

Ridge turned onto the walkway to his mother's stucco cottage. Bhrava Saruth paused to tear a few lavender stalks from bushes. He raised them to his nose to sniff, then looked down at his chest. Looking for someplace to tuck them? Between one eye blink and the next, a pocket formed. He tucked the purple flowers inside.

"It would have been useful if you'd waited thirty seconds to do that," Ridge said, reaching for the doorknob.

"What?"

"Never mind."

He started to open the door without knocking, since there was a rule that sons could simply walk into their parents' houses, but he had better give her some warning since he had arrived with a guest.

He knocked and called, "Mom?"

"In here, Ridgewalker." She sounded like she was in the living room.

"Are you decent? I have company."

"Decent?" The door opened, revealing Mom in sandals and a paint-spattered smock. "Do you think I run naked around the house all the time when you're not here?" She peered past him to Bhrava Saruth, not looking particularly abashed by her quasi-public comment. Her voice sounded hoarse. Ridge hoped she hadn't been crying or terribly distraught by her morning experience.

"Good to see you, Mom," Ridge said, though it had been less than a week since they'd seen each other. His mother had taken control of the wedding planning without asking and had been visiting frequently. Too frequently, apparently.

"I'm glad you're here, Ridge. We need to talk. And..." She looked to Bhrava Saruth. "I know we've met, but I've forgotten your name. You're Tylie's friend, aren't you? An artist?"

Had someone introduced and explained Bhrava Saruth that way? Ridge couldn't remember, but he wasn't surprised. He opened his mouth to give her a true introduction, but the dragon spoke first.

"I am the god, Bhrava Saruth!"

Mom's mouth dangled open, and then she broke into a coughing fit.

Ridge dropped his face in his hand but gave the dragon his best baleful look through his fingers.

"I thought we were no longer hiding truths from her," Bhrava Saruth said.

"Mom," Ridge said, lifting his face and extending his hand toward her, then patting her gently on the back. She was still coughing. She'd probably been so shocked, she'd swallowed her tongue. "This is Iskandia's gold dragon ally, Bhrava Saruth," he said. "We told you whatever we told you because you'd decided dragons weren't real, and we didn't want to alarm you."

"I..."

Ridge lifted his eyebrows, hoping more was coming, but she seemed stunned.

"Do you want to change, so she can see the real you?" Ridge asked the dragon, then peered left and right to the houses on either side, checking to make sure nobody was in sight. The lots here weren't that close together, but someone sitting on their porch would definitely notice a dragon appearing in Mom's yard, even if it was starting to get dark.

"I would be most pleased to show your mother my true majesty."

Ridge, hoping that wasn't an innuendo, extended his hand toward the yard.

Bhrava Saruth ambled back a few steps and then, before their eyes, blurred and changed shapes, from human to dragon.

Ridge stood close to his mother and rested a hand on her shoulder. Sardelle had said she'd seen Phelistoth, but two dragons in one day might be overwhelming.

Bhrava Saruth rose on his hind legs and stretched his wings, or maybe stretched all his muscles, like a dog getting up from a nap. Then he lowered his head on his long neck until it was level with Ridge's. He looked into Mom's eyes, his own deep green orbs compelling.

Majestic, am I not? You are an artist, yes? You may draw me if you wish.

Ridge eyed his mom, afraid the telepathic contact—he assumed it was her first—would send her over the edge. He squeezed her shoulder, worried that she hadn't moved, hadn't reacted at all.

"You're not going to faint, are you, Mom?"

Finally, she stirred, wrenching her gaze from the dragon. "Ridgewalker Meadowlark, I am a strong, independent woman. I do *not* faint."

A neighbor comes outside, Bhrava Saruth announced.

He blurred and shifted shapes again, this time, turning into a golden ferret, a creature that Fern had seen before. Her mouth dangled open as he chittered and ran into the house. Numerous feline screeches and hisses came from the living room.

"Oh dear," Mom said. "He won't harm my cats, will he?"

They are chasing me! Bhrava Saruth cried into their minds. *Me. The god Bhrava Saruth. Back, feline antagonizers.*

"I don't think so." Ridge draped an arm around his mom's shoulders, half afraid to let her go lest she pitch over, despite her strong independence. "Let's go inside, Mom."

The living room smelled of fresh paint, and Ridge paused before an easel set up in the center of it. What looked like it would become a lighthouse on a rocky point in a storm was taking shape.

"How about the kitchen?" Ridge suggested when he spotted Bhrava Saruth perched on the back of the couch, gazing down at five cats, his green ferret eyes gleaming with power. They'd stopped hissing and were staring raptly at him.

Not sure if he was gathering feline followers or simply ensuring they did not eat him, Ridge led his mother to the kitchen, shutting the door behind him.

"Can I get you something, Mom?" He noticed a kettle on the stove. "Tea?"

Mom shook her head and closed the mouth that kept dangling open. "No, no, you sit down. We need to talk. I'll get you some tea. Are you hungry? You must be. I'll make you something to eat too."

Ridge wanted to object but thought she might gain some comfort from going through the familiar actions of taking care of him. He slid into a chair at the small kitchen table. He debated making small talk before launching into what he'd come to discuss, but after starting out by introducing a shape-shifting dragon, there seemed little point in discussing the weather.

"As you might guess," Ridge said, "Bhrava Saruth is magical. All the dragons are."

"Magical. Humph." His mother strode to the sink, grabbed a paintbrush, and started washing it out. Vigorously. "There's no such thing as magic."

Ridge did not know what to say. Argue and convince her? Let her deny it if that made her happier? Maybe Sardelle had been mistaken and his mother hadn't seen the floating rocks. Or she had seen them but hadn't grasped the meaning. Or had denied the meaning.

"Just tricks." Mom paused to cough again.

Ridge frowned, hoping she wasn't coming down with a cold. When he'd first moved her out of the poor section of the city that he had grown up in, she'd been delighted, and she still seemed to enjoy her peaceful semi-rural cottage with the seventeen cats. But she was about to turn seventy, and even though she got around fine and didn't need anyone's assistance—as she reminded him whenever he broached the subject of moving her closer—he didn't know who would care for her out here if she were to get sick. The neighbors were nice enough, but perhaps he should offer to help move her into one of the vacant houses on the street where he and Sardelle lived. She might make them both crazy if she visited every day—or multiple times a day—but it would be easy to keep an eye on her then.

"Those dragons know a few tricks," she added when she recovered. "That's all."

"But you've decided that dragons do indeed exist?"

"I don't know. It could be people tricking me. Like that strange boy." She pointed a dripping paintbrush toward the living room.

"You can go rub his belly if you want to convince yourself he's physically there and real. Er, assuming he's still in ferret form."

"I really don't know why you would be involved with this, Ridge. Tricking your own mother. And Sardelle! I thought she was so nice, so mature. Above this kind of thing."

"She *is* nice, Mom. Uhm, does that mean you saw the rocks?"

She gave him a scathing look and went back to scrubbing the paintbrush. That one would be completely devoid of paint soon. Also bristles.

"I should have told you from the beginning, Mom," Ridge said, "but I knew you didn't believe in magic, and I didn't think you *wanted* to believe in magic."

She grunted without looking back. It sounded like agreement.

"But Sardelle is a sorceress. From another time period."

Mom froze, staring down into the sink.

Ridge debated how much of Sardelle's story he should share. Was that enough? No, with so many people knowing the rest of it, she would hear it sooner or later.

"I met her when I was stationed up at Galmok Mountain, where she'd been hibernating in a stasis chamber for three hundred years. She was effectively trapped in the rocks there, but our miners found her. At the time, I barely believed in magic myself, but I'd encountered some enemies with a few tricks, as you call them, so I wasn't completely unaware. But I had no idea there were people who did good things with magic. Like Sardelle. She's gone into battle with me and helped me defend the country, but she's first and foremost a healer. And a historian. Now that she's met cousin Lilah, they're getting along nicely."

Mom was still staring into the sink, her back rigid.

"I know Sardelle would like it if you would come back with me and talk to her. She's distressed that you walked in on dragons and magic lessons this morning when you weren't prepared. Her family is long gone, and she doesn't have anyone left, so I know she was really touched when you accepted her so easily. And she'd be very upset to lose your good opinion of her."

"Ridge." Mom clunked the paintbrush down on the counter and turned to face him. "This is extremely immature of you. I don't understand why you're making up these stories and trying to trick me. Do you think I'm old and senile? To believe your fiancée is three hundred years old? Why are you doing this when the wedding is so close? This isn't a joke. I've waited your whole life for this. For a wedding and babies. Is that even—was any of it ever real?"

Upset by her distress—and denial—Ridge rose and went to hug her, but she pushed him away and turned back to the sink.

"Mom." He rested a hand on her shoulder, her very tense shoulder. "I know it's hard to believe. I've had almost a year to get used to it now. That's the only reason I'm calm about it. I was also shocked at first. But this isn't a trick or a joke." He grimaced, mad at himself because he'd teased her and played a few pranks on her in the past. Not for nearly twenty years, but he could somewhat understand why she would be suspicious of him.

She only shook her head, refusing to look at him or acknowledge his touch.

At a loss for how to make her believe him, he said, "Shall I ask the dragon to come in and show you some magic?"

It was half joke, but half serious. Maybe if she saw plates and tea kettles floating around the kitchen under Bhrava Saruth's command, she would begin to grasp that magic was real.

"*No*," she said emphatically. "No more tricks. Go away and leave me alone. I'm very upset with you, Ridgewalker."

"Mom..." He stopped, having no idea what else to try. It stung that she didn't believe him and that she thought he was capable of planning this elaborate ruse to tease her. To hurt her. Logically, he understood that she was having trouble processing this and groping for a way to explain it, but it still upset him.

The tea kettle whistled. She shrugged her shoulder away from his touch and stalked to the stove.

Ridge let his arms drop, watching her glumly.

"Please go," she said without looking back. "If you insist on this farce of a wedding, you'll do it without me."

Reluctantly, Ridge headed toward the door. In a couple of days, he would try again.

She coughed as she removed the kettle, her shoulders hunching. He frowned. He would come back tomorrow. To make sure those coughs were due to emotion, not some encroaching illness.

She lifted her hand to her face. Wiping her eyes?

Ridge paused with his hand on the door. Damn it, he didn't want to leave her like this. Maybe he could find someone more trustworthy—at least in her eyes—to confirm what he'd said.

"Mom," he said, inspired by the thought. "I know I'm sarcastic and make jokes, and maybe you don't trust my word, even though I'd never lie to you about something as serious as this. But will you talk to the king? If I can get you an audience?"

Once again, he wished he hadn't been so flippant with Angulus that morning. Especially if he was going to ask for favors. Still, Angulus liked Sardelle, and he'd met Mom briefly and ought to remember her—if by the cat-shaped soaps she'd foisted on him rather than anything else. Ridge thought he might take a few minutes out of his schedule to talk to her about this.

"You can talk to him about this," Ridge continued. "You know he's a serious man and wouldn't lead you astray."

Mom kept her back to him. He did not think she was excited about the idea, but he was positive she would be polite and wouldn't wash paintbrushes while the king was talking. Getting her to agree to go to the castle might be difficult though. Unless Angulus would have his people send her a summons. She *couldn't* say no to that.

"I'll set it up," Ridge said, heartened by the idea, even though he cringed at asking Angulus for a favor. But he would. If it would help his mother believe the story and maybe bring her back into the wedding planning process—and into trusting Sardelle—he would do whatever it took.

* * *

Night had fallen by the time Sardelle, Cas, and Kaika reached the harbor. In a city the size of Pinoth, there were always dozens, if not hundreds, of vessels docked, everything from the Iskandian navy warships, to commercial fishing boats, to private yachts, to merchant freighters from around the globe. Between all their crews and the people who lived near the waterfront, Sardelle would have thousands of auras to search through while hoping to find a familiar one. It helped that Tolemek had dragon blood, but even so, this was a daunting task.

Have no fear, Jaxi thought. *I am an excellent searcher.*

Like a bloodhound?

Like the powerful sorceress I am.

"Let's start at the port authority office," Kaika said. "There should be someone there around the clock, and they'll have a record of all the ships that have legally entered the harbor."

"You think kidnappers would enter legally?" Cas asked, her head turning left and right to observe everything as they walked along the waterfront.

Sardelle doubted they would find Tolemek out in the open, but it didn't hurt to look. Maybe they would stumble across one of the kidnappers who had been sent out to buy groceries, ideally in exotic garb that would mark him or her as a foreigner. Not that exotic garb was that atypical here. Enough trade and tourism came through Pinoth that foreigners weren't that uncommon, especially here by the waterfront.

"They would have a hard time entering the harbor *illegally*," Kaika said. "The navy keeps an eye on who comes and goes. Just try to take a berth without paying a docking fee and signing the registry. I'll go flash my rank and my best smile and see what I can learn."

Kaika chopped a wave and jogged toward an office still lit for the night.

Sardelle stretched her senses out toward the docks. On her first broad brush of the area, she didn't sense Tolemek's familiar aura. Minutes passed as she painstakingly went from ship to ship.

Cas paced at her side, peering out at the docked craft and eyeing every passerby. The foot traffic dwindled as the night grew deeper.

"Anything?" Cas asked after ten minutes.

Jaxi, are you searching too?

Yes. I don't sense him. And we know that my powers are far greater than yours.

But not your modesty.

No, because false modesty is tedious.

"Sorry, no," Sardelle said, aware of Cas looking expectantly at her.

Sardelle gazed bleakly around the harbor, up to the castle, and over to the butte that held the flier hangars. Even though the waterfront spanned miles, she had a feeling she would have sensed him if he had been out there. Under normal circumstances. But if his kidnappers had magic—and the sticky substance she'd found suggested at least one among their party did—they could be camouflaging Tolemek's presence. It wouldn't take someone powerful to do that, just someone with some experience. And then it would take someone with the power of a dragon to see through it.

"Phelistoth is who we need," Sardelle said.

Cas looked at her again.

"I was thinking that a dragon would see through any magical camouflage that the kidnappers could be employing to hide Tolemek. I don't know if Phelistoth would be eager to help, but Tylie would, and she could likely talk him into assisting."

Sardelle had debated going back to the house earlier, before accompanying Cas to the harbor, to tell Tylie that Tolemek was missing and perhaps get her help finding him, but a part of her had hoped they might find him right away without having to worry his sister.

Jaxi? Can you reach Tylie from here? The house, several miles away, was out of Sardelle's range. *Or Wreltad? Let one of them know?*

Is that wise? She might run out to look for him, and it's awfully late for that.

She may be the best one to help us find him. I should have gone back and gotten her earlier. Besides, if she goes out with Phelistoth, it's not like she's going to get mugged.

Unless he's distracted by the wares from the cheesemonger's store when hoodlums chance across her.

The cheesemonger should be closed by now, Sardelle thought dryly. *Besides, she's not without defenses despite her disinterest in hurling fireballs around and harming people.*

"That will be good if we can get a dragon to help," Cas said, "to double-check, but it's possible he's not here. If they took him aboard a ship, it could have already sailed. We don't know when he was taken, whether it was last night or early this morning, but it's likely it's now been a full night and day. Let's see what Kaika has learned."

She started walking toward the port authority office, and Sardelle trailed behind her.

"You mentioned the airfields, too," Cas added. "He could be there. Or he could also have been taken on a train."

"Yes, there are many possibilities, but all searching will be easier with the help of a dragon. We'll let Tylie know what's going on and hope she can convince Phelistoth to help with the hunt."

I'm talking to Wreltad now, Jaxi said.

Good. Sardelle paused to sweep her senses across the harbor again. Since she had already done a more thorough check, she didn't expect to find anything. But for a second, she thought she felt a familiar presence out near the breakwater, much farther out than she'd been looking before. Frowning, she faced the distant rocks that protected the city from the fury of the ocean. She didn't see anything out there, but she sensed... She wasn't sure what.

Now that she looked closely, there was nothing there, but for a second, she'd been certain she had felt someone in the distance, someone with Tolemek's taciturn and occasionally grumpy aura. But as she swept back and forth with her senses, all she detected was empty water.

Jaxi? Do you sense anything out there?

Rocks and fish. Seaweed.

But definitely not people or a boat?

No.

"Sardelle?" Cas asked, having stopped when Sardelle stopped.

"I'm... not sure. I thought I sensed something for a second, but Jaxi didn't catch it, and I don't feel it now. Maybe my mind was playing tricks on me." She did not say more, not wanting to get Cas's hopes up. Besides, she could have sworn that whatever—or whoever—she had sensed had been underwater. But that couldn't be unless there had been a ship with a deep draft. But a ship couldn't have moved away that quickly, and anything that large she would be able to see with her eyes, even in the night.

"Sorry, all," Captain Kaika said, walking back up to join them. "The handsome young man working nights in the port authority office showed me the logs from the last couple of days, and nothing stood out. A few foreign freighters arrived, but familiar ones that come by regularly on their trade routes." She held up a piece of paper. "I did get their names and berths, just in case we want to visit and check them out. Question the crew. It's always possible the kidnappers stowed away or paid for legitimate passage... before they turned to their life of crime."

Cas took the paper from her. "Let's check them. Sardelle, you would be able to tell if someone was lying to us, wouldn't you?"

Sardelle pulled her gaze back from the breakwater and focused on them. "Most likely, yes."

"I'm going to leave that excitement to you two," Kaika said. "Another handsome man is waiting for me to enjoy dinner with him." She winked and lifted a hand.

Cas offered a curt wave and headed toward a gas lamp to check the names under the light.

Sardelle wanted to head home for dinner with *her* man, too, but she had promised to help Cas. And wherever Tolemek was, he might need their help badly.

She couldn't help but peer out toward the breakwater again as Cas headed off toward the first foreign freighter, wondering what exactly had tugged at her senses out there.

Chapter 6

Tolemek woke with his head pounding and his sinuses feeling like they were stuffed with cotton. He was glad that the room he was in was dim, but that was all he was glad for. As soon as he tried to lift a hand to scrape gunk out of his eyes, a clink sounded, and he met resistance. Shackles.

His wrists were chained to each other and to his ankles. Another chain locked his ankles to the base of the table. The iron links were rusty, and the chain looked to be decades old, but he doubted tugging at it would break the links. Especially from his awkward position.

He lay curled on his side on a gritty metal floor, as if someone had dropped him there and left him. Judging by the way his entire body ached, that someone had beaten on him first. Or maybe he was simply stiff from lying there for however many hours it had been. However many days?

He glanced down at his fingers, remembering the web-like substance that had defeated him. Someone must have washed it off—with some acid, judging by how raw his skin felt—but he could feel small bits still stuck to his hands when he rubbed them together. At least it wasn't enough to impede him now. Of course, the shackles handled that.

Tolemek turned his head slightly, trying to pick out his surroundings as he used his fledgling magical powers to stretch out with his senses. They didn't tell him much, except that he was alone in the room. Or the cabin? The cramped space and metal walls and ceiling made him think of cabins on an ironclad. The bench and table he lay between were both bolted to the floor—or deck. Except he didn't feel the sway of waves he would expect on a ship, even one nestled in a dock someplace.

A faint rustle came from the other side of the room, and he shifted and pushed into a sitting position so he could see past the table. The largest hawk he had ever seen perched on the back of a chair, preening under one huge wing with its beak. The thing was three or four feet in height. At least. He was surprised it did not tip over the chair with its weight.

More alarming, he hadn't sensed it with his magic. And he didn't sense it now. Could this be some illusion?

His senses were weak compared to Sardelle's and even Tylie's, but he was sure he should have detected another being in the room with him, even a feathered hawk being.

The bird lifted its head and stared at him with beady eyes. It was positioned between him and what appeared to be the only exit, a metal hatch with a wheel for a latch. A coincidence? Or a deliberate positioning?

As his brain slowly kicked into gear, Tolemek realized he could be looking at something he'd only heard about before: a shaman's familiar.

Neither Cofah nor Iskandian sorcerers typically had them or *had* had them historically speaking. He remembered Sardelle speaking of a shaman she'd battled who'd had a giant owl familiar. At the time, the shaman had been working with the Cofah, but hadn't *been* Cofah. Dakrovian? Tolemek couldn't remember if she had said. That might have been the language he'd heard those people using in his lab. He knew a smattering of Trade Dakrovian, but there were dozens of languages on the continent, and he seemed to recall that a different trade tongue was used at the southern end.

The door creaked open. No, the *hatch*. This was definitely a ship.

A man in buckskin clothing, or something similar, stepped inside, ducking his head for the low hatchway. Fringes and feathers dangled from his tunic, and he wore moccasins with intricate beadwork on the tops, but from the neck up, he looked like some nobleman out of the Iskandian capital in a brown bowler hat and spectacles, with a perfectly waxed mustache, the ends groomed into tips that curled up. Tolemek would have no trouble describing the man—his kidnapper?—to the police, should he get the chance.

The police wouldn't find you here, my friend, the man spoke telepathically into his mind.

"I guess that answers my question about whose familiar that is," Tolemek croaked, his throat feeling like it was lined with sandpaper. Maybe telepathy would be easier. Except that he was ill-practiced at it and might embarrass himself.

Realizing the man had read his thoughts, Tolemek attempted to erect a mental barrier around his mind, something Sardelle had been showing him how to do. Unfortunately, he'd been so busy with his chemistry work that he hadn't had time to come by for many lessons.

"Yendray is my name," the man said in Cofah, sliding into the chair, not caring that the giant hawk was still on the back and loomed over his head. The hawk didn't seem to care either. Tolemek sensed something magical about the man, an item in one of his pockets, perhaps. Some artifact? "I'm sure you're not pleased to meet me, given the situation, but I am pleased to meet you, Mr. Targoson." He had a pleasant, lilting accent, and he tipped his hat along with his introduction. "I've followed your work."

"Ah," Tolemek said neutrally. "I don't suppose it's my healing formulas that have you excited."

He didn't want to spend time with anyone who'd been inspired by the deadly substances he'd made over the years.

"I'm sure they're useful, and I wouldn't mind purchasing the recipe from you, but I confess that it's your formulas with wartime applications that would be of ultimate use to me."

"In doing what?"

"Uniting my homeland and turning it into a world power that can compete with the likes of Cofahre and Iskandia."

"Your homeland being Dakrovia?"

"Jlongar Jalak, yes. My older brother is the chief there, as our father was before him. My family has brought stability to our little area and united the three contentious tribes in the south around it, but you must admit that our continent as a whole is not taken seriously by the world. Even if it's no longer as trendy for the empire to kidnap people and turn them into slaves as it was in centuries past, we're still exploited for our crops and other resources."

"Kidnapping *is* tedious," Tolemek said.

"Have no fear. I do not intend to make you a slave."

"Very comforting. Do you intend to release me from my shackles?" The chains clinked as Tolemek lifted his hands a few inches.

"I have considered it, but you do have a reputation to consider, Mr. Targoson. Deathmaker." Yendray tipped his hat again, then, seeming to notice some speck of dirt on it, removed it and brushed at it with his fingers. "Even though my men searched you thoroughly, I fear you could cleverly devise a way to escape if your hands were free. To be honest, I thought it would be harder than it was to capture you, especially since apprehending you was our backup plan, only to be employed if we ran into you in your laboratory. We'd hoped to get in and out without encountering you, but as it turns out, it was fortuitous that you were still at work for the day. Since we did not find *nearly* enough of what we sought."

Tolemek did not know what to make of his chatty and even personable kidnapper. Was he the man in charge? It sounded like he might be. How many people did he command? Just the ones that had broken into Tolemek's lab? Or a whole Dakrovian strike team?

"And what is it that you sought?" Tolemek asked.

"You do not sense it on me?" Yendray reached for his pocket.

Before he pulled it out, Tolemek realized what the man reached for. Not an artifact, but something far more familiar. He should have recognized it immediately.

Yendray withdrew a stoppered vial, one Tolemek knew to be one of his own. The dark red liquid inside filled it only a third of the way full.

"You came for the dragon blood?" he asked.

"Indeed. I heard from a Cofah acquaintance that you and a team of Iskandians stole a significant amount from the empire this past autumn. Excuse me, that would have been *spring* in your hemisphere. That same acquaintance, one of the scientists who was working for the emperor on weapons using the blood, had to flee Cofahre after he and his team were blamed for the utter destruction of a secret laboratory within a manmade volcano."

"Unfortunate," Tolemek murmured when the man paused. Perhaps a prompt here and there would keep Yendray speaking. He definitely had a chatty streak. It was almost as if Yendray considered him a colleague rather than a kidnapped enemy chained to the deck.

"He's working in Jlongar Jalak with me now. We're remaking some of the imperial tools and weapons, and I'm contributing some of my own ideas, naturally. One does hate to be derivative. But—" he spread a palm toward the ceiling, "—we have a problem."

"No dragon blood?"

"No dragon blood. My colleague smuggled a small amount out of the empire when he left. Less than this." Yendray wiggled the vial. "We've already used it in our experiments. We need much more for what we wish to create."

"Such as super weapons?" Tolemek hardly thought it would take more than an organized militia and modern rifles for someone to unite the tribes of Dakrovia. If the books and newspapers could be believed, most of them lived deep in the jungles and ran around in loincloths while waving spears.

"In order to create quasi-intelligent weapons powered by magic and the most efficient fuel known to man." Yendray wiggled the vial. "As I'm sure you know, the Cofah were powering rockets and craft akin to the Iskandian fliers with it."

Tolemek thought about pointing out that the light sources taken from Galmok Mountain were actually more efficient energy sources, since they didn't *ever* seem to run out of power. But he didn't want to give this man any ideas about something else to steal. It was possible that mages of this era could not replicate the *Referatu* light sources. Sardelle had said she might be able to figure out how to make them, but as far as Tolemek knew, she hadn't managed it yet, and the Iskandians were still mining the centuries-old artifacts out of Galmok.

The hawk, apparently bored by the conversation, went back to preening under its wing. It almost knocked Yendray's bowler off, but he straightened it without glancing back.

"The question is," Yendray said, holding Tolemek's gaze, "where can we find the rest of the dragon blood you took from Cofahre? I understand that backpacks full of vials were taken."

"What was in my lab is all that's left," Tolemek said, not looking away from Yendray's gaze in the hope that he would believe the lie.

"Come now, Targoson. I'm sure you haven't used it all in your experiments since then. A little goes a long way, as you have no doubt discovered."

Tolemek did his best to shrug, which wasn't easy with his wrists chained to his ankles. "If there's more, I don't know where it is. I was given a couple of vials to work with at the beginning of the summer, and that's all I've seen lately."

He knew very well where the rest of the vials were. In a vault in one of the basements in the king's castle. But he did his best not to think about that and to keep a mental wall around his thoughts.

Yendray narrowed his eyes, staring directly into Tolemek's.

Tolemek felt something brushing at his mind, almost like someone with a rake trying to scrape away leaves to reveal the grassy yard beneath.

"I see I should have tried to get that information before you started guarding your thoughts," Yendray said, leaning back in the chair.

The hawk squawked a protest when the hat bumped its feathered chest. It flexed its wings and flapped them for balance.

"Apologies, Brukko," Yendray murmured.

The hawk quieted and found its balance again. It glared at Tolemek, as if he were to blame for the upset.

"There's not any more dragon blood in Iskandia," Tolemek said.

Had Yendray come to him in peace, as a fellow colleague interested in science, Tolemek might have been willing to share a vial or two, especially if it was clear the Dakrovian weapons wouldn't be used against Iskandia or Cofahre. Uniting the tribes there might actually make sense, since they always seemed to be at war. But since the shaman had kidnapped him and was trying to strong-arm him into giving away the location of *all* the vials, Tolemek was disinclined to help.

Further, it seemed unlikely that Yendray could get into the castle to steal them without hurting—or killing—people along the way. Even though Tolemek wasn't a native and hadn't sworn an oath to defend Iskandia, like Cas had, he found himself inclined to protect the people he'd come to know and care about, and maybe the country as well. King Angulus had been a lot more accommodating to him than Emperor Salatak ever had been, and he even liked the man. Tolemek would hate to see him get hurt because he inadvertently blabbed the location of the vials.

He would also hate for Angulus to think he'd colluded with the Dakrovians or perhaps been bribed by them. The Iskandian king seemed a fair and reasonable man, but if he was led to the wrong conclusion, he could take away Tolemek's place in his country with a wave of his hand. He grimaced at the thought of losing his home there with Cas.

"I'm afraid you'll have to go find a dragon willing to share some with you," Tolemek said firmly—Yendray was still watching him through slitted eyes. "And if you could return me to my lab, or at least a dock somewhere in Iskandia before you leave to hunt for it, I would appreciate it."

"I'm sure you would." Yendray stroked one side of his mustache. "I could argue that you have dragon allies and could far more easily obtain more blood than I."

"They haven't shown any interest in sharing their blood with us. In fact, Phelistoth was quite irritated when he recovered from his illness and learned that he'd been used so. Perhaps if you were to take some pastries to the gold dragon, Bhrava Saruth, he would trade some of his blood to you."

"That seems unlikely."

"It depends on how good the pastries are, how heavily frosted. And if you also offer belly rubs."

Yendray snorted. "Yes, I'm positive a dragon wants a human rubbing its scales. That sounds like a good way to get oneself bathed in fire and eaten."

Clearly, the man had never met Bhrava Saruth.

"I was hoping it would be easy to get information out of you," Yendray said, "but I'm not surprised it is not. Fortunately, I came prepared. I have a truth serum that I can use on you. It's possible since you are a shaman of sorts yourself that you may be able to resist it, but I doubt it."

As he rose to his feet, someone outside knocked on the hatch.

Yendray walked over, opened it, and leaned out. He asked a question in his own language, and a woman responded. Tolemek couldn't understand any of the words. It definitely wasn't Trade Dakrovian.

Yendray nodded and looked at him again. "I'm afraid our truth-telling session will have to wait a little while. It seems you have friends who are searching for you. Have no fear. I'll see you again shortly. Brukko, keep an eye on him."

For the first time, the hawk squawked. It sounded like a complaint. Or a sarcastic comment about how he'd already been doing that.

"So mouthy for a familiar," Yendray said, smiling.

He tipped his hat toward Tolemek and the bird, then ducked and stepped through the hatchway.

Tolemek tried to see into the dim corridor outside to get a better feel for what kind of ship this was, but all he glimpsed was more gray metal before the hatch clanged shut again.

He sighed and looked up at the bird, wondering what the odds were of outsmarting it and finding a way out of his shackles before Yendray returned.

***

Cas dismounted from her horse in front of the house she'd grown up in, the manicured lawn of the sprawling estate mostly dark, though the driveway to the portico was well-lit. Surprisingly well lit. She eyed what had once been gas lamps and realized her father must have found a way to get electricity out here. She'd heard lines were being run throughout the city, but mostly for the government's use so far. The army fort had gotten access earlier in the summer, and there was supposed to be a big ceremony at the castle later in the week to showcase the installation of electrical lights there.

Supposedly, the stuffy officials that reigned in the historical registry office said which buildings could receive upgrades and which couldn't, and had kept the king from making that change to the castle for years. Since it had been so devastated by the sorceress's attack, Angulus must have made the argument that as long as they were rebuilding so much from scratch, maybe it was time to modernize a few things.

A few lights were on in the house, glowing powerfully from behind curtains, and her father's black steam carriage was parked under the portico, so Cas knew he was home. She had visited him a couple of times this summer to shoot at the range out back, but she still worried he might feel she only came to see him when she needed help. She had debated all the way out here whether she truly wanted to ask him for that help, especially since her father didn't have any great love for Tolemek. But Sardelle hadn't found anything at the harbor—questioning the foreign freighter captains hadn't resulted in anything—and Cas also hadn't learned anything at the airfield, where only one commercial dirigible had been docked.

Aware that time could be of the essence—what if his kidnappers wanted to question, or interrogate, Tolemek about one of his concoctions and then get rid of him once they had what they wanted?—she felt she had to use every resource available to her.

Not sure where in the house her father would be, Cas tugged on the ostentatious doorbell rope instead of knocking. It was late, but she assumed from the lights that he was still awake. Perhaps not surprising for an assassin, he had always favored night and was more likely to be asleep in the mornings.

He came to the door himself, still mostly dressed for the day in black trousers and a gray long-sleeved and high-necked shirt that seemed warm attire for a summer evening. His sandy hair was impeccably trimmed and combed, as usual.

"Caslin," he said, no hint of surprise in his voice. He stepped aside and gestured for her to come in.

She wondered if he'd heard of Tolemek's disappearance—with his network of contacts, he had a tendency to learn about things as quickly as the heads of military intelligence.

"Good evening, Father." She stepped into the grand foyer, marveling at how bright it was now, almost as if sunlight streamed through the high windows.

"It's a little dark for shooting on the range," he observed.

"Yes, I came because… I'm hoping you can assist me with something." She hated asking him for anything, hated being anything but a woman capable of handling her own problems, and had to fight back a wince.

"Your pirate is missing."

"He is. And he's really more of a chemist and advisor and provider to the crown than a pirate these days."

"So I understand."

Cas took a deep breath and faced him. "I've been to his lab, and we believe whoever took him came most recently out of Dakrovia. But we weren't able to find any ships in the harbor or at the airfield that might belong to the kidnappers, nor any records of ships like that having recently left."

"You believe he was kidnapped rather than killed," her father said, making it more of a statement than a question.

"There wasn't a body."

"But there were bullet holes, suggesting the attackers wouldn't have cared if they killed him."

"You know more about this than I expected," Cas said. For

a ludicrous moment, she wondered if *he* had kidnapped—or shot at Tolemek—but her father wouldn't have used Dakrovian magic. Nor would he have likely shot and missed. Besides, he'd passed up the chance to assassinate Tolemek earlier in the year, a chance offered by the Cofah emperor himself.

"I keep an eye on him."

"Er, why?"

"Because you are involved with him." Her father's lips thinned.

"I thought you made your peace with him at General Zirkander's barbecue earlier this summer. He's turning himself into a successful businessman in addition to someone useful to our king and country."

"Nevertheless, I feel it's important to watch him, to ensure you continue to be safe around him, both because of what he was and is, and because..." He extended a hand to her. "You are my daughter."

Cas thought about pointing out that she could take care of herself and she didn't need her father spying on her boyfriends, but that seemed an arrogant thing to say, considering she'd come to ask him for help. Besides, if he was having someone keep an eye on Tolemek, maybe that someone had seen something.

"You don't have any more information than I do, do you?" Cas asked. "I know you're good at finding people. I was hoping you could help me find him."

"I'm *excellent* at finding people."

Since Cas wanted something, she decided not to remark on his lack of humility.

Her father strode into one of the hallways off the foyer, waving for her to follow. When he stepped into his office, he flicked a switch, and lamps came on around the room. Judging by his pleased smile, the electrical upgrade to the house was still very new, and he was pleased—or smug—about having it.

He opened one of the file drawers in his desk and withdrew a folder. "You said you suspect a Dakrovian connection?"

"At the least, the kidnappers made a stop there on their way here. A Dakrovian bomb was used. A Farongi grenade, Captain Kaika said."

"That reminds me of something in one of my weekly reports. You may know I subscribe to the Watchers' Guild and get updates from around the capital, so I can more easily find people when the time comes."

Cas had no idea what the Watchers' Guild was, but she made an encouraging noise. If he had a lead, she wanted it.

"Here we are." He plucked a red pen from a holder and underlined a few lines in a paragraph two thirds of the way down the page of a pamphlet that had been printed with a press. "Lady Masonwood, a very distant relation to the king, as you would guess, is the purveyor of the Sophisticated Hem, an upscale clothing shop in the merchant quarter. Most of their wares cater toward noblewomen shopping for dresses and the latest female fashions, but her male colleague is a haberdasher and maintains a corner of the store for noblemen and those of affluent means seeking the latest in hats, ties, sashes, and the like."

Cas listened in bewilderment, wondering what this could have to do with kidnappings.

"Due to the reputation of the shop near and far, it's not uncommon for men and women who have recently come into an influx of funds to go there and shop. I've caught two thieves over the years because of Lady Masonwood's tips to the guild."

"A noblewoman related to the king is associated with this Watchers' Guild?"

"Oh yes. Quite a few nobles have been recruited into its ranks. I do believe people of that ilk enjoy slumming with the demimonde. Adds an air of excitement to their lives. But my point, as I'm certain you're wondering, is that a Dakrovian man came in this week and bought a hat, insisting on paying in Jlongar Jalakian gold medallions because he didn't have any of the local currency. It made an impression on Lady Masonwood because foreigners don't generally come through her door, and if they do, they're well-known and well-traveled businessmen capable of paying in any number of currencies."

"I don't know, Father. It seems like a stretch. Why would a kidnapper go hat shopping?"

He closed the folder. "I don't know, Caslin, but Farongi weapons are made in Jlongar Jalak."

She nibbled on her lip. That *was* quite the coincidence.

"Sometimes, it's the smallest of mistakes that allow you to locate the man you're tracking. And sometimes, you have to follow dozens of leads before finding the one you need. I'll give you the report so you can read through and see what else might tie in with Targoson, but I definitely recommend questioning Lady Masonwood and seeing if she remembers anything. Such as where he's staying." Father eyed her uniform as he handed the pages to her. "She will assume you can't afford her wares and try to shoo you out of the store if you walk in wearing army clothing. Be prepared to let her know who you are up front, and don't be intimidated, not that I expect you would be. However, if you wish, *I* can question her."

As much as she wouldn't have minded her father's help, Cas suspected his method of questioning would involve removing some fingernails. Unless she learned that this Lady Masonwood had been the one to blow up Tolemek's lab, that would seem extreme.

"I'll handle it, Father. I do appreciate the offer of assistance. And this." She held up the report.

"Of course." Father clasped his hands behind his back.

Cas groped for something else to say to him—it seemed she should stay for more than five minutes, given how seldom she came to visit. But he hadn't invited her to stay for a late dinner or anything like that, and she hated to presume. She looked at his desk, thinking a daily newspaper might suggest a topic of discussion, then stirred in surprise when she glimpsed a familiar pale blue envelope. She had recently received one exactly like that.

"General Zirkander invited you to his wedding?" she blurted, then promptly wondered if she'd been mistaken. Maybe pale blue envelopes were fashionable this year, and everyone was using them. It was true that Zirkander had invited her father to that barbecue, but she was positive he had been trying to help Cas mend fences with him, not that he'd truly wanted her father at his house.

"He did."

"But Zirkander *shot* you this spring. I mean, you deserved it since you were getting in the way of our mission and working against the king…"

Her father's eyebrow twitched. "Perhaps he's inviting all the people he's shot in an attempt to make amends and start his life anew."

"I don't think most of the people he's shot are still alive. Or are Iskandian."

"I shall consider myself special then. Normally, I would not accept an invitation to a pointless social gathering, but there's quite a buzz in the capital and even beyond about the famous—or infamous—pilot getting married. It was written up on page twelve." He waved to the guild report. "Some influential people will be there, including, it's speculated, the king himself. Likely a dragon or two, as well, though I have no interest in them. A dragon is unlikely to wish to hire me."

"To assassinate people?"

Cas's mind boggled at the idea of Zirkander's wedding being a networking event for entrepreneurial assassins. Wouldn't it mostly be army officers? Since Sardelle didn't have any family of her own, Cas didn't think she had invited a lot of people outside of Zirkander's sphere of acquaintance.

"Naturally. It *is* my profession."

Cas reached for the invitation. "May I see it?"

"If you wish. I assume you received one of your own?"

"Yes." Cas wondered how many other people had. Zirkander kept saying he and Sardelle were having a small wedding by the pond near his house, but she knew everyone in Wolf and Tiger squadrons had been invited, and she couldn't imagine it had stopped there. A networking event. She shook her head.

She pulled out his invitation. Even though Zirkander and Sardelle had hand-written short personal notes on hers, she didn't expect this one to hold more than the generic date, location, and request for a response that was printed on all the cards. But Zirkander had written on the bottom of this one too.

Ahnsung —

Come join us, and I'll let you watch Lieutenant Ahn hit me with a brisk ball again. Also, if you promise not to stab anyone on my lawn, I'll reserve a piece of cake for you.

— Ridge

Cas snorted. His note to her had been irreverent, too, unlike Sardelle's far more proper invitation, and she wasn't surprised that he'd adopted a similar tone for everyone. She was a little surprised that he'd personalized all the invitations and wondered when he'd found time. Whenever she saw him lately, he was on some errand or another, off to do a task that required his input or signature. From what Cas had seen, being a general and being in charge of an entire division of the army was far more arduous than simply flying and maintaining one's own vehicle.

"My own wedding to your mother was a small, simple affair," Father volunteered, surprising her. "Her parents did not approve of me, if you can imagine."

"Because of your profession or because you were aloof and cold?"

There went that eyebrow again. Maybe she shouldn't be so frank with him. She'd tap-danced around such questions as a teenager, but these days, she found herself disinclined to do so.

"I was cordial with them," he said. "To the best of my ability. You know I find it difficult to exude affability."

Yes, Cas had inherited that difficulty from him.

"And at the time, they believed I ran a small landscaping business. Even though I made it clear that I was not impoverished, they did not feel I was good enough for their daughter. As you know, I've not spoken to them since your mother passed. By that time, they had learned of my true work, and of course they blamed me for her death. Rightfully so, I admit, but it was always a regret of mine that they wanted nothing to do with you after that." He spread his hand, as if to say the ways of human beings perplexed him. Maybe they did.

He hadn't admitted his fault or his regret to her before, and Cas did not know how to respond. She didn't remember her mother's parents and didn't know if they were even alive still, so she couldn't say she missed them, but she had occasionally felt a dearth of family when she'd been growing up. It had only been she and her father, and various servants and tutors, for most of her childhood.

"Did Mother want children? Me?" Cas thought of her conversation with Tolemek, still regretting that she'd stiffened up and walked out, perhaps hurting him.

"She did. I was less certain it was a good idea, given my work and the possibility that enemies might strike at any family I formed, but she convinced me otherwise. And I was somewhat intrigued by the thought of having children who would carry on the family business." He lowered his spread hand, shrugging a little.

Yes, she knew that part of the story. "I've never imagined myself having children."

He tilted his head. In disappointment?

He was always so hard to read. She doubted she would have brought this up if he hadn't started sharing first.

"I guess Tolemek has," she added.

"Ah."

Again, she couldn't read him. She didn't know if he was disgusted by the idea of them having children or relieved Cas didn't want them. Maybe he hoped their relationship would dissolve, and she'd find someone more appropriate. Someone less Cofah. Less former pirate.

But he didn't say any of that, and she told herself it wasn't fair to assume.

"I need to find him," Cas said. "So I can talk to him about it again. And just because. I don't want to lose him."

His lips thinned, and this time, she was sure there was some disapproval in his eyes. Still, he clasped his hands behind his back and said, "Are you sure you do not wish me to question Lady Masonwood?"

"No, thank you. And actually, I know someone who needs a dress. Maybe I can convince her to shop for it there. Lady Masonwood may be more willing to gossip to clients."

"I hope your someone is financially well-endowed."

"Uhm." Cas knew generals made more than lieutenants, but she also knew Zirkander had a lot of houseguests he had to support. She also didn't know if Sardelle earned money of her own from tutoring. As far as Cas knew, Sardelle wasn't on the king's payroll, though she should be, given all the assistance she'd given Wolf Squadron and the city as a whole. "I'll check." Cas held up the report—she would look through the rest of the pages later—and headed for the door. "Thank you, Father."

"You are welcome." He followed her into the hallway and toward the foyer. "Caslin?"

She paused at the front door. "Yes?"

"I did enjoy seeing you pelt Zirkander with that brisk ball." His eyes glinted. "Even if that dragon-in-disguise thwarted most of your team's attacks, you got in a few good hits."

It bemused Cas that General Zirkander, brave pilot and hero of Iskandia, knew so many people who liked to see him hit by balls. She understood that her father didn't care for him because he'd been a big part of why she had become a pilot, but so many of his superior officers seemed to have similar feelings toward him.

"I'm glad it pleases you to see me hit things, Father."

He made a vague salute-like gesture and let her walk out without further comment.

As Cas strode down the driveway, she considered how early she would have to get up to visit Sardelle in the morning before work. She had to convince her that the Sophisticated Hem was the ideal place to shop for her wedding dress.

Chapter 7

Sardelle wasn't surprised when she sensed neither Tylie nor Phelistoth at the house when she returned. Earlier, Jaxi had told Wreltad that Tolemek was missing, so Tylie had likely left right away to find Phelistoth and hunt for her brother. She hoped they had more luck searching for Tolemek than she, Cas, and Kaika had.

She did sense Ridge sitting alone on the sofa, neither eating dinner nor reading. He seemed morose, and she quickened her pace, remembering that she'd asked if he would be home for dinner, implying that *she* would be.

How long had he been waiting? Was he disappointed she wasn't there with something ready to eat? Neither of them was overly domestic—Fern had been the one to teach her how to bake cookies and tarts—but since she was the one whose work usually took place at home, she'd gotten in the habit of purchasing or making dinner for them—and their frequent visitors.

When she stepped inside, only one of the gas lamps brightening the house, Ridge rose from the couch to face her. He smiled, though it seemed forced. Had something happened?

"Are you all right?" she asked, brushing his mind.

"Yes. I was just sitting in the mostly dark and thinking. Sorry I didn't start something for dinner. I was, uhm, rehearsing something."

An image of his mother's house flashed through his mind, followed by one of Angulus in his office.

"You went to see your mother?" she asked.

"Yes. I'm still working on convincing her that magic exists and that you're wonderful, and that we're not playing an elaborate prank on her."

"Oh." That wasn't quite the reaction Sardelle had expected from Fern, but it did seem more natural for her—for anyone who had spent seventy years not believing in magic—than a rush to find rope to hang witches.

"We'll get it straightened out." Ridge came around the couch, offering his arms. "I have a plan."

"Should I be worried?"

"Not at all. Everything will go forward without a hitch. The wedding will be lovely. Mom will be there to hug us and wish us well."

Sardelle could tell from his surface thoughts and emotions that he wasn't entirely positive that would be the case, but whatever this plan was, he seemed hopeful. She stepped into his arms for a hug, happy to rest her head and the day's disappointments on his shoulder.

"Any luck with Tolemek's lab?" he asked.

"There were a couple of clues, but no luck finding him yet. We're not sure the kidnappers are Dakrovian, but they seemed to have at least done their shopping there before coming over. We checked the harbor, but neither Jaxi nor I could sense Tolemek's presence there. Cas went off to check the airfield, though I'm not sure if she'll find anyone there at night to question. She's determined though. Understandably so."

"Yes. I'd search night and day if you were missing."

"Thank you." She leaned into him, enjoying the hug, and not wanting to step away.

"I assume you'd do the same for me," he said in a leading tone.

She grinned and thought about pointing out she already *had* done that. Recently. But he seemed in the mood for levity, so she asked, "Who's left in the world who would bother kidnapping you?"

"Lots of people. I'm a very important person these days, you know. I'm integral to the operation of the army, and I know lots of secrets. They would pay a lot to get me back."

"Is that true? You told me all you do is get General Chason coffee at your staff meetings."

"I do, but I hear secrets while I'm pouring it."

"I suspect most of your enemies would rather shoot you than kidnap you."

"To keep me from being mouthy?"

"Precisely."

"That's possibly true. I guess me being dead would obviate the need for you to search night and day for me. Would you at least use your powerful magics to utterly annihilate the bastard who killed me?"

"I definitely would. And Jaxi would help."

Naturally, Jaxi spoke into their minds. *I am much better at utter annihilation than Sardelle.*

I'm afraid I can't deny that, Sardelle said, switching to telepathy.

"I feel better now," Ridge said, "knowing that two sorceresses would be eager to slay my killer."

As you should, Jaxi thought. *It's an honor that not many people earn.*

Ridge released Sardelle. "Were you searching for Tolemek all this time? Why don't you relax—" he waved to the couch, "—and I'll make something to eat."

"I would like that. I'll light some lamps."

"For a romantic evening at home? It didn't escape my notice that the house is dragon- and student-free tonight. Is Tylie looking for Tolemek?"

"Yes. With Phelistoth's help, maybe she'll have luck finding him. She has more of a link to him than I do, so she might be able to sense him from farther away than I can." Sardelle almost told Ridge about that moment when she thought she'd sensed Tolemek in the harbor, but she suspected her mind had been playing tricks on her. She almost hoped it had, since she'd seemed to sense him under the water. She hated to imagine someone killing him and dumping his body over the side of a ship.

"I suppose it's not right to get romantic when a friend is missing." Ridge moved into the kitchen and lit the lamps in there.

"That's not going to stop you from trying, is it?" she called through the doorway.

"Absolutely not."

Sardelle snorted softly.

"Before I left, I did send out word to Wolf Squadron. They'll go out tomorrow to fly up and down the coast and search for any suspicious ships. Or suspicious anything. From the air is my preferred way to search."

"Good. There's only so much area that Tylie and Phelistoth can cover."

Sardelle hung Jaxi on the rack next to the fireplace and headed for the kitchen. She would happily let him prepare something, but sitting on that couch wasn't her idea of relaxing.

If you're not careful, you'll fall through one of the bullet holes, Jaxi said.

My butt is large enough that I doubt I'm in danger of that.

Soon, it'll be larger. Are you going to tell Ridge about Ridge Junior tonight?

I don't think he's going to lobby for a child to share his name. Also, I'm not sure butts get bigger during pregnancy. Other things, perhaps.

Sardelle considered Jaxi's question. Would this be a good time to tell him about the baby? They would have privacy, assuming Bhrava Saruth didn't show up, but their friend was missing and Ridge's mother was distraught. It worried Sardelle that he hadn't been able to toss a few jokes, give his mom a hug, and bring her around. She'd always suspected her magical career would be more of a sticking point for Fern than Ridge had assumed.

Everything gets bigger. Trust me.

I know you don't speak from personal experience, Jaxi.

No, but I witnessed two of my handlers giving birth. Several times. Their butts got bigger when they were pregnant. Every time. And things went downhill from there.

You're truly making me look forward to my experience as a mother.

Just promise me you won't hang me on the wall with nothing to do for fifteen years while they're growing up. That happened once. It was intolerable. Just because you're a mother doesn't mean you have to stop hurling fireballs and incinerating people.

I'll keep that in mind.

The kitchen was still warm from the summer sun that had streamed through the windows that afternoon. Ridge had removed his cap, draped his uniform jacket over the back of a chair, and rolled up his shirtsleeves. Seeing his bare, muscled arms made her think that romance wouldn't be such a bad idea after all. After dinner. Thus far, he'd stirred embers to life in the cook stove, retrieved a skillet from the rack, and scrounged a can of beans from the cupboard.

"Will we be having more than beans?" Sardelle slid into one of the chairs at the table, content to watch him prepare their dinner, even if it would likely be a limited offering. Ridge had spent most of his adult life eating meals in the mess hall or the Officers' Club, and it was a foregone conclusion that he'd never had to cook for himself when he'd lived with his mother.

"We'll soon find out." Ridge headed for the icebox. "I suppose it depends on how many dragons have been through since the last time I went to the butcher shop and the cheesemonger."

"The cheese, I can alas attest, met a premature end. This morning, I saw Phelistoth cruise through with a wedge in his hand before he headed out to nap in the sunbeam."

"Being a dragon is a demanding job, isn't it? Hah, I see slabs of..." He pulled out a brown bundle, opened it, and sniffed. "Pork chops. Excellent."

"I believe there are some vegetables in there too."

"Yes, and if we leave them alone, they'll still be there tomorrow." He flashed her a grin. "I like to contribute to vegetable conservation efforts."

"Are you truly forty-one years old? And a general? It's hard to imagine such a mature individual not interested in eating his vegetables." Sardelle shook her head and left her seat at the table to see what they had. The dragons never touched the greens—they seemed to share Ridge's dietary preferences of meat, cheese, and sweets.

"I just don't want to deprive tomorrow's vegetable eaters of sustenance."

"Uh huh. Scoot over. Your mother brought over some carrots, zucchini, and green beans." She grabbed the veggies and made a mental note to use her magic to refreeze the ice block later. The ice man had stopped coming by the house after glimpsing a dragon flying over the pond one morning.

"We already have vegetables." Ridge held up the bean can.

"Those are swimming in bacon fat and maple syrup."

"Which makes them the perfect vegetable."

She stuck an elbow in his ribs as she navigated past him to grab a knife and the cutting board. He squeezed her before grabbing another pan and throwing some more wood in the stove.

"It actually feels strange with nobody else in the house," Ridge said as Sardelle set to work on cutting the stems off the beans and slicing the carrots. "I've gotten used to Tylie being here most of the time. And her dragon."

Thinking of Jaxi's comment, Sardelle wondered if this would be a good time to mention that someone else would be there with them full-time soon. She wasn't sure why she was having a hard time bringing this up. Because they hadn't planned it together, she supposed. And Ridge hadn't been exuberant when she'd brought up the idea of children before.

"Ridge?" She paused, then cleared her throat. "There's something I need to tell you."

"Should I be worried that you sound nervous about it?"

"I'm not sure. I *am* nervous. But it's because I'm concerned about what your reaction will be, rather than because I don't want the thing I have."

"That was vague. If one of my lieutenants came in talking like that, I'd be positive he crashed his flier."

"The only thing I ever fly is a dragon."

"I saw that dragon today. He didn't appear recently crashed. He hugged me."

"While in dragon form or human form?"

"Human form. But he was wearing a dress, so I would have found it less alarming if he'd hugged me as a dragon."

Sardelle smiled but didn't inquire further on Bhrava Saruth's clothing choices. She needed to blurt out her news before she lost her nerve.

"Sardelle?" Ridge turned from the pork chops starting to sizzle in the skillet. He took her hands and turned her to face him. "I'm easy to talk to, aren't I? What's going on?"

"You are," she agreed, gazing into his eyes. If she hadn't had the ability to sense a person's emotions, their *real* emotions, she might not have been worried. She was positive he would smile and be supportive. She just wasn't positive his first genuine response would be pleasure.

He lifted his eyebrows.

"I'm pregnant," she said. "It wasn't intentional. If it had been, I would have at least waited until after the wedding, and of course asked you if you were ready. But I must not have been diligent enough one night with my precautions. Possibly, it was a futile hope to believe I could thwart a dragon's blessing forever." She could hear her voice and how rapidly she was speaking and forced herself to stop talking, especially since Ridge seemed to have stopped hearing anything after the first couple of words.

"Pregnant?" he whispered and looked down, as if the evidence would already be on display.

"Pregnant." She was tempted to lock down her senses so she wouldn't be aware of his first reaction, but she couldn't make herself do it. She wanted to know what he felt, and she hoped... she wouldn't be disappointed.

He kept gaping for a few seconds, stunned by the news, but once he recovered, a goofy smile spread across his face. "That's much better than a crash."

"Is it?"

"You don't think so?"

"I do, but I wasn't sure if *you* would think so. If you believed you were ready for this. I know you're busy at work right now and—"

He stepped forward and wrapped her in a hug, kissing her temple before burying his face in her hair. "*Much* better," he said.

She sensed contentment from him. Pleased contentment. And a bit of relief that she hadn't had bad news.

She hugged him back, fiercely. Relieved he didn't consider this bad news.

They clung to each other in silence for a long moment before Ridge drew back, only enough so he could grip her hands again and gaze into her eyes. "I should have told you before, but I got distracted by having my memory stolen and that whole sorceress-in-the-castle event. Back when I was in the middle of crashing…" He pointed his chin in the direction of Galmok Mountain. "One of my last thoughts, what I thought would be my last thoughts before I died, was regret that I hadn't told you I was honored that you wanted to have my children. I know I'm busy, but I'll try to be less busy and come home to see if you need anything. Now and after." He looked down at her stomach again. "Did it just start? How long—er, do you know?"

"It's recent," she said. "I think it may have been the night of your proposal."

He grinned. "Technically, that was *your* proposal."

"Only because you were taking forever with yours."

"I wanted it to be perfect."

Perfectly terrifying, she thought, remembering having dinner and sex on a stone arch a thousand feet above Crazy Canyon. But she caught herself returning his grin, pleased he'd enjoyed the night and pleased he wasn't horrified by this new development.

Ridge's grin faded as another thought came to his mind, followed by a sense of determination.

"I need to talk to the king tomorrow," he said with resolve.

"About my pregnancy?"

"No. I have a favor I need to ask him. But actually…" He tilted his head thoughtfully. "Can I tell him you're going to have a baby? That may sway him in case my charisma doesn't."

"Charisma? I don't think he sees you as charismatic."

"Unfortunately, I know this. If only he were a twenty-year-old soldier with a love for beer. I can always win those types over."

"I'd be alarmed if such a man were ruling the nation."

"You don't think he would be delightfully enthusiastic?" Ridge asked.

"Not delightfully so, no."

"Angulus was young when his father died. I forget the exact age, but in his twenties."

"I suspect he was a similar man in his twenties as he is now."

"Possibly so. He didn't invite me in to chat often then. Oddly." Ridge extricated one of his arms and leaned back to flip the pork chops.

Sardelle supposed she should return to cutting vegetables if she intended for there to be anything green with their meal. "You can tell him if you want. In my day, a pregnancy wouldn't have been a secret for very long. Any healer—and many sorcerers in other disciplines as well—would notice the extra aura early on."

"Do you still miss those days?" He shifted back and wrapped both arms around her again as the scent of their cooking dinner filled the kitchen.

She smiled, appreciating his warmth. With Ridge so busy at work, they didn't get as many quiet nights like this as she would have liked. "I do. And I miss the people. Though I *have* started appreciating some modern conveniences."

"Personally, I couldn't imagine living in a world without fliers."

"The main modern convenience I was thinking of is the widespread availability of indoor plumbing."

"Toilets aren't nearly as enjoyable as fliers."

"We may have to agree to disagree there."

"Goodness, you're a strange woman." His eyes crinkled, and he bent his head to kiss her.

She kissed him back, and they might have gone on doing that, but one of their stomachs growled, and they broke apart with a laugh.

Ridge checked the pork chops while Sardelle returned to cutting vegetables.

"Airships aren't bad either," Ridge said. "Did you have those in your time?"

"We did not. Just sailing ships. We also didn't have steam carriages, locomotives, dragons, or anything besides horses and horse-drawn wagons really."

"No submarines either, I suppose." He tossed a grin over his shoulder at her. "Have you been on one of those?"

"A submarine?" Sardelle asked, not familiar with the term.

"They're as claustrophobic as a casket, and I hear they smell like dirty socks after a few days with cooped up soldiers who have no way to bathe out there. But Angulus thinks they'll prove as important to warfare and defending the country as my fliers. If you can imagine that. He approved development of the prototypes about ten years ago, and the naval shipyard in Church Rock is building a bunch of them now. I think there are four or five out patrolling the coast at any given time. I got to ride in one a couple of years ago and share my thoughts on whether there was a way for them to attack airships and fliers. Not likely, but they could take out regular steam and sailing ships without being seen. Quite the engineering marvels. Almost as good as toilets." He removed the skillet from the stove. "Oh, forgot to warm up the beans."

Sardelle was staring at his back and didn't respond. He'd formed an image of the craft—a type of long cylindrical underwater boat—in his mind as he'd been speaking, so she'd gotten the gist. She thought of the harbor, out by the breakwater where she'd thought she'd sensed someone. Tolemek. But then there'd been nothing there. Nothing on the *surface.*

"Do other nations have these submarines?" Sardelle asked.

"I believe the Cofah are working on some of their own but aren't quite as far along as we are. I'm not sure about any smaller countries. It's possible. There are spies everywhere, so it's hard to keep military secrets a secret for long."

I didn't sense an underwater boat out there, Jaxi said.

Neither did I, but I sensed... something. Someone. Under water. Briefly. We know Tolemek's kidnappers either have a shaman with them or have access to someone who can make magical items. What if they have one of these underwater boats and, when they sensed me searching for Tolemek, camouflaged it? That could explain why I only glimpsed something. It sounds like such a craft would be easy to hide from the port authorities too.

That seems like a stretch. Such a vessel would still have to come above the surface in order for people to get out. Or for kidnap victims to get in.

True. If I hadn't sensed anything, I'd agree and wouldn't be thinking along these lines. There's no real evidence. But I'll at least mention the possibility of this kind of transportation to Tylie, so Phelistoth can be on the lookout for it.

How's a dragon going to see something underwater?

With magic, presumably. Sardelle assumed a dragon would have no trouble sensing something, even deep down in the ocean. Assuming he knew to look for it.

"Are you chatting with Jaxi or having deeply thoughtful thoughts?" Ridge turned away from the stove—he'd dumped the beans in a pot to heat them up.

All chats with me are deeply thoughtful, Jaxi informed them both.

"I guess that answers my question." Ridge's lips twitched. "Sort of."

Sardelle patted him on the side. "I'm not sure anything will come of my thoughts, but there's nothing more to be done tonight. Why don't we have our dinner and enjoy each other's company?"

"I'm always amenable to enjoyment."

"I'm glad to hear it."

"I'm already enjoying the fact that the vegetable cutting hasn't progressed much. I guess we'll have to save them for tomorrow. Darn."

Oh, please, Jaxi said. *Do you not know that a powerful sorceress can instantly mince carrots?*

Sardelle felt a stirring of power, and seconds later—it wasn't quite an *instant*—the green beans and carrots lay cut into neat piles, ready for a pot.

"Your sword is trampling all over my enjoyment," Ridge said.

"Swords can't trample. They slice, dice, cut, and stab."

He eyed the vegetables. "So I see."

"She's merely helping you be a good role model for your future child."

"I can accomplish that by eating green beans?"

She kissed him. "It's a start."

***

Ridge watched the Wolf Squadron fliers take off as he walked up the long road to the castle, seagulls squawking overhead, perhaps complaining about the noisy propellers. As always, he wished he were going with them, even if it was just to search up and down the coast for signs of kidnappers.

But he had to talk to Angulus, to ask for his favor. He didn't have an appointment and hoped the king could make time to see him. Usually, Angulus was the one to summon *him*, not the other way around. The day before had been an anomaly. During which he'd *also* been asking for a favor. Ridge winced. He didn't like being a burden on anyone. Or a pest. When he'd been asking for favors on behalf of Bhrava Saruth, it hadn't seemed so bad, since Angulus owed the dragon too. But this was definitely a personal favor.

"Sire, I know you're busy, but would you go speak to my mom for me?" he muttered to himself.

Maybe he should attempt to speak to her again himself without bothering Angulus. But that hadn't gone well the night before. And after the news Sardelle had given him, that they were going to have a baby, he knew he had to do everything he could to ensure his mother reconciled with Sardelle. She could help Sardelle with woman things—there would be woman things with a pregnancy, wouldn't there?—before the baby was born, and then she would definitely want to be involved afterward. She'd been saying how much she wanted a grandchild for twenty years, as if Lieutenant Zirkander would have made a good father.

He shuddered at the idea. But now... Was he more mature now? The idea of being a good role model for a kid and knowing wise things to say to guide it scared him more than a little. Not to mention the fact that the baby would presumably grow up to have some magical powers. Ridge wouldn't have a clue what kind of wisdom to offer in regard to that.

Still, he had been more pleased than worried by the news. He'd thought she had been working up to telling him something dreadful.

Sardelle would be a great mother—he had no doubts about her parental abilities—and he could at least be a good provider. Maybe he should buy the house they had been renting to ensure their child—or eventually children?—would have a nice place to grow up. He would have loved the woods and that pond when he'd been a kid. He ought to be able to scrounge together the money for a down payment, especially if those dragons stopped eating all his groceries for a few months. Maybe he could sell the cabin out by the lake.

After the honeymoon. He couldn't get as much time off as he would like, but he planned to whisk Sardelle out there for a few days of privacy, relaxation, and enjoyment. Vegetable-free enjoyment if he had his way. He'd ordered a couple of upgrades to the cabin since the last time she had been up there, and he hoped she would like them.

"General?" someone asked.

Ridge halted and looked up, realizing he'd almost run into the closed wicket gate. Which would have been rather pathetic given that the main gate next to it was open, a delivery truck waiting there while a pair of guards inspected it.

"I'm here to see the king," Ridge said to the man who had stopped him.

"Yes, sir. You can go in. I just didn't want you to—" The guard glanced at the closed gate.

"Crack my forehead on that? I appreciate the help. I wouldn't want a big ugly scar or a broken nose, right?"

"I wouldn't think so, sir. You might not get as many photographs in the newspapers if you weren't, uh—" The man waved at Ridge's face.

"Dolons thinks you're pretty, sir," one of the guards checking the vehicle called with a wink.

"I didn't say that," the first guard blurted.

"That's good," Ridge said, "because I would much rather be handsome." Though if a broken nose would get the journalists to stop writing about him—and how Sardelle was supposedly witching him into marrying her—then it might be worth it.

Ridge waved at the guards, including the one blushing

furiously, and headed up the drive into the courtyard. He was surprised he'd gotten in so easily, but he had just come up the day before, and the guards were all familiar with him. He expected more resistance at the castle door itself. The guards there knew who was on the list for appointments with the king and who wasn't.

"Hello, gents," Ridge said amiably to the two stern-faced guards when he reached the stairs. "Would one of you ask the steward to pass on to the king that General Zirkander would like to see him whenever he gets a minute? I don't need long. A quickie between meetings is fine."

He braced himself to be told to run along, that the king didn't have time for impromptu meetings. Hells, Ridge didn't usually have time for them himself, and he was a lot less special than a king. He'd had to come in early this morning to get through his paperwork and see Wolf Squadron off before sending his aide to the staff meeting so he could make time for this.

"A quickie?" came a woman's voice from behind him. "He usually reserves those for me."

Ridge turned to find a smiling Captain Kaika walking up in uniform, a folder under her arm.

"Oh? I can see where he would prefer your curves to mine, though I wouldn't imagine that outfit inspires a lot of passionate tearing off of clothes."

"No?" She slid her finger down the buttoned flap. "The more that's covered up, the more there is to tease a man's imagination."

"If you say so."

"Trust my wisdom in these areas. You need to report to Angulus? Me too. Come on in."

Kaika patted one of the guards on the shoulder and walked between them. Neither protested her unannounced entrance.

Ridge hazarded walking past after her without asking for their permission. The guards exchanged looks with each other but didn't stop him or say they would have to check with the steward first.

"Huh," Ridge said, catching up with Kaika and walking at her side. "You're like a walking key."

"I can get you in through the secret door at the Sensual Sage too." She smirked. "In case you and Freckles want to experiment."

"Freckles? That's your name for Sardelle?"

"It is."

"She's a lovely, serene, and wise woman."

"With freckles." Kaika turned toward the stairs that led up to the private suites.

As Ridge followed her, it occurred to him that Angulus might not be delighted at seeing them walk in together. Even though he and Kaika had never dated, dallied, or spent any time together outside of work, he'd caught Angulus squinting suspiciously at him a few times when they'd traded jokes in front of him. As if it was Ridge's fault that Kaika was as quick to make a snarky comment as he was.

"You can go first," Ridge said when they reached the office door. "I'll wait."

"You're going to wait outside while we have our quickie? Won't the noise bother you?"

"That's not really why you're here, is it?"

She grinned wickedly at him, then knocked. "Nah, somehow I became the military liaison for Tolemek's kidnapping case. I've got Bitinger's report on the lab." She held up the folder. "Not that his people found more than Freckles and I did."

The door opened, and two men walked out in blue velvet suits and puffy round hats that only someone in the nobility would wear. Their expressions seemed irritated—or perhaps constipated—so they must not have cared for how their meeting went.

One of them bumped Kaika's shoulder as they pushed past her and Ridge. The man curled a lip at her, as if his clumsiness was her fault. He opened his mouth, as if to inform her that soldiers should get out of the way when the nobility passed through, but he glanced at the open door behind him and didn't say anything.

"That is a man in need of a quickie," Kaika announced as the pair moved away. She didn't bother to speak quietly.

Ridge almost asked if she was offering but noticed Angulus coming to the door and kept his mouth shut.

Angulus started to smile when Kaika turned toward him, but he spotted Ridge, and his expression grew more masked. Ridge felt uncomfortable intruding on what had likely been the start of a private moment—it was good to know that Kaika could make the king crack a smile now and then—and he waved for her to go in first. His favor request could wait.

But Angulus waved both of them in. "An update on Tolemek?"

"Got the report from Intelligence, Sire." Kaika walked in and laid the folder on his desk. "There's nothing there that I didn't already tell you about. Sardelle is more useful than that Bitinger was. Maybe you should ask her to work in Intel."

Ridge was busy being pleased by Kaika complimenting Sardelle—and calling her by name—and almost missed Angulus looking at him with raised eyebrows.

"Unfortunately, I don't have any other leads on Tolemek, Sire," Ridge said, realizing the king thought he had something to report. That made him feel disingenuous, like he had been invited in under false pretenses. "I just sent Wolf Squadron out to look for suspicious activity along the coast, but we're mostly hoping to get lucky."

"Hm." Angulus opened the folder to look at the report inside. "I would like to recover him for reasons of national defense, of course, but I also feel responsible for this. It seems likely word got out about something he was working on for me, and someone decided to extract information from him."

"Or for me." Kaika leaned her hip against Angulus's desk. "That explosive was my idea."

"I doubt it's about that. But Tolemek has worked on a number of secret projects for me, some employing very cutting-edge technology and biochemical methodologies. And he's seen my rockets."

Ridge opened his mouth, but shut it again, biting his lip to keep from making the joke that begged to be made. It was almost as if Kaika read his mind, because she smirked over at Ridge, and then asked Angulus, "Should I be jealous about that? I thought we were practicing monogamy this summer."

Ridge rubbed his face to cover up the smirk tugging at the corners of his lips. If *he'd* made the joke, Angulus would have glared at him.

Angulus merely raised an eyebrow at Kaika and said, "He saw my rockets this spring. Before you started visiting the castle."

"Oh, I guess that makes it acceptable then."

Ridge was proud of himself for keeping his mouth shut. Though he vowed to add *visiting the castle* to his repertoire of euphemisms.

"They weren't able to come up with a list of the contents of his vault, I see," Angulus murmured, then looked up at Ridge. "I don't suppose Lieutenant Ahn would be helpful in putting together a list?"

"I can ask, Sire. I don't think she's particularly interested in his work though, so she may have never seen inside the vault. She calls his painstakingly crafted original formulas *goos*."

Kaika shook her head and folded her arms over her chest. "Pilots."

"What do you call them?" Angulus asked her.

"Gunks."

"Much more erudite."

"You know what a scholar I am."

"Indeed. Did the guards have to remove many grenades and guns from you on the way in?"

"Nah, I've learned to leave them in the officers' billets when I come to the castle."

"I didn't think you were comfortable having them so far away."

"I'm making sacrifices for you."

"I'm very appreciative."

Ridge rubbed the back of his neck and made a point of not looking at them or noticing how they were smiling slightly and gazing into each other's eyes as they bantered. He wished he'd stayed in the hallway and was thinking of slinking out and waiting for Kaika to leave, no matter how long that took, before knocking again.

"I got the architect's drawings with the builder's stamp of approval this morning," Angulus said, shifting his attention to Ridge. "They're ready to start tomorrow."

"For Bhrava Saruth's temple? Good. I'm sure he'll be pleased."

"How, by the blessings of all seven gods, did you get those people ready to build so quickly? Architects take weeks if not *months* to draw up blueprints. I'm aware of this because of the copious repairs I've had to have done to the castle this year."

"Er, yes, Sire," Ridge said, trying not to wince as he remembered dropping off the sorceress who had wreaked havoc on his castle. Admittedly, Angulus had been the one to blow up that wine cellar or whatever it had been in the back, but it was all still Ridge's fault.

"I asked a question, Zirkander. *Yes* isn't the appropriate answer."

Kaika snickered.

"Uh, about how they got it done so quickly? I sweet-talked everyone, sir. Promises of beer, barbecues once the temple is built, offerings of dragon-god blessings and flier rides."

"So, they were more motivated by the notion of spending time with you and getting drunk than they were by the money I pay them?"

"I don't think they particularly care if I'm involved, Sire." Why did Ridge feel like he was walking on quicksand? This was the last thing he'd expected to be tied to the train tracks for. He'd just been trying to get things done in a quick and efficient manner. "The dragon blessings were key."

"I doubt that," Angulus muttered, sharing an exasperated look with Kaika. She merely shrugged.

"I'm sure they're being extra careful and taking more time for you because the castle is an important historical structure," Ridge said, "and you're obviously very important to please. It's probably different with a temple for a dragon. If a stone falls from the ceiling and crushes someone in the temple, Bhrava Saruth can use his magic to heal that person."

"I'd say you're an awful diplomat, Zirkander, but these finished blueprints suggest otherwise. At the least, you've got a gift for bribing people."

"That's possibly true."

"Do you have anything else to report?" Angulus asked Ridge and glanced at Kaika, something in his eyes suggesting he anticipated spending some private time alone with her before she left.

"On Tolemek?" Ridge asked. "No, Sire. I actually came to ask for a favor, but I can wait in the hall while you two frolic between the sheets together. Or on the desk. Whatever is appropriate at lunchtime."

Kaika smirked. Angulus appeared less amused.

"A favor?" he asked.

"A small one, Sire." Ridge slipped a hand into his pocket to surreptitiously rub his dragon figurine for luck. "I wouldn't ask, but, uhm, I think my mother trusts you more than she does me."

"Why does that surprise me very little?" Angulus asked.

"Because you're the supreme ruler over the entire country, and I'm…"

"Trying?" Angulus suggested.

"Unconventional," Ridge said.

"Does she trust the cats more than she trusts you?" Kaika asked.

"Likely so. The cats didn't play pranks on her when they were younger."

"What's the favor?" Angulus asked.

He hadn't issued a long-suffering sigh before asking, so Ridge chose to find that promising. "My mother has very recently had her beliefs shattered, first by stumbling across a dragon lying in my backyard, and then by having a sorceress—or sorceress-in-training—stumble across her. While performing magic."

Angulus tilted his head. "She didn't believe in dragons?"

"Or magic."

"But Sardelle…"

"Hence my problem," Ridge said. "Mom isn't talking to Sardelle now, and she's angry at me because she thinks we're all playing some elaborate hoax to trick her into believing magic is real when it's not, and—Kaika, stop smirking."

Kaika had her fingers pressed to her lips, but it didn't matter. Ridge could still tell.

"It's really more of a grin, General," she said.

"Then stop grinning."

"I'm trying. It's difficult."

"Are you saying you never told your mother Sardelle is a sorceress?" Angulus sounded genuinely surprised.

Ridge lifted his shoulders. "Mom doesn't believe in magic. She would have thought we were kooks. But with the wedding coming up and Sardelle now pregnant, I don't want any dissension between the two most important women in my life. I want them to get along, to like and support each other."

"Sardelle is pregnant?" Kaika asked. "Do you by chance know when the baby was conceived?"

Ridge frowned at her. "I'm not helping you win the baby pool."

"Oh, you heard about that, did you?"

"I don't know how *you* heard about it. I thought it was strictly between pilots and the ground crew in the flier battalion." Ridge stuck his hands in his pockets and looked at Angulus, hoping his request hadn't sounded as pathetic as he feared. A grown man coming in to see the ruler of all of Iskandia about a domestic misunderstanding. "Sire, I believe my mother would believe *you* if you told her magic exists."

Angulus gazed back at him, his face difficult to read. Was he amused? Exasperated? Utterly flummoxed because Ridge had come here for this? Ridge didn't know; too bad he didn't have Jaxi here to read the king's mind.

Angulus finally pulled out an appointment book, laid it on his desk, and flipped through the next few days. Ridge bit his lip again to stop from asking if he had quickies scheduled in. Why was it so hard not to be irreverent?

"She has a long ride in, doesn't she?" Angulus asked. "The day after tomorrow at three past noon?"

"That will be fine, Sire. Can you possibly have your secretary send her an official summons?"

"Because she won't trust *you* if you relay the summons?"

"That's a distinct possibility, Sire."

"Zirkander, what have you been doing to this poor woman?"

"Nothing." Ridge lifted his hands. "It's just that when something she deems impossible happens, she has a hard time believing it."

"Mm."

"Is anybody else amused that a general and a national hero has mom problems?" Kaika asked.

"Only you," Ridge told her.

"I'm mildly amused," Angulus said.

Ridge backed toward the door, relieved Angulus had said yes, and figuring he had better give them their privacy. "Permission to go, Sire?"

"Yes."

Ridge told himself he walked out of the office and the castle in a stately manner befitting his rank, but it was possible he fled in ignominy.

Chapter 8

Weeks ago, when Sardelle had envisioned acquiring a wedding dress, she had assumed she would go with Fern and let her pick out something whimsical, or perhaps let her choose fabric that she would turn *into* something whimsical. Fern already had her measurements and had made her two dresses. They were brighter and perkier than Sardelle normally chose for herself, but she was happy to wear them occasionally to make Ridge's mother happy. Alas, she didn't know if she dared show up at Fern's house right now.

What she hadn't imagined, when thinking about choosing a wedding dress, was going shopping with two women in uniform, Cas and Kaika each armed with pistols in holsters. Though Sardelle wore a blue summer dress and sandals, Jaxi was also belted to her waist, and she worried the merchants would think they were being invaded. Maybe she needed to send Lilah into the shops first. Ridge's cousin, and one of Sardelle's newer friends, Lilah wore a modest gray skirt and blouse, the entire ensemble free of weapons.

Weapons or not, none of them looked like they belonged on the street Cas had turned down. Gleaming black and silver steam carriages were parked on the sides of the wide boulevard, most with chauffeurs reading newspapers or magazines from the front benches while they waited for their employers. Men and women in custom-tailored clothing, many attended by what Sardelle assumed were maids or shopping assistants, strolled along the sidewalks and wandered into stores.

A few glanced toward her little group and pursed their lips. Sardelle didn't know if the gesture was for their modest clothing or for the weapons or for both.

"You say we may get a clue to Tolemek's whereabouts at the shop you're leading us to, Cas?" Sardelle asked.

Tylie and Phelistoth hadn't come back to the house yet, so she didn't have any more leads than she'd had the night before. When Cas had arrived early that morning, circles under her eyes suggesting she hadn't slept much, and mentioned an eccentric Dakrovian foreigner being spotted at a clothing shop, Sardelle had been willing to go along and check. Lilah hadn't started her classes yet, so Sardelle had swung by her apartment to collect her, and Kaika seemed to have been assigned to Tolemek's case, so she'd been easy to pull away from work. Sardelle was fairly certain Jaxi had been in contact with her because Kaika had been waiting when they'd ridden into the city.

You're welcome, Jaxi said. *We may have to use some magic to convince this storeowner to assist us. I can already tell she's going to be snooty.*

You've located her? Sardelle peered at the shop names farther down the boulevard. She hadn't seen the Sophisticated Hem yet.

No. Call it a hunch. I do believe the shop is on that corner next to the gold-gilded dragon fountain breathing not fire but a stream of water out of its nostrils.

That almost looks like Bhrava Saruth.

Maybe his magnificence has inspired sculptors of late.

Very possible, but that statue looks to have been there for a lot longer than he's been in town.

"I see it." Cas pointed to the corner Jaxi had identified.

"Next to the garish statue with the runny nose?" Kaika asked.

A woman strolling toward them along the walkway, with a somber-faced older man carrying shopping bags behind her, curled a lip when she caught Kaika's words, and gave her a long dismissive look up and down.

"Common filth," she said, raising her nose as she strode past their group.

"Does that mean you don't want to get randy with me later?" Kaika winked at her. "I was hoping to bag a noblewoman when I came down here."

The woman threw a horrified glance over her shoulder and

practically leaped into the next doorway. The man gave Kaika a more speculative look before following his wife—or was she his employer?—inside.

"I learned that move from Captain Blazer," Kaika said. "It tends to shut up snobby women quickly."

"What happens if they're interested in being bagged by you?" Cas asked.

"It hasn't happened yet. Should I be worried about my allure?"

"Is it rude of me to find it remarkable that she dates the king?" Lilah asked Sardelle as Cas and Kaika, their destination in sight, surged into the lead.

For a moment, Sardelle was surprised Lilah knew about that, but then she remembered Lilah had spent a number of days researching bones at Galmok Mountain with Captain Kaika as her bodyguard. Kaika might have admitted to spending time with Angulus, but she didn't brag about it or mention it to many people, as far as Sardelle had observed. She found it more likely that Therrik, who'd learned about the relationship a few months ago, had said something.

"I believe Angulus enjoys her refreshing bluntness," Sardelle said.

"Actually, he likes my ass." Kaika winked again and gave one of her back cheeks a slap.

Lilah lifted her eyebrows. "She *is* blunt."

"Refreshingly," Kaika said.

They reached the corner in front of the Sophisticated Hem, and Cas paused, regarding Kaika with a concerned expression.

"Perhaps Sardelle and Professor Zirkander should go in," Cas said, "while we…"

"Blow up that runny-nosed dragon fountain?" Kaika asked.

"You didn't bring explosives with you, did you?" Lilah asked.

"I *am* on duty. Looking for kidnappers."

The question, Jaxi said, *is not whether she brought explosives but how many she brought.*

You, being a sentient soulblade, no doubt know the answer, Sardelle replied.

Naturally, but I don't want to spoil the guessing game for anyone.

Cas turned to Sardelle, pulled a folded piece of paper out of her pocket, and held it out for her to read. "This is the incident that the proprietor reported, a man paying for a hat in Dakrovian coin. I'm hoping you can use your telepathy to learn more about the man and especially if she has any idea what part of town he's staying in." Cas shifted her weight back and forth, glancing at a pair of well-dressed women who sashayed out of the shop. "Maybe I should go in and ask the questions. I'm just not very... I mean, even when I'm not in uniform, I don't look like I fit in here. I'm just like Kaika."

"You're supposed to sound reverent and awed when you say a sentence like that," Kaika observed.

After Sardelle read the snippet, she looked at Cas. "Unless I miss my guess, you're the only one of us who grew up in a wealthy household."

"But my father's money is new money, not old noble money. There's a difference. Besides, I learned about guns and bows, not dresses and shoes. You always look regal and serene, Sardelle, even when General Zirkander is flying upside down with you in his back seat."

"I don't think that's true, but I will thank you for the compliment." Sardelle returned the paper to her. "Lilah, will you accompany me inside to see if I can find a dress?"

She hoped Lilah wasn't offended that *she* hadn't been identified as regal and serene. Probably not. She was scrutinizing an old plaque on the dragon fountain. She drew a notebook out of a purse stuffed with no fewer than three paperbacks and scribbled something down.

Sardelle waited until she was done writing to touch her arm. "Lilah? Will you help me find a dress?"

"Oh yes, of course." Lilah wedged the notebook inside her purse between the books. "I just wanted to make a note of that. I believe I spotted a factual error. If so, the plaque should be corrected."

Sardelle eyed the patina on the old plaque, guessing it had been in that spot for decades, if not centuries. She doubted anyone would rush out to have a new one made, but she didn't say so.

"Make sure to get a dress with inside pockets and straps," Kaika suggested. "To hold grenades and knives."

"I have Jaxi. I don't need grenades and knives."

"Then make sure to get one that matches her scabbard. I assume you'll be walking down the aisle with her?"

"Of course."

Kaika gave her the thumb-to-fingers circle gesture that the pilots favored. It seemed to mean both ready and good.

"Can you actually afford the clothes here?" Lilah murmured as she and Sardelle headed for the entrance.

Unlike most of the other shops, the Sophisticated Hem had no large display windows. Instead, the storefront was castle-inspired, with formidable stone walls and high, narrow windows reminiscent of arrow slots. The heavy oak door was bound with iron bands full of rivets, and the small window in it was covered with bars.

"I don't know," Sardelle said. "But it doesn't hurt to browse. And question the owner."

"I'm surprised Fern didn't offer to make you a dress."

"She did, but then... I'm not sure if she's talking to me now."

Lilah looked at her in surprise.

"She found out I'm a sorceress."

"I didn't think she believed in magic."

"She does now," Sardelle said glumly, pushing up the heavy door.

Polished hardwood floors lay inside, with few racks and display cases cluttering the area. A small selection of gowns hung on wooden dummies near the walls, and steps in the back led to an area of jewelry, scarves, and men's and women's hats.

A graying lady in an elegant summer-green dress and short jacket strolled toward them. Sardelle lifted her chin and did her best to look regal, as Cas had called her. And like someone who could afford expensive clothing. Technically, she could conjure nucro bills into existence, but she didn't think Angulus would appreciate her flooding the capital with counterfeit currency.

"Greetings, my friend," the woman said—was this the Lady Masonwood that Cas's report had mentioned? She came forward to clasp Sardelle's hands. "The future Mrs. Zirkander, isn't it?"

"Ah, yes." Sardelle did her best to rein in her surprise at being recognized. "Please call me Sardelle."

"I've seen your picture in the newspapers."

Sardelle attempted a smile, but she was taken aback, both at being recognized and also at being greeted so enthusiastically. The former usually did not lead to the latter, not in this century.

Jaxi snickered into her mind.

Do you know something I don't know, Jaxi?

Usually.

Are you reading this woman's thoughts?

If I am, it's certainly not my fault. She's spewing them all over the place, much like the water shooting out of that fountain's nostrils.

"It's lovely to make your acquaintance, Sardelle. I am Lady Masonwood, only a distant relation to the king. Are you here to see my dresses? I may be able to offer you a discount in exchange for..." Masonwood looked at Lilah, then also at a pair of young, well-dressed women perusing the racks, and finally at a gentleman in a suit working in the hat area. "Assistance," Masonwood finished in a whisper.

She released Sardelle's arm, stepped back, and said, "Stay here, please. Look around. I'll return shortly." Masonwood started away, but turned back, raising a finger. "Don't leave. Promise me you're staying, yes?"

"Yes," Sardelle said.

As the woman hustled through a doorway on one side of the show room, Jaxi snickered again.

Are you going to enlighten me? Sardelle asked her.

Where would the fun be in that?

You remember that it's not appropriate to read people's minds, right? We've had this discussion before. You never used to do this in our century.

Our century was ridiculously stuffy when it came to that kind of thing. The freedom of this lawless era is growing on me.

"That's not the greeting I expected," Lilah said.

"Nor I." Sardelle ignored the glances the young women were sending in her direction and headed for the wall of dresses. Though she had come because of Cas's lead on Tolemek, it would be convenient if she could get the dress selecting out of the way, and if this Lady Masonwood truly wished to give her a discount, perhaps the garments would be affordable.

"What do you think she wants?"

"Healing of some sort would be my guess. It *is* what I'm known for."

"Is it?" Lilah trailed her to the dresses. "The newspapers have highlighted your ability to control Ridge and magically coerce him into marrying you."

"No need to bring that up." Sardelle wondered if everyone in town, or in the whole country, had seen those ludicrous articles.

Lilah smiled slightly. "I don't know who these people are who think someone tricking Ridge into marrying her would be a good idea. I'm surprised..." She glanced at Sardelle, then said, "Never mind," and stroked the sleeve of an ivory gown.

"I think his mouth fools a lot of people into not realizing he's a good man who loves his job, his country, and is loyal to his friends," Sardelle said.

Lilah's cheeks grew pink as she pretended to examine the gown. "I suppose he is. Honestly, I still don't know him that well. He was a trying young man."

"So he tells me." Sardelle didn't take offense at Lilah's comments. She hoped Lilah and Ridge got a chance to spend more time together now that she lived in the capital. They didn't seem to have much in common, but family was important, something Sardelle hadn't realized fully until hers was gone. "I imagine Therrik was a trying young man too."

"He still is." Lilah smirked. "But if he likes you, he can be quite personable."

"How do you get him to like you?"

"I caressed his weapon."

"You were taking advice from Kaika, I see."

Her smirk deepened.

Sardelle glanced toward the side doorway, but Lady Masonwood still hadn't returned.

She's washing her feet in the lavatory, Jaxi informed her.

Ah.

I'm not sure whether to be alarmed or bewildered that such information doesn't surprise you.

I'm going to guess that she needs something... attended. By a healer. I hope you brought gloves.

"Ridge was wondering," Sardelle said, moving over to look at the next dress in the row, "how you're getting along here in the capital. And with Therrik."

"I'm delighted that Vann has been sent back down to the capital from that remote outpost, even if he didn't get the job I encouraged him to apply for. We've been enjoying each other's company. He helped me move into my new apartment."

"You aren't having any problems with his surly tendencies?"

"No problem at all. As I said, he isn't surly with those who don't irk him."

"I can only imagine since my very existence irks him." Sardelle smiled.

"I'm hoping that one day, he'll learn to mistrust those with dragon blood less. He has his reasons for hating magic, and I understand why he does, but it's not right for him to loathe everyone he meets that falls into that category. But you can tell Ridge that Vann and I are getting along nicely. He needn't worry about me."

"Good. And I will tell him. Do you like this green one?"

"Mm, not enough lace to fit in with current fashion, from what I've seen. I don't follow popular trends, admittedly, but I went to the weddings of two colleagues in the last year, and they assured me they were dressing in line with the modern fashion coming out of the capital."

"How *much* lace?" Sardelle always felt lace was something that should be reserved for undergarments.

Yes, I believe your soul snozzle enjoys your lacy underwear, especially the pair that's almost see-through. Jaxi made a thoughtful hm noise in Sardelle's mind. *It's possible it's the see-through aspect that appeals to him more than the lace itself.*

Thank you for the analysis, Jaxi.

You're welcome.

"You could attempt to set some trends." Lilah lifted the sleeve of a beige dress with fringes. "This might fall nicely on you. And here's an inner pocket. For your grenades."

"Jaxi would be affronted if I felt the need to carry explosives. She's quite capable of melting, incinerating, and blowing up things. Though I do hope none of that will be necessary at my wedding."

"Let's hope. Are you allowed to try on dresses?" Lilah looked toward the man in the suit, but he was working on a hat, snipping pieces of felt all over a work table, and ignoring them.

Surprised Jaxi hadn't chimed in on the incineration and explosion subject, Sardelle silently asked, *Is she still washing her feet?*

No, she's spritzing perfume on them now. The scent of rose petals.

"I do like that one," Sardelle said of the beige dress. "Neutral colors tend to match the leather of Jaxi's scabbard nicely. I suspect she'll glow a little as I walk along too."

"Is that desirable?"

"She thinks so."

Lady Masonwood returned and bee-lined for Sardelle, barely glancing at Lilah.

Sardelle groped for an opening to ask about the Dakrovian customer. Maybe subtlety didn't matter that much. Masonwood shouldn't have a reason to protect the man if she'd reported on his comings and goings to a guild that sold information to people like Ahnsung. And Jaxi, an expert at snooping into people's minds, ought to be able to pluck the information from Masonwood's thoughts if Sardelle merely brought the Dakrovian up.

"I was hoping you could help me, Sardelle," Masonwood said. "You are a true healer, aren't you? I looked you up after the dragon attacks on the city a couple of months ago."

"Yes, I'm happy to assist with ailments."

Sardelle resisted the urge to crinkle her nose. Jaxi had been right. Rose petals. The scent of the perfume wafted strongly from the woman.

"Though my dress-shopping assistant, Professor Zirkander, was actually hoping to do some research on your clientele for a demographics paper at her university," Sardelle said, gesturing at Lilah. "Would you mind answering a couple of questions for her before we go back to check out your problem?"

Sardelle was on the verge of attempting telepathic communication with Lilah for the first time to explain herself, but Lilah turned toward Masonwood and extended her hand.

"Yes, I teach demographics and economics, and research and write papers, naturally. I have over forty-seven publications out there in respected journals." She glanced at Sardelle, a hint of a what-next look in her eye.

"She's curious about non-local clientele," Sardelle said, speaking quickly because Masonwood wore a puzzled—and slightly impatient—expression. "Do you get many people in here from other nations, or is it predominantly local Iskandians?"

"Well, we're known far and wide, you understand. It's rare for the Cofah to come here, but we occasionally get well-off merchant captains visiting Jolof—" she waved to the felt-clipping haberdasher, "—and traveling business mavens on occasion, but only those who have the leisure to stay a while, as we custom-fit our clothing, and while we will deliver, we don't risk shipping overseas through the freight service."

"Have any Dakrovians been in, by chance?" Sardelle asked.

Masonwood tilted her head in a puzzled look.

She's thinking of a man that came in her shop wearing buckskins and a bowler hat, Jaxi told Sardelle, *but she's also thinking it strange that you're bringing this up. It's possible Lilah isn't a convincing economics professor. It could be her boobs.*

Pardon?

She's well-endowed.

That's not allowed in the academic world?

It seems rare.

"Occasionally," Masonwood said, shrugging. "May I convince you to look at something for me?" She pointed to the side doorway.

"Of course." Sardelle trailed her into a short hall that led past changing rooms, an office full of packages being prepared for shipping, and a lavatory.

When Masonwood turned into the lavatory, Sardelle suspected she was in for toenail fungus, warts, or bunions. She decided that if she got a discount on a dress for healing such things, she wouldn't mention it to Ridge.

You don't think your soul snozzle would be amused?

Too amused, likely.

Maybe there's a package for Tolemek's kidnappers in that stack. Do kidnappers get deliveries?

That's a good question. If he came here to shop, and they custom-tailor everything...

When you asked Masonwood about foreigners, a couple of names popped into her mind. Vark Something and Yendree J-something.

So, you think we should root through the packages and see if any are going out to a Something? Sardelle asked.

Sorry, she didn't stop to spell them for me. Those probably aren't the exact first names either. Who knows if she was even thinking of them correctly. But she also had the thought that she needed to get those packages mailed out to them. I can sift through that shipping preparation area to see if there's a match—or a close-enough match—while you're rubbing her feet.

Would it be helpful if Cas, Lilah, and Kaika help? Sardelle asked as Masonwood gestured to two padded stools next to a steaming pool. There were changing rooms behind the pool, along with toilets in private stalls filled with candles and potpourri. This store had a fancy latrine. Maybe the woman lived in the apartment above and came down to use it for bathing. Or maybe one regularly took a dip after purchasing a dress.

Help with the foot-rubbing? Doubtful.

With the searching.

Only if they can distract that hat-snipping man and sneak back without being noticed. It would be much easier for me to read the labels. I'll begin now.

"It's my feet, dear. I've had these dreadful—oh, I don't know exactly what you call them—bumps—for years, and they're impeding my comfort when I walk."

I believe the medical term is warts, Jaxi said.

Just look at those packages, please. As Sardelle sat on one of the stools opposite Masonwood, she switched her telepathic focus to Cas. She didn't often speak that way to her, but had before, and didn't think Cas would find it too jarring. *Cas? We believe a couple of foreigners, possibly Dakrovians, have been here recently and made purchases. There's an office back here with boxes due to go out. If you can slip into the hallway and into it, perhaps you'll find something if you poke around.*

Sardelle didn't add that she would be shocked if this actually led to Tolemek's kidnappers, both because she didn't want to deflate Cas's determination and because she didn't have any better ideas. Once Phelistoth or Bhrava Saruth came within her range, she would mention the submarine possibility to them. With their powerful magic, they might be able to detect such a conveyance from dozens of miles away, especially if it employed a magical power source, as the army's fliers did.

I've got the proprietor distracted, Sardelle added, sensing Cas conferring with Kaika. Sardelle broadened her range to include her. *We're in the back, but the man is still in his part of the shop. You'll have to distract him somehow to get past to snoop.*

Oh, I can distract a man, Kaika replied, the grin coming through the telepathic link. *No problem.*

Good. Jaxi is already looking.

You left your sword in the office? Cas asked.

No, she's looking from my hip.

I see why you need us, Kaika thought.

I heard that, Jaxi said, speaking to all of them. *I'll have you know I read all the books in the prison library at Galmok Mountain from under thousands of tons of rocks. I'm positive I'll find the right package before either of you gets back here.*

"I can make those go away," Sardelle said when Masonwood thrust a foot into her lap.

"Oh, wonderful. I've tried all manner of poultices and tinctures. It's really quite embarrassing. It's summer, and I'm unable to wear sandals for obvious reasons."

Sardelle didn't think the warts were that noticeable, since they were between the woman's toes, but she could understand them making walking uncomfortable. "Just give me a few moments, and I'll take care of them."

Have I mentioned how exciting it is to watch you handle women's feet? Jaxi asked.

You haven't.

Good.

Shouldn't you be focusing on finding those packages before Cas does? Since you made that claim?

Oh, I will. I can do many things at once. It's part of the gloriousness of being a soulblade.

"I can hardly wait," Masonwood said. "Did you come in for a wedding dress? I would be most honored to have you choose one from my collection."

"I did," Sardelle murmured, her eyes closed so she could concentrate, though she also brushed the woman's mind, curious to find out if she was telling the truth. Even though Masonwood wanted something and had a reason to be nice, this wasn't the reception Sardelle had expected.

"I'll discount it deeply and sell it at cost. I don't suppose you could get me an invitation to the wedding?" Masonwood smiled, the words surprisingly genuine. "I've tried to use my connections to Angulus to get an invitation, but it seems General Zirkander is only inviting military personnel. Or so we all thought. Then I heard that assassin Ahnsung got an invitation. Imagine!"

"He's the father of one of Ridge's pilots," Sardelle said in explanation, though it had surprised her, too, when Ridge had addressed that particular card. She had signed the invitation but hadn't written anything else on it, having no idea what to say to the man.

"Mm. Many noblewomen are distressed that they haven't been invited. Oh, we know *he's* not of the nobility, but he's been such a dashing hero flying in and out of the capital these past twenty years. One tends to forget that he has dubious origins. Some of my younger associates are terribly jealous of you, my dear, but I just think it's so romantic that the great General Zirkander has fallen in love and is getting married. Some author will pen a tale about it, I'm certain."

Sardelle decided it would be petty to mention that the author would probably neglect to mention her in it, instead putting some more socially acceptable woman in the role of wife-to-be. Instead, she smiled and released Masonwood's bare foot.

"Is that better?"

The woman wiggled her toes, then bent as low as she could manage to examine them. "I don't feel the bumps there anymore. This is wonderful."

You may want to delay her a little longer, Jaxi said. *We're still looking. Lilah, Cas, and I. Kaika is simultaneously flirting with the haberdasher while asking him to show her hats for her boyfriend. The haberdasher sees nothing odd about this. He's wondering what her boobs look like under her uniform.*

Sardelle lifted a hand as Masonwood started to rise. "Perhaps I should check your other foot too. Warts are viral and can spread."

"Oh dear." Masonwood plopped back down onto the stool and lifted her other foot for Sardelle.

"I'm sure I could send you an invitation to the wedding," Sardelle said, doing a cursory examination. She decided not to mention that Masonwood would be doing her a favor in coming, since her side of the guest list had been so sparse. She'd already invited the woman who had trimmed her hair the month before and the postman who delivered their mail—he had been delighted. "Just let me know where to have it sent."

"Excellent, excellent."

We've got something, Jaxi said. *A package addressed to a berth in the Ambergull harbor.*

That's a hundred miles down the coast.

Hence why it's being shipped instead of sent out by bicycle deliverer, I imagine. It's the Yen- name. Yendray. I was close. This package is the only thing addressed to a wharf.

Excitement stirred in Sardelle's breast. Maybe this would turn into a viable lead after all.

Can you tell what's in the package? she asked.

A hat. It's covered with rabbit fur that's been dyed blue. I have a feeling Tolemek has an eccentric kidnapper.

I'm not sure if that's a good thing or a bad thing.

What if the man was mad? Some delusional megalomaniac who wanted to take over the world with Tolemek's concoctions?

I don't know if hat fur necessarily denotes that degree of madness, Jaxi said, *but if nothing else, I think we'll be able to identify him if we spot him.*

Agreed.

Chapter 9

Cas and Kaika jumped off the steam wagon that had given them a ride back to the fort and ran for the front gate. They had left Sardelle and Lilah at the Sophisticated Hem—apparently, Sardelle had established some rapport with that Masonwood woman and felt obligated to buy her dress there. But Sardelle had promised to find General Zirkander and catch up with Cas and Kaika on the way to Ambergull. Cas knew Sardelle could throw magical wind at Zirkander's propeller to make the flier go faster.

As she ran, Cas clenched the address she had scribbled down in her hand, glancing at it often, though she already had it memorized. Wharf B Berth 12 in Ambergull. She had no idea why the Dakrovians would have docked a hundred miles down the coast after kidnapping Tolemek, but this was the best lead she had.

The gate guards, recognizing them and seeing the determined expressions on their faces, waved them through without asking for identification. Cas headed straight to the tram at the back of the fort that led up to the hangar butte.

"Do you need to ask General Zirkander or your squadron leader for permission before taking off?" Kaika asked as they jumped into the tram car waiting at the bottom of the cliff.

Cas waved for the operator to send them up. "I should. And if they're up there, I will."

"And if they're not?"

"I'll round up who I can to go check out Ambergull. If there's a big Dakrovian or pirate ship docked down there, we may need backup."

"I'm a little distressed you didn't let me swing by the armory to pick up some explosives. I hardly have any with me."

"There's a small armory in the hangar. Maybe it can supply you." Cas paced in the small tram car as much as she could. Three short steps, turn, three short steps, turn again…

"Most of the ordnance up there is designed to be dropped from above."

"If they have Tolemek, I'll be happy to fly you over their heads to do that."

"We should probably get him out of their ship first," Kaika said dryly. "Which likely means boarding it. We'll need some of your best fighters along. If your flier squadrons *have* any best fighters."

"Captain Blazer is an experienced warrior."

"Yes, I've seen her boxing medals. We can throw some gloves on her and send her in first. She'll have to let the kidnappers know that the only valid targets are above the waist, otherwise no points for them."

The tram clanked as it reached the top of the butte. Cas jumped out and ran for the hangar door. She knew Zirkander had sent Wolf Squadron out to search up and down the coast for suspicious activity and didn't know who would be inside, if anyone. She hoped not to run into Colonel Coyote from Tiger Squadron, as he might not give her permission to take off. She intended to go regardless of what any of her superior officers said, but there would be fewer repercussions if she left without asking for permission than if she was denied permission and left anyway.

The door opened before she reached it, and two ground crew soldiers carrying a dented propeller between them strode out ahead of Zirkander. Cas came to an abrupt halt. His face and hands were as greasy as those of the ground crew.

"Sir," she blurted. "We have a lead."

"So I heard," Zirkander said.

"Sir?"

"From Jaxi. She keeps me apprised of everything she thinks I need to know. Leads to find kidnapped friends, the color of the dress Sardelle picked out, the warts she healed… The important things in life." Zirkander pointed his thumb through the doorway.

"Tranq is still out with most of Wolf and Tiger Squadrons, but Duck, Pimples, and Blazer just got back. Take them with you to Ambergull."

"Ah yes," Kaika said. "Duck and Pimples. Preeminent pugilists, I'm sure."

Zirkander looked at her.

"Captain Kaika believes we'll have to forcefully board the ship and fight our way to Tolemek," Cas made herself explain, though she was antsy to rush into the hangar and jump in her flier, "not simply drop bombs on it from above."

"No bombs? And she's still willing to go along?"

"I like to clobber things with fists and bullets too," Kaika said.

"And here I thought Angulus was civilizing you."

"Nah, I'm wilding him."

"That's alarming. Ahn, Sardelle is on her way here. We'll be right behind you. If she senses Tolemek on a ship and thinks we need to board, we'll let Jaxi lead the way."

"Last I saw, Jaxi was attached to Sardelle," Kaika said.

"Yes, I believe that's still the case," Zirkander said.

"You're going to send your fiancée in first against kidnappers?"

"She's a very capable woman." Zirkander grinned. "Don't worry, Kaika. I'll let you go after her."

"Thoughtful, sir. Thank you."

Cas bounced on her feet, not in the mood for banter. "Permission to go, sir?"

"You're still here?" Zirkander jerked his thumb toward the fliers again.

Cas bolted.

The hangar doors stood open as she ran toward one of the two-seaters, the sky outside gray. The workday had nearly ended, but the long summer days meant they could reach Ambergull before dark. Though maybe it would be better to arrive *after* dark.

"Nice of you to come to work, Ahn," Duck called, waving a thermos as he munched a sandwich. "You've been scarcer than bees in the winter these last couple of days."

"Looking for Tolemek. Mount up. We're heading to Ambergull."

"So we heard." Duck nodded toward Pimples. "Just having a snack first. You don't want cranky, hungry pilots along, do you?"

"I think she just wants to find her cranky, hungry pirate," Blazer said from her own flier. She was loading fresh ammo for her machine guns.

Another time, Cas might have asked how the day had gone and what she'd found to shoot at while she was out there. But not now. She climbed into her cockpit, powered up the craft, and ran through a quick check.

Thankfully, the others finished what they were doing—or eating—and pulled themselves into their own cockpits. Pimples and Duck took their one-seaters, and Kaika pulled herself into a two-seater with Blazer. Cas rubbed the triggers of her machine guns, hoping she got a chance to shoot the kidnappers who had blown up Tolemek's lab.

"Are we certain Tolemek is in Ambergull?" Blazer asked over the communication crystal as Cas guided her flier toward the open doors, taking the lead.

"Not certain, ma'am, no."

"Too bad. I know Pimples is concerned that his special cream will run out, and there'll be nobody around to resupply him."

"That would be tragic," Duck said. "That Cofah princess might stop writing him letters if she knew what he really looked like."

"He could always apply some makeup," Blazer said, "to hide his pimply-ness. Women have been doing that for ages."

"Makeup could only improve his face," Duck said.

"The wit in this hangar is almost as sharp as the edge of a spoon," Pimples said.

A soft drizzle fell as Cas sailed off the butte and into the air. Eddies tugged at her wings, but she had no trouble turning south as soon as she had some altitude. She passed over the hangars and then the lighthouses, stone hotels, and manors perched along the rocky coast.

"Captain, you got your wedding present picked out for the general and Sardelle yet?" Duck asked.

"I got a pattern picked out," Blazer said.

"You going to knit Sardelle some boxing gloves, so she can pummel the general when needed?"

"Nah, making them something useful for the house."

"What?"

"You'll see it if you visit for one of the general's barbecues and consume the typical amount of beer and sarsaparilla," Blazer said.

"That clue doesn't help me as much as you might have thought," Duck said.

"That's all you're getting. I don't want to ruin the surprise. You'll have to come up with your own gift idea."

"I had an idea, but Pimples said Sardelle wouldn't like it."

"I believe I said *nobody* would like it," Pimples muttered.

"It was hilarious. General Zirkander would *love* it. I may still go back and get it."

Kaika said something from the back seat that Cas didn't hear. Blazer responded with, "They don't need another cat."

"...lonely."

"Two cats make more cats."

"...can happen anyway... neighbor cats."

Cas caught herself glancing over her shoulder as the team flew down the coast, hoping to spot Zirkander on the horizon. He wouldn't put an end to silly conversations, but at least *this* one might end.

Fortunately, it fizzled off on its own. A few more debates came up over the course of the flight, and some of the light faded from the gray cloudy sky. Somewhere behind those clouds, the sun sank toward the horizon.

Cas spotted the river mouth that marked Ambergull and stirred in her seat.

"Anyone know where our dragon allies are?" Pimples asked. "I bet they'd have an easier time finding Tolemek."

"I believe Tylie and Phelistoth are out looking for him," Cas said when nobody else answered.

"I believe Bhrava Saruth is lounging on his new island and sighing in delight as workers prepare to break ground," came Zirkander's voice over the crystal.

"Sir." Duck twisted in his seat. "How far back are you?"

"About fifteen miles behind you, Jaxi tells me." Zirkander paused. "She also tells me that Bhrava Saruth isn't actually in the city. She's not sure where either dragon is."

"Collecting more worshippers, no doubt," Blazer said.

"Phelistoth doesn't collect worshippers," Zirkander said. "He doesn't even like people."

"Just what you want to hear about your ally dragon."

"He's less an ally and more the dragon that's living here while Tylie does her sorceress training."

"So, the delusional dragon who thinks he's a god is our only true ally?" Blazer asked.

"Likely so."

"Comforting."

Cas turned her flier to head up the river. In a few miles, Ambergull would come into sight. "Can Sardelle or Jaxi tell if Tolemek is in the city from where you are, sir?"

After a pause, Zirkander answered. "Not yet."

Cas hoped that meant they were simply too far away to detect people, not that Tolemek wasn't there.

She headed in, not intending to wait for the others.

* * *

The hawk was sleeping. At least, its eyes were closed. Whenever Tolemek shifted, clanking his chains too loudly, the oversized bird would open one yellow eye to look balefully at him.

Tolemek sat, leaning his back against a bench built into a bulkhead—he was now positive he was on a ship, even though it surprised him that he couldn't feel the waves rocking it at all. His chained ankles kept him from going far—he'd barely managed to reach the pot that he assumed had been left for biological needs. He'd also been left water, but no food. Judging by the pitiful whines coming from his stomach, it had been some time since he'd been kidnapped.

The room—cabin—he had been chained in seemed to be a compact mess hall, with the table and benches taking up much of the space. He could see built-in cabinets against the bulkheads near the ceiling, but with his ankles chained to the base of the table, he couldn't reach them. Too bad. He would have liked to look for some lubricant that might let him slip free. Assuming nobody had left the key lying around.

He wished he had a way to communicate with Tylie or Cas over a long range. As far as he knew, nobody knew where he was or where to look for him. If he was indeed in a boat, he could be halfway to Dakrovia by now. He hoped not. Maybe the ship remained near the coast of Iskandia, meaning there was hope for escape. If Yendray wanted dragon blood, he might even still be lurking near the capital.

Tolemek lifted his shackles, looking at them with his eyes and also examining them for weaknesses with his mind. He wished he'd spent more time working with Sardelle, training to learn how to apply his magic to more than making formulas. Being able to bend or break or melt metal would be a handy skill to have now.

Soft scratches came from the hawk when Tolemek used his senses, its talons on the back of its chair as it adjusted its position. Both of its eyes were open now. Had the creature felt him using a hint of magic? Would it warn its master?

Tolemek's stomach growled. Wasn't there a kidnapping rule about feeding one's captives?

The hatch creaked open, and Yendray walked in carrying a paper sack and wearing different headwear from last time, a brimmed hat with a green feather sticking out at an angle.

"Fresh snacks," Yendray announced, hefting the sack.

The hawk squawked, the piercing noise echoing in the mostly metal cabin.

Tolemek's stomach growled again, though he didn't have high hopes for food that came in a crinkled and stained brown sack.

Yendray switched to his native tongue to murmur sweet nothings to the hawk. He withdrew something as he approached. Was that a dead *mouse*?

He tossed it to the hawk, and the giant bird flapped its wings and caught it. The tail of the furry gray snack was rigid. Definitely a dead mouse. Very dead.

The hawk gobbled it down, but also croaked something that sounded vaguely like a protest.

"Sorry, my friend. I don't know where to acquire live ones here. Unless the scientist over there can suggest a place."

"To acquire live rodents in the capital? Yes, I get them for my snakes. I can tell you the name and address of my supplier if you'll simply let me go."

"We're not in the capital now. We had to leave last night when someone came looking for you. I hadn't realized Iskandia was endowed with many mages, but I definitely sensed someone searching for us. Fortunately, I have the ability to hide our presence—and yours too. But we left the area in case a further search was forthcoming. Also, I have a package to pick up." Yendray smiled and touched his hat.

That explained why Yendray hadn't returned the night before to interrogate Tolemek. They must have been moving the craft from the capital or somewhere near it to... wherever they were now.

"Where are we?" Tolemek asked. "I might still be able to recommend a rat supplier."

"Hm, even though I've built some magic-dampening elements into this boat, I'd hate to have you telepathically tell someone. It's much better to keep you in the dark. At least until you tell me where I can find that dragon blood."

"I told you I don't know."

"And I'm positive you're lying. But we'll find out soon enough." Yendray dipped a hand into a pocket and pulled out a vial.

Tolemek grimaced, disgusted with himself because he hadn't found a way to escape from this man yet. Simple iron chains should not be able to hold a scientist. Even if they had been designed to thwart dragon-blooded magic users. If he could access a cabinet with a few chemicals in it, he could surely come up with a way to escape them.

"Something that needs to be ingested?" Tolemek eyed the liquid in the vial. "Or simply inhaled?"

He had never managed to make a truth serum strong enough to work without the target ingesting it. If this odd man had accomplished what he hadn't, he would be irked.

"You're welcome to breathe it in, and we can test how effective a few fumes are," Yendray said, "but I've always had to throw a few drops in people's mouths to get it to work."

"I hope you're not expecting me to open up and show you my tonsils."

"Not even if I add it to something tasty to eat?" Yendray shook the brown bag.

"Like a dead rat?"

"Brukko likes them. Admittedly, not as much as the living ones. Do remind me to question you on the location of a good purveyor of live mice."

"Right. I'll be sure to do that." Tolemek glowered as the Dakrovian stepped closer, his earlier thoughts returning to mind, that if he blabbed the location of the vials and Angulus found out, the king might kick him out of Iskandia, leaving him once again without a home. Without *Cas*. She loved her job, and he couldn't imagine her leaving it and all her friends for him. He couldn't imagine himself *asking* her to.

Yendray bent, and Tolemek shifted his weight, hoping for an opportunity to thwart his captor. Since he was still chained to the table, he wouldn't be able to spring at the man, but if Yendray bent down, Tolemek could grab him and—

Power flattened Tolemek to the deck like a two-ton invisible weight settling atop him. Abruptly, it was difficult to even breathe, much less think of attacking.

"The iron chains should limit your use of power somewhat," Yendray commented. "They do not affect mine."

Tolemek growled. It was all he could manage.

Yendray removed the cap of his vial. The greenish brown liquid inside looked about as appealing as mud.

"Now, if you'll be so kind as to open your lips for me. No?"

Tolemek clenched his teeth.

It didn't matter. Yendray twitched a finger with his free hand, and some magical force shoved Tolemek's jaws apart.

Fear rushed through Tolemek, and he wondered if this man was more powerful than Sardelle. If so, what would happen if she found Yendray and confronted him?

Yendray tipped the vial to pour in a few drops. Tolemek tried to jerk his head to the side but didn't manage to move it more than a half inch. The viscous liquid struck his tongue.

It was surprisingly sweet, but that didn't make him want it. He tried to spit it out. Yendray dropped his hand over Tolemek's mouth, covering his lips and nose. The same weight that flattened Tolemek to the deck seemed to flatten his tongue to the back of his throat. He couldn't have spat even without the hand there.

He didn't swallow, but he doubted it mattered. He sensed the liquid dissolving on his tongue, finding a way into his bloodstream.

What was that sweet flavor? Glycerin? He supposed it would make the stuff more palatable if Yendray were trying to sneak it into someone's food.

Tolemek snorted at himself. The ingredients hardly mattered at this point. Though glycerin had a slippery quality that made it a decent lubricant. Too bad he couldn't break that vial over his wrists. Maybe he could have tugged them out of the shackles.

Yendray recapped the vial and set it on the table. Some of the weight pressing down on Tolemek faded.

"Feel like talking to me, my good alchemist?" Yendray asked.

"Is that me?" Tolemek muttered, though he had no wish to speak at all.

"Naturally. What do you call yourself?"

"The Iskandian capital awarded me a degree that makes me a doctor."

"A doctor? Odd. Do you heal people?"

"With my healing salves, yes."

"Is dragon blood one of the ingredients?"

Tolemek, seeing where the line of questioning would lead, did not want to answer, but his conscious brain no longer had full control over his body, his words. He almost seemed a distant observer watching this from the outside.

"No," he heard himself answering.

"But you've made other formulas with dragon blood."

"Yes."

"What were they?"

"Acids for fighting dragons. Acids that can eat through their scales."

"Ah, that would be useful, but I'm more interested in a power source, I admit. Where are you storing the dragon blood that the Iskandians took from the Cofah?"

Tolemek tried again to exert his influence, to keep his tongue from flapping, but Yendray's concoction was more powerful than the one he had once made during his pirate days. Simply being aware of what was happening did little to help him fight its influence.

"*Where* is the dragon blood?" Yendray repeated.

"King Angulus is the one to dole it out to me as needed. I assume he keeps it in the castle in a vault somewhere."

"You're not positive it's there?"

"Not positive, but he's always had some when I've been there and requested it."

"Hm. I—" Yendray frowned and looked upward.

The weight on Tolemek disappeared as the man seemed to concentrate on something else. Tolemek tried to employ his own meager senses. The iron shackles might have dampened his ability to do so, but he got a sense of people and ships around them, something he hadn't felt the last time he'd attempted to figure out where he was. They had to be docked in some harbor.

"Damn," Yendray said. "It's that same woman."

He sprang to his feet. "Come, Brukko. I may need you to distract them."

The hawk flapped its wings and followed Yendray out the hatchway, half-flying, half-walking to make it through. Tolemek would have thought it one of the craziest things he'd seen if his brain weren't still running off-kilter.

His eyes focused on the vial still resting on the table. With the hawk gone and the hatch open, this might be his chance.

Chapter 10

"WE'RE ONLY A FEW MILES behind the others now," Sardelle said from the back seat of the flier.

"Thanks for the boost." Ridge waved back, indicating the magical wind giving the craft more speed.

The rest of the squadron has reached a city on a river and are turning toward the docks, Jaxi informed them. *It was a little village during our time, Sardelle. I don't remember the name.*

"It's Ambergull now," Ridge said. "A big port a few miles up the river."

Your people are heading in to land. Cas is leading them. Though this is odd. She seems surprised by something. Alarmed, even. They all do.

"No idea what?" Ridge glanced back at Sardelle. "I haven't heard of any trouble down south, unless it's the kidnappers themselves."

He had little idea who had taken Tolemek—Sardelle had said it might be Dakrovians—but he hadn't imagined a band of opportunistic thugs thinking a frontal assault on four fliers would be a good idea. They wouldn't have fliers of their own. What would they be attacking in? An airship?

Sorry, I'm not sensing anything, Jaxi said after a moment. *No airships or fliers aside from those of your people. But they've aborted their landing, and they're swooping all about over the river.*

I don't sense what they're fighting, either, Sardelle added. *But a couple of them are firing machine guns. Kaika is digging in her pack for an explosive.*

"I'm taking us in," Ridge said, pushing his flier to maximum speed. "Report, Wolf Squadron."

"We've got a battle going on here, sir," came Pimples' terse voice.

Someone else cursed. Duck?

Ridge squinted through his goggles, trying to grasp what was going on. He could make out the fliers swooping, twisting, and taking turns firing toward an area in the sky over the river, but he couldn't yet see their target. The deepening twilight did not help.

"Fighting what? Report."

The only good thing was that Ridge didn't think it could be a dragon. Dragons were larger than the fliers, so he would have seen one of them.

I am sensing a dragon in the distance, Jaxi said, *but I believe—yes, that's Phelistoth. He and Tylie are heading up from the south. I'll tell Taddy and Tylie what I know, but they're still miles away. I'm not sure they'll arrive soon enough to help with... whatever your people need help with.*

"Uhm," Duck said. "It's sort of embarrassing, sir."

"Report anyway," Ridge said.

"Looks like a giant hawk, General," Blazer said, her words hard to understand, as if she was clenching one of her cigars in her teeth. She probably was.

"Did you say a *hawk*?" Ridge thought he saw something now. A dark shape twisting and diving with just as much speed as the fliers—and more agility. If it *was* a hawk, it was much bigger than a typical one.

"Looks that way, sir," Duck said. "It's a real uppity one. I shot at it—I thought I *shot* it—but it didn't seem to do anything."

"It's got some kind of magic protecting it, I bet," Pimples said. "Like a dragon!"

No, like some shaman's familiar, Sardelle said into Ridge's mind, with a mental sigh.

A cousin to that owl we fought at Magroth? Ridge asked.

That's what I'm guessing. As with that owl, I can't sense it. I can see something with my eyes, but nothing with my mind.

"Get Kaika in close enough to throw bombs at it," Ridge said, approaching and joining the rest of the squadron in the Flying Badger formation they were using to attack without getting in each other's sights. "It's a shaman's familiar. It'll take a lot to kill it, but I blew one up with a bomb once. They're not immortal and not as impossible to hurt as dragons."

"Those are the prettiest words I've heard you say, General," Kaika said, slapping Blazer on the back and pointing over her shoulder. "Get me snuggled up to it."

"How about I fly upside down so you can fall on its back and snuggle there?" Blazer said.

"It doesn't look big enough to ride, or I'd be game."

The hawk came into Ridge's machine-gun sights as Duck veered left and Ridge's flier momentarily led the formation. Even though he knew better, that bullets would do little to hurt it, he fired. Maybe he could distract the overstuffed bird while Sardelle and Jaxi did something.

He had a better look at the creature now. The brown hawk was several times normal size, and with its wings spread, it seemed even larger than a man.

It twisted and spun in the air, and Ridge couldn't tell if his bullets hit. The hawk flapped up and banked hard, then flew straight at him.

The air grew brighter beside Ridge, and he flinched as a fireball roared away from the flier and toward the creature. The hawk started to twist away from it, but a gust of wind hammered it, knocking it into the fireball's path.

Ridge heard the familiar's alarmed screech over the roar of his propellers. He hoped Jaxi's fire incinerated it instantly.

Unfortunately, the bird flapped away from the ball of flame as it dissipated. Ridge couldn't tell if it was injured. It kept flying, not appearing hampered or noticeably charred. Ridge got a few more shots in before he flew past it, making room for the next flier to swing into the spot he'd left.

I think it's stronger than that owl, Jaxi said. *More resilient.*

Just what I wanted to hear. Ridge banked to pull back into the end of the formation for another run. He glimpsed people out on the docks below, gaping up at the sky.

As Jaxi hurled another fireball, Sardelle said, *I'm looking for the shaman. If a familiar is in the area, you can bet its master is.*

Even more good news.

If his familiar is more powerful than the one we faced before, the shaman will be too.

Ridge sighed and told himself it would still be better than fighting a dragon. He hoped that was true.

Jaxi cackled. *Got it.*

Ridge was on the verge of congratulating her, but the hawk came into view ahead, flying out of another fireball.

Damn, Jaxi added.

"It's hard to get my passenger close enough to throw bombs when there are fireballs all over the place," Blazer said.

I'm being careful not to hit any of the fliers.

"Jaxi promises not to incinerate you," Ridge said. "Why don't you two coordinate and try throwing a bomb at the same time as her fireball is on top of the hawk. Might give it some extra boom."

"I don't need extra boom," Kaika yelled from Blazer's back seat. "I've got plenty of boom."

"Let's see it then." Though Ridge hated to miss a turn at shooting something, he veered away without firing so he could make room for Blazer and Kaika. It wasn't as if his guns were doing anything.

But the hawk wasn't interested in letting him veer away. It flapped its powerful wings and flew after Ridge.

"Hang on, Sardelle!" he yelled over his shoulder, then threw his flier into a dive.

The wide river lay below, and Ridge spun, picking up speed as his craft plummeted toward it. He glanced back. The hawk was right behind them.

Ahn and Pimples tried to flank it, angling fire at it from the sides, but once again, the bullets did nothing.

Ridge pulled up at the last moment, the belly of his craft skipping off the water. He stayed low, flying past the fingers of the docks stretching into the water. The hawk stayed right behind him, gaining ground. He'd hoped it might be too slow to pull up and would plunge into the water, but he wasn't surprised it hadn't been.

Up ahead, Ridge spotted the city's massive dry dock extending into the river, the berth capable of housing an ironclad warship.

He flew toward it, though he couldn't see around its tall walls yet. Orange light flared behind him, Jaxi hurling another fireball.

I think I singed it that time, Jaxi said.

I don't sense the shaman anywhere, Sardelle admitted. *The hawk may be buying him time to escape. Or he could be camouflaging himself. I'm attempting to knock the hawk back so it won't follow you.*

The flier jerked and shuddered, and it was as if they were flying through soup instead of air. Its belly dipped for the water, and Ridge pulled up, trying to compensate.

Sorry, we're working on that, Sardelle said.

The familiar has a few tricks, Jaxi growled into Ridge's mind.

The soup disappeared, freeing up the flier's wings, but they had lost speed and time. When Ridge glanced back, the hawk was close enough to bite their tail. But it didn't *want* the tail.

"Duck!" Ridge yelled to Sardelle.

She dropped low in her seat as the hawk flapped over her and straight for Ridge. He ducked down but didn't release the flight stick. He pulled up on it, and the hawk slammed into the back of his seat. Wings battered Ridge. He pushed the flight stick forward, and the flier dipped toward the river.

Some invisible force struck the hawk—it almost knocked Ridge's cap and goggles off too. A talon gouged him in the cheek as the creature launched itself from the back of his seat. He jerked an arm up to protect his head, but it flapped away. He spotted Sardelle, almost falling over the side of the flier as she drew back, blood on the tip of Jaxi's blade.

"Thanks," Ridge rasped, not quite sure what had happened, but knowing he didn't want to let that bird get close again. His cheek flamed with pain, and blood dripped to his chin.

"Are you all right, sir?" Blazer asked from wherever the rest of the squadron was.

"Yeah," Ridge said, feeling foolish for multiple reasons.

He'd broken the formation they'd been carefully flying in and unintentionally led their target away. If he and Sardelle did not finish it off, he would feel extra foolish.

We poked it good, but it's relentless, Jaxi said. *It's coming back down.*

They were still flying low, almost skimming over the river. As Jaxi had promised, the hawk veered toward him again. Maybe it had decided Ridge and Sardelle were the most likely of the group to trouble it.

Ridge spotted the hulking dry dock facility again, and on impulse, he turned into it. He was going too fast, and he knew it. Reckless, General Ort would have called him.

A ship filled the dry dock space, not a warship but a great freighter. There wasn't much room to maneuver.

Aware of the hawk soaring around the corner after him, Ridge jerked the flight stick, tilting their wings and turning the flier on its side. He flew between the wall of the dock and the hull of the craft with scant inches to spare.

A clunk came from behind him, but he couldn't glance back to check on it. He didn't dare. They had already passed most of the ship and the back wall of the dry dock loomed ahead.

Still flying sideways, Ridge tilted his craft toward the sky again, then twisted and flew upside down over the deck of the ship, heading back toward the river. He spotted the hawk standing on the bottom of the dock, its wings blackened. It seemed dazed. Had he caused it to crack its head on the ship? He hoped so.

Jaxi hurled another fireball at it. Shouts of alarm and fear came from the deck of the freighter. Fortunately, her ball of flame spun down between the hull and the dry dock wall where it wouldn't hurt anyone—except its target.

The hawk tried to leap aside, but it seemed disoriented. It bumped into the wall, then disappeared as the fireball swallowed it.

Ridge took his flier out of the dry dock and shot across the river. The rest of Wolf Squadron was doing the equivalent of aerial pacing.

"Now would be a good time for bombs," he announced, craning his neck to look back.

The hawk recovered, and it leaped off the bottom of the dry dock, heading out toward the river again. Did it seem slower? More charred?

"Coming in at it," Blazer said.

Jaxi flung a fireball as the hawk flew out of the dry dock. It skimmed under Blazer's flier to strike the creature as Kaika dropped a bomb on it. The explosive ignited as soon as it reached Jaxi's flames.

A thunderous boom rang out, and Ridge felt the blast wave from across the river. He banked, intending to go back in to attack the creature again if needed.

The hawk dropped into the water. Stunned? Dead?

Pimples, Ahn, and Duck headed in to finish it off, but the creature's wings fluttered. Ridge thought it would try to launch into the air again, but instead, it pointed its beak downward and dove, disappearing beneath the surface. Pimples and Duck fired, their bullets splashing into the water. If they struck the hawk, Ridge couldn't tell.

"Is it dead?" he asked over the communication crystal. Maybe someone else had a better view. *Sardelle?* he added silently, twisting to look back at her.

She sat calmly with her soulblade resting across her lap. Ridge was relieved that she did not appear wounded. She must have done a better job of ducking than he had.

"Well, it's gone, sir," Duck said. "But it looked like it propelled itself underwater rather than simply sinking. Can magic hawks swim and hold their breaths?"

"Probably," Blazer said.

I can't tell if it's alive or dead since neither Jaxi nor I can sense it. Sardelle leaned forward and rested a hand on Ridge's shoulder, her gaze locking on his cheek. *I'll heal that as soon as we get a chance.*

That bad, huh?

It looks painful.

It does sting a little, but since I didn't get rabies the last time a magical bird maimed me, I'm not too worried about it. Unless you tell me I should be worried. I'd hate to be rabid for our wedding.

That would disturb the guests, she said.

Ridge turned back forward to ensure he wasn't on course to run into a tree or building. He guided them up the river, searching for sign of the hawk—or the shaman Sardelle had mentioned.

Fortunately, most of them are military and understand these things happen, he added.

Perhaps this is the time to let you know I invited a noblewoman from the capital today.

Oh? You don't think your haircutter and the postman will be uncomfortable in the presence of nobility, do you?

Let's hope not.

"I don't see it anywhere," Pimples said. "I'm going to hope it's dead."

"Permission to land and check the berth, sir?" Ahn asked, her voice tense. "I'm hoping a shaman's familiar means we're close to finding Tolemek."

"Permission granted. We'll come down too."

Ahn was already veering for the docks. Ridge hoped for her sake that Tolemek was close, but he feared that if he was, the shaman would be too.

* * *

Tolemek strained and grunted, his fingers brushing the glass vial perched tantalizingly close to the edge of the table, but he couldn't quite grasp it. Sweat dribbled from his temple. It was hot and stuffy in the cabin, and his efforts made it seem more so.

He shifted, pulling every millimeter of length he could from the spot where his chain was bound, then he reached again. His knuckles bumped the vial. It wobbled, and he cursed, afraid it would fall and roll farther away from him.

Voices came through the open hatch. He couldn't understand them, but they sounded choppy, urgent. He hoped whatever was going on would keep Yendray and whoever else worked on the boat busy.

The vial tipped over.

"Damn it." He tried to lunge after it.

But it rolled toward him instead of away. He jerked his chained wrists down as it fell off the table and caught it before it shattered on the deck.

Tolemek carefully extracted the stopper. The vial was about two-thirds full, but it wasn't a large container. He feared it wouldn't be nearly enough to be helpful, but he carefully dribbled some of it between his skin and one wrist shackle, then did his best to mash the iron against his flesh and spread the liquid around. He dripped a few more drops on the bottom of his wrist, then stoppered the vial and set it on the table.

The sounds of more voices came from the other end of the corridor outside his hatch. A thrum started up, and the deck vibrated. An engine?

Tolemek had no idea where he was, but he had a feeling it would be better for him if the craft stayed where it was. He tugged on the shackle, trying to pull his lubricated wrist and hand through it. If he managed to escape, maybe he could sabotage something on the vessel on his way out.

Tendons ground painfully against bone, and even with the lubricant, the shackle scraped off his skin, but he managed to yank his hand free.

"One down," he breathed, grabbing the vial to apply the substance to the other wrist.

Unfortunately, he didn't have enough for the shackles around his ankles, nor would it have worked anyway. He still wore trousers and boots.

With a grunt of pain, he twisted and yanked his other hand free. He unfastened his boots and socks, and eyed his feet and ankles, as well as the tiny amount of serum left in the vial. As he'd suspected, there was no way his big feet would slip through the shackles, even if they were lubricated.

At least with his hands free, he could stand up. He almost cracked his head on the surprisingly low ceiling when he did. The chain allowed him to take a step in each direction from the table. He pulled open the cabinets he had been eyeing earlier.

The craft lurched, and he stumbled against the wall—the hull. They were definitely going somewhere.

Tolemek recovered and opened the cabinets mounted near the ceiling, hoping for some chemical goodies he could put to use to free his ankles and perhaps create a weapon to help him escape the ship.

Instead, he found bowls, cups, crackers, sardines, and lard. Not overly helpful.

He rummaged through the food stuffs he could reach and also found some vinegar in the back. He tugged out that and a wooden cup, setting them on the table. With his limited magical powers, he thought he could evaporate the water in the vinegar, leaving only the acetic acid. It was a weak acid, only mildly corrosive to metal, but the chain wasn't in that great of shape. Maybe he could pick on one of the rusty spots, especially if he could caress the acid a bit with his power to intensify its effectiveness. He'd done such things before, but not while wearing iron shackles. Since iron had a tendency to dampen magic, he worried he wouldn't be able to draw on enough power.

"Won't know until you try," he muttered, standing barefoot on the deck and staring down into the cup.

Steam rose from the vinegar as he concentrated. His head soon ached from the effort, and an acrid scent rolled out of the cup, making him think of Cas's comment about inhaling fumes and withering balls. He backed up slightly, then refocused.

More shouts came from the front of the boat, making him extra aware of time passing, but most of the water eventually disappeared, leaving the acid nearly pure. He left just enough water so it wouldn't crystallize, then took his cup to the deck. He spread the substance on the rustiest, weakest-looking links on the chain. Normally, he could have used his power to assist the corroding along, but he wasn't able to affect the iron itself. He was forced to wait, hoping the acid was strong enough to do something.

A hatch clanged somewhere in the craft, and Tolemek worried he was out of time. He braced his bare feet against one bench and his back against another, gripped the chain with both hands, and pulled and twisted. It didn't give right away, but he did feel a faint shift, the link stretching. He heaved several more times.

Finally, one rusty link pulled open. It was enough. He slipped the links apart, and he was free. Sort of. His ankles were still shackled and attached to each other, but he could take short steps. With luck, that would be enough.

As he stood, Tolemek had the sensation of movement, the deck vibrating under his bare feet. He still didn't feel the familiar movement of a ship bobbing in the waves. Wherever they were, it had to be a very calm day out there. The voices at the end of the passageway were also calm now. Yendray might return at any moment to question him further.

Carrying the end of his chain so it wouldn't drag on the deck, Tolemek hunted around for a weapon. There didn't seem to be a damn thing, unless he wanted to hurl crackers at his enemies. At a loss for a better idea, he fastened the lid on the lard container and took the tub, imagining himself like Captain Kaika hurling a bomb down a passageway.

When he reached the hatchway, he peered into the gray metal corridor outside. The ceiling was low out there too. This entire ship had a claustrophobic feel to it.

He could see the backs of men's shoulders up ahead. They were sitting and facing away from him in a cabin or engine room of some sort at the end of the narrow passageway. One had a hand on a set of levers rising from the deck.

Tolemek didn't want to go toward the men, but he didn't see many other options. Built-in bunks lined one wall, some with curtains drawn across them, with a single closed hatch in the wall opposite them. Did that lead to a set of stairs heading above decks?

Since the men's backs were toward him, Tolemek crept toward the hatch. There was a big wheel to turn the lock, no simple latch or doorknob. He imagined it creaking uproariously as he moved it.

He was almost to the hatch when someone walked out of that forward compartment, not one of the men in chairs but Yendray. He strode straight for the hatch, a distracted look on his face, but he spotted Tolemek and blurted a startled curse in his language.

Afraid he would hurl some magic, Tolemek threw the tub of lard at him.

Startled, the shaman threw up his arms to knock it aside. Tolemek sprinted for the hatch. The tub clunked to the deck, lard spattering everywhere, and Yendray attacked Tolemek's mind, mental claws seeming to gouge deep into his brain matter.

Roaring, Tolemek launched himself at the man. He poured his pain and frustration at this whole situation into a punch, slamming his fist into Yendray's face. His foe tumbled back, slipped on the lard, and crashed to the deck.

A part of Tolemek wanted to leap onto him, grab him by the front of his shirt and shake him until he cried out in surrender, but the two men up front sprang to their feet. They wore pistols on their belts and each reached for them.

Tolemek wheeled open the hatch as fast as he could. He jumped into a tiny chamber as a pistol fired, the bullet clanging off metal inches from the back of his head. He whirled and yanked the hatch shut behind him, though he feared all he was doing was locking himself in a closet. Utter darkness filled the tiny space.

"Breyatah's Breath, what *is* this place?"

He spun around and patted on the opposite side, finding another wheel marking another hatch. Maybe the stairs were behind it.

Before he could turn the wheel, it creaked, spinning of its own accord. He groaned, imagining some army on the other side.

The hatch behind him creaked, someone spinning the wheel to open it, as well. He grabbed it from his side, trying to keep them from succeeding. The outer hatch opened with a *suck-hiss* sound.

Water rushed in, startling Tolemek. He barely had the presence of mind to gasp in a lungful of air before icy water flooded the tiny closet. In the dark, cold, and wet, he was completely flummoxed, but he knew that hatch was open, so he pushed off toward it, still hoping for stairs or a ladder. *Some* kind of escape.

Something brushed his shoulder. He pushed past it, knuckles grazing a strange texture. Feathers?

His bare foot scraped against metal. He pushed off it, reaching out with his senses and trying to figure out where he was—besides completely underwater now.

To his surprise, his senses, which hadn't worked at all before, did now. He could tell that he was not only in water, but in the ocean. No, this was a river. He sensed banks in the distance. And he sensed air above him. Surprisingly *far* above him. Thirty feet? Forty?

He paddled toward it, kicking awkwardly with his ankles still chained to each other.

Clangs and thuds echoed through the water from beneath him. Fearing pursuit, he swam faster than he ever had before. If not for his dragon-blood-aided senses, he wouldn't have known which way was up and which way was down. His lungs burned, and he fought the urge to inhale.

Finally, his hands and head broke the surface, and he sucked in clean fresh air.

For the first time, he saw lights, and he peered toward one of the river banks. He had come up downstream from a city. What city, he had no idea. Was he even in Iskandia still? He did not know how long he had been unconscious, only that his stomach was growling with hunger, and he wished he'd grabbed some of those crackers.

Hoping for a friendly port and no angry pursuers, Tolemek swam toward the lights.

Chapter 11

Cas walked out on Wharf B, Berth 12, an unassuming wooden platform that led to nothing. She stared glumly at the empty water surrounding it. Only a couple of gas lamps burned nearby on the wharf, but they provided enough light to tell that there weren't any ships here. Had there ever been?

If not for the hawk, Cas would think this had been a bum lead. The familiar must have been guarding *something*. But if some ship had taken off while the bird had been battling them—or distracting them?—surely, she would have noticed it. Once she'd realized her bullets couldn't take down their magical foe, she hadn't been a hundred percent focused on the battle. If a ship had sailed away from the wharf, she definitely would have seen it.

"Nothing, huh?" came General Zirkander's voice from behind her.

Cas shook her head.

He walked out to join her, a deep cut on his cheek dripping blood down to and off his chin.

He must have noticed her looking at it because he waved to it and said, "The bird got me. But don't worry. Sardelle assures me she can make me pretty again by the wedding."

"By healing the wound?" Blazer asked, following him out. "Or by applying some rouge and a wig?"

"A wig?" Zirkander scraped his fingers through his short hair. He had either left his cap and goggles back in his flier, or the hawk had gotten them. "That doesn't seem necessary. I've gotten compliments on my hair from ladies. It's thick and soft, and one woman liked that it's always playfully tousled."

"What woman was that?" Sardelle walked out behind Blazer, her eyebrows raised.

"Er, nobody. I mean, a woman from long ago. It might not even have been a woman. Come to think of it, I believe General Ort was the one to say that."

"Smooth, sir," Blazer said. "More likely, Ort told you to put your cap over your thick, tousled hair, since that's what regulations require outdoors."

"Yes, that's probably how it went. I misremembered."

Captain Kaika elbowed Sardelle. "Are you really going to marry him?"

"Likely so. Since we're already living together, it seems like the appropriate thing to do."

"You're living with dragons, too, but you haven't mentioned marrying them."

"I think there are rules against marrying outside of your species. And the dragons aren't there *all* the time."

"It would have been convenient if one had been here for this fight," Duck said.

"That's the truth," Pimples said. "I'm afraid we didn't even finish off that big bird."

Cas felt the dock was growing too crowded, especially since it was missing the one person she longed to see. She gazed out at the dark water, having the niggling sense that she had just missed him. Would she get a second chance to—

"I sense Tolemek," Sardelle blurted.

Cas whirled toward her. "What? Where?"

"Swimming." Sardelle extended a finger toward the dark water. "He's all right. Jaxi is talking to him and guiding him toward us."

Cas squinted into the gloom. She *did* see a dark head out there. Where had he *come* from?

"Remember that discussion we had about underwater boats?" Sardelle asked Zirkander.

"Submarines? I remember."

"I think we may be dealing with one, but I can't sense it at all. Neither can Jaxi. I believe our shaman may be riding around in it and camouflaging it. If he helped with the construction, he may even have used his magic to build the camouflage into the hull. Like creating an artifact."

Zirkander grunted. "That'll make it hard to find him. Submarines are sneaky even without magic bits."

Cas barely listened to them. As long as Tolemek made it back to them, what did it matter if the submarine got away? So long as the shaman hadn't done anything vile to him. Her gut clenched with worry as she imagined him having been tortured and questioned.

She gripped Sardelle's arm. "He's not injured, is he? He's not swimming very fast."

"His ankles are chained together," Sardelle said. "That's slowing him down. As for injuries, he seems to have some scrapes and bruises, but nothing major."

"He's going against the current," Zirkander pointed out. "Maybe Jaxi can give him a lift."

"She's discussing it with him now," Sardelle said. "Apparently, pride is a consideration."

"Pride?" Cas asked. "If she can help him, ask her to do it, please. He can blame it on me."

You can address me directly, Jaxi thought into Cas's mind. *I'm usually aware of the thoughts of those around me. I like to know when people are planning inimical things.*

Does that usually happen in a group of General Zirkander's pilots?
No, they're much more likely to be planning their next witty joke.
If you could help Tolemek, I would appreciate it.
Already doing it.

Cas looked back to the water and had no trouble making out Tolemek this time. He now floated over the river, heading rapidly in their direction. He lifted his hands, as if fearing he might crash into them, but Jaxi set him gently down on his butt at Cas's feet.

She dropped down and smothered him with a hug, not caring that he was soaking wet. He returned the hug, wrapping his arms around her and pressing his forehead to hers.

"Tee," Zirkander said. "Nice feet. Is that why you were kidnapped? For your boots?"

Tolemek scowled up at him. "This reunion would have been perfect if you hadn't been here, Zirkander."

"What? How can it be perfect when you look like a drowned rat? A chained and barefoot drowned rat."

"As opposed to a well-shoed rat?" Kaika asked.

"Exactly," Zirkander said.

"Cas," Tolemek murmured, turning his face back toward hers and kissing her.

Her cheeks warmed because they had so many onlookers, but she'd been worried enough about him that she didn't think of pulling away. He drew back, cupped her cheek in his hand, and gazed into her eyes. She gazed back, wishing she had some of Sardelle's telepathy so she could privately tell him how worried she'd been and that she loved him.

"I didn't know what happened to you," she whispered.

"I should have left a note." One corner of his mouth twitched upward. "While they were shooting at me."

"You definitely should have. Please be more considerate next time you're kidnapped."

"I'll try."

Small bursts of flames appeared on both of his shackles, and the metal fell away from each of his ankles. Tolemek, still gazing at her, barely seemed to notice. Cas assumed Jaxi or Sardelle had been responsible.

"How long do we have to let them make moon-eyes at each other before we can ask what happened?" Zirkander whispered loudly to Sardelle. "And if all of Iskandia is in danger?"

"You're the general," she murmured. "Aren't you in charge of this mission?"

"Am I? Wonderful." Zirkander raised his voice. "All right, you two can use my cabin by the lake to rest and relax and reacquaint yourselves with each other's naked bits, but Tee, can you brief me first?"

Tolemek sighed and pushed himself to his feet, water sloughing from his sodden clothing. It was the same clothing Cas had last seen him in days earlier. She hoped to drag him aside soon and get her own debriefing from him—and also apologize for stalking out so abruptly after he'd brought up children. The offer of the general's cabin actually intrigued her. Assuming the city wasn't in danger, she would love to go off to a quiet place in the woods with Tolemek. It would be easier to talk if they had a couple of days of privacy.

"A Dakrovian shaman is working with his brother, who is the chief of Jlongar Jalak," Tolemek said. "They want to unite all the squabbling tribes there and take control of the continent. With the help of dragon blood."

"Is *that* what they were looking for in your vault?" Sardelle asked.

"So I was told. I have no way to know if Yendray—that's the shaman and the only person I spoke to—was telling me the truth."

"Yendray." Cas touched the pocket that held the address for the hat package. "That's who Masonwood sold the hat to and what led us down here."

"Hat?" Tolemek asked.

"Long story," Zirkander said. "Keep going with yours."

"Phelistoth is coming," Sardelle said, looking toward the southern horizon.

"Tell him he's late." Zirkander nodded to Tolemek to continue.

"There's not much more to tell," Tolemek said. "I gathered he didn't particularly want to kidnap me or do me any harm, despite his kidnapping buddies being perfectly willing to shoot up my lab. He just wanted to find out where I was keeping the dragon blood since he only found a half a vial in my vault."

"Did you tell him?" Zirkander asked.

Tolemek winced. "I don't know exactly where it is, but I'm pretty sure it's in an iron-lined vault in the king's castle. And under the influence of his truth serum, I did tell him that. Less than an hour ago. You should have come to rescue me earlier, Zirkander."

"Who said we came to rescue you? I was just looking for some oversized magical birds for my squadron to battle in training exercises."

"That was his familiar."

"So we gathered." Zirkander looked at Sardelle, then around at Cas and the others. "We better get back to the city and warn the king. I assume us charring and mangling the hawk isn't going to stop this Yendray from going after the dragon blood."

"If the hawk is what I brushed against on the way out of his underwater boat, it's still alive."

Zirkander sighed. "Of course it is."

* * *

Sardelle sat on the front stoop while Tylie practiced her healing skills on a wounded frog she'd found by the pond. It lay motionless in her hands while she worked on it, only its eyes moving slightly.

Sardelle was surprised Tylie had been out roaming the muddy path that morning. They'd all had a late night, flying back from Ambergull, and then heading to Tolemek's lab. He had insisted on checking it for himself and then cleaning up while assuring Tylie that he was fine—she and Phelistoth had landed on the riverside wharf shortly after Jaxi had lifted Tolemek out of the water. Sardelle had sensed that Cas wanted to drag Tolemek off so they could have a private night together, but she didn't know if Cas had ever managed that. Several Intelligence officers had come out to the lab to question Tolemek as Sardelle and Ridge had been leaving.

The newspaper boy is coming, Jaxi announced from her rack in the house. *In case you want to tell Tylie not to use her magic for a couple of minutes.*

To an outsider, she should just appear to be holding that frog.

You say that as if that in itself isn't odd.

Well, I think the newspaper boy, postman, and all our neighbors have already identified us as odd.

What neighbors? Nobody has built in the lot across the street, and the people next door moved out shortly after we moved in. Right after their first dragon sighting, I believe.

The newspaper boy rode into sight on his bicycle, peering warily at the house as he came around the trees. He twitched when he saw Sardelle, then stopped, putting his feet on the dusty road. He plucked a rolled newspaper from his canvas tote and, from at least a hundred feet away, lifted his arm to throw it.

"Here, ma'am."

The newspaper sailed up and landed on the walkway in front of Sardelle with impressive accuracy. She started to call a thank you, but he was already wheeling away at top speed.

The neighbors might not be the only ones who've seen a dragon down this street, Jaxi observed.

He seemed alarmed by the sight of me. Sardelle merely sat on the stoop in a summer dress, holding a couple of menus from the caterers she and Ridge were debating on. Watching Tylie work with the frog made her decide to cross off the "frog legs" option on one of the menus.

Maybe he reads the newspapers as he delivers them and has learned of your witchy ways.

Well, no wedding invitation for him. Since the boy had disappeared, Sardelle used her power to levitate the newspaper into her hand. She doubted she wanted to read it, fearing some new slander about her might have been printed, but she glanced down at the front page anyway.

Construction of Dragon Temple Underway on Island North of City.

"Huh." That wasn't what she had expected to see. She was also startled that the byline belonged to that same female reporter who had been writing all those tales about her controlling Ridge.

Expecting a public outcry or some kind of protest about the temple being built on the king's land—which was usually reserved for recreational use by Iskandian subjects—she skimmed through it.

It doesn't sound like an outcry to me, Jaxi said. *Look at the third line. The great and benevolent god, Bhrava Saruth?*

I... see that. The entire article was flattering toward Bhrava Saruth and also stated that his temple would be a magnificent place where humans from far and wide could come to be blessed and, if need be, healed.

Maybe he shape-shifted into that journalist's form and came into the newspaper office to write the article himself.

We have seen him emulate people perfectly. Sardelle remembered the time Bhrava Saruth had shifted into Ridge's form.

That might explain why he wasn't around yesterday. Or at least why we didn't sense him around. He could have been writing up this propaganda.

Or maybe he was simply influencing the woman and coercing her to do so.

Sardelle couldn't quite imagine Bhrava Saruth impersonating a journalist to write a story about himself. Despite his claims of being cunning, he didn't seem tricky or deceitful. He was up front about what he wanted, and he seemed to take it for granted that his followers would provide it for him.

She could imagine him adopting his handsome human form to flirt with the journalist while gazing deeply into her eyes and earnestly explaining his godly desires. While inviting her to a bedroom.

Either way, if he was in human form, it's unlikely we would have detected his aura from very far away, Jaxi said.

Sardelle nodded. She'd observed before that the dragon presence, something she could usually sense for miles, was far diminished when one shape-shifted into another form.

Look at the last line. Jaxi snickered. *I wonder how many people will show up to help.*

The closing line invited stalwart humans interested in assisting with the construction to show up each morning for the assignment of tasks.

Hm. I wonder if the construction workers Ridge has talked into the project will be pleased to have helpers or annoyed because they'll be untrained and get in the way.

It's possible nobody will show up. Jaxi sniffed. *I wouldn't.*

I don't know. I would think curiosity might bring some people out. Though my understanding of the location is that it's difficult to get to without a ship.

Maybe Bhrava Saruth will volunteer to pick people up each morning at one of the city squares and fly them over.

"All better," Tylie announced, setting down her green patient and lifting her hands.

The frog loosed a few ribbits and bounded toward the pond.

"Good work, Tylie." Sardelle lowered the paper, deciding she would wait until later to flip through the rest of it. With luck, the female journalist's focus on Bhrava Saruth would keep her distracted, and she wouldn't write any more articles about her and Ridge. "Perhaps you'll end up specializing in animal healing rather than human healing. Though you can certainly do both."

"Animal healing?" Tylie, barefoot and in a sleeveless summer dress with fresh paint spatters on it, spun toward Sardelle with her hands clasped in front of her. "Is that truly a specialty?"

"Animal husbandry and healing, yes. The sorceresses who went into that in my time tended to help with domesticating wild animals and keeping already domesticated ones healthy and happy. Sometimes, they would have a herd of goats or similar creatures that they traveled with to help farmers clear brambles and weeds before cultivating land."

"A herd of goats?" Tylie appeared inordinately pleased by that idea.

She's not keeping them here, Jaxi said. *It's bad enough she has turtles, ravens, rabbits, owls, and that cat Kaika brought as a housewarming gift. The cat is the only normal thing in the house.*

"Eventually." Sardelle smiled and ignored Jaxi. "If that's of interest, it wouldn't hurt for you to sign up for some classes at one of the pre-universities in town. It wouldn't be a bad idea for you to learn the basics, but you could also start studying the veterinary sciences. It's good to understand things from a mundane scientific viewpoint as well as from a magical one."

Sardelle had been meaning to suggest classes for a while, since she'd learned that the sanitarium where Tylie had been held for years hadn't given her any schooling. Sardelle loved teaching history and magic, but she was still three hundred years behind on a lot of her own studies, so there were others who could teach other subjects better. It hadn't stopped feeling strange to her that what had been current events in her day were now historical events to everyone alive today.

Doesn't the king want her to become a powerful sorceress who can help defend Iskandia against dragons and various human evils? Jaxi asked.

Maybe, but she loves animals, and I haven't noticed that she loves hurling fireballs, or even studying how to make fire.
Which is inconceivable. Fire is fun.

"Maybe I would be better at working with animals than at finding people." Tylie grimaced, and Sardelle sensed her distress at having been so slow to locate Tolemek. She had expected it to be easy with Phelistoth's help.

"Cas followed quite the trail of breadcrumbs to find him," Sardelle said. "With that shaman muffling his aura, it's not surprising that even a dragon didn't sense him until you were right on top of him."

Tylie shook her head, clearly disappointed in herself. "He's my brother. I should have known where he was."

Someone's coming, Jaxi said.

Pardon? Sardelle looked toward the street and stretched out her senses.

A fancy steam carriage turned off the main street and is heading this way. It has the royal emblem on the door.

Sardelle nodded, also sensing it now that she was looking. Jaxi had been assiduous in warning of visitors since the Fern incident.

Sardelle rose and smoothed her dress. She didn't recognize the driver or the two young men inside, but she assumed from the emblem that Angulus had sent them.

The carriage rolled into view, black, blue, and gold, not a dent or speck of mud on the exterior. Fluffy gray plumes wafted from the smokestack in the back.

A driver on the bench up front nodded to Sardelle, then maneuvered the vehicle so that it faced back up the dead-end street before stopping in front of her walkway. The side door opened, and one of the men stepped out wearing the king's colors and carrying a small beige envelope. One of the king's uniformed guards watched from the doorway, a short sword and pistol on his belt. He appeared more bored than alert.

The king's men, at least, seemed to have gotten over their fear of mages and magic. Or maybe Angulus intentionally picked people unlikely to be concerned about her reputation.

"Ms. Sardelle Terushan?" The man with the envelope stopped in front of her and bowed.

"Yes."

"The king requests that you come with us to attend a meeting at the castle." He offered her the envelope.

Sardelle was tempted to ask what kind of meeting and with whom but doubted the man would know. She withdrew a card and recognized Angulus's small,tidy writing.

Sardelle,

I'm certain you are busy, but if you are able to break away from your projects, please join me for a meeting this afternoon. I hope it will benefit you.

~ Angulus

"Of course I'll come." Sardelle nodded to the man. Selecting meals for her wedding and watching Tylie heal a frog hardly constituted busyness.

"Excellent." He bowed again and offered his arm.

"One moment." Sardelle jogged inside to grab Jaxi off the rack.

The king's man raised his eyebrows at the addition of the sword, but his arm remained out, and all he said was, "This way, ma'am."

Tylie, Sardelle asked silently, *will you be all right here alone?*

She almost asked if Tylie wanted to come along, but had no idea what this was about, so decided not to presume it would be permitted. Besides, the last time Tylie had been at the castle with her, she'd put a ladybug in Angulus's lute. Something about insect eggs inside of it that the ladybug would enjoy munching on.

Yes. I'll find more injured animals to practice on. Tylie skipped toward the path that led to the pond.

At least she likes to be useful, Jaxi said as Sardelle climbed up into the carriage. The velvet-lined seats had the perfect amount of cushioning, and the interior smelled of some pleasant floral perfume. *To small animals with broken things.*

There's nothing wrong with caring for animals as a profession.

I can't imagine healing frogs pays well.

She'll find a way to earn enough to live on. The animal husbandry specialists were in quite high demand with farmers and ranchers, as you may recall.

Taddy will be bored out of his mind. He likes to slay things in noble battle, you know.

From what I've observed, Wreltad is more interested in spending time with Ridge in the duck blind and debating the merits of engines and aerodynamics.

Jaxi snorted into Sardelle's mind. *They're the ones who should have been bonded.*

Perhaps so.

"You seem calmer about going to see the king than the last woman we picked up and delivered to the castle," the guard sitting across from her said.

"Oh?" Sardelle asked. "Who was she?"

"General Zirkander's mother."

Sardelle's calmness evaporated. Did this mean Fern had also been invited to the meeting? If so, what was it about? *Her?*

Even though she knew she needed to find a way to get Fern used to the idea of a sorceress as a daughter-in-law, she hadn't planned to do it in front of Angulus. How had he even found out? Surely, *Ridge* wouldn't have asked the king to talk to his mother about her. Would he?

Jaxi, do you know anything? Sardelle had spent the night before with Ridge, and he hadn't said anything about this. Why wouldn't he have warned her?

Only that it would be amusing if Fern showed up with a basket of cat soaps for the king.

Sardelle dropped her face in her palm. *You're not as helpful as you think you are.*

No? Should I heal a few frogs on the way to the castle?

I've seen your idea of healing, incinerating whatever the offending thing inside a person's body is.

That works fine in some cases. Bullets. Arrowheads. Lances.

Sardelle looked out the window as the carriage turned onto the main street into town and ignored the rest of Jaxi's list. She told herself that Angulus was an ally, even a friend, and that he wouldn't put her in an awkward position intentionally.

That didn't keep her from feeling nervous as the carriage rolled closer to the castle.

Chapter 12

THE MAN WHO HAD DELIVERED the envelope led Sardelle all the way through the castle and to the door to Angulus's office, the one upstairs and in the back, attached to his private suite.

Sardelle smoothed her dress, wishing she had run into the house to change into something more formal instead of only grabbing Jaxi.

Only. Jaxi made a sniffing sound in Sardelle's mind. *As if I'm not the most important thing in the house to grab.*

You definitely are. If ever there's a fire, I'll grab you first.

And wave the flames toward Ridge's couch, I hope.

I fear that monstrosity may be fire retardant.

I could test that theory, Jaxi said as Sardelle's guide knocked on the door.

She patted her hair to make sure it was all still back in a neat braid.

"Come in," Angulus called from inside.

The man pushed open the door, stepped in, and presented her as, "Ms. Sardelle Terushan here to see you, Sire."

Then he stepped back, letting her take his spot, and closed the door as he exited.

Angulus wasn't the one occupying his chair behind the desk. Fern sat there, dabbing a handkerchief monogrammed with the king's initials to her eyes. She lowered it when Sardelle entered, her expression growing difficult to read.

A tray of fresh cinnamon buns rested on the desk next to a basket of homemade soaps, the latter a gift she'd presumably brought to him. Sardelle couldn't tell from the door what shapes they were carved into, only that they were different colors.

Worried the meeting wasn't going well—what exactly was this about?—Sardelle looked to Angulus, who leaned against a bookcase nearby. For a moment, she thought something might have happened to Ridge. Why else would his mother be in tears?

No, this is all about you, Jaxi said, *and the shattering of long-held beliefs.*

"Good afternoon, Sardelle," Angulus said gravely. "I'm glad you were able to make it."

"Of course, Sire." Sardelle curtseyed, then nodded to Fern. "Mrs. Zirkander."

Sardelle usually called her Fern—Fern had insisted on that—but didn't know where she stood with the woman now.

"We've been discussing the return of magic into the world," Angulus said, "and how it's getting harder to ignore it these days."

"Are you really three hundred years old?" Fern blurted, then glanced at Angulus and shrank back into the chair, as if she wasn't sure she should speak.

"I was born more than three hundred years ago, yes," Sardelle said, "but I was trapped in a stasis chamber for most of that time, placed into a sort of hibernation where I didn't age and wasn't aware of the outside world. As far as I know, I'm essentially thirty-five years old, but during the time I slept, everyone I knew, including all of my family, passed away." She didn't want to appeal for sympathy from Fern but thought the information would answer a few questions Fern might have had about Sardelle over the months they'd known each other, such as why her side of the wedding guest list was so small.

Fern bent forward and coughed into the handkerchief.

She doesn't appear all that enlightened, Jaxi said.

Fern coughed long enough that Sardelle was tempted to reach out with her senses to see if something more than a cold was troubling her. But right now, she was afraid to presume to touch her, physically *or* magically. Fern was a stringy, strong woman, used to living alone and fending for herself most of the time. It was hard to imagine her contracting some debilitating illness.

"I didn't see Sardelle's stasis chamber," Angulus said when Fern stopped coughing, "but I've seen other examples of the technology. The dragons that have returned to the world all came out of frozen states. I know because I was the one to inadvertently let one out. And then he let others out. Including the one who is somehow getting free press in our reputable city newspapers." Angulus frowned over at Sardelle, as if she would know something about it.

She lifted her hands in innocence.

Reputable. Jaxi sniffed. *Has he not seen the drivel being printed about you? Next thing you know,* The Pinoth Observer *will be speculating on clockwork automatons controlling the government and men giving birth to babies.*

"I understand, Sire," Fern said quietly, looking at the soap basket instead of at either of them. "I saw one of the dragons."

"And you saw some magic being performed, too, did you not?"

Her voice grew even softer. "Yes, Sire."

Fern wrung her hands in her lap. Sardelle wanted to use her power to comfort her with soothing waves of energy, but once again, she was afraid to do anything.

"Do you want to see any more examples of it?" Angulus asked. "I'm sure Sardelle could give a demonstration."

"No, Sire."

"It's been very useful to have her here helping the country against Cofah invaders, enemy dragons, and a sorceress who wanted to kill me and take over the country. She *did* kill many of the regional lords that were here for a meeting." Angulus winced at the memory. "Sardelle has been one of our few magical allies, and we've been lucky to have her."

"Magical," Fern mouthed, shaking her head.

Angulus frowned and met Sardelle's gaze, opening his palm toward the ceiling. He seemed at a loss. Sardelle wondered how long this meeting had been going on.

"I know you think General Zirkander—Ridge—has been teasing you about magic," Angulus said, "but that's not the case. He's... a loyal and trustworthy man when he's not being an irreverent pain in the ass."

Fern lifted her chin and met his eyes for the first time since Sardelle had come in. "Ridgewalker is a good man. I know he is. I just didn't know…" She lost her certainty as she glanced at Sardelle again.

"And Sardelle is a good woman," Angulus said. "I would certainly welcome her into my family if she were marrying any of my children." His lips twisted in a wry expression.

Sardelle wasn't sure if it was because they weren't that far apart in age or because he lamented that he didn't have any children.

I guess Captain Kaika hasn't shown any excitement about giving him heirs, Jaxi said.

Any heirs Kaika produced would be… problematic.

Because she would insist on teaching them the finer points of demolitions?

Because they're not married.

Technicalities. If he dies without any children from legitimate marriages, I'm sure the nobility will go hunting for half-noble babies that they can stick on the throne. It would be crazy to put someone in charge of the country who's smart and wise and a capable leader. Much better to stick with bloodlines.

I hope you're not sharing these thoughts with Angulus.

Of course not. I haven't observed that he enjoys my delightful presence in his mind. Oddly.

Fern coughed again.

Concerned, Sardelle started to stretch her senses toward her, deciding Fern need never know. But she grew aware of a powerful presence approaching and paused.

Your god seems to be heading this way, Jaxi said. *Uhm, and he's carrying someone. Is that normal?*

How would I know?

You're his high priestess.

You're with me every time I interact with him. You see him as often as I do.

Not by choice, Jaxi said.

I could leave you home with the couch more often.

Did I mention how much I enjoy interacting with dragons?

"Sire?" Sardelle decided she should warn him since it appeared that Bhrava Saruth was heading straight toward the castle. Would he land in the courtyard? On the rooftop?

"Hm?" Angulus had walked to Fern's side and laid a hand on her shoulder, but he looked up at her address.

"Bhrava Saruth is heading in this direction."

Angulus's lips thinned. He must have truly been irked by that newspaper article.

"I think he might land inside—"

The large windows behind Fern flew open, and a hulking gold form appeared in the air outside.

Fern shrieked and ran around the desk. Angulus also backed up a few steps, though he faced the window instead of looking away.

Bhrava Saruth alighted on the ledge, scrunching his body and using magic so he could balance there while bending his long neck down to stick his head inside. Sardelle would have been impressed at his contortionist's skills if she hadn't been busy gaping at the person clasped between the dragon's jaws.

The man screamed, flailing, his feet dangling above the king's rug. Fern shrieked and ran for the door, almost bowling Sardelle aside in her haste to escape. She sprinted into the hallway and didn't look back.

Greetings, high priestess and human king, Bhrava Saruth spoke into their minds, heedless of the screaming man dangling from his fangs—and the fleeing Fern. *It is I, the god Bhrava Saruth, and I have captured an evil Cofah spy.*

"And you brought him to my office?" Angulus looked like he had more scathing words in mind, but one did not irk one's dragon allies, however irking they were.

Of course, human king. I caught him spying on the island where my temple is being constructed. He was peering down from a cliff and had inimical thoughts in his mind. Clearly, he is a threat to Iskandoth. Do you wish to interrogate him now? Or shall we simply execute him?

The man shrieked and flailed some more, apparently privy to Bhrava Saruth's telepathic communication.

It was hard to get a good look at his face as he struggled mightily to escape, but he did have darker skin than typical for an Iskandian. Still, Sardelle didn't think it was as dark as that of most Cofah—not as bronze as Tolemek's flesh. And the man wore clothing typical of Pinoth's latest fashions.

I don't think spies usually dress in military uniforms from their country, Jaxi told her.

"Put him down," Angulus said as he walked toward the door, looking like he meant to call in his bodyguards.

Are you certain, human king? He is most nefarious and untrustworthy. I do not wish you to be in danger of—

The ripping of clothing tore through the office, and the man plopped to the rug. The entire back of his shirt hung from one of Bhrava Saruth's fangs. The man yelled and ran toward the door.

At first, Sardelle thought he was fleeing, hoping to escape the dragon through the most viable exit. But his eyes bulged in recognition as Angulus came into his sights, and he yanked a dagger out of a belt sheath.

He sprang at Angulus with the blade.

Though startled, Sardelle raised a barrier between the two men, even as armed bodyguards rushed in through the door and Angulus leaped back, jerking an arm up in a block. The man struck Sardelle's barrier and bounced into the air. Rifles fired, and bullets slammed into his chest before his feet touched down. She felt his pain as he cried out, tumbling back against the desk.

More guards rushed in, and they piled on the man, searching him for weapons and flinging them away. As they hoisted him to his feet, Sardelle sensed that one of the bullets had found his heart and that he would die soon. Unless she intervened. Should she?

She looked at Angulus. He appeared more stern and angry than afraid.

"Sire," she said. "Do you want him alive for questioning?"

Too late, Jaxi said.

She looked to the man as the bodyguards dragged him toward the doorway and realized Jaxi was right. "Never mind, Sire. It's too late. Your bodyguards have deadly aim."

"They're trained for that," Angulus said grimly. He looked toward his window.

Bhrava Saruth still crouched there, his talons gouging deep scratches in the painted sill. He was using his large pink tongue to try to flick the remains of the man's shirt from his fang, and he appeared unaware of them observing him. Finally, he drew his tongue back into his mouth, and Sardelle sensed a tendril of magic being drawn upon before the garment burst into flames. Ashes trickled to the floor.

"What in the hells just happened?" Angulus asked.

Cofah spies are despicable, Bhrava Saruth said. *Killing you was not even his mission. I believe he simply saw an opportunity and took it. I did not intend to let him go. Human clothing is very fragile.*

"Sardelle?" Angulus asked. "*Was* that a spy?"

Sardelle had no idea, though she was inclined to think so after he'd attacked Angulus.

Actually, Jaxi said, *I was peeking into his thoughts before all that craziness happened, and he did seem to be a spy. He was terribly panicked at having been caught and worried he would be punished by Inquisitor Arkos—I do not know who that is. I don't remember inquisitors from my day.*

"That's the head of the emperor's—now Prince Varlok's—intelligence division. Huh." Angulus looked at Bhrava Saruth again, his expression softening. It wasn't exactly friendly, but he did appear less irked. "You say he was at your island?"

The future home of my temple, human king. Which I am most excited to see completed. I caught him spying on its construction.

"Why would the Cofah be concerned about Bhrava Saruth's temple?" Sardelle wondered.

Why would anyone? Jaxi asked.

High priestess. Bhrava Saruth swung his head to look into Sardelle's eyes, and the ledge he balanced on creaked. *Your sword is being mouthy again.*

Yes, it's her special talent.

I intentionally did not include him in my telepathic communication, Jaxi said. *He's a gold-snouted eavesdropper.*

"Perhaps," Angulus said after a thoughtful silence, "the Cofah are concerned about the cordial relationship we share with Bhrava Saruth and the fact that he's fought on behalf of Iskandia several times now. They may see the establishment of a nearby residence for him—"

Temple, Bhrava Saruth corrected. *A divine temple suitable for a dragon god.*

"Yes," Angulus murmured. "The Cofah may see it as a sign that we've established a permanent alliance with Bhrava Saruth and that if they make any aggressive moves on our country, they'll have to deal with him."

I shall nobly battle and defeat those Cofah mule molesters.

I'm going to laugh my scabbard off if he nobly breaks that window sill and falls into the courtyard.

"That's good to hear," Angulus said. "It's also possible there are spies in the city, as there usually are, looking for information on Emperor Salatak's whereabouts."

Sardelle nodded. It had been a few months now since the kidnapping, but the empire surely hadn't given up on finding its missing emperor. She had no idea where Angulus had stashed the man, but she did trust that he hadn't killed Salatak, that he was in exile somewhere secret.

"The spies may also have seen the *front*-page newspaper article and decided to investigate the temple for themselves," Angulus said.

"That seems possible, Sire."

"I'll alert Intelligence with what we know. They're already trying to figure out if this Dakrovian shaman will strike again. I'm sure they'll be delighted to have more trouble." Angulus stepped over to the doorway and looked both ways in the hallway outside. He murmured a question to one of the guards stationed out there, then leaned back in. "Sardelle, do you know which way Fern went?"

"Ah." Sardelle felt embarrassed that she'd forgotten about Fern in the chaos. She reached out with her senses and frowned when she didn't find her in the castle anywhere.

She's in the carriage we arrived in, halfway down the hill into the city, Jaxi said. *She must have told the driver her meeting was over.*

"Oh dear," Sardelle said.

Angulus raised his eyebrows.

"She left."

Angulus pushed a hand through his curly hair. "I meant to alleviate her concerns, not add to them."

"I think she may just need some time to get used to the idea of... everything."

"Perhaps. She didn't seem herself though. Granted, I've only met the woman once, but she has a cold or something and looked quite distraught. Sardelle, I'm not in the habit of having women flee my castle in distress."

"I think she was more distressed by the dragon than you, Sire."

"Who would be distressed by a *friendly* dragon?" Bhrava Saruth asked, hopping down from the window sill, now in his human form, blond locks falling about his face—and into his eyes. "Perhaps I should have changed into this unassuming shape earlier? I've been told that it's most appealing to females." He stopped in front of the desk and pointed at the cinnamon bun tray. "Are these for me? Did you anticipate my coming?"

Angulus wriggled his fingers at them. "Go ahead. Mrs. Zirkander wasn't interested in them. Sardelle, I need to talk to my people about the spy right away and make sure nothing is afoot for tonight."

"Tonight, Sire?"

"The Festival of Lights I've let myself be talked into. Guests will be arriving early this evening." He pushed his fingers through his hair again. "Is it terribly unkingly to wish I hadn't agreed to it and that I could simply curl up in my favorite chair with a book?"

"I think it's human."

He started for the door but paused and looked back. "You're invited, of course. If you didn't know. I believe my steward already invited Zirkander and some of our hero soldiers, but hero sorceresses should receive invitations too." He smiled, though it appeared frazzled.

"Thank you, Sire."

"And, ah, I don't want to presume, but I would appreciate an invitation to your wedding."

"Oh, I filled out a card for you weeks ago, Sire. But Ridge took it and mentioned wanting to deliver it personally." She pursed her lips. "I hadn't realized he hadn't already given it to you."

"Ah? Then I am invited? Good. I didn't want you to think I wouldn't make the time to come." He gave her something akin to a military salute. "Good afternoon."

He disappeared into the hallway, leaving Sardelle frowning slightly. Why hadn't Ridge already given Angulus that invitation? She knew they butted heads from time to time, and that Ridge wasn't positive where he stood with Angulus after the incident with the sorceress, but he'd spoken to the king numerous times in the last few weeks. Why couldn't he have left the invitation on Angulus's desk at one of the meetings?

"Delicious." The smacking of lips followed the word. "Better than freshly caught sheep."

Sardelle looked over at the demolished tray of pastries and almost commented on the dragon's insatiable appetite but noticed something white on the rug in front of the desk. She walked over and picked it up, then realized it was the handkerchief Fern had been coughing into. She spotted blood on it, and her stomach dropped.

"She's got more than a cold," Sardelle whispered, lamenting that she had been interrupted and hadn't had a chance to thoroughly examine Fern. "Bhrava Saruth?"

Bhrava Saruth lowered the tray from his face. Had he been *licking* it? "Yes?"

"Do you have time to help me find someone?"

"Of *course*, high priestess."

Do we need his help to find Fern? Jaxi asked. *She's most likely on the highway with that carriage taking her home.*

We don't have a steam carriage of our own, and it's a ways to the army fort where we might be able to get a horse. A dragon would be convenient and allow us to catch up with her.

What about the light festival? The king very pointedly invited you. Don't you think he'll be disappointed if you're not here?

Fern needs help. You should know I would prioritize healing someone—Ridge's mother!—over anything else.

Yes, I do know that. I just object to riding on a dragon with frosting all over his nose.

One can't be picky about one's allies.

Not even a little bit? I feel that hygiene should be considered when choosing an ally.

"I can carry you wherever you wish to go," Bhrava Saruth said. "Are you ready now? Follow me."

He left the tray on the desk, ran to the window, hopped on the ledge, and sprang outside. Sardelle didn't see whether he landed before changing into his normal form, but she sensed it when his powerful dragon aura returned. Even if he was a goofball, she genuinely appreciated his willingness to help.

Yes, Jaxi said, *but can we just use the door?*

***

Ridge scrawled his signature on a requisition form, barely glancing at the text. The paperwork had stacked up during the days he'd been arranging the temple construction, begging the king for favors, and chasing down the coast after Tolemek. This was at least the hundredth thing he had signed this afternoon.

After moving it to the side, he set down his pen and shook out his hand, eyeing another stack waiting for him. He was tempted to take off early and fly out to see his mother—her meeting with the king should have been earlier that day—to see how she was doing. But he had better complete every duty assigned to him first. Since Angulus had deigned to see his mother, the least Ridge could do was stay abreast of all the work related to the flier battalion and flight academy. Besides, he still hoped to ask Angulus to be his kin watcher at the wedding. Staying in his good graces was important.

A solid knock sounded at the door.

"Come in," Ridge said, shaking his hand again. Funny how all the gripping and maneuvering he did with his flier's flight stick never caused cramps but scribbling recommendations and signing his name over and over did.

The door opened, and General Ort strode in, his uniform as precisely pressed as always, his gray hair impeccably combed even though the cap tucked under his arm had likely lain atop it recently. His boots gleamed like gold coins in the sunlight slanting through the window.

"General Ort," Ridge said, standing and starting to salute before he caught himself. He'd had his new rank for months and still forgot he didn't need to salute generals. "Vilhem," he added, knowing Ort would correct him if he didn't do it himself. Even if he still couldn't get used to the idea of calling him by name. "Am I in trouble?"

"Do you feel like you should be?" Ort asked as Ridge waved him to one of the two chairs in front of the desk. Ort carried a folder as well as his cap.

"Usually."

"I understand the king was impressed that you've already got everything in place for Bhrava Saruth's temple." Ort eased into the chair. "Albeit less impressed that the dragon is getting a temple."

"Impressed?" Ridge leaned back in his own chair. "That's not the impression I got when I spoke to him about it. He mostly seemed irritated. Apparently, his castle renovation hasn't come together as quickly."

"Mm."

Ridge, wondering what had brought Ort to his office, asked, "You're still coming to the wedding, right? To stand at my side to attest that I'm fit to marry Sardelle?"

"I believe my job as one of the two kin watchers for the male member of the wedding party is to judge whether *she's* fit to marry *you*."

"Yes, but we all know she is. I'm the questionable one."

"I won't argue with you about that. I'm actually here on another matter—" Ort lifted the folder, "—but before I get into it, I've been instructed to ask, on my oldest daughter's behalf, if you have any spare wedding invitations."

"For her? Certainly. I would have sent her one, but I didn't know she would be in the city."

"She's coming for the wedding. And I believe she was hoping to get five invitations for her local friends here. Actually, she asked for ten, but I think those were to barter to people who want to go and who would trade her favors or goods in return." Ort pressed his lips together. "Wedding invitations hardly seem like they should be used as currency."

Ridge blinked, surprised Ort's daughter Thami would come all the way up here for his wedding. They had met a few times over the years, but Ort had generally been careful to keep his daughters out of Ridge's orbit. Apparently, a teenaged Thami had made the mistake of admitting to having a crush on him however many years ago that had been. Ort had found that extremely unacceptable. Thami was close to thirty now, if Ridge recalled correctly.

"I've been personalizing them, rather than just handing out blanks," Ridge said, "but I guess I can scrounge some up for her to give to friends. Though I'm a little puzzled as to why anyone who doesn't know me or Sardelle would want to come."

He and Sardelle had decided to have a simple wedding in the backyard at the house, overlooking the pond. But if more people than they had planned on wanted to come, he would have to look for a larger venue. Would it be too late to find something appropriate? He feared it might be.

"Please, Ridge. Thanks to those hundreds of newspaper articles over the years, *everybody* knows you. Or feels they do. I understand your wedding has been deemed the social event of the year."

Ridge stared at Ort. If it had been anyone else, Ridge would have been certain that was a joke, but stolid General Ort rarely made jokes.

"You must have known," Ort said.

"Uh, no, and I can't imagine it. Especially not with that journalist saying all those nasty things about Sardelle controlling me and using magic to force me into wedding her. What's her name? Dunberry. Dumbberry. Something like that. Can you believe she had the gall to ask me for an invitation the last time she cornered me coming out of the fort? I'm half tempted to start flying everywhere I go, so I can ensure I don't run into her again."

"It must be a burden being a man of such renown." Ort's dark eyes twinkled.

"It's a burden being teased by my commanding officer. General, I think you've spent too much time around me." Ridge pointed at the folder. "What did you come to see me about?"

"The report you turned in last night."

"I put in everything Tolemek told me." Ridge, knowing a copy would go to Ort, the Intelligence unit, and the king, to be pored over by countless staff members, had done his best to be complete.

"So I gathered. I have a copy here." Ort opened the folder, skimmed the first page, then closed it again. "You recommended extra guards at the castle and that the navy deploy its own submarines to keep an eye on the harbor and surrounding waters."

"Yes, that's right. I talked to Sardelle, too, and she thinks she can put some magical alarms around the castle so they'll be tripped if someone with dragon blood flowing through their veins attempts to sneak in."

"You're not supposed to hypothesize in reports, naturally, but you've had as much experience with these vials of dragon blood as anyone. Do you think this shaman is likely to risk his life to acquire our supply? It seems that making a deal with a dragon might be safer."

"I believe Phelistoth and Bhrava Saruth have both been asked if they would voluntarily share some of their blood, and neither liked the idea. Phelistoth since he'd already had so much of his blood extracted without his permission, and Bhrava Saruth because—" Ridge shifted his voice to emulate that of the dragon's, "—a god does not give his blood to his followers." Ridge cleared his throat. "I don't imagine the Cofah-friendly dragons are much different, and I don't know if any of the dragons we inadvertently let out of that cave prison decided to claim Dakrovia."

"So, your answer is yes, you deem it likely this shaman will break into the castle."

"Was I too longwinded?" If so, that amused Ridge. He'd always considered Ort the longwinded one.

"I deem it likely, too, and suggested to the king this morning that he move the dragon blood. To somewhere only he knows."

"So the Dakrovians would have to kidnap *him*?"

Ort's brow furrowed. Maybe he hadn't thought that could potentially happen. "We wouldn't let it be known that the king is the only one who knows the location. And he should be hard to get to at any time of day."

"They might guess he'd be the one to know where it is though, since Tolemek, under the influence of a truth serum, said the vials are in the castle now."

Ort spread a hand. "I still think they should be moved."

"I'm not arguing against that, sir. Vilhem. Just saying the king's bodyguards should be extra vigilant because he might be seen as a likely resource."

"They should *always* be vigilant."

"True, but they don't have much experience dealing with magic. Who does in this era?" Ridge stroked his jaw. "As I said, Sardelle mentioned setting some traps, but that may take a few days. Maybe Therrik should be added to the castle duty roster for a while. He and Kasandral can stalk around, looking for evidence of magic use. The sword is apparently like a hunting dog that can lead him to sorcerers. And shamans, presumably." Ridge remembered trailing Therrik through the castle earlier that summer as Kasandral led him to the collapsed rubble that Angulus and the sorceress had been under.

"Are you actually recommending Therrik for something?" Ort's gray eyebrows arched. "I didn't think you cared for the man."

"I don't, but recommending him to be Angulus's hound doesn't seem that much of an accolade."

Ort snorted. "I'll pass the idea on to the king. I'm meeting with him and Admiral Hamilin later to discuss submarine deployment and the likely capabilities of one piloted by a shaman."

"Good. You might want to get Therrik in the castle before the Festival of Lights tonight. I'm sure there will be legions of people milling around, cadging free food and drinks up there. I know most of the high-ranking officers were invited."

"Seven gods, I forgot that was tonight. Do you think the shaman has heard about it? He might figure that's the ideal time to sneak in and raid the vault."

"Possibly. He was in the capital long enough to shop as well as kidnap Tolemek. He's clearly not so pressed for time that he can't read a newspaper here and there."

Ort thumped a fist on the chair and scowled out the window, then shoved himself to his feet. "Damn, I thought we'd have days before he made another move. That's only hours away. How could I have forgotten?"

"Because the festival doesn't sound that exciting? Other than the free food. Someone waits until dark, flips a switch, and electrical lights go on." Ridge shrugged.

"With thousands of people watching from the city and hundreds of guests in the castle. As you said."

Seeing Ort's distress was starting to worry Ridge. He hadn't even planned to go to the event. The hangars had gotten electricity earlier in the year, so he no longer found turning on lights that enthralling. But maybe Ort was right and the shaman would use the festivities as a distraction to sneak in. He grimaced at the idea of some Dakrovian dribbling the equivalent of one of Tolemek's goos down Angulus's throat to question him.

"Get Sardelle and meet me at the castle, Ridge. We'll need someone who can detect magic use. I'll see about tracking down Therrik, but I need to talk to Angulus as soon as possible too."

"Now? I was going to..." Ridge stopped himself from saying he'd planned to check on his mother, since Ort was scowling at him. That had definitely been an order, not a request. They might be the same rank now, but Ort had seniority. Besides, Ort was right. The safety of the king had to be placed above visits to one's mother. "Yes, sir. I'll go find her now. Maybe one of the dragons is around too and could be of assistance."

"Good. Make it quick."

Ort almost ran as he left the office, closing the door with a loud thump.

"And he wonders why I still call him *sir*," Ridge said, grabbing his uniform jacket off the back of his chair.

Chapter 13

The wind beat against Cas's goggles and tugged at her scarf as she brought her flier in for a landing. Pimples, Duck, and Crash had already pulled into the hangar. She swept down, opting to practice a wheeled landing rather than using the thrusters, and made it smoothly. She would have been pleased with herself, but she felt useless at the moment, since neither she nor anyone else on Wolf Squadron had caught sight of that shaman's submarine.

That had been their sole purpose in heading out that day, even if it had been an idealistic one. They had been looking for an underwater craft that wouldn't be visible unless it rose to the surface. Colonel Tranq had reported that submarines did do that from time to time, so there had been a chance they would spot it, but not today.

As soon as she parked her flier inside, Cas hopped out and jogged to the back to attend to biological needs. The lavatory in a little corridor at the rear of the hangar was a popular pit stop after missions, but she didn't see anyone else, so figured she wouldn't have to wait. Then a black-clad figured stepped out of the broom closet opposite the lav.

She let out a startled cry and threw up her hands in a semblance of defense before she recognized the man. Her father. He gazed blandly at her, his hands clasped behind his back.

"You all right, Raptor?" Pimples called back.

"Yes," she yelled over her shoulder. "Just slipped on a puddle." She lowered her voice to a whisper to address her father. "What are you *doing* here? You're not allowed in the fort without an escort. Probably not at all, given your profession."

"That is indeed true. However, I came to relay some information to you." He didn't bother to explain how he had gotten into the fort or up the tram and onto the butte.

"It couldn't have waited until I was at home?"

"You weren't at home last night."

"No, I was getting Tolemek."

"So I heard. I shall offer my congratulations on your successful reunion with your pirate."

However awkward-sounding the words, they surprised Cas, and she squinted at him, trying to decide if he was being genuine. He wasn't generally tactful when it came to her relationships.

"Thanks. What's the information?"

"There is a reward out for the dragon blood that your people brought back from Cofahre this spring. I've only just learned about this, so I believe it's been recently placed. The job of retrieving it wasn't given to me specifically, merely put out on the market where many of my colleagues seek out employment opportunities. Since I have numerous clients that keep me busy, I don't typically take on jobs like that, but I still peruse the offerings to see what's going on in the city and what my contemporaries are up to."

"And they're up to looking for dragon blood?" Cas grimaced. Had that shaman decided to hire freelancers instead of attempting to steal it himself? "How good is the reward? Any idea how many people might try to find it? It didn't say where the dragon blood was located, did it?"

"It's an excellent reward in untraceable silver nucro coins. Many will be tempted, though I suspect few will make a serious attempt at getting it, since the dragon blood is believed to be stored in a vault deep within the king's castle."

Cas's grimace deepened. Tolemek believed that was its location, so it did seem likely. She would have to tell General Zirkander about this.

"No idea who offered the reward, I suppose?"

Father shook his head. "It's to be turned in to a middleman, one who is often used for this kind of thing, and who has already been given the funds for safekeeping. There also seems to be a competing faction that is offering a much smaller reward. They want to see the dragon blood utterly destroyed instead of stolen, believing neither the Cofah nor Iskandia should be able to use it to make super weapons."

Cas didn't necessarily disagree with *that* sentiment, but she was duty-bound to protect the king's interests.

"All right," she said. "Thank you for the warning."

He inclined his head. "You are welcome."

"I'm going to assume this means you aren't taking on the job for yourself."

"I am not. I have other work that will take me out of the capital for a while. Do you wish to shoot when I get back?"

The one father-daughter bonding thing they did. She never knew what to talk to him about when they were out there on the range behind the house, but as odd as it was to her, he seemed to appreciate merely shooting in silence with her. And since he'd done this favor for her—risking sneaking into the fort to deliver the message—she could find time to go out there with him.

"Yes," she said. "I need to get back to work." Actually, she needed to use the lav, but her statement was still true.

"Of course."

She glanced over her shoulder to make sure nobody else was ambling in their direction. When she looked back, her father was gone. She peeked into the broom closet, but it was vacant. He'd either sneaked out the back door or into the men's lav. Did assassins ever use the facilities while they were illegally trespassing? She had no idea.

* * *

As Tolemek reached the bottom of the long winding street that led up to the castle, a steam carriage rumbled up behind him. He shifted to walk along the side so it could pass, though he was half-tempted to ask for a ride. He didn't mind a little exercise, but he wanted to get up there and in to see the king before Angulus stopped taking appointments for the day.

The night before, Tolemek had said everything he thought he had to say to the army's persistent intelligence people—their insistence on questioning him for hours had kept him from having the conversation with Cas that he'd longed to have since before he had been kidnapped. Only after the officers had left had Tolemek realized he should advise the king to move the dragon-blood samples out of the castle. Maybe Angulus would reach that conclusion on his own, but Tolemek felt compelled to suggest it before taking off for the day. Taking off and finding Cas.

He wanted to bring her dinner—or should he take her out to dinner?—and explain that he'd been premature in discussing children and that he understood if she didn't want to have them. He hoped she would change her mind someday, but he thought he could live with it if she didn't. He might be disappointed, but he didn't want to lose her.

The carriage slowed down instead of passing him, the uniformed driver pausing to look down at him from her bench.

The door opened, and a familiar head poked out with a general's army cap perched atop it.

"What do you want, Zirkander?" Tolemek asked.

"Peace for Iskandia, a beautiful wedding with Sardelle, and a dragon that doesn't eat all my cheese." Zirkander offered a lopsided smile. "Also, to give you a ride up if you want it."

Tolemek grumbled but pulled himself into the carriage. Zirkander would likely have an easier time getting in to see the king than he would, so he might as well tag along.

Tolemek sat on the bench opposite Zirkander. "What in all the hells would you do for a living if Iskandia found peace?"

"My mom has offered to teach me how to make soap and candles. I bet I could figure out how to shape them into fliers."

"The newspapers would definitely stop printing articles about you if that became your new career."

Zirkander's expression grew a touch wistful as the carriage rolled into motion again. Maybe he was fantasizing about making flier soaps at that very moment.

"You going to see the king?" Zirkander asked. "Or just heading up for the festival?"

"I want to warn him to move the dragon-blood samples," Tolemek said.

"Ah, I'm on my way to do the same thing, per General Ort's orders."

"The king has probably already thought of it on his own."

"Probably. I'm also supposed to find Sardelle, so she can be on hand for the festival and hopefully detect magic in use. But she wasn't at the house." Zirkander spread his hands. "I'm hoping she or Jaxi will contact me at some point so I can let them know. You're not able to sense them or where they are, by chance, are you? I know you've had a few tutoring sessions with Sardelle."

"I had to throw a tub of lard at my captor to escape. My magical talents are nascent at best."

"Too bad." Zirkander draped his arm across the back of his bench.

"I'm surprised you're riding around in a carriage. It doesn't have wings."

"Which *is* a shame. I usually take a horse around town, but this one was on its way to the vehicle pool when I was on my way to the stables. I decided to requisition it for my purposes. This rank ought to come with some privileges, right?"

"You couldn't have requisitioned one without bullet holes in it?" Tolemek stuck his finger in a round gouge in the wall near his bench.

"Well, it's an army vehicle, not some fluffed up carriage used to tote noblemen about. You can't expect luxuries like upholstery and velvet cushions."

"Or walls without holes in them?"

"Precisely."

Zirkander gazed out the window overlooking the harbor and the butte at the far end where his flier hangars perched. They were nearing the top of the hill, so they had an impressive view.

"Do you want to have children, Zirkander?"

Zirkander's eyebrows arched. Perhaps it had been an abrupt question, but they were almost to their destination, and Tolemek had been wondering earlier that day whether Zirkander and Sardelle had ever had a conversation similar to—and similarly awkward to—the one he'd started with Cas.

"I didn't think I did, but then Sardelle and I had a chat, and she has since convinced me I'd be a good father."

"So, she lied to you."

Zirkander smirked. "Possibly so. I'm not the one in the relationship who can read minds. Technically, she may have only suggested that I wouldn't be a horrible father, as I'd always assumed."

That admission surprised Tolemek, and he squinted at Zirkander, trying to tell if he was lying—or making some joke. If he was, it wasn't obvious. His smirk had faded, and he looked out the window again.

"So, she convinced you that you *do* want children." Tolemek couldn't help but wonder if he could do the same with Cas, but he didn't want to pressure her in any way. Maybe he was dwelling too much on it, especially considering they had only been together for six or seven months.

"Mm, she knocked aside the main obstacle that was in the way of me thinking I should have kids. I actually do like them, you know. They're fun, especially when they're old enough to talk. Kind of like young lieutenants."

Tolemek wasn't sure exactly what the main obstacle was for Cas. Maybe she was simply young and wanted to focus on her career. Which made sense. He had to remember that she was several years younger than he, even if she *was* the mature one.

"Have you been talking to Sardelle?" Zirkander asked.

"No. Cas."

"Has *she* been talking to Sardelle?"

"I don't think so. About what?"

"Never mind." Zirkander leaned closer to the window, then grabbed the horn in the corner. "Corporal, slow down again, will you?" He lowered it and told Tolemek. "Another hitchhiker."

Before Tolemek could peer out the window to see who, Zirkander opened the door and stuck his head out. "Care for a ride, Ahn?"

Tolemek blinked. Cas? Why was *she* going to see the king?

"I'm almost to the top, sir."

"Yes, but I have your boyfriend in here, and he said he'd feel like a lazy lump if he got a ride while you walked all the way to the top."

Tolemek pushed Zirkander back into his seat so he could lean out and offer a hand to Cas. Also, because he was being a pest.

She wore her army uniform, as usual, and looked to have come from work. When she saw him, she climbed in and sat on the bench beside him.

"Are you also going to warn the king to move the dragon blood?" Tolemek asked.

"Er, how did you know?" Cas asked.

"It's the trendy thing today." Zirkander draped an arm over the back of his bench again.

"Actually, sir," Cas said, looking at him, "I wanted to warn him that there's a reward out there for it now. I went to your office to tell you and then General Ort's office to report to him, figuring I should go through the chain of command. But neither of you was in your office."

"That's because generals get to spend their days having long lunches, gambling at the horse races, and leaving early to drink at the Officers' Club."

"I don't believe you, sir."

"Good. And don't believe it from anyone else, if they ever try to push that spiel on you when offering you a promotion. Where did you hear about the reward? And do you know who's offering it?"

"My father. He came to see me at work."

"Random civilian assassins aren't supposed to be let into the fort."

"I told him that, sir. But he told me that his contacts mentioned a job being put out to his network of associates. Someone knows the government or the army has all those vials of dragon blood we brought back from Cofahre, and they're offering a substantial sum for it. There's a middleman involved for the delivery, so he doesn't know what nation. The payment is in Iskandian nucros, so it might be someone other than the Dakrovian shaman."

"Oh?" Zirkander asked. "Does he not know how to use a money exchanger?"

"He didn't when he went hat shopping."

Though Zirkander didn't seem to find anything unusual about the comment, Tolemek gazed at Cas in surprise. "I may have to ask you later what route led you to find me down in Ambergull."

"It's a somewhat interesting story."

"All right," Zirkander said. "We'll add that to the list of things to tell the king. Speaking of chains of command, I suppose all this should go to his internal intelligence man, but I have another reason to want to check in with him. I hope he doesn't think it odd that I've come to visit him three days in a row."

"Maybe he'll think you harbor secret romantic feelings for him," Tolemek said.

"Sardelle might be distressed to hear that," Zirkander said.

"And Captain Kaika," Cas put in.

"I don't know about that," Zirkander said. "She seems flexible about her romantic feelings."

"You don't think she would mind being replaced?"

"I just imagine her inserting a newcomer into the equation. Angulus would be the one likely to object."

Cas wrinkled her nose.

"We're being passed," Zirkander said, peering out the window as the carriage slowed. They had reached the portcullis, and not soon enough for Tolemek's comfort. The conversation had taken an alarming turn.

"That's Colonel Therrik," Cas said. "With Kasandral on his back."

"Looks like he ran up the hill," Zirkander said. "Show off."

"Should we be alarmed by his appearance? With that sword?" Tolemek imagined Therrik having been called in to combat the shaman.

"I requested it, actually," Zirkander said.

"That didn't answer my question."

"I suggested he be added to the castle guard for a few days, in the hope that Kasandral will get all green and glowy if a shaman sneaks in and starts throwing magic around. As to whether that should alarm you, I always find it alarming when Therrik is stomping around with that sword."

One of the gate guards knocked on the door, then opened it to look inside.

"General Zirkander, Dr. Targoson, and Lieutenant Ahn to see the king," Zirkander said.

"The king is very busy in preparation for the festival. He may not have time to see you."

"We'll take our chances." Zirkander saluted cheekily at the man.

Tolemek half-expected the guard to tell them to turn their bullet-ridden box around and drive back down the hill.

A second guard came over, this one an older veteran that Tolemek had seen often when visiting the castle. "They're all on the guest list for the festival." He nodded at Zirkander and kept speaking to his colleague. "Whether the king will have time to see them or not is questionable, but they're all entitled to graze at the buffet and watch the lamps get turned on."

"I'm on the guest list?" Cas asked.

"Park over there," the guard told the driver, stepping back and closing the door.

"Did you not get the invitation?" Zirkander asked. "All of Wolf Squadron and Tiger Squadron were invited, and some other soldiers who have distinguished themselves."

"Maybe I did. I've been distracted." Cas brushed Tolemek's thigh and met his eyes.

"I didn't mean to be distracting," Tolemek murmured as the wheels bumped over cobblestones toward an area filled with other carriages, most a lot more luxurious than the army's utilitarian vehicle. He wrapped his fingers around hers. She initiated physical contact so seldom that he had learned to appreciate the times she did.

"If that were true, you wouldn't still have that ghastly hair," Cas said.

"I did trim it."

"I don't believe you." She squeezed his hand.

Zirkander reached for the handle, probably intending to flee before they started gazing dreamily at each other, but the door was yanked open before he touched it.

Therrik loomed there, his sword in hand. Tolemek released Cas's hand and reached for one of the vials in his belt pouch—after the kidnapping, he had vowed not to leave his home without some protective measures.

"*You*," Therrik snarled, looking straight at Tolemek.

"Good evening, Colonel Therrik," Zirkander said. "Are you the valet for tonight's proceedings? I'm afraid I don't have a bag or large purse for you to carry for me."

"I sensed someone with dragon blood." Therrik hefted Kasandral, displaying its faint green glow. "I thought it might be the shaman."

Zirkander shooed him back so he could climb out. "I don't give rides to shamans, only my officers. And their hairy boyfriends."

Therrik growled but backed away from the carriage.

"Colonel," the captain of the guard said, coming up to him and lifting a hand. "I believe you'll find it most useful if you go inside and guard… the thing it is you were brought here to guard." Judging by the perplexed and faintly annoyed furrow to his brow, he hadn't been told.

"I'd love to if I knew where it was," Therrik said. "Zirkander, go let the king know I'm here with the sword and ask him where he wants me." He eyed the well-dressed guests arriving, some stepping out of carriages, some handing horses off to stable boys. "I'm going to mingle and make sure none of the guests are more than they seem."

"Mingle?" the guard captain balked. "You'll alarm people with your huge sword."

"That happens a lot." Therrik strode away without looking back.

The guard captain strode after him, voicing further protests.

"Does that man know you outrank him?" Tolemek asked Zirkander as he climbed down from the carriage.

"Not that I've noticed."

Cas hopped down beside Tolemek before he could offer a hand. Not that she needed it.

"I can pass along your information to the king if you two want to stay out here and enjoy the festivities." Zirkander waved toward the gardens at the side of the castle where tables and a stage had been set up. A brightly dressed pair of women were already juggling there, tossing flaming torches back and forth to each other. "Since we all have the same message, more or less," he added.

"Yes, sir." Cas appeared relieved. She had probably thought it presumptuous for a lieutenant to go see the king in the first place.

Tolemek saw the king frequently enough that he wasn't intimidated by him, but if Zirkander wanted to deliver his message, that was fine with him. As Therrik seemed to believe, it would probably be better to stay out here and keep an eye on the guests—and watch for any with buckskins or peculiar hats—than loitering in Angulus's office. Besides, Tolemek wouldn't mind attending the entertainment with Cas. It wasn't quite the romantic dinner he had envisioned, but perhaps she would enjoy an evening away from work. Too bad she was still dressed in her uniform. She would likely feel more relaxed in some civilian clothing. He certainly wouldn't mind seeing her in one of her summer blouses or that dress she had with the hem that floated around her knees, revealing far more bare skin than her uniform did.

"Tolemek?" Cas poked him in the arm.

Realizing she and Zirkander were both looking at him and waiting for an answer, Tolemek cleared his throat. "Yes, by all means, go chat with the king, Zirkander. We'll enjoy the juggling, and it looks like a music troupe is setting up too."

"Such a shindig just for turning on some lights," Zirkander said.

"I bet the castle will look striking all lit up, sir," Cas said. "A lot more impressive than the hangars. They hardly have any windows, so you can't even see the lights from outside."

"All right. Have fun and stay out of trouble." Zirkander saluted Cas, flicked a wave at Tolemek, and strode toward the castle doors.

"My lady." Tolemek offered Cas his arm. "Will you accompany me to the event?"

"Gladly." She slipped her arm through his, and they strolled in the same direction that other guests were heading. "Maybe we'll get lucky, and there won't be any trouble tonight."

Therrik stalked past in front of them, shaking his sword and growling to himself, or perhaps to any guests with a smidgen of dragon blood in their veins.

"I wouldn't take that bet," Tolemek murmured.

Cas sighed wistfully.

Chapter 14

EVEN THOUGH BHRAVA SARUTH FLEW far faster than any steam vehicle on land or sea, he and Sardelle left the castle later than Fern had, and Sardelle didn't spot the carriage until it was turning off the highway and onto the street with her house.

Would you mind setting down a few houses away, Bhrava Saruth? I can get off and walk the rest of the way, and perhaps you can go find some sheep to hunt.

Sheep? It's getting dark.

Don't animals like to head to streams to drink before nightfall?

High priestess, it is most ignoble to attack an animal when it's drinking. Besides, your mate's mother bakes many sweets. I have enjoyed her dragon-horn cookies numerous times. What is that brown substance they are dipped in?

Chocolate.

It is delicious, Bhrava Saruth said, drawing out the word with loving enthusiasm.

I don't think Fern will be in the mood to bake tonight. Sardelle thought of the blood on the handkerchief. *She may also not be in the right state of mind to appreciate your... you.*

But we have already met. Bhrava Saruth swooped straight for the rooftop of Fern's house. *I could turn into a human so I can fit inside. Then I can help you comfort her. Perhaps I should turn into a ferret. Are ferrets not cute and comforting? Oh, but her cats did not respect me properly when I was in that diminutive form. I believe they thought I was hunting competition. As if the god Bhrava Saruth would deign to eat mice.*

I think she may need healing more than comforting. Since Sardelle hadn't examined Fern yet, she didn't know exactly what was wrong with her. If she had some illness that was beyond Sardelle's healing abilities, perhaps it would be good to have the dragon nearby. She had seen Phelistoth wave his hand and heal people that would have taken her hours to attend.

Yes, I could heal her certainly. Do you think she would wish to become my worshipper then? Since her son helped with the design of my temple, I am certain she will want to come visit it when it is complete.

Undoubtedly. Just let me go in first, please.

As you wish. Perhaps I will see if those pigs next door would like to accept me as their god. For dumb animals, pigs are quite clever, you know.

This should prove interesting, Jaxi told Sardelle.

Me attempting to get Fern to let me help her?

Bhrava Saruth being trailed by a squadron of loyal pigs.

Ah.

Sardelle didn't hear any alarmed shouts when Bhrava Saruth settled on the peak of the roof. It was dark enough that the chauffeur driving the king's carriage might not have noticed him soaring overhead.

As Sardelle slid off his back and searched for a way down from the roof, the carriage door slammed shut. Magic wrapped around Sardelle as Bhrava Saruth lifted her into the air and down to the path beside the house. She landed between the bench and pottery shed and remembered the conversation she and Ridge had shared there, about Apex's death.

Voices drifted back to her, the king's man asking if Fern needed anything as he saw her to the door.

"I'm quite fine, young man. Perfectly capable of seeing myself to my own door. I appreciate the ride, but you needn't worry about me." Fern coughed.

"Are you sure, ma'am? You don't sound well. Maybe there's some neighbor who could stay with you or at least look in on—"

"I don't need any help. Please, return to your master. I have cats to feed."

Indeed, plaintive meows came from the front of the house. Sardelle sensed at least a dozen of them converging on Fern, wondering where their human caretaker had been all day.

"Yes, ma'am." The man squawked as he almost tripped over a cat.

"Careful, young man. That was Mimi."

"Sorry, ma'am." A quick thud of steps was followed by a door slamming shut.

Sardelle waited until she sensed Fern step into the house before moving up the path. Even then, she had trouble making her legs propel her along. Fern hadn't been happy to see her at the castle, and Sardelle doubted she would want to see her now, either. But if she was ill... Sardelle couldn't let her sit there alone and miserable. If she had to, she could wait until Fern went to sleep and possibly heal her without waking her, but Sardelle would prefer to have her permission.

At the front door, she started to knock, but realized she was standing in the dark. She focused on the lantern mounted on the wall, and a small flame flared to life.

I could start a nice bonfire if you need more light.

Not necessary.

It's dark inside too.

Sardelle sensed that Fern had gone in and lain down on the couch, promising the cats she would feed them soon, that she needed to rest first.

Sardelle took a deep breath and knocked. Fern didn't answer. She was still awake, but she lay on the couch with her eyes closed and didn't open them.

The door wasn't locked. Sardelle opened it enough to poke her head into the dark room.

"Fern? May I come in?"

The mumbled response could have been a positive or a negative. Sardelle went in anyway. She thought about lighting lamps, but Jaxi beat her to it.

It was muggy inside, the house heated from the day in the summer sun, and the air smelled of paint and cats. Sardelle waved a few windows open and used her power to bring in a breeze and push out the stale air.

"Fern?" She approached the couch warily.

"Sardelle?"

"Yes, it's me. I was worried about you this afternoon. I came to see how you're doing."

"Nothing wrong with me," Fern said, though she didn't open her eyes. "Just a little tired and—" She broke off into a series of wracking coughs.

"I can see you're going to be more stubbornly independent than Ridge is."

Fern opened her eyes. They were bloodshot, and she looked exhausted.

"He brings his slivers and hangnails to me for treatment," Sardelle said. She knew for a fact that Ridge was more of a baby about those kinds of things than he was about bullet wounds and gouges from giant feathered familiars.

"Yes, he's only selectively brave. I don't know how a man can risk his life going into battle in those crazy fliers every day, but then get ashen and think he's going to die if he drinks milk that's gone bad."

"I suppose pirates and enemy soldiers kill you quickly. Food poisoning might be a slow, torturous way to go."

"He was captured by the Cofah once and tortured. With more than bad milk."

Sardelle nodded. "He told me some about that, but not much. I don't imagine it's an experience he wants to relive."

"He just says something flippant if you try to get him to be serious."

"I have noticed that tendency." If talking about Ridge helped Fern relax and gave them some common ground, Sardelle would happily speak about him.

"He didn't get that from me. Or from his father."

"The flight academy?" Sardelle suggested. "His pilots all seem to be crafted from the same pattern."

"A dreadful pattern. Like those terrible dragon-print skirts all the girls are wearing this summer. He is a dear boy, though. He worries about me and cares far more than he lets on." Fern closed her eyes for a moment.

As cats milled about Sardelle's feet, some rubbing her calves, she let her senses trickle toward Fern, examining her lungs first.

She burrowed down to see with her mind what she never could have otherwise without a microscope.

It wasn't a cold or simple virus, but a fungal infection. Farmers' Rot? That was what they had called it in her time. Windstorms could stir up the fungus in the dirt, and if enough was inhaled, it could infect people's lungs. It was more common inland where it was drier, but there were plenty of farms and exposed earth in this area, and Fern spent a lot of time out in her garden.

"Can I get you some tea, Fern?" Sardelle asked.

"No, you're the guest." Fern struggled to sit up. "I'll get you some. I need to feed the cats too."

"I can handle it. Why don't you rest?" Sardelle did her best to influence her with a calming sensation, a desire to relax. "Seeing the king is stressful."

"Seeing a *dragon* fly through the window is stressful."

"That is true." Sardelle didn't mention that Bhrava Saruth had been on her roof recently. Now, she sensed him several miles away. Communing with pigs, perhaps. "Let me get that tea started. Kitties, follow me for dinner."

She didn't have Tylie's knack for animals, but she touched their minds gently, conveying the idea that food awaited in the kitchen. Since they already suspected that, they were easy to sway. A few cats Sardelle hadn't noticed earlier appeared, making the total at least fifteen. She wondered how Fern afforded feeding them all.

"They *are* following you." Fern turned her head to watch the procession into the kitchen. "Even though you're a—uhm."

Because she was a sorceress, Sardelle thought, but she didn't want to bring up magic and distress Fern further.

"They know there's food through this door, I'm sure." Sardelle lit lamps and opened more windows in the kitchen. She found a turkey leg and a ham hock in the icebox, and a whole array of bowls lined up by the wall. She didn't know how much the cats ate but carved some meat into each container.

I'll get the tea kettle, Jaxi said.

Don't heat it too quickly. We don't want Fern suspicious that her tea has been poisoned by magic.

My magic is sublime, not poisonous.

I know that, but we're still working on her.

She's oddly heartened by the fact that the cats followed you, Jaxi said. *She believes animals can tell if a person is kind and good. She's trying to decide if they know about your witchy ways.*

Lovely. Sardelle returned the ham to the icebox, and the meows lessened as the cats dug in.

She thinks they do since she believes cats are perceptive.

The tea kettle whistled.

That water boiled extremely quickly, Jaxi. Especially given that there's no wood in the stove.

Details, details. It's summer. Who wants to heat up a stove when a little energy applied directly to the water will do?

Sardelle selected a pleasant lemon-smelling tea from one of a handful of unlabeled bins, found a couple of strainers, and poured two cups. She didn't truly think Fern would suspect the beverage poisoned or tainted, but it might make her feel better if they both drank.

She's half-asleep.

Good. It'll be easier to heal her if she's not awake and fighting me. Dealing with a fungal infection is more work than healing a cut or a broken bone.

Fern's eyes opened when Sardelle returned.

"The cats are eating ham," Sardelle told her.

"Good." Fern shifted to a sitting position to accept the cup. "I've been so tired this week, Sardelle. I'm not used to getting sick. Other people get sick, and I take care of them. That's how it works."

"It sounds logical to me." Sardelle sat on the chair near the couch.

Fern coughed, fighting to keep from spilling her tea. Sardelle was tempted to sit beside her and rest an arm around her shoulders but feared being pushed away. She would let Fern finish her tea, then see if she could use her power to tempt her to relax, to fall asleep. It would take her about an hour to work on that infection, she judged.

Fern drank from her cup. "My stomach muscles and back

hurt from all the coughing I've been doing. Do you think it's something bad?"

"Nothing you won't recover from."

Especially with your help, Jaxi said.

"You're a very strong woman," Sardelle said, hoping Fern wouldn't see it as unwelcome flattery. She truly *was* strong, living alone out here with her husband rarely heard from and even more rarely seen.

"If I *don't* make it," Fern said, wrapping her hands around the cup, "I want you to know… Look, I'm a little scared of what people have been saying this week. *Doing.*" she glanced warily at Sardelle.

Sardelle resisted the urge to interrupt her, to tell her that she *would* make it, that she would heal her as soon as Fern fell asleep. Instead, she sipped her tea and tried to look encouraging.

"But I can tell that you care about Ridge and that he adores you. And you don't seem to mind that he's sarcastic and leads a maniacal life at times." Fern pursed her lips. "I haven't noticed that his promotion has kept him out of the sky or from doing crazy things."

Sardelle decided not to mention how Ridge had almost died at Galmok Mountain. Despite his fears about being chained to a desk as a general, he did still manage to get himself in trouble frequently.

"And you're nice. And helpful." Fern glanced at the door as a large black cat ambled out of the kitchen, its belly full.

Sardelle smiled, finding the praise encouraging. Until Fern broke into another coughing fit.

"I better get some rest," Fern said when she finished. She set the cup on the table and lay back on the couch again. "But just in case, I want you to know, I'm happy he's found you. And that you're getting married."

"Thank you. I'm glad to hear that."

"I do hope to live long enough to see babies. Witches can have babies, right?" Fern twisted her neck to look at Sardelle.

"Yes." Sardelle decided not to correct her on terminology. "And actually… it's early to make announcements, but I told

Ridge, so I should tell you too. I'm pregnant. If all goes well, next spring, Ridge should be a father."

"Truly?"

"Yes."

"And I'd *finally* be a grandmother. If I live that long."

"You will. You can't pass away with so many cats relying on you. And birds." Sardelle glanced toward the cages hanging from the ceiling. Maybe because night had fallen, the various birds inside hadn't made much noise when people had come in.

"Will the baby be... uhm."

"Magical?" Sardelle guessed. "It's likely he or she will have a little aptitude, but lots of people with dragon blood never do any training and lead perfectly normal lives." She didn't know if she should hint at that, since she would naturally want to teach her own child enough magic to defend himself or herself—and help others if possible. But Fern had plenty of time to get used to that idea. Most children didn't show any aptitude until they were four or five. "He or she could grow up to be an artist or a pilot."

"Seven gods, not that." Fern managed a wan smile before breaking into another coughing fit.

She sounds awful, Jaxi said. *I'll put her to sleep if you don't.*

Will you also heal her?

No, that's your job. Unless you want me to try to incinerate microscopic fungi spores.

I'll take care of it. Sardelle sent a gentle feeling of weariness toward Fern.

She probably hadn't been sleeping well of late because it didn't take much magical influence to convince her to close her eyes and relax. As sleep overtook her, Sardelle shifted positions to sit next to her on the couch. She remembered healing Duck in this very spot.

Your memories of this house aren't particularly inspiring, Jaxi said as Sardelle settled in, closing her eyes and touching Fern's shoulder.

There were some good times here.

Are you referring to when you and your soul snozzle rutted with abandon against his mother's door?

Not... specifically.

I don't remember anything else good happening here.

I'll see if I can make a list later. After Fern is better. Now, if you'll give me some solitude, please.

As you wish. I'll see if Bhrava Saruth has succeeded in accumulating a vast pig following yet.

v

Ridge knocked on the king's office door, though the lack of guards standing beside it suggested Angulus wasn't in. He arched his eyebrows at the guard who had accompanied him up here.

"Sorry, sir. He has a meeting with General Ort and Admiral Hamilin soon. He should be back here shortly."

"Maybe he wanted to catch the juggling act."

"Not particularly," came Angulus's dry voice from the stairway. He strode down the hall, wiping his hands as if he'd just been doing some dirty manual labor. Four expressionless bodyguards trailed him. "Lady Covewatch arranged the entertainment. She arranged this whole festival. Thought the city needed a chance to see that the castle is still in good condition—or should I say that it's in good condition again—after the various attacks this spring. She did pointedly bring in a music troupe with lute players for my listening pleasure, which I appreciate, but I'd appreciate it more if I didn't have to give a speech afterward."

Ridge had a vague notion of Lady Covewatch being some well-connected noblewoman, social maven, and relative to Angulus, but he didn't think he had ever met her. The queen had always arranged festivals and social events when she had been alive. Ridge imagined Captain Kaika doing those things someday, but he highly doubted she and Angulus would ever get married. In part because of her lack of noble blood and in part because of... everything else.

"Are you supposed to be this candid with your military officers, Sire?" Ridge stepped aside so Angulus could enter his office.

"Probably not, but my bodyguards grow weary of me complaining solely to them."

The two bodyguards in the back exchanged quick glances with each other. In agreement? The ones in the front remained stoic and expressionless, as seemed to be a requirement for the job.

"Come in, Zirkander. I was expecting Ort. Is he coming?"

"Yes, Sire. We met this afternoon, and he went off to find Therrik to protect your castle from magic users." Ridge followed Angulus into the office, stopping on a rug and clasping his hands behind his back. "I'm not sure where Ort is now, but he must be on his way. He also asked me to find Sardelle so she could lend her efforts to defending the castle, but I wasn't able to locate her."

"She probably went after your mother." Angulus glanced at a window with extremely large and fresh gouges in the sill.

"Is my mother all right? I was wondering how the meeting went."

"It could have been better. We were interrupted by a dragon bringing me a Cofah spy."

"Oh? I have news for you that may be related to that."

Angulus blew out what might have been an exasperated breath. "You're making it sound like my castle is in danger of being besieged at any moment, despite the fact that my intelligence officers haven't suggested anything more than increased security and an escalation to a higher threat level until we find this Dakrovian shaman. Care to explain?"

"Certainly, Sire. First off, the assassin Ahnsung told Lieutenant Ahn that he's been made aware of a large reward that's recently been posted for the acquisition of your dragon blood. Second, Ort and I thought the shaman, if he knows about this festival, might try to sneak into the castle tonight while there are people roaming everywhere to try to get it. We don't have any evidence. Just guesses."

"I've arranged for the dragon blood to be moved."

"Good." Ridge remembered Angulus's hand dusting. Had he moved it himself? "That should take care of part of our problem, assuming the blood is insulated somehow. I know Sardelle can sense it from quite a distance, so I assume this Dakrovian could too."

"It's in the same iron boxes that it's been stored in here for months. Sardelle said she couldn't sense the blood unless she was right next to the boxes, and even then, the signature was faint."

"And it's going somewhere more secure than the castle?"

"It's going somewhere I don't think most people will think to look for it." Angulus smiled tightly.

From his vagueness, Ridge assumed he wouldn't be told the location. That was fine with him. He couldn't hide his thoughts from mages—as past experiences blatantly showed him—so he would rather not have that knowledge.

"That's all I have to report, Sire. Oh, and that Therrik is on the grounds with Kasandral. He reported to the captain of the guard, I believe, but asked me to see if you want him somewhere specific." Asked. Ordered. Ridge decided not to worry about semantics.

"Somewhere he won't alarm Lady Covewatch's guests overly much."

"Too late for that. He almost made Tolemek wet himself when he yanked open the door to our carriage, green sword blazing."

Angulus's eyebrows twitched, and Ridge reminded himself that urination shouldn't be mentioned in the presence of royalty.

"I've worked with Dr. Targoson often enough now to know he's not easily alarmed. It's more likely, he reached for some vial to throw at Therrik."

"Yes, I'm sure that's it, Sire."

Footsteps pounded in the hallway outside, and the bodyguards stirred near the still-open door. One reached for a pistol, but stopped before he touched it, so Ridge assumed someone familiar was coming.

"General Ort and Admiral Hamilin here to see you, Sire," one of the guards announced, holding a hand up to stop the men.

"Let them in," Angulus said. "It sounds like my submarine meeting just got more interesting."

"Sire," the two gray-haired officers said as one as they stepped in, both saluting.

Admiral Hamilin, a block of a fellow with jowls that flapped when he walked quickly, ignored Ridge and addressed Angulus first.

"I have an update on the enemy submarine, Sire. As you ordered, I brought up two of our submarines from Doloon Base, and they're patrolling the harbor and coastline near the city. One of them spotted an unknown craft only a couple of miles to the south of the butte—they drew close enough to get a visual on it. It seemed to be heading for the harbor, and our submarine gave chase, but the enemy disappeared from sight and also went silent to our craft's listening station. I received my last update less than thirty minutes ago. They haven't been able to relocate it and now—" Hamilin gestured to Ort.

"A fire mysteriously started in the harbor, Sire. A large one. It's threatening two canneries, a warehouse, and all of the second section of docks."

"Maybe Therrik should take the sword for a visit down there," Angulus said.

"I bet it's just a distraction, Sire," Ridge said. "Damn, I wish I'd been able to find Sardelle. Shall I take a flier out to my mother's house to see if she's there? Or I could run back to my house. Tylie was there, as well as the soulblade Wreltad. He's useful."

Ridge now wished he'd thought to grab the soulblade and bring him to the castle. He'd been skeptical that anything would truly happen tonight, so soon after they had routed the shaman—or at least his hawk. A foolish assumption.

Angulus scowled. "That's the sword that wiped your memory and made you think it was a good idea to bring an enemy sorceress into the castle, isn't it?"

Ridge fought not to squirm under Angulus's glower. "I didn't think it was a *good* idea. It was more that I had no choice because I was powerless to fight them." He grimaced. That didn't make him sound any better. "Wreltad didn't approve of what his handler was doing, and he is on our side now. I'm sure he could help in this. Though I would rather find Sardelle."

"I'd definitely prefer Sardelle," Angulus said. "Though I'd like to think our military capable of dealing with one shaman." His scowl wasn't as harsh for Ort and Hamilin, but they both winced. "Now I wish I'd kept Bhrava Saruth here too."

"I don't think you can keep a dragon against his wishes," Ridge said.

"I could have had more cinnamon buns brought up."

"Ah, that would have done it."

"I've alerted the infantry company captains, and we've got men patrolling the waterfront as well as helping the firemen, Sire," Ort said. "But it seems this shaman has some way to turn invisible."

Everyone looked at Ridge as if to ask whether that was possible. As if he was an expert on magic.

"I know Sardelle had a hard time detecting the submarine," Ridge said. "Even Phelistoth did, it sounds like. Tolemek implied this shaman is a scientist, or at least a chemist, like him. Sardelle mentioned he might have constructed the submarine with lasting magic built into it. I know she can make it so people look right at her and don't see her."

"Wonderful," Angulus grumbled. "Dismissed." He waved at Ort and Hamilin but held a hand up to Ridge. "Zirkander," he said as the other men walked out, "tell Therrik to patrol the grounds. No, I better come tell him myself. And yes, as much as I hate to rely on Sardelle, it might be a good idea to have her here. Something is clearly afoot. You can take one of my fliers parked in the back."

"Yes, Sire."

As they headed for the door, a strange sensation came over Ridge, like ants crawling on his skin. Magic.

Angulus paused and frowned at him.

"Do you feel something too?" Ridge asked.

"Yes."

The door slammed shut in front of them.

"Er," Ridge said, "I hope that was just one of your guards thinking you wanted some private time."

"Alone with you?"

"I'm charming and sexy, Sire. Sardelle told me so."

Apparently not deeming that worth an answer, Angulus ran to the door and grabbed the knob. He tried to turn it, but it didn't budge. He pulled on the door, but it also did not budge.

He cursed and ran to the back door, the one that led to the rest of his suite. He was able to open it, and disappeared into his sitting room, but more curses soon flowed out of it. Ridge had a feeling all the doors leading out of the suite were locked now.

Ridge knocked on the main door and called, "Are any of the king's stalwart guards out there? Anyone with a key? Or a sledgehammer?"

Angulus ran back into the office, and Ridge thought he might glare at that last comment—his castle had taken enough damage already this year—but he ignored it and went to try the window.

Ridge knocked again. There were always at least two guards out there if Angulus was present. Could they not hear him? Or had something been done to them? Ort and Hamilin had *just* left. What could have happened in that thirty seconds?

"This window was opened a few hours ago," Angulus growled, rattling the panes as he tugged at the latch. "I *know* it works."

He grabbed a heavy stone tape dispenser off his desk and smashed it against one of the panes, but it made a strange twang noise and bounced off.

"What the hells?" he demanded.

"I believe someone wants you to stay put, Sire."

"That's unacceptable."

Ridge decided this wasn't the time to make further jokes about his charm and sexiness. He tried banging on the door again, the very stout oak door that wouldn't have been easy to force open even if it weren't magically reinforced. Once again, nobody answered.

Chapter 15

"Y OU'LL HAVE TO LEAVE YOUR pistol here, Lieutenant," a guard standing next to something that looked like a mobile closet said. Or maybe it was a mobile armory. "No weapons allowed in the gathering." He nodded toward the jugglers and lute players. People with painted faces and wearing colorful costumes ambled through the crowd, offering to do tricks for people.

Cas reluctantly pulled out her pistol. Other men and women in uniform had done the same, laying them in slots with names on them in the armory. She supposed she wouldn't need her firearm to munch on snacks and watch a lutist play.

"*He* has a weapon." Tolemek pointed at Therrik's back. He'd strode through the checkpoint with Kasandral in hand, the sword no longer glowing now that he'd moved away from Tolemek.

The guard's lips thinned in disapproval. "He's special."

"No kidding," Cas said.

After handing over her pistol, she stepped forward and waited to see if Tolemek would be patted down. She hadn't seen any of the other guests getting that treatment, but many of the guards still mistrusted him and remembered his moniker of Deathmaker.

The guard did eye him, but he didn't wear any open weapons, and the man waved him through.

"Are you armed with any potions?" Cas murmured as he stepped up to her side again.

"You mean scientific formulas?"

"I suppose."

"Then possibly so, but I wasn't removing them to stick into that grubby weapons locker. There were grease stains and who knows what else in the cubbies."

"And here I've been told I was the one with the sharp eyes."

With her sharp eyes, Cas noticed a large boxy steam wagon rolling out from behind the castle on the far side. The man driving it didn't wear a uniform that would have identified him as one of the king's men, nor was the royal emblem on the side of the vehicle.

"If that were coming in instead of going out, I would deem it suspicious," Cas said.

Tolemek turned to look. Before he could answer, Therrik strode up to them and squinted at the vehicle. The driver didn't look at anyone, simply maneuvered the wagon carefully past people as he headed for the gate.

Therrik lifted Kasandral enough to display a faint green glow coming from its blade.

"That's for that wagon, sir?" Cas asked him.

"I think so. I'm getting the urge to go over and smash it."

"Quash it," Tolemek said and pointedly turned his back to the wagon. "I believe the king may be taking our advice and moving the dragon blood."

"Right now?" Cas followed his example and turned her back, not wanting to draw anyone's attention to it with their interest, especially if Tolemek was right. "When all these people are here?"

"Better now than after the shaman arrives," Tolemek said.

"I suppose. I wonder where the king is having it taken."

"Some bank indistinguishable from another, I imagine."

Therrik stared at the wagon for a few seconds longer, but finally grunted and turned around. He muttered something under his breath. The command words ordering the sword to stand down?

"I'm surprised Kasandral sensed it," Tolemek said. "I can't say that I did. The vials must be in iron boxes."

"It's a sensitive sword." Therrik's head whipped in another direction.

Cas looked in time to spot a side door in the castle opening and closing. Servers had been bringing food and drinks out through it, but she didn't see anyone near it now.

"I think the sword felt something else." Therrik strode in that direction, mowing over a few guests in his way.

"Are we going to help?" Tolemek asked.

Cas doubted Colonel Therrik would *want* their help, but she worried that self-opening door signified someone magical sneaking into the castle. She couldn't stay and munch snacks and watch juggling if the king was in danger.

"Yes," she said firmly.

"I was afraid of that."

Cas jogged back to retrieve her pistol. She wished she had her sniper rifle. It seemed a far more fitting weapon to unleash on a shaman.

The guard protested the weapon pickup, but one of his peers had joined him at the stand and gripped his arm.

"That's Raptor from Wolf Squadron. If she wants a firearm, let her have one."

"But—"

Cas didn't hear the rest. She took a few steps toward the gate, as if she'd only been collecting her pistol because she was leaving, then holstered it, joined Tolemek, and headed for the door. Therrik already stood there, a hand on the knob and the other gripping Kasandral. He squinted suspiciously at the low hedges lining the castle wall on either side of the door, then strode inside.

Cas hurried to catch up with him. She had no delusions about finding a shaman who didn't want to be found without the help of magic.

In the servants' corridor inside, Therrik almost knocked over a woman heading out with a tray. She tottered, bumping her shoulder on the wall as he passed. Her tray wobbled.

Therrik barked an apology but didn't slow down. Cas paused to make sure the woman didn't drop the tray, then ran to catch up. Up ahead, Therrik veered into one of the kitchens.

"Is he stopping for a snack?" Tolemek muttered.

"Probably not."

"Is the *shaman* stopping for a snack?"

"You know him better than I do."

Tolemek grunted in vague agreement.

"Maybe we can grab some flour to throw at him if he's

invisible," Cas said as they ran toward the kitchen. She imagined the castle's entire guard regiment leaping on a man invisible but outlined in white flour.

"I don't think that's how it works. It's less that the person is actually invisible and more that he's fiddling with the minds of observers so they don't realize they see him. I have vials of my smoke-grenade formulas with me in case invisibility *is* the problem."

"Fine, then. I'll grab something else to throw at him."

"Usually, you throw bullets."

"Shooting up the castle may be frowned upon."

A clatter and a shriek came from the kitchen.

"Did that ape knock more people over?" Tolemek asked, picking up speed and pushing through the door first.

Plumes of black smoke wafted out.

"Fire!" someone cried.

Cas groaned. She doubted *Therrik* had started a fire.

* * *

High priestess, are you awake?

Sardelle grimaced. She believed she'd annihilated the dangerous microscopic fungal infection that had spread through all the tiny airways of Fern's lungs, but she had wanted to do another thorough check of the woman before pulling out of her healing trance. Or being pulled out by a dragon.

I'm healing Fern, she responded. *What is it?*

He's back on the rooftop, Jaxi informed her. *Maybe he wants to complain that pigs don't make good followers.*

As this time of night, I'd think all the pigs would be asleep.

Sardelle opened her eyes and focused on the dark window near the door. She had lost track of time but suspected she had been working for at least an hour. Fern slept on the couch, breathing easily, the fever that had gripped her gone. Sardelle sensed that her lungs, though still raw and tired, were doing much better.

There are fires in the city, Bhrava Saruth said. *By the docks and in the castle. I believe there are enemy saboteurs afoot. If they molest my temple site, I shall char them into ashes.*

Fires? Sardelle lurched to her feet. *Jaxi, do you sense that?*

Not from way out here. I might be able to if someone's gargantuan dragon aura wasn't dampening my range.

Can you fly us back there, Bhrava Saruth? Sardelle grabbed the tea cups and hurried to take them into the kitchen. She thought about leaving a note for Fern, but if that Dakrovian shaman or someone else was causing trouble in the city, she couldn't tarry.

Of course, high priestess. Shall I bless your mate's mother before we go? I would very much like her to become one of my worshippers. She has good hands.

Uh, Jaxi thought. *I don't want to know what that's in reference to.*

I think she's petted him in ferret form. Bhrava Saruth, I'm sure a blessing would be useful, and I would appreciate it even if she's sleeping and won't realize what happened.

As she finished the words and stepped back into the living room, a golden glow swept slowly over Fern from head to toe.

Perhaps we can tell her that I blessed her, Bhrava Saruth said. *Otherwise, she may not fully realize the perks of following me.*

He's not into doing anonymous good deeds, is he? Jaxi asked.

The glow faded, and Sardelle did one more check to make sure Fern was doing well before she headed for the door. Fern radiated vitality and slept comfortably. Good.

Anonymity doesn't get you offerings of tarts. Sardelle snatched Jaxi's scabbard and headed outside, closing the door softly.

That would be tragic.

Bhrava Saruth alighted on the walkway in front of Sardelle, lifting her with his magic so that she settled on his back again.

There aren't any other dragons attacking the city, are there? Sardelle asked. *That would explain fires burning.*

Not unless they are cleverly hiding their auras from me. This is very unlikely. Few of the dragons left in the world are clever.

I wonder if he's including Phelistoth in that statement, Jaxi said as Bhrava Saruth sprang into the air.

Sardelle didn't answer her. Instead, reminded of Phelistoth, she asked, *Bhrava Saruth, is Phelistoth within your range? Can you ask him to bring Tylie to the city in case we need help?*

She would like to think that they could handle a single shaman without the help of multiple dragons, but just because Tolemek had only spoken to one man capable of wielding magic did not mean there weren't more. And just because Bhrava Saruth didn't sense an enemy dragon didn't mean there couldn't be one in the city, shape-shifted and up to no good.

Phelistoth! We do not need him. He is a Cofah dragon.

He's been helpful to Iskandia thus far. Just round him up if you can, please. If you do, I'll ask Fern to bake something just for you.

Very well.

As the dark countryside passed below them, and the wind tugged at her hair, Sardelle hoped Angulus was all right. A fire at the castle. Somehow, that seemed more ominous than one in the harbor. Either way, she feared Ridge would be in the middle of the trouble. She hoped he and all their friends were also all right.

Chapter 16

Ridge tried the door again, frowning when it didn't budge. From what he had learned of magic, whatever the shaman out there was doing to keep them locked in should only work as long as he was concentrating on it. Unless he had applied some magical artifact or tool to the doors and windows—or potion, Ridge added, thinking of Tolemek's concoctions. But how would the shaman have gotten close enough to do so with all the guards in the hall? And what kind of weird alchemical formula could have made all the glass in all the windows—Angulus had tried applying the heavy tape dispenser to the rest of them, as well—too strong to break?

A muffled scream reached Ridge's ears. It sounded like it came from downstairs. He thought he detected a hint of smoke in the air and worried the castle might be burning down around them.

He jogged to the window and peered out. He could just make out the stage, and the jugglers still seemed to be performing. Whatever was happening inside must not have become common knowledge outside yet.

"Zirkander." Angulus strode into the office from the sitting room. "Make yourself useful."

He carried a rusty pickaxe that looked like it had been removed from a wall mounting and an axe made from...

"Er, is that bronze, sir?" Ridge caught the axe when Angulus tossed it to him.

"One of my ancestors used it to slay a sea monster, or so the plaque says."

"Sea monster?" Ridge mouthed. Some dragon hybrid from ages past?

Angulus strode to the door to the hallway. "The pickaxe was a gift from miners after they found a lucrative diamond at the newly opened Masonwood Gems on my great-great-great grandfather's land. I'm not sure about the integrity of the wood haft after all these years, but both tools looked more promising than the tape dispenser. Or the centuries-old flintlock above the fireplace."

"I have my pistol, if we think shooting things would be useful." Ridge had contemplated firing at one of the windows earlier, but he doubted a bullet would have any more luck piercing a shaman's magical protection than a tape dispenser. He'd seen too many bullets bounce off Sardelle's magical shields. Besides, he didn't want to go down in history as the person responsible for killing a king if the bullet took a bad bounce.

"Doubtful."

With a mighty swing, Angulus slammed the pickaxe into the door. Ridge expected to see and hear wood splinter, but the tool bounced off without leaving a dent.

Angulus growled, then took a couple of steps to the side. He tapped at the wall in a few places with the flat end of the pickaxe, found a spot he liked, then stepped back and took another mammoth swing. The pick smashed into the plaster coating, and lath underneath it snapped.

"Hah," Angulus said, tugging the tool out. "No magic protecting the walls."

"I guess the shaman assumed a king wouldn't destroy his own office to escape."

"Then he doesn't know me very well." Angulus slammed the pickaxe into the wall again.

"Perhaps more royal visits to Dakrovia would be in order." Ridge walked over to help, careful not to get in Angulus's swing path.

Angulus shot him a dirty look, then pointed to the small hole he'd created. "This is going to have to be a lot bigger for us to get out. Alternate with me."

"Yes, Sire."

Ridge did his best to be useful, but the axe was duller than the head of the sea monster it had slain thousands of years ago.

The tape dispenser might have been a better tool. But he and Angulus did make progress, however ugly, so he kept his mouth shut.

Unfortunately, someone must have decided the interior castle walls should be extra thick, perhaps so the king wouldn't be subjected to hearing the voices of people walking past in the hallway. They found another layer of lath and plaster behind the first.

"I can't believe nobody is hearing this and coming to check on you," Ridge said as they toiled.

Another scream drifted up from the level below. It belonged to a woman.

"I hope it's because they're down there, helping out with that." Angulus gritted his teeth and swung with more ferocity, though by now, they were both breathing heavily.

A bead of sweat ran down the side of Ridge's face. As determined as Angulus was, he had to pause to take a break, dropping the head of the pickaxe and leaning on the end of the handle. The plaster-covered tip of that pick didn't look any sharper than Ridge's bronze-age tool.

He used the axe to clear away shards of plaster. He saw with some satisfaction that they had broken all the way through in a couple of places. The studs in the wall would be problematic, but at least they were making progress. Ridge decided not to point out that Angulus would likely be much safer if he stayed in the office, that this shaman didn't seem to want to kill people. Maybe, once he realized the blood was gone, he would leave the castle.

Or *was* it gone? Had Angulus actually gotten it off the grounds or just loaded it into a wagon somewhere?

Angulus waved for him to back up so he could resume swinging the pickaxe.

"Tell me something, Zirkander," he said between swings.

"Yes, Sire?"

"Why haven't I gotten my wedding invitation yet? Sardelle says she signed one."

That wasn't the question Ridge had expected. He kicked some of the plaster on the floor out of the way.

"Because I actually wanted to ask you…" Ridge groped for eloquent words, which was hard to do when he was dripping sweat and cutting a hole in the wall.

"I'm not mad at you anymore about the sorceress." Angulus glanced at him between swings. "If that's what you're worried about."

"I have wondered about that. I certainly feel guilty. Logically, I know I couldn't have stopped her—I tried to crash my flier into the ocean and kill us both rather than bring her into the castle. But it's like Ahn and Kasandral, I suppose. Knowing you couldn't stop it doesn't mean you didn't still do it. And people died because of it."

Angulus stopped, leaning on the pickaxe to catch his breath again. "Logically, I know a lot of things too. But humans fail at being logical a lot."

"They do indeed," Ridge murmured quietly, studying the hole instead of meeting Angulus's eyes.

"I didn't realize you'd tried to crash."

"They read my every thought. Eversong and what was, at the time, her soulblade. They wouldn't let me do anything except their wishes. I was just the puppet."

"I can't imagine what it would have been like, ruling a thousand years ago when dragons and powerful sorceresses were prevalent and even the norm. Those rulers must have often felt like puppets themselves."

"Likely so."

Angulus hefted the pickaxe again. "So, I'm invited to the wedding?"

"Yes, Sire. You always were. I've just been trying to get up the courage to ask you to be one of my kin watchers."

Angulus paused mid-swing and stared at him for a moment. Which was somewhat alarming, since the pickaxe was raised over his shoulder. But Angulus soon recovered from whatever surprise he felt.

"Of course I will."

"Good. Thank you." A ridiculously intense wave of relief flooded through Ridge. He told himself this wasn't something he should be thinking about right now, but after having tried to figure out a way to ask him for weeks, he couldn't help but be glad he had finally done it. And Angulus had said yes. Ridge truly hadn't been certain he would.

"I'm a bit surprised though," Angulus said as he returned to swinging. "You're Lord Popularity with the common soldier. Don't you have a lot of colleagues that you're good friends with that you'd rather have at your side?"

"Most of my good friends that I came up through the ranks with are dead."

Angulus squinted at him, as if he thought it might be a joke. Ridge wished it were. But Angulus saw the reports. He had to realize how deadly the job was, how few people retired from Wolf Squadron. Or any of the squadrons. If they were lucky, they were only injured and medically retired.

Angulus seemed to realize it wasn't a joke. He frowned and swung the pickaxe again.

"Not that I wouldn't have punted them to the side for you, Sire," Ridge said, figuring Angulus knew how to handle his levity more than his seriousness. "Mox, Digger, and Antar would have understood."

"I appreciate what you and your people do for the country, Zir—Ridge," Angulus said. "I probably don't say it often enough. I know the medals stop meaning much after a while. Or so I assume. Nobody ever gave me a medal. Sometimes, I'm envious of you for that. For a lot of things."

"Oh?" Ridge didn't know what to say to Angulus's seriousness any more than Angulus knew what to say to his. "If you come to the wedding, I'm sure I can find one to give you."

"Very generous, but I think I'll survive without you donating one of your medals to me."

"How about a piece of cake?"

"That I'll take."

Angulus grunted, lowered the pickaxe, and shoved at the broken plaster on the far side of their hole. His fist went through to the other side. He pulled back bloody knuckles, but he barely seemed to notice the injury. He stuck his entire arm through and patted around, trying to reach the doorknob.

Ridge doubted the magically barricaded door would be easier to open from the other side. Angulus cursed and drew his arm back.

He stuck his head into the hole. "Captain Targeer, Yorx, where are you?"

"Magically convinced to be elsewhere, I imagine." Ridge hefted the axe. "I think we can clear a little more and get out. If we suck in everything we've got to get past the studs."

Angulus growled, drew his head back, his curly hair coated with plaster dust, and waved for Ridge to get to it.

"We'll get out," Ridge repeated, hoping to reassure him. "And find the shaman who's sneaking around in your castle."

He still didn't think it was the best idea for the king to go roaming when intruders were around, but if his liege wanted to escape and pummel the enemy, it was Ridge's job to help him.

Together, they tore away the last of the wood and plaster. Ridge squeezed out between the studs, flopping into the hallway without any grace. Angulus, broader of chest and shoulder, had no room to spare, and snarled as he got stuck. Ridge gripped his shoulders to help pull him out. Angulus grunted and looked like he left most of his chest hair on the wood supports, but he finally tumbled out.

"Maybe," he said, wincing, "I should get a medal after all."

"A medal *and* cake."

Ridge helped him to his feet, and they took off down the hall.

* * *

Tolemek paused in the smoke-filled kitchen because Cas did. She gaped at the fire, then joined in with the cooks and servants hurling pots of water on the fire. Therrik, however, had continued on, bypassing the fire and heading for a door at the back of the kitchen, one that looked to lead down to a basement. Tolemek didn't know this part of the castle well. But he did know why this fire had been started.

"Cas, it's a diversion," Tolemek called into the chaos.

She paused, and their eyes met through the smoke.

"I'm following Therrik." He didn't want to order her to come with him, but he pointed in the direction the big colonel had gone and hoped she would.

Coughing, Tolemek ran down the stairs that Therrik had taken. He tugged out one of his vials of knock-out liquid as he went, one that would turn to gas when he broke it open and the substance contacted air.

He entered a narrow storage corridor that looked like it led to wine and root cellars. It was dim, with only a few old gas lamps burning on the walls, their plumbing visible along the mortared stone, an addition that had come long after the original basement had been built.

Tolemek ran to catch up with Therrik, keeping his thumb on the stopper of his vial. Usually, he built grenades to house the knock-out liquid, grenades that couldn't be activated simply by dropping them, but his lab was still a shambles, and all of his already-made devices had been destroyed or stolen. He had been lucky to find the ingredients to put together a few vials.

"Is he going to steal dragon blood or *wine?*" Therrik growled after poking his head into a cellar full of valuable vintages, the dusty bottles lining the walls in special shelves.

The stone hall continued on, numerous side passages opening up, and Tolemek wouldn't have been surprised if more than potatoes and wine existed down there. He'd heard that a great deal of the expansive basements had been damaged during the sorceress's attack, but this section appeared to be the original castle construction.

"Sword's getting brighter," Therrik whispered, still leading. "And pulling me this way..."

"I can't tell if any of the dragon blood is still here," Tolemek whispered. "I don't sense it, but it was probably shielded by iron, regardless."

He remembered the black steam wagon Cas had looked at earlier, the way she'd squinted suspiciously at it. Tolemek suspected it had been loaded up with the valuable vials of blood.

Would Yendray grow frustrated and lash out if he located the king's vault only to find it open and empty?

"Don't remind me you're one of them," Therrik growled, not looking back.

He turned a corner and sniffed. Tolemek also crinkled his nose. A sweet-smelling smoke lingered in the air, and he slowed his steps, worried the shaman might have deployed a knockout gas of his own. It didn't smell like the compound Tolemek created, but there were other ingredients that could produce the same effect. Further, a shaman more talented than Tolemek might be able to make a protective barrier the way Sardelle could, so he wouldn't be affected by the tainted air.

Tolemek paused, on the verge of sharing a warning with Therrik. The smoke was thicker up ahead.

"I see something," Therrik whispered before Tolemek could speak.

Therrik rushed forward, and Kasandral's glow flared from dull to bright, washing the stone walls in green. He jumped around a corner, the smoke half-obscuring his movements, but the sword swept forward, trackable by its glow.

"That smoke—" Tolemek started his warning, but a *boom* ripped through the air.

The stone floor quaked, hurling him into the wall. A cloud of smoke flowed toward him, its acrid scent plaguing his nostrils as he righted himself. Crumbling mortar trickled from the walls, and several stones fell from their homes, clattering to the floor.

Ahead of him, Therrik roared. Something—his sword?—clanged against stone. Or was that metal against metal?

Tolemek lifted his vial but waited, using his senses, trying to detect what was ahead of him and if anyone was coming.

Another clang bounced down the stone hall, and the hazy air stirred. A figure ran into view, shrouded by smoke.

Tolemek judged from the sword-fighting noises that Therrik was far enough ahead that he wouldn't be in danger of friendly fire—friendly knockout formulas. Tolemek held his breath and threw his vial at the floor in front of the figure, then skittered backward to get out of its range.

He almost tripped over his own feet and realized that he was more sluggish than he should have been. His legs felt like lead.

Ceramic shattered, some vial or container hitting the floor in front of *him*. The smoke-shrouded figure had retreated, and Tolemek couldn't see him anymore, but he sensed someone in the hallway ahead of him. Green smoke flowed up from the floor, mingling with the rest.

Still holding his breath, Tolemek forced his rubbery legs to propel him backward.

Someone brushed his arm from behind, and he almost exhaled in surprise. Cas pushed him to the side and fired her pistol into the smoke as the sounds of a sword fight continued to come from around the corner.

Someone cursed in a foreign language, and the figure appeared right in front of Tolemek. A man in buckskins. The Dakrovian threw something as Cas fired again, this time, taking him square in the chest. Their enemy pitched backward, but his vial struck the ground, shards of ceramic flying as more green smoke flew into the air.

Cas hunched forward, coughs wracking her body.

Tolemek wanted to grab her, hoist her over his shoulder, and retreat, but with his limbs still rubbery from the first concoction, he feared they would both pitch to the floor if he tried.

Besides, Cas didn't seem interested in retreating. She heard the clanging of swords and ran forward, even as she gripped her stomach and spat, as if she could eject the foul smoke that way. Tolemek glimpsed tears streaming from her eyes as she ran around the corner, but she led the way with her pistol, not letting the discomfort stop her.

Tolemek forced his legs to work, to drive him after her. He would have left Therrik to fend for himself, but he had to back up Cas. She had only come down here because of him.

As he rounded the corner after her, Tolemek almost tripped over a body, a long-haired man wearing beads and buckskins... with a huge sword gash across his throat. Lifeless brown eyes stared at the stone ceiling. It wasn't Yendray. The other man hadn't been, either.

Cas coughed up ahead. In front of her, Therrik leaped through a huge, warped hole in an iron door—an iron *vault* door. He disappeared inside, but a moment later, another explosion went off. He flew backward, cracking his head on the edge of the hole on his way to slamming into the wall opposite the vault. He crumpled to the floor but did not release Kasandral.

Fighting coughs, Cas leaped to the opening in the vault door.

"Wait," Tolemek ordered, his voice raspy. He'd finally had to take a breath and inhale the tainted air. It was a sulfur mustard gas, and his nostrils and eyes and throat all burned.

Cas paused before running inside. Tolemek charged up beside her, stumbling on his malfunctioning legs, and threw a knockout vial into the vault.

"Back," he rasped, reaching out to grab her arm.

She fired into the vault before letting him tug her away. Therrik jumped to his feet, shaking himself like a dog, as if he hadn't been hurt at all, at least not enough to notice.

A gun fired, but it wasn't Cas's this time.

Therrik whipped Kasandral across his chest, the magic of the sword making his movement faster than humanly possible. A clang sounded as he deflected a bullet. He charged into the vault again.

"Don't, you idiot!" Tolemek yelled, backing away from the vault himself.

Damn it, hadn't Therrik seen him throw the vial? Maybe he was holding his breath...

Fighting coughs, Cas dashed snot away from her nose with one hand while keeping her other trained on the vault. More clangs and bangs came from inside.

Someone rushed out. Not Therrik.

"Yendray," Tolemek blurted. He could barely see the man with all the smoke, but he was wearing that stupid bowler hat.

Cas fired. Her bullet bounced straight back, almost striking her in the shoulder.

"Shit," she cursed and ducked as it ricocheted off stone.

Tolemek flattened himself against the wall and grabbed her, pulling her back too. He sensed the protective barrier around

Yendray even though he couldn't see it with his eyes. The shaman sprinted away from the vault, away from Therrik and that sword.

"Out here, Therrik," Tolemek yelled and jumped in front of Yendray's path.

The shaman didn't seem to be carrying a weapon. Maybe if Tolemek could at least get in the way, he could delay him until Therrik ran out with Kasandral. The sword could pop that magical barrier with one swipe.

Yendray stopped and yanked a small pistol out of a holster under his tunic. "Apologies, Deathmaker," he said, not sounding breathless at all from dealing with Therrik. "But I can't have you following me."

Tolemek cursed, sensing the shaman lowering his barrier, but only long enough to fire. He flung himself to the floor as Cas tried to knock the man's arm away. She was partially successful, but the bullet still struck Tolemek in the shoulder. He hollered as fiery pain exploded in his body.

Cas yelled in fury and aimed her pistol after the shaman, but Tolemek sensed Yendray had already raised his barrier again.

"Don't," he gasped, not wanting to be hit *twice*. "He's protected."

Cas swore and ran after Yendray, but she smacked into an invisible barrier that now stretched across the corridor. She stumbled back, almost dropping her pistol.

Tolemek gritted his teeth and gripped his wound. Hot blood warmed the palm of his hand, and another wave of pain went through him at the touch.

"Therrik," he called, his voice still hoarse. "The shaman left."

"Which *one*?" Therrik snarled, his voice sounding hollow from within the vault.

"The one in charge. The one I *think* is in charge." Speaking hurt, so Tolemek slumped against the wall and gave it up.

Cas rushed back toward the vault and peered inside. "Damn, sir."

Therrik stepped out of the hole, smoke wreathing him.

"He went that way." Cas pointed down the corridor. "There's a magic barrier that I ran into, but Kasandral—"

"On it."

With the point of the sword leading, Therrik ran past Tolemek without a glance.

Cas tore her gaze from the vault and ran to Tolemek. She slipped a supportive arm around his waist.

"What's in there?" he rasped. "He didn't get the blood, did he? I didn't see him carrying anything."

"I don't think so. There are three dead men and women—Therrik's work—and then a bunch of remains of boxes and shelves that were blown up. Some gems and gold ingots on the floor among the bodies."

"Not the prize Yendray sought."

"Apparently not. We better get you up to find a doctor. Or Sardelle."

"I don't think she's here." Tolemek pushed away from the wall, letting Cas guide him in the direction Yendray and Therrik had disappeared.

"Too bad. I think that sword surprised the Dakrovians—that's what we believe they are, right?—but the leader had some tricks ready to play."

"I saw. And felt." Tolemek gritted his teeth. "There must have been more than one shaman, or Therrik wouldn't have been thwarted, even momentarily."

He didn't like the big colonel, but he had no problem acknowledging that he was a superbly well-trained fighter. He hoped Yendray ran into trouble and that it gave Therrik—and Kasandral—the time to catch up with him. If not, the Dakrovians might keep trying to find and obtain that dragon blood.

"Maybe." Cas looked at his face, worry in her eyes.

Tolemek attempted to smooth his own face. "I'll be fine. It's just my shoulder."

"You don't need that shoulder for mixing goos?"

"I've done it one-handedly before. Cas?"

"Yes?" Cas peered around the corner before leading him around it and back toward the stairs.

"I've been meaning to tell you… the other night, before all this happened, I didn't mean to imply that I wanted to end our relationship. If you don't want to have children, I understand that. Maybe we could just get a dog."

"Don't you already have over fifty snakes, lizards, and other reptiles?"

"Those aren't pets. And don't live in the house."

"Thankfully," she murmured.

As they headed up the stairs, some of the horrible smoke lingering in the air, his shoulder bumped the wall, and he winced and sucked in a pained breath.

"Is this the best time for this discussion?" Cas asked.

"I thought we should have it before I die."

"Do you have bullets elsewhere that I should know about?"

"No, but the night is young." Tolemek managed a smile, though he was sure it was wan and half wince.

"Well, I'm glad to hear that you don't want to break up. I don't either. I'm just—look, I'm only twenty-four. It's possible I may feel differently someday, but children are the furthest thing from my mind now. And I don't want you to assume that I *will* feel differently." She raised her voice to be heard over the shouts and clangs still coming from the kitchen—there was even more smoke on this floor, albeit normal smoke, not anything designed to deter enemies. "I don't dislike children, but I love my job. I don't want to stay home and raise babies."

"Understandable, but just something for you to keep in mind... I could potentially set up a laboratory on our own land, especially if we buy that house in your father's neighborhood that we talked about. There would be plenty of room. And if I did that, I could possibly care for children."

"You barely remember to eat when you're working."

"If I get around to hiring an assistant, he or she could remind me to eat. And feed children. This would be years away, of course. I'm sure I could get it figured out by the time you were ready. *If* you ever decide you're ready. That's all."

"Hm."

Did that *hm* sound thoughtful rather than dismissive? He wouldn't push further. He just wanted her to know it was an option for the future if she one day changed her mind. If not, he would understand.

Shots rang out in the courtyard. The music that had been playing in the background halted.

"I think we know which way Yendray went," Tolemek muttered.

"Yes." Cas tried to walk faster but glanced at him and made herself slow down again.

"You don't have to wait for me. Go help. I'll find a nurse myself. Or at least someone with bandages." Though he would rather have painkillers at the moment. He wished he'd thought to bring along tubs of his healing salve.

Cas hesitated.

Tolemek extricated himself from her grip. "Go," he said again. "Catch up, and when Therrik knocks his shields down with that sword, you can shoot him."

"Therrik or the shaman?"

Tolemek snorted and handed her a vial of the knockout liquid. "Both."

Cas kissed him, then ran off down the corridor, disappearing into the kitchen. Tolemek knew she would be out in the courtyard in an instant and hoped she could help. He slumped against the wall and closed his eyes, wishing he had more to offer her.

Chapter 17

As Cas burst out the servants' door in the side of the castle, an explosion ripped through the courtyard. People screamed and dove for cover under tables and hedges. The jugglers had already leaped off the stage, and she spotted a lute player racing toward the back of the castle.

She let the smoke guide her toward the source of the explosion—it had come from the front of the castle, the drive that led in through the gate.

With her pistol in one hand and Tolemek's knockout potion in the other, Cas raced toward the smoke. A groan followed by clanks sounded. The gate being opened? She couldn't see it through the smoke. A huge black pall had descended on—or arisen from—that entrance area.

Shots fired from that direction, and she winced, hearing bullets ricocheting off the stone wall. Were the guards firing blindly into the smoke? Or were they hitting the shaman's barrier as he ran out?

The guards must have seen her approaching because they stopped firing. Cas raced into the thick of the smoke, veering toward the gate, but she almost tripped over a man lying on the cobblestone drive. She accidentally kicked something, and metal scraped as an indignant flare of green light came from the ground. Kasandral.

"Colonel Therrik?" Cas blurted, crouching to pat his chest. She could barely make out his form in the haze and couldn't tell if his eyes were open or closed.

He groaned. His clothing was tattered, and her hand encountered blood.

"He's getting away!" someone yelled. "Somehow, he got the locked gate open."

"Get a wagon! He must be going to the harbor!"

Not sure if Therrik would regain his senses in time to help, Cas holstered her pistol and grabbed Kasandral. She hated that blade and had no interest in wielding it, but it would be far more useful against a shaman than a firearm.

Hunt! it seemed to cry into her mind as her fingers wrapped around the hilt.

She shuddered. She knew it wasn't sentient and didn't talk, not the way Sardelle's soulblade did, but it definitely had a strange sentience of a sort, and right away, she felt it tugging her toward the gate and beyond. It wanted to lead her to the shaman.

"Fine with me," she muttered and jumped to her feet. "I'm borrowing your sword, Colonel," she said, in case he was conscious enough to understand, then sprinted away.

She thought she heard a combination groan and grunt that sounded like a protest, but she couldn't wait to see if Therrik roused himself.

As she raced through the open gate, she was in time to glimpse someone running off the winding road that led down into the city. The figure veered toward the slope. That slope was comprised of massive black boulders that formed a large part of the hill the castle perched atop, the ancient stone structure overlooking the capital from this high point on the north end of the harbor. It had to be close to a thousand feet down to the water from the spot where that man—it was too dark to see details of his clothing, but she assumed it was the shaman—had veered off the road.

Cas ran after him, dreading the idea of scrambling down those huge jagged rocks in the dark, but maybe she could catch up to him before he made it far. He had to think that he was fleet of foot enough to beat the steam vehicles that would take the winding road down to the harbor.

"So am I," she growled as she ran.

The shaman had disappeared from sight, but she knew where he'd gone off the road. Kasandral flared with a hungry green glow. The sword also knew.

As soon as she reached the spot, Cas ran out on the rocks. The blade's glow lit the way, and she spotted the shaman less than fifty feet away.

He glanced back at her as she navigated down the boulders as quickly as she could, and she braced herself for some magical attack. Kasandral should protect her from a direct attack, but the shaman could make the rocks shift under her feet, and that would be just as effective at slowing her down.

Instead, he ran out to the end of the spit of boulders he was on and leaped into the air.

Cas halted and gaped. The slope wasn't sheer enough that anyone could jump out and land in the water—besides, a fall from this height would kill a person, even if he *did* land in the harbor.

But he didn't fall as one would expect. Some magic buoyed him up, and he floated downward, skimming above the rocks.

Cas groaned. Of course, she should have guessed a shaman could levitate his way out of danger. It would only take him a minute to get to the bottom instead of the ten or more it would take her to climb down. She had no hope of catching him.

Unless…

Cas hefted Kasandral over her shoulder and took aim, as if she were preparing to hurl an axe at a stump. She was known for her marksmanship and could hit targets with rocks as well as with bullets, but the shaman had already descended halfway to the bottom, and the sword wasn't balanced for throwing. Still, she had to take the chance. It wasn't like the shaman could pick up the magic-hating blade.

Sighting along her other arm for assistance, Cas lined up her shot and threw the sword. It flared with even more light as it spun through the air. She held her breath, afraid she hadn't timed the shaman's descent well—or that he could speed up at will—and that it would clank uselessly off the boulders near him.

But the blade flashed green as it appeared to strike his magical barrier right above his head. He had time to throw his arms up and jump to the side before the blade penetrated it, but Cas thought it still clipped him in the shoulder. A pained scream rose up from below, seeming to confirm that.

She smiled grimly, glad to repay the wound Tolemek had received to *his* shoulder.

Alas, the blade did not embed itself in the shaman. After striking the man, Kasandral fell to the rocks next to him. The sword continued to glow, but it couldn't do anything more by itself.

The shaman spun, the green glow coming from beside him highlighting the anger on his face, and Cas realized she was vulnerable now. He threw his arm up, fingers splayed, and a huge ball of fire roared up the mountainside toward her.

Cas dropped to her stomach between two boulders. The heat made the attack feel like an inferno roaring past her, and she feared all her neck hair would be scorched off. Fortunately, the brunt of it missed her.

Hoping the boulders protected her somewhat, she yanked out her pistol. Maybe his protective barrier would still be down.

Before she could take aim, the rocks rumbled and shifted around her. Thunderous snaps and cracks came from the top of the slope. Horrified, she realized he'd started a landslide. Right above her.

***

"Where are you going?" Angulus demanded when Ridge ran out one of the side doors of the castle and headed straight for the rear yard. Angulus frowned at gunfire and smoke at the other end, near the front gate.

"To where I can be most useful," Ridge said, having a hunch that the continued fire meant the shaman was protecting himself, the same way Sardelle did when people fired at her. He pointed toward one of the king's two fliers, both waiting on the landing pad in the back. "The air."

The flier bullets wouldn't be any more useful than those from guns if the shaman had a barrier up, but he could definitely do something about the Dakrovian's escape submarine. If he meant to board it, then it had to be above the surface somewhere. Ridge didn't know how much of it would be visible, but he hoped his bullets would cut through the water and hit something critical. If he had to, he would crash the flier into the submarine to damage it enough to keep it from operating.

"Fine," Angulus said. "I'm going with you."

"Probably not a good idea, Sire," Ridge called over his shoulder as he raced around the corner of the building and the fliers came into sight. His plan to crash the flier was a last resort, but he definitely shouldn't fly anywhere with the king if he had that in mind.

To his surprise, two other people were running toward the fliers, Captain Kaika and Lieutenant Pimples.

Technically, Kaika was pulling Pimples toward the fliers. He gripped a stuffed pastry in one hand and didn't look like he had flying in mind. A small satchel flapped against Kaika's hip as she tugged him along.

"Ma'am," Pimples blurted, food still in his mouth. "I'll come. I just need a second to chew."

"Chew while you fly."

"Kaika," Angulus blurted, running right behind Ridge.

"Can't talk now, Angulus," Kaika hollered, though she gave him a cheerful wave as she stopped at the side of one of the fliers. "There's a troublemaker afoot. He just ran out the front gate with Lieutenant Ahn after him." She spun toward Pimples and pointed to the cockpit. "Up, up. Let's go."

"I'm going, I'm going." He stuffed the pastry into his mouth so he could use both hands.

He needn't have bothered. Kaika grabbed his legs and shoved him so hard that he tumbled into the cockpit face first.

"Those *are* my personal fliers, Kaika," Angulus said, managing to sound dry even though he was out of breath.

"Which means they'll be perfect for mowing down enemies of the crown." Kaika placed her satchel in the back seat with enough care that Ridge suspected she had raided the castle's armory for explosives.

Ridge veered for the cockpit of the second flier, not objecting to Pimples and Kaika taking the other. If Kaika truly had explosives, they ought to be more effective at destroying a submarine than bullets. So long as they could strike at it before it descended below the surface. Once it was far enough underwater, nothing except another submarine would have a chance at getting at it.

A startled curse came from the side yard of the castle, and smoke flowed out of one of the open windows. Ridge scrambled into the cockpit and fired up the craft, hoping it would be easy to spot the enemy once he was in the air.

For a moment, Ridge thought he would have to talk Angulus out of coming along, but Angulus heard that curse and stopped at the edge of the landing pad to look back at the castle. He seemed to remember that his duty was here, not hunting down enemies.

"Go get him, Zirkander," Angulus said, meeting his eyes and nodding. "You, too, Kaika."

"I'm more than ready to do so." Kaika waved from the back seat, then thumped Pimples on the shoulder. "Get this bucket in the air."

"Bucket?" Angulus asked. "Really, Kaika, those are the most advanced fliers we've got."

Ridge's thrusters roared to life, and he didn't hear her response, but he was positive it was a sarcastic one. He lifted off, angling over the castle and toward the wall and the harbor beyond. Pimples, half a pastry still stuffed in his mouth, came right behind him.

"You enjoying that dessert, Lieutenant?" Ridge asked after tapping the communication crystal to turn it on. He also tugged his dragon luck charm out of his pocket and gave it a quick rub.

"I *was*. Then chaos broke out. I'm still confused about what's going on, sir."

"We're going after a submarine. And a shaman if we see him along the way."

He's on the waterfront path below the castle that leads to the docks, Sardelle spoke into his mind. *He jumped down from the road to the castle, then used magic to slow his fall and carry him away from Cas and Kasandral.*

Sardelle, Ridge replied silently. *Where have you been? I've been missing you all day.*

Out helping your mom.
Helping? Is she all right?
Sardelle hesitated. *She should be fine now.*

Ridge wanted to pump her for more details, but the road and the rocky slope down to the harbor were in view now. He spotted a small green glow from halfway down the hill. Was that Kasandral? What was the sword doing lying by itself on the rocks?

Where are you now, Sardelle? Ridge wanted to go down and retrieve the sword—it was far too valuable a tool to leave down there, but they had a limited time to find and stop this shaman before he escaped.

Almost there. Bhrava Saruth is giving me a ride. Oh dear.
What?
I sense Cas on the slope, well above the sword. She's been buried by a rockfall.
Hells, can you and the dragon get her out?
Of course.
Pimples, Kaika, and I will deal with the shaman.
He's almost to the docks.

Ridge flew down toward the trail and sailed in circles as he squinted into the gloom below. The path wasn't lit, and the gas lamps burning along the docks and in the city dulled his night vision. Further, the fire that General Ort had reported still threw flames into the night from one of the canneries on the waterfront. Ridge finally spotted someone running off the path and onto the waterfront street that led to the docks.

Ridge wanted to open fire right away, but steam carriages rumbled along that same street. Worse, he spotted dozens—no *hundreds*—of people out along the waterfront, enjoying the evening air. And probably waiting to see the castle lights come on.

"Gonna be waiting a while now, I bet," Ridge grumbled.

Since he couldn't fire, he brought his craft lower to trail after the Dakrovian. Once he got out on the docks, closer to his submarine—and hopefully farther from people—Ridge would open up.

"Ma'am," Pimples said, "we can't drop bombs. There are people everywhere."

"Just get me in close. I've got excellent accuracy."

Ridge flew over a well-lit pier where a black carriage was parked in front of an armored ironclad, loading some cargo. Odd, considering the hour. But there wasn't time to worry about it. Both carriage and ship appeared Iskandian.

"Close *where?*" Pimples asked. "Which pier is he going to run down? There are a hundred."

"Just circle and watch and see."

The shaman glanced behind him as he weaved through the crowd of people along the waterfront, people now gaping at the fliers. Ridge realized it probably looked like he and Pimples were doing a strafing run and meant to attack. He lifted an arm and waved, trying to appear friendly. Maybe people would think this was part of the festivities.

Not unless you do some of your loopy rolls in the air, Jaxi spoke into his mind.

Jaxi, are you powerful enough to create a barrier to stop that man from reaching his destination? Ridge glanced over his shoulder, wondering if Sardelle and Bhrava Saruth were close enough now to help.

He spotted the great gold dragon landing on the road near the castle and peering down the slope. Huge boulders flew into the air before bouncing and clattering downhill. Sardelle slid off Bhrava Saruth's side, running to the edge. Ridge gulped. If Cas had been buried by those huge boulders, she couldn't be in good shape.

Uhm, I tried, but he evaded me, Jaxi said. *He's quite powerful for a mage in this era.*

Ridge turned his gaze back to the waterfront in time to see a splash. The shaman kicked his legs and disappeared under the surface.

Imagining the fleeing man using his magic to dive deep, too far for bullets or bombs to reach, Ridge groaned. But then he spotted gray metal in one of the berths at the end of the pier. It looked more like an oval garbage lid than a boat of any kind, but he recognized it immediately, the hatch of a submarine and a portion of the hull around it, all that needed to be above water for someone to access the craft.

Ridge flew straight toward it. "Follow me, Pimples. Kaika, I've got something for you to bomb."

"The vile enemy that violated Angulus's castle?" Kaika asked.

"Whatever gets you excited about dropping bombs."

"I think that's everything, isn't it, sir?" Pimples asked.

Ridge flew low, just above the masts and smokestacks of other berthed ships and took careful aim with his machine guns. He doubted the bullets would damage the metal hull of the craft, but the docks were dark around it, and he wanted to highlight the spot for Kaika.

As he closed, the submarine started to sink. Ridge cursed. Did the shaman have some way to get aboard from underwater without flooding the vessel? He didn't think any Iskandian submarines had features that allowed that.

Before the vessel completely disappeared, he rained bullets down. They clanged off the hatch and hull, not doing any obvious damage, but he hadn't expected them to. He flew past, making room for Kaika and Pimples, before banking to come back around.

He was in time to see Kaika dropping a compact package from the back seat of Pimples' flier. The gray metal hatch had already disappeared under the water. Would the bomb have any effect?

The package blew an instant before it would have struck the water, and fire filled the night sky. The boom echoed across the harbor, and hundreds of people along the waterfront gawked toward it. Wood split, and boards flew.

Ridge winced at the damage to the docks, worried they had not harmed the enemy at all and had only damaged their own infrastructure.

But as the light faded and the smoke cleared, the top of the submarine came into view again, bobbing up to the surface. Was it his imagination that the hatch was tilted to the side? Did that denote damage?

"Drop another one," Pimples blurted encouragingly, coming back around.

"Wait," Ridge barked as the hatch opened. "Someone's coming out."

But Kaika had already dropped another bomb. Ridge winced as someone stuck his head out, looked up, and yanked his head back inside. A second later, the bomb plummeted through the hatch.

The second explosion wasn't as flashy or loud as the first, since it was muffled inside of the submarine, but he saw the hatch ripped off and plumes of smoke pouring out.

Ridge rubbed his face as he circled with his flier, knowing the crew member must have been blown into tiny pieces. He reminded himself that these people had chosen to steal from Iskandia—and tried not to think about how his team had stolen the blood from the Cofah to start with—even if they hadn't been successful.

Though he didn't know that yet. Had the Dakrovians found some of the dragon blood in the castle or had Angulus sent it away in time? Maybe that shaman was lugging some in a bag. Or stuffed in his pockets.

Ridge flew low as the warped submarine tipped sideways, allowing water to seep through the open hatchway. There was nowhere for the shaman to retreat to now, but Ridge guessed he wouldn't go back to the waterfront where he could be more easily apprehended. More likely, he would swim out to the breakwater and try to find a way out of the city and to safety.

"That *was* some pinpoint accuracy, ma'am," Pimples said, flying low to check on the submarine—the wreck. "You should've been a flier pilot."

"Sitting in a chair all day sounds boring to me," Kaika said.

"But it's a chair in the *sky*."

"That makes it less boring?"

"Of *course*." Pimples demonstrated by spinning his craft upside down.

"The shaman is still out here in the harbor, as far as I know," Ridge said, flying over the gentle waves. He wished he had

Wreltad or Jaxi along so one of the blades could have lit up the dark water. Or simply told him where their enemy was. "Come help me search for him."

"Yes, sir." Sounding sheepish, Pimples righted his craft. "But how can he still be alive if he's underwater? Magic?"

"I'm assuming he has a way to make a bubble around himself. Or breathe under there somehow. I suppose he could be hiding under the piers out of our sight too." Ridge glanced toward the slope. It would have been handy to have Sardelle's or Bhrava Saruth's help locating the Dakrovian, but they were busy retrieving Lieutenant Ahn.

Hoping she had survived that landslide, Ridge looked back toward the water. A man popped to the surface right in front of him. Still wearing his hat.

Ridge reacted on instinct, firing first, knowing a shaman would have no trouble flinging an attack at him, even from in the water.

The Dakrovian jerked in surprise, trying to duck back down, but one of Ridge's bullets seemed to catch him. In the arm? The shoulder? In the dark, Ridge had a hard time telling. He *could* tell that the subsequent bullets bounced away before striking the shaman.

"He's over here," Ridge said as his flier took him past the spot where the man treaded water. "He's got his shields up. Some bombs might help."

"Bombs *always* help," Kaika said.

Ridge banked to come around again, hoping the shaman would struggle to keep his defenses up if he'd been wounded. He expected the Dakrovian to be gone, to have submerged again, where he would be an impossible target. Instead, the man continued to tread water. He glared defiantly as Ridge lined up to fire at him again.

The shaman raised an arm out of the water, something clenched in his hand. A grenade? Some chemical device?

Ridge could tell he was the man's target, but he also remembered all the times Sardelle had warned him not to shoot while she had a barrier up to protect them, that the bullets would bounce back at them. If this shaman meant to throw something, that ought to mean his barrier would be down… at least for a second.

Ridge barreled ahead, meeting the man's defiant glare. He gripped the triggers of his machine guns but held his fire until—there. As the Dakrovian hurled the object, Ridge held down the triggers and fired repeatedly. He tilted his wings as he rained down bullets and rolled sideways, hoping to avoid the projectile.

He was sure he'd timed it right, that the object would sail past without quite touching his flier, but the projectile changed its trajectory as it neared him. It darted to the side as if it were some living thing, right toward the cockpit. Ridge tried to duck, but it slammed into his shoulder.

He winced, anticipating an explosion, but the dull thump didn't hurt as much as he expected. The object didn't simply bounce away though. Whatever it was *burst*. A strange liquid or goo spattered all over him and the cockpit.

Ridge tried to adjust the flight stick, since he had passed the shaman's spot and was heading straight for the docks, but it was a struggle to move his hands and arms. By the glow from his power crystal, he saw strings of white gunk all over him, and his stomach sank into his boots as he realized he couldn't move. He was like a fly caught in a spider web, and he was going to crash.

Chapter 18

Sardelle sensed Cas alive and in pain under the rocks, but she couldn't imagine how she'd survived being buried by what appeared to be tons of boulders.

As Bhrava Saruth watched from above and shifted rocks out of the way, Sardelle picked her way down the slope as quickly as she could.

Hold, high priestess. I have not moved enough boulders yet. Allow the god Bhrava Saruth to expose your companion, so we can more easily help her.

Worried about Cas, Sardelle didn't want to deal with the dragon's pomposity, but she made herself pause. He was helping, and he could free Cas much more quickly than she could.

Before her eyes, dozens of boulders flew into the air at once, as if they weighed no more than grains of sand.

Sardelle conjured a light to brighten the slope, more for her benefit than Bhrava Saruth's. As soon as she could see pale flesh—an arm—among the rubble, she hurried down, hardly caring that a few more boulders were still flying into the air.

"Cas!" she called. "Can you hear me? I'm coming."

Sardelle didn't get an answer. She realized Cas had lost consciousness. A blessing for her, given how severe her injures were.

As soon as Sardelle reached Cas, she knelt and rested a hand on the dirty, tattered shoulder of her uniform. Blood smeared Cas's face, and lumps were already swelling.

Allow me to heal your companion, high priestess, Bhrava Saruth said. *Your mate is in trouble and may need our assistance. Also, a shaman's familiar just flew out of a wrecked underwater boat. We must make haste to join the fray.*

"My mate?" Though Sardelle's instincts made her want to heal Cas as quickly as she could, she couldn't help but lift her head to look down at the harbor. The last time she had checked, Pimples and Ridge had been piloting their craft to hunt for the fleeing shaman.

Her eyes bulged as she spotted one of their fliers—*Ridge's* flier—skipping across the water like a stone. A stone heading straight toward the docks.

She sensed that Ridge was conscious but angry and alarmed—for some reason, he couldn't move, not enough to manipulate the flight stick.

Help me, Jaxi. Sardelle drew on her power to create a stiff wall of wind in front of Ridge's flier, hoping to slow it down.

But she was more than a mile away and struggled to affect the air from that distance. Then Jaxi's energy flowed into her, increasing her power. The wind gathered, pushing against the nose of the flier. It started to slow, but Sardelle grimaced, certain it was too little too late.

Then a third being added energy to theirs. Bhrava Saruth.

The flier halted, its propeller inches from the end of a pier. Sardelle sensed Ridge's relief, though he was still frustrated that he couldn't move and couldn't go help the others to make sure the shaman was dead and the submarine destroyed.

Given time, she might have been able to figure out how to disintegrate the strange magical webbing that held him, but Cas groaned, and Sardelle had to shift her attention back to her.

Ridge, we're coming to help, she told him telepathically. *We just need to heal Cas first.*

I believe you already *helped.* His response was dry despite his frustration. *Don't think I don't notice these things.*

She smiled. *It would be a lonely wedding if you weren't there with me.*

You think so? I keep getting requests for extra invitations. I think there are going to be a lot of people there.

"Sardelle?" Cas rasped.

"Yes, I'm here." Sardelle still had her hand on her shoulder, and she examined Cas with her senses only to find that the grievous wounds had already been healed. Only a few superficial scratches remained.

Yes, Bhrava Saruth announced. *I was interrupted when I realized that the mate of my high priestess and my first worshipper in this time was headed for certain doom. And now I must go assist him again, because an overly large bird is flying toward him with evil intent.*

Bhrava Saruth leaped into the air, the wind from his wings stirring Sardelle's hair as he flew past her. She looked up, worried anew for Ridge, but she told herself that Bhrava Saruth could handle any shaman's familiar. Still, she would hurry down to help as soon as she could.

"How are you feeling?" Sardelle asked Cas.

"A lot better than expected." Cas eyed the rocky sides of what had almost become her grave.

"Can you get up? Our people are still in trouble."

A boom floated up from below. Kaika dropping another explosive, Sardelle assumed.

"Are *in* trouble?" Cas tried to push herself into a sitting position. "Or *are* trouble?"

"Both of those things." Sardelle helped her sit up.

"Cas!" Tolemek called from the road above. "Where are you?"

Sardelle had let the light fade, and she reignited it so he would see them down here on the slope.

"And where's my sword?" came another demand. Therrik stood up there next to Tolemek, and a steam carriage waited behind them.

Sardelle sensed that both men were in pain from injuries. Whoever this shaman was, she was glad she hadn't had to battle him herself, though she felt guilty for arriving late to the fight.

"We better get up there," she told Cas. "They both need a healer, and they have a carriage that can take us down to the waterfront more quickly than climbing."

Cas rose to her feet, a touch shaky. Sardelle would heal the rest of her injuries as soon as she knew that nobody else was in more dire need.

The shaman levitated himself down the rocks, Jaxi said.

How lovely for him.

I could levitate you if you aren't comfortable doing it yourself.
The steam carriage will be fine.
How pedestrian.

"The sword." Cas groaned and looked back. "I can't leave it down there."

"Yes, you can. You're injured."

"Not that injured. Thank you for that."

"You have Bhrava Saruth to thank actually. He was faster than I."

Cas wrinkled her nose. "Does that mean I have to rub his belly?"

"He'll probably try to get you to worship him too."

Rocks shifted above them. Therrik was picking his way down the slope while grumbling about lieutenants presumptuously taking his sword. He shot dirty looks at both Cas and Sardelle.

Maybe she would let *Bhrava Saruth* heal his injuries. Then he could be indebted to the dragon. She wondered if Bhrava Saruth would like to have his belly rubbed by a surly colonel.

Cas frowned after Therrik, probably feeling she should have been the one to go after the sword. Sardelle put an arm around her back and pointed her up the slope. Tolemek waited at the top, looking like he also meant to pick his way down, but Sardelle sensed a lot of pain from him, so she held up a hand, hoping to stop him.

As she and Cas made their way up, he insisted on coming down partway to meet them.

"Tolemek was shot in the shoulder," Cas told Sardelle. "He needs your help, too, please."

"The enemy shaman?" Sardelle asked.

"Yes."

As soon as he was close enough, Tolemek rushed forward and hugged Cas with one arm. "The guards said you were completely caught in an avalanche," he said, his voice agonized.

"I was hoping nobody saw that," Cas said.

"Sit down, please, Tolemek." Sardelle hated to hurry their reunion, but she wanted to get that bullet out of his shoulder as quickly as possible in case Bhrava Saruth had more trouble with the hawk than she expected. Or in case nobody could figure out how to get Ridge out of his flier before it sank.

Alarmed at the thought, she glanced toward the pier where he'd almost crashed. His craft was floating on the water rather than sinking down, its light weight and the wings keeping it aloft. Good.

"Sit?" Tolemek let go of Cas. "That sounds difficult. Mind if I just collapse?"

"Not at all," Sardelle said.

She and Cas helped him to a relatively flat spot, and Sardelle set to work on his injury.

***

The flier bobbed quietly in the waves of the harbor, the propeller bumping against the end of the pier. Ridge still had power, as the glowing energy crystal attested, but the craft wasn't going anywhere until a crane lifted it out. Unfortunately, Ridge couldn't go anywhere, either, not until someone came along to lift *him* out. Or cut him out, more likely. It might take a soulblade to do it—the magical webbing had hardened, and moving seemed more impossible than ever.

Booms came from out in the harbor. Ridge hoped that was Kaika and Pimples dropping bombs on the head of the shaman—and that they were getting through the man's barriers. He wished he could help. Or even turn to look.

As the last of three explosions died away, a piercing screech came from behind Ridge, from closer than the explosions had been.

Reflexively, he tried to spin his head around to look for the source, but of course, he couldn't move. Another screech sounded. Closer, this time. He groaned, certain the shaman's familiar was back. If he was its target, there was not a damn thing he could do.

The ropes of webbing smothering Ridge and the entire cockpit abruptly burst into flames. He let out an unmanly squawk, terrified the crazy familiar was going to burn him to ash. But the flames disappeared without harming him—he barely felt the heat—and the webbing disappeared with them.

Though he wasn't sure what had happened, Ridge didn't hesitate to grab his pistol and whirl in the direction of the screeches.

He was in time to see a golden dragon-shaped arrow slam into the side of the feathered creature. They were so close to the flier that Ridge lifted his hands to protect his face, expecting blood and guts to spatter him. But Bhrava Saruth's momentum carried the hawk all the way to the next pier before they splashed into the water. Feathers flew as the dragon tore the hawk to bits. As large as the bird had been, it was small compared to Bhrava Saruth, and its magic couldn't compare to that of the dragon.

Ridge looked away, trusting that particular nemesis wouldn't rise again.

"Sir?" Pimples asked over the communication crystal. "Are you all alive over there?"

"Surprisingly, yes. I'm not even injured." Ridge turned in the direction of the other flier, finding it against the dark sky by its propeller noise. "I don't suppose you have good news about the shaman?"

"Actually, I think we got him, sir."

"*We?*" came Kaika's voice from his back seat. "I was the one dropping bombs on his head."

"But I flew you close so you could do so, ma'am. I'm integral to missions. Everyone says so."

"Is that true, General?" Kaika called.

"Well, I imagine at least someone might have said so once."

"Ha ha, sir."

I can confirm, Bhrava Saruth announced into Ridge's mind, *that the enemy shaman and his pesky pet bird are dead. Also, their underwater boat has filled with water and now rests on the bottom of the harbor. It has been my pleasure to assist you in this manner.*

Thank you, Bhrava Saruth, Ridge said with genuine gratitude, knowing he'd been close to becoming a hawk snack.

You may leave your gratitude in the form of baked sweets at my temple when it is completed.

Ridge slumped back in his seat and closed his eyes. *I'll be glad to do so.*

Excellent. You are a very good worshipper.

Ridge snorted and wondered if pastries from Donotono's Bakery would do or if the dragon expected homemade goodies.

* * *

Tolemek sat among the rocks, his eyes half-closed as he watched the harbor and Sardelle worked on his shoulder. It itched like mad, but the wound already hurt less. She had removed the bullet, leaving the bloody lump on the ground beside him.

Cas sat on his other side, her arm around his back, lending her support. It seemed odd that she was the less injured of the two of them, thanks, he understood, to Bhrava Saruth. His heart had dropped into his boots when he'd heard from the guards that the shaman had dropped tons of boulders on top of her. He'd resolved in that instant not to worry about the future and children again, so long as the gods saw fit to keep her alive and give her back to him.

Irritated grunts came from below as Therrik, Kasandral in his hand again, climbed back up toward the road. Tolemek didn't know how the sword had ended up way down there, but he admitted smug pleasure that the colonel had been forced to retrieve it. Therrik must have decided the battle below had wrapped up sufficiently and that he and the blade weren't needed.

"I learned something tonight," Cas said.

"That life is short—and can sometimes be prematurely *shortened*—and that one should appreciate it with the people one loves, rather than arguing about small matters?"

"That Dakrovian shamans are hells to kill."

"Ah. Also an important lesson."

Cas smiled and patted his stomach, careful not to disturb Sardelle, whose hand rested on his warm, itchy shoulder as she sat beside him, her head bowed.

An Iskandian ironclad belched smoke out of its stack and left the dock. It was at the far end of the harbor from where all the fighting and bombing had taken place, but the captain must have decided to wait to leave until any potential obstacles had been cleared away. Tolemek was surprised the ship was departing at night.

The sky brightened behind Tolemek. He twisted his neck, half-expecting some magical attack or bomb dropping.

Distant claps and cheers erupted from the men and women still crowding the dock. The castle was alight, almost blazing with light. Sconces all along the outer wall beamed, and white illumination poured from the windows of the higher levels and towers visible above it.

Tolemek snorted. "I guess someone determined that the lights *would* go on tonight, no matter what else happened."

"One can't let the schemes of enemies interfere with one's festivals," Cas said.

An explosion tore through the night, and Tolemek jerked his gaze back to the harbor. His first thought was that Kaika had somehow set one of her bombs off by accident. But more explosions followed, and they didn't come from the pier where the two fliers were parked and other soldiers had gathered. No, they came from that ironclad.

It had almost reached the mouth of the harbor to head out to sea. But it wasn't going anywhere now.

Whatever bomb had been set off had opened up a huge hole in the side of its hull, and flames still spilled from it. Tolemek suspected its coal bins were burning down in the boiler room.

"Uh, that didn't appear to be accidental," Cas said. "I've heard of catastrophic boiler failures before, but..."

Sardelle lifted her head and gazed down at the flames pouring from the ironclad.

"That was no accident," she said grimly. "That's the ship that was carrying the dragon blood to... wherever Angulus meant to hide it."

"How do you know?" Tolemek remembered the carriage that had left the castle. Had it been taking its secret cargo down to the harbor to load onto that ironclad?

"I sense it. I didn't before the explosion, but the iron it was boxed in must have been destroyed, because I sensed it strongly there for a moment. Now... I believe all the vials were destroyed, and it's dissipating into the water flowing into the hold."

"Did the shaman do it?" Tolemek asked, feeling confused. Yendray had wanted the dragon blood for himself, not to see it destroyed.

"No, the shaman is dead, and I believe the team that infiltrated the castle with him is too." Sardelle shook her head slowly, her gaze locked on the burning ship. "So many people killed, and for what?"

"My father said there were rewards out there for the dragon blood," Cas said. "One for its acquisition and another for its destruction. Someone must have decided the latter was easier to accomplish."

"Seven gods." Tolemek rubbed his face, thinking of all the formulas he'd crafted using it. Most had been designed to harm dragons, but there had been the potential to do much, much more.

"I guess nobody's going to turn it into a super weapon now," Cas said.

Tolemek hadn't even wanted to do that. He'd just found it an incredible substance, an energy source that could be magically programmed with simple commands.

"Not unless Bhrava Saruth volunteers to donate some of his own," Cas added.

Tolemek shook his head, having a hard time imagining Bhrava Saruth allowing a needle between his scales to draw out his divine blood. And he already knew Phelistoth resented that the Cofah scientists had taken his blood while he'd been unconscious. He had already stated he would never allow such a thing again.

"We may simply have to go forward without it," Tolemek said. "And hope no more enemy dragons come to visit us, because I hadn't had time to make much more of the acid I crafted from the original stuff, acid that can eat through dragon scales."

"Let us hope Bhrava Saruth's presence in the city keeps other dragons away." Sardelle patted Tolemek on the back and rose to her feet. "I need to do a little more work on you later, but the worst has been healed. I'm going down there to help. There are injured people still alive on that ironclad."

She picked her way up the hillside, using the glow of her soulblade to light the way.

Tolemek sighed and leaned against Cas, gazing down as the flames continued to burn on the sinking ship. These weren't the lights he had expected to watch tonight, but at least it should mean that nobody else would attempt to break into the castle anytime soon.

"Maybe I'll spend a little less time working going forward," Tolemek said.

"Have you found your assistant?"

"Not yet. But I'd like to be home more often to spend more time with you."

"I'd like that. I'd hate to go shopping for wedding presents alone."

"Then again, I do have a lot of work to do to get the lab fixed up again…"

She poked an elbow into his ribs. "You're not getting out of shopping with me."

He sighed and hugged her close, wishing they were gazing out on the stars and the city lights, not a burning ship and a burning cannery. He hoped that the future would be more peaceful than the last week—than the last *year*. At least for a while.

Chapter 19

The early afternoon sun gleamed on the calm waves lapping at the hull of the yacht, the yacht taking the wedding party to the newly named Temple Island. Ridge smirked, thinking of Bhrava Saruth's suggestions for names. Divine Destination. Palace of the God. The Dragon God's Sublime Residence. And the eponymous Bhrava Saruth Isle.

"Does that smirk mean you approve of our transportation?" Sardelle linked arms with him as she joined him at the railing near the bow of the yacht. She was even more beautiful than usual with carved bone clips holding her hair back from her face, her blue eyes almost matching the clear sky, and an elegant orange—or saffron, as Lilah had corrected him—dress that reminded him of autumn foliage and seemed a nod to the end of summer. "Or are you having irreverent thoughts?"

"You know me well, and you can read my mind. What do you think?"

"Irreverence. Even though I'm not attempting to read your thoughts right now."

"It's not really necessary, is it? I'm an open flight manual." Ridge patted her arm with his free hand.

"*I* certainly approve of our transportation. It was considerate of Angulus to let us use his yacht for this short trip. I must say, private sailing vessels have improved vastly since my day."

"Are you referring to the lavatory facilities?" He grinned, thinking of their recent discussion on modern conveniences, particularly indoor plumbing.

"Not specifically, but I assume they're wonderful. Did you know there are stabilizers built into the yacht to make the ride less bumpy on days when the waters are rough?"

"Fortunately, there's no need for them today." Ridge waved toward the clear blue sky. "It was kind of the gods—the real ones—to grant us good weather for the wedding."

That was never a guarantee along this section of the coast in Iskandia. That morning, a dense fog had socked in the city, and Ridge had worried it might turn into rain clouds, despite Phelistoth's promise that the sun was out above it. The dragon had been busy chugging coffee at the house, not flying high to personally check on meteorological events.

"Yes, and maybe with the dragon blood gone, nobody will have a reason to come looking for it, and the gods—and the Cofah—will grant us some peace for the next year. Or twenty." Sardelle rested a hand on her stomach.

Ridge assumed it would be some months before signs of the pregnancy were evident, but he smiled, already wondering what their child would be like.

"Peace for a while wouldn't be bad." He thought of Tolemek's question about what Ridge would actually do with himself if peace came to Iskandia. Ridge didn't truly wish to make soap or candles. But he could understand why Sardelle would want an uneventful future for the raising of their child. Or children? Would she want to have more than one? Ridge had lamented at times that he'd been an only child, especially since it hadn't always been safe in his neighborhood to go out and find playmates. He had always been delighted when the whole family had gotten together, giving him the chance to romp around with his cousins. "Though a pirate attack now and then would be all right. My pilots need more than practice maneuvers to stay at peak performance."

"Your *pilots*."

"Yes. I get plenty of practice doing my job of sitting at a desk and signing papers."

"How many times have you actually sat at your desk this past month? Between Tolemek's kidnapping, the dragon-blood incidents, and the building of the temple, I know you haven't been in your office very often."

"Enough to keep my penmanship skills honed." Ridge

mimicked writing in the air in front of them. "My name is long. It takes regular practice to be able to sign it."

"I've seen your signature, Ridge. It's a small R, a couple of bumps, and a large Z."

"But the Z has a little flourish. That adds to the difficulty level."

She shook her head but shifted to kiss him, so she couldn't have been too disappointed by his handwriting efforts.

"Aren't you supposed to wait until the priest waves his hands over your head to do that?" came a familiar grumble from behind them.

"Therrik." Ridge reluctantly released Sardelle and turned to face him, hoping Cousin Lilah would be with him. Alas, she was at another railing, chatting with Lieutenant Ahn and Tolemek about something. "How'd you get on this yacht? The regular guests are supposed to be on the ferries."

He waved toward the ships sailing out of the harbor behind the king's yacht, far more people than he had expected packing the decks. What if there wasn't enough cake for all those he had promised a slice to? He was positive he hadn't invited so many people, even allowing for the extra blank invitations he'd given to General Ort's daughter, Lieutenant Pimples, and Captain Kaika. Maybe someone had forged some invitations, though it was puzzling to imagine someone bothering. Unless they were dying to attend the unveiling of the structure on Temple Island.

Given the *size* of the structure, Ridge was surprised it wasn't visible from the capital. If only those pesky cliffs didn't get in the way…

Therrik lifted his chin. "You know there's nothing regular about me, Zirkander."

"I hope that statement doesn't relate to your latrine habits."

Sardelle swatted Ridge.

Therrik's eyes narrowed. "I miss the days when we were the same rank so I could shove you up against walls and mash your windpipe."

"You weren't supposed to do that when we were the same rank, either."

"Are you sure? It seemed right."

"Positive."

Therrik glanced down at a bracer on Ridge's wrist. "That doesn't look regulation."

Ridge wore his full dress uniform, including the pistol and saber, though he doubted he would have to stab or shoot anyone today. The army blue and gray didn't nod to autumn the way Sardelle's dress did, but she had promised him he was dashing in his uniform. The leather bracer did have a somewhat fall feel, and it was large enough that he'd been able to clasp it on the outside of his sleeve so people would see it.

"Sardelle gave that to me when she proposed. She made it. I forget the exact meaning, but I believe it means she's claimed me as hers." Ridge grinned at her.

"*She* proposed?" Therrik asked. "The *man* is supposed to propose."

"Only if you're a stuffy noble locked into a long-past century," Ridge said.

"Don't you know how to do anything right, Zirkander?"

"When someone deigns to marry you, you're welcome to do it your way."

Therrik looked over at Lilah, and Ridge winced. The last thing he'd wanted to do was put thoughts of marriage to his cousin in Therrik's mind. He kept waiting for Lilah to come to her senses and find a nice, polite academic to date.

I believe she's attracted to Therrik's warrior physique, Sardelle said into his mind, a smile flirting with her lips. *It can be hard to find sufficiently muscular academics.*

I'm sure there must be some out there. She needs to look harder.

Lilah must have noticed Therrik's attention because she smiled and waved at him across the deck. They held gazes for a long moment, ignoring the guests, servers, and royal bodyguards meandering between them.

Ridge wondered if he was too high ranking and mature to make a gagging noise.

I would, Jaxi spoke into his mind. *They're thinking about rutting. Make sure to stick your finger way back into your throat to ensure it sounds authentic.*

Thank you for the tip.

You're welcome.

"Aren't you allowed to modify the dress code somewhat as a general?" Sardelle asked. "I could have sworn that when we ran into that General Brastbore in the citadel, he was wearing a hat from his favorite hook ball team, and he proclaimed he'd created Alternate Hat Day."

"You can do days like that, yes. For your unit. Alas, Therrik isn't in my unit, so I can't make him wear bracers." Ridge, suspecting Therrik was too busy fantasizing about Lilah to hear him, added, "Or bracelets. Or other jewelry. Too bad. Some nice heart-shaped earrings might soften his flinty appearance."

"Doesn't your yap ever stop, Zirkander?" Therrik turned back to him, a scowl replacing his moon eyes.

"Rarely. Was there a reason you came over to listen to it?"

"Yeah. To congratulate you on your wedding. If you had to marry a witch, you picked a good one." He stuck out his hand.

Ridge glanced at Sardelle, hoping she wasn't offended. *Is he joking or being serious?*

I believe he's earnest in his congratulations. However dubious an addendum that was to them.

Huh.

"Figured I'd get that in before your legions of fans swarm you," Therrik added, glancing toward the trailing ferries.

"I'm convinced those people are just coming for the free food and to see the dragon temple, but thank you." Ridge clasped Therrik's hand. By silent agreement, they kept the handshake very brief.

"I still can't believe the king had a temple built for a dragon." Therrik curled his lip. "As if we want those dragons to stick around."

"A certain general talked me into the idea," Angulus said, walking toward them.

Therrik's eyebrows flew up, and he spun around and saluted. Ridge didn't think he'd ever seen anyone sneak up on the colonel or catch him by surprise. It was probably just because so many people were wandering around on the yacht.

"This particular dragon *has* been helpful." Angulus stopped in front of their group, two of his bodyguards alert just behind him.

Maybe it was Ridge's imagination, but they seemed extra diligent ever since he and Angulus had been trapped in his office without any of them. The captain of the guard had been chagrined to learn that Angulus had been forced to wield a pickaxe to escape, even if Angulus himself had appeared proud of the blister the work had earned him.

"He healed a pilot," Angulus added, "destroyed a shaman's familiar, and offered me a secret spot in his temple as a place to store the dragon blood. A shame the cargo didn't actually make it there."

So *that* was where the blood had been heading. Huh.

"Yes, Sire," Therrik said. "I'm sure I was mistaken. Building a, uh, structure for a dragon is perfectly reasonable."

"Shouldn't you yell a warning to the people behind you when you back up that quickly?" Ridge muttered.

Sardelle swatted him again. Angulus raised an eyebrow in his direction.

"You're welcome to call it a residence, Therrik," Angulus said. "That's how Zirkander sold me on it."

"How about a stable?" Therrik asked.

"Greetings, human friends," came a cheerful voice as the human-formed Bhrava Saruth ambled toward them wearing his flowing *kryka*, a loose vest, and more necklaces than should be legal.

He spread his arms as he approached, displaying tufts of blond armpit hair. Something about a dragon's transformation into a human being so complete that armpit hair was included flustered Ridge. Or maybe it was that Bhrava Saruth deemed clothing that revealed such hair appropriate for a wedding.

"Is this not a lovely day to celebrate the opening of my temple?" Bhrava Saruth lowered his arms. Thankfully. He smiled at them all, though his eyelids shivered as he met Therrik's gaze, and Ridge suspected he'd heard—or sensed—that stable comment. "I have invited any humans who seek healing or blessing to come today."

"During the wedding?" Angulus asked.

Ridge groaned silently and looked at Sardelle. *Is that why all those people we don't know are coming?*

Hm. She tapped her chin and gazed back at the ferries. *A few, perhaps. But my understanding is that your wedding has been deemed the social event of the season.*

Our wedding. And that can't be possible. Unless it's been an extremely slow season.

You underestimate the interest the Iskandian people, especially those in the capital, have in you. They think of you as their hero. I understand there's talk of a statue being erected, though oddly, Angulus hasn't signed off on it yet.

A statue? That's even crazier than a temple. I don't want a statue. Ridge wouldn't mind seeing a statue of one of the original models of fliers, perhaps with an educational plaque underneath, in a prominent location in the city—right now, people had to go to the flight museum to learn about the history of the craft—but definitely not one of him.

Statues aren't about the person represented; they're about the dreams and ideals of those who put them up.

Ridge made the face that comment deserved.

"I can do the blessings before the ceremony," Bhrava Saruth said. "There will be festivities before my high priestess and her mate join, yes?"

Ridge didn't know what to think when nobody batted an eye at the dragon's reference to Sardelle as his high priestess. Even she seemed bland and almost accepting of the title these days.

"That will be an excellent time for people to come worship me and see my throne. Do you think they're bringing offerings?" Bhrava Saruth rose on tiptoes to peer past Angulus's shoulder and toward the ferries.

"*Throne?*" Therrik asked.

Angulus dropped his face in his hand, maybe already regretting that he'd donated land for the temple. Residence. Stable.

"It is a marvelous *temple,* fully furnished with divinely approved—and dragon-sized—seating areas similar to nests."

Bhrava Saruth smiled at Ridge, probably reading his thoughts. "Though I do intend to take alternate forms when I bless my worshippers. This makes them less nervous."

Ridge imagined a ferret on a throne rising on its hind legs and waving its paws as it offered blessings.

"I must go and prepare for the arrival of the guests." Bhrava Saruth clapped his hands together, then leaped onto the railing, sprang away from the yacht, and switched into his dragon form while airborne. He flapped his wings and flew north faster than the ships were traveling, then banked and disappeared into the gap in the cliffs leading to his little cove.

"Your wedding is going to be weird, Zirkander," Therrik said.

"Your bluntness refreshes like a spring… flood."

"I'll show you what a wedding is supposed to be like when I get married. Pardon me, Sire." He bowed to Angulus, then headed over to Lilah.

"*When?*" Ridge gripped the railing for support. Therrik was assuming that would happen?

You seem to have put him in the mood for pledging his eternal bond—and virile manhood—to Lilah, Jaxi observed.

His virile what? He's not going to propose to her now, is he? Ridge stepped away from the railing, barely aware that Angulus was talking.

Relax, hero. He's just starting to think about how he might go about proposing. Doing it on a boat heading out to a fake god's temple isn't his idea of romantic.

I'm terrified to imagine what his idea of romantic is.

Yours was proposing from on top of a giant rock.

Crazy Canyon is known around the world for its natural sandstone arches. They're geological marvels.

Uh huh. Trust me. Therrik can't do any worse.

Angulus cleared his throat. "Zirkander, are you listening to me?"

"That's the expression he gets on his face when he's chatting telepathically with Jaxi, Sire," Sardelle said.

"He looks constipated."

"That sounds about right."

Ridge tore his gaze from Therrik's back, though he didn't want to. He wanted to observe the man to make sure he didn't drop down to one knee and pull out a promise necklace.

I assure you that he isn't carrying, holding, or wearing any jewelry, Jaxi said. *Bhrava Saruth already fulfilled the maximum allotment of necklaces allowed on board when he visited the yacht.*

"I asked if you were nervous, Ridge," Angulus said dryly, meeting Sardelle's gaze.

"About my cousin's future? A little, Sire."

Angulus's brow furrowed. Ridge assumed he hadn't heard about Therrik's love life. Or didn't care. Ridge would like to not care as well, but as long as his family was involved...

"About the wedding," Angulus said.

"Oh! I am a little concerned about the venue and the dragon that just flew ahead to prepare his throne, but I'm not nervous about marrying Sardelle." Ridge gripped her hand. "Especially now that my mother has decided she will make an acceptable daughter-in-law and future mother to her grandchildren. I do thank you for talking to Mom, Sire."

"You're welcome, though I believe Sardelle healing her of a medical condition had more to do with your mother coming around."

"Possibly. It's difficult to dislike someone who saves your life from a horrible disease."

"Or a horrible dragon," Angulus said. "Just ask Therrik. He was forced to stop calling Sardelle names after that."

"Mostly," Sardelle murmured.

He's not still calling you a witch behind my back, is he? Ridge asked silently, assuming she was monitoring him.

Not often. Lilah punches him when he does.

She's a good cousin.

Yes, I like her. We have many common interests. That's why I asked her to be one of my kin watchers, even though that's frowned upon, inviting someone from the groom's family to inspect him.

Yes, especially when she might give a less than stellar review of my attributes. Ridge smirked. He might have objected to Lilah as one of Sardelle's kin watchers, but most of the women that she had come to know well in the months since she'd joined him in this time were either his relatives or his officers. He wished her family were still alive so she could have invited them.

He supposed Lilah would do a better job of uttering the lines than Tylie—he knew Sardelle had been thinking of her at one point. The last he'd seen Tylie, her sandals had disappeared—again—and she had been leaning over the railing, staring blankly into the water.

Actually, she was speaking with dolphins, Jaxi said.

Ah. Is it as fraught as speaking with dragons?

You would have to ask her, but they seem to be amenable creatures.

"It looks like we'll arrive shortly." Angulus nodded toward the opening in the cliffs ahead without commenting on the distracted—or constipated—expressions of all the people engaging in telepathic communication around him.

"Excellent." Ridge turned toward the railing and rested a hand on Sardelle's back as she also turned. A flutter teased his stomach. Maybe he *was* nervous.

"I look forward to seeing the venue," she said as Angulus turned to talk to the skipper. "I've heard that most brides see and approve of the event space *before* the day of the wedding."

"The finishing touches were still being, er, finished yesterday."

"Is that supposed to make me more nervous? Or less?"

"I—" Ridge placed a hand on his chest, "—would have been perfectly happy having this at home in the yard as we originally planned. You and my mother were the ones to decide the area wasn't suitable."

"That's because more and more people kept getting invited. Our yard isn't *that* large."

"People could have flowed out into the trees and over to the land by the pond. Nobody uses those areas except for us, anyway."

"The land by the pond is all mud and reeds. Reeds coming up out of mud."

"Clearly, we would have put the lesser guests out there." Ridge looked over his shoulder at Therrik.

Sardelle shoved her shoulder against him. "He's too heavy. He would have sunk into the mud."

"Darn."

***

Sardelle gripped Ridge's arm as the king's yacht swung into the little cove, curious to see what the temple looked like. She vaguely remembered flying over this island on journeys up the coast but was fairly certain it had only been a lump of stone a couple of square miles in size.

Gasps of surprise mingled with oooohs as the temple came into view. Sardelle blinked up at columns that stretched up to a massive slanted slab of a ceiling half as high as the surrounding cliffs. Sixty feet? Seventy? It was high enough that a dragon could fly straight in between the widely spaced columns without having to draw in his wings. Maybe that had been the point, though all she could think was that it was gargantuan for those with human proportions. Most of the inside stood empty, but rooms with ceilings of more modest heights lined the sides of the grand entryway.

The temple as a whole took up the entire front half of the island, which had been leveled recently, with wide marble steps leading up from a newly installed docking area. One that could easily accommodate a dozen ships. Bhrava Saruth must have been expecting hordes of people to visit him.

"I still can't believe you managed to get that built in *weeks*, Zirkander," Angulus said, standing with the yacht's skipper a few feet behind them. "Things like that took lifetimes to build back in the era when slaves pulled slabs of rock out of quarries and across the desert on logs."

"Well, this is the modern era, Sire," Ridge said over his shoulder. "Also, Bhrava Saruth was quite willing to exert some effort to help with the construction. We used him to lift the heavy things. He's more efficient than slaves. Doesn't necessarily eat less."

"What would I have to feed him to get him to repair the hole in my office wall?"

"That hasn't been done yet? Sire, you're the king."

"You noticed. Excellent."

"What I mean is, how can anyone be prioritized above you?"

Angulus sighed. "It's not me. It's the historical society that always gets so worried about renovations to their aged and venerable castle."

"Hasn't most of it been destroyed by enemies at this point?" Ridge asked. "Are there really any stones in it that are more than fifty years old?"

Sardelle sensed Angulus narrowing his eyes without looking. She thought about kicking Ridge's foot with the pointed toe of her shoe, but he'd polished his boots for this. It would be a sartorial crime to sully them.

It's not too late for him to back out as kin watcher, she told him silently, knowing how much it had meant for Ridge to ask Angulus and have him agree. *Better be nice.*

"Do you want me to get the same architect to come to the castle and take a look, Sire?" Ridge asked.

"Will I have to pay her in beer?"

"I think professionals prefer payment in nucros. With a beer bonus." Ridge turned back, giving Sardelle a squeeze, as if to ask if he'd been nice enough.

She leaned on his arm as the yacht came around the island to head in to the dock, bringing more of the interior of the temple into view. The very colorful interior of the temple. All manner of trellises and gazebos covered with flower arrangements had been brought in.

"That's a *lot* of flowers," Ridge said.

"Was that Bhrava Saruth's work? Or Fern's?"

"They weren't there yesterday. I don't think Bhrava Saruth is that aware of the existence of flowers. He was more concerned that a huge throne carved from marble be installed."

"She must be feeling a lot better if she arranged all that." Sardelle glanced at the sole ship currently tied at the docks, a barge that would have been capable of bringing in all the woodwork and flowers. Not to mention the tables that the crew were carrying off it now. A few people in cooks' whites waited on the deck for their turn to move things—Sardelle recognized the name of the catering company they had chosen on the aprons tied about their waists.

"Nothing could energize her more than being in charge of her only son's wedding." Ridge lowered his voice and leaned his temple against hers. "I really appreciate you taking care of her. I thought she just had a cold. I didn't know mushrooms were growing in her lungs."

"Fungi," Sardelle corrected, bemused at the notion of toadstools sprouting up inside of human organs.

"Aren't mushrooms fungi?"

"All mushrooms are fungi, yes, but not all fungi are mushrooms."

"I love it when you say smart sciency things to me."

"I love how impressed you are by basic biology."

"We're clearly made for each other."

I may gag, Jaxi announced.

I thought you did that earlier when Vann was having snuggly thoughts toward Lilah. Sardelle may have eavesdropped on Jaxi's conversation with Ridge.

I did. I have excellent gag reflexes. I can gag all day. Look, you're making the king uncomfortable with your gooey talk.

Sardelle leaned away from Ridge to look back, mildly concerned Angulus truly *might* be uncomfortable.

But he wasn't even looking at them. He was gazing toward the bow of the yacht. Admiring the splendor—or at least massiveness—of the temple? Ah, no. His gaze had locked onto the person walking toward them. Captain Kaika.

The last Sardelle had spoken with her, she had been debating between wearing her army uniform to the wedding or something "fun and slinky." She'd said she would let the weather decide, since the army uniforms were "itchy when hot."

She wore a silvery-blue dress that flowed from her shoulders down to her muscled calves while hugging enough of her body in between to turn eyes. Her form was more athletic than voluptuous, but several male sets of eyes followed her stroll toward Angulus—including his. He lifted an arm, and she ambled up to his side for a hug and to give him a butt pat.

Sardelle was surprised at the open display of affection, since, as far as she knew, they were still keeping their relationship quiet. But then, this was his yacht, and he had only invited a couple of dozen people on board, those close to him and to Ridge and Sardelle. Perhaps there would be less hugging once they were on land. Or perhaps not. Weddings tended to put people in the mood for love. Everyone except soulblades.

I can't help it that I have taste. I am pleased, however, that you and your soul snozzle are getting married.

Thank you.

And that you chose a dress that will complement me nicely when I start glowing a pale blue.

You're going to glow for us? Should we feel honored?

Obviously. I'll wait until the priest officially marries you, and then I've got some fireworks planned. Taddy is going to help.

Oh? A hint of wariness crept into Sardelle as she looked toward Tylie's spot—she'd switched from communing with dolphins to chatting with a seagull perched on the railing next to her. She wore one of her usual cotton dresses, this one not splattered with paint, and had Wreltad's scabbard slung over her back on a strap. *Should I be worried? You're not going to try to blow off the roof, are you?*

It would take more than the power of two soulblades to budge that roof. It must weight fifty tons. Given time, I could melt it...

Not necessary. I'm sure Bhrava Saruth wants his human friends to be protected from the rain when they visit.

It's cute when you insist on calling them friends instead of followers.

I endeavor to be cute, Sardelle replied.

It's even better when Ridge calls it a residence instead of a temple. I like Therrik's label even better.

A stable?

Indeed.

You have not stepped onto my island yet, high priestess, Bhrava Saruth's voice boomed in her mind, *and already, I can hear the mouthiness of your sword.*

Considering dragons have no ears, he can hear a lot from very far away, Jaxi observed.

I'm sorry she hasn't yet come around to worshipping you, Bhrava Saruth, Sardelle said. *One day, when you finally win her over, it will be a great triumph.*

This is true. The other soulblade has already agreed to worship me.

What? Jaxi asked. *Taddy, that's not true, is it?*

I agreed that he was a magnificent dragon, Wreltad spoke into Sardelle's mind. *It seemed wise.*

You're not the fearless warrior you think you are if a little dragon worries you.

He's a large dragon. And you're only being snippy because the fireworks display I have planned is grander than what you've been thinking of.

You don't know my thoughts, Taddy. I only told you my fake *plan. Because I knew you would turn it into a competition.*

"Sardelle?" Ridge extended a hand toward the gangplank where their kin watchers had already filed off and onto the docks.

"I'm ready." She walked with him. "But I should warn you that there may be explosions after our kiss."

"Naturally." He winked at her.

"I mean from external sources."

"Oh? I didn't see any place for Captain Kaika to smuggle explosives in that dress of hers, but I also didn't search her purse. I assumed the king's guards would handle that."

"The soulblades are planning… It sounds like it's turning into a competition."

"Ah. Should we be flattered to know they care enough to try?"

"I don't think so." Sardelle went ahead on the gangplank, following the rest of the guests, people gawking as they approached the temple. It was even larger up close.

"You're sure?"

"I believe they're using us as an excuse for showmanship."

Really, Sardelle. You know me better than that.

You're scheming something new right now, aren't you?

Maybe.

"Will it top my mother's flower displays?" Ridge waved to Fern, who stood on the steps of the temple, pointing servers with platters toward tables.

"It may *burn* your mother's displays."

"Flowers are known to be disposable pleasures."

"Not *instantly* disposable. You may be thinking of tarts." Sardelle released Ridge's arm and nodded to Fern. "I'm going to go check on your mother. Make sure she's doing all right."

"I suspect she'll complain, tell you how stressed she is, and also be completely self-satisfied and pleased. I... Hm, I better go check on that development."

They had reached the walkway leading from the docks up to the temple steps, and Ridge was pointing to a table at the top of those steps and off to one side. More specifically, he pointed to Lieutenants Duck and Pimples, who were holding a box and arguing with one of the king's bodyguards. All manner of wrapped boxes and bags sat on the table. Wedding presents, Sardelle presumed. The bodyguard was holding his hand up, preventing the lieutenants from placing their box on the table. Well, whatever dubious thing was in there, the box was too small for it to be furniture.

"Yes, those are your men," she said. "You should be able to handle anything they might have brought."

"My men have interesting tastes."

"I never would have guessed."

Sardelle climbed the steps and went to the left, toward Fern, as Ridge walked toward Duck and Pimples, a slightly worried crease to his brow. She hoped they hadn't brought something living. As much as she'd appreciated the sentiment behind the kitten that Captain Kaika had brought as a gift earlier in the summer, their house was awfully busy these days with furred, feathered, and scaled creatures coming through, some as permanent residents, some as Tylie's woodland friends. Some as dragons in unexpected forms.

"Sardelle," Fern exclaimed, spotting her from several paces away, smiling and lifting her hands.

Sardelle suspected nothing would get past her today. As she directed people here and there, she was akin to a squadron commander directing her pilots into battle.

"Good afternoon, Fern," Sardelle said, bowing her head.

Fern clasped her hands. "You're so beautiful in that dress. I must admit, I was worried when my illness—thank you for making me that tea and helping me feel better—prevented me from joining you to shop for it, especially when I heard that some of Ridge's officers accompanied you." She shook her head, the most aghast expression on her face. "I feared they were some of the same ones that picked out that dreadful couch."

"Actually, I believe they had that couch handmade to their specifications."

"That doesn't make me feel better, Sardelle."

"But no, I'm positive that Cas—Lieutenant Ahn—had little to do with that couch. I don't think Kaika did, either, since she's not one of his pilots."

"Mm, and Lilah went with you also, didn't she? I must say her tastes run toward the staid and academic, don't they? I just wasn't sure. But this is a fabulous dress. So elegant!"

"Thank you. Lady Masonwood picked it out for me. She has a shop in town."

"Oh yes, I've heard of it. But her clothing is so expensive, dear. However did you manage… Do witches make a lot of money?" Her aghast expression turned to one of puzzlement.

"Not as a general rule." Sardelle decided not to correct the witch usage. She was pleased Fern was back to being warm and enthusiastic toward her. "Unless they're entrepreneurial. And then there are of course ways to use one's talents. In this case, Lady Masonwood gave me a deep discount in exchange for wedding invitations. I believe I saw her coming out on the king's yacht."

"The king's here now, isn't he? I better go greet him. And nobles are coming too?" Fern gripped Sardelle's arm. "I must say that it's daunting interacting with these people." She glanced over Sardelle's shoulder and pointed at a young caterer bearing casks labeled as mead and wine. "No, no, not there. *There.*"

Sardelle couldn't imagine anything would daunt Fern for long today.

"And what is going on at that gift table now?" Fern pursed her lips, her gaze shifting focus to where Ridge had joined Duck and

Pimples and the bodyguard in a discussion about the box. "Some of the king's men arrived early and have been checking the packages to make sure no weapons or suspicious substances join the collection on the table. I certainly hope nobody is planning to use your wedding as a venue for attempting an assassination of the king. That would be completely unacceptable."

"I agree with that." Sardelle cocked an eyebrow as guests from the first ferry disembarked, including Cas's assassin father, Ahnsung. Ridge *had* invited him, she reminded herself.

A troupe of musicians started playing from within the temple.

"Oh no. They're going out of order. I need to talk to them." Fern released Sardelle's arm with a pat and said, "You look fabulous. And so does Ridge. Enjoy yourselves."

She hastened into the interior, waving her hands as she approached the musicians.

"How is she doing?" Lilah asked, coming over to join Sardelle while Therrik strode to the gift table carrying a small box.

Sardelle's mind boggled at the idea of him giving her and Ridge a gift. She assumed Lilah had picked it out and simply put his name on the card.

"She seems healthy and vibrant," Sardelle said.

"That's good. My mother would wither up into a husk if I asked her to plan my wedding. My late husband's aunt and mother handled most of the planning for ours."

Sardelle thought about asking her if she would rely on some relative of Therrik's if they were to get married. She'd heard that his parents were long gone. But she decided not to bring that up—Ridge would have a fit if she asked encouraging questions about that union.

"Ours was much smaller than this though," Lilah said. "I hardly know any of these people. This is almost a..."

The musicians started up again, this time playing a slightly different song. Sardelle could barely tell the difference and assumed it was the work of the same composer.

"Circus?" Sardelle asked.

"Well, festival, at least."

It is entertaining, Jaxi said. *At least so far. I'm dying to see if the bodyguard allows the ticking box to go onto the gift table.*

Duck and Pimples' gift? It's ticking?

Actually, I gather that's Duck's gift. Pimples joined in with Beeline and Crash and got Ridge—technically, both of you—a subscription to a cheese-of-the-month club.

If we're being technical, that sounds like a gift for Phelistoth.

Ridge likes cheese.

Yes, but he makes the mistake of bringing the cheese he buys home where dragons can find it. What's Duck's gift? Have you snooped?

Sardelle supposed she should wait to be surprised, but she wasn't sure she *wanted* to be surprised in this instance. Earlier in the summer, she had been glad she'd had some warning in regard to the couch. If she'd had to wait for it to be unveiled, she might have fainted in front of everyone.

I don't snoop. I observe.

Through walls and boxes and other opaque structures.

It's not my fault I'm extremely qualified to observe. To partially assuage your curiosity, I shall let you know that it's immature and gross. Is it comforting to know that the person who thought such a thing would make a good wedding gift is one of those responsible for defending the country from enemy incursions?

Not comforting, no, but not that surprising.

Alas, the non-magical people around will have to remain in the dark unless they open it up. Which Duck is forbidding. The king's bodyguard is concerned that it might be a bomb.

"It's less alarming than I expected," Lilah said.

"Duck's gift?" Sardelle asked before realizing Lilah couldn't—shouldn't—know anything about that.

"The temple. I was expecting something garish, and while it's not exactly modest or modern, it's vaguely appealing. Karudian-inspired, unless I miss my guess. It looks like a new version of one of the three-thousand-year-old temples the Karudians once built to honor what they believed were dragon gods. I suppose the architect knew that history and thought it would be appropriate."

"I think Bhrava Saruth just liked the columns." Sardelle decided not to mention the throne, especially since she hadn't seen it herself yet.

"They are lovely columns." Lilah quirked one corner of her mouth. "Will you be expected to perform rites out here? As a dragon's high priestess."

"I hope not. It's not that conveniently located to the house."

"That being your *only* objection, of course."

"Of course."

Over here, human visitors, Bhrava Saruth's voice sounded in Sardelle's mind. In everybody's mind, judging by all the people who looked into the interior. *I have blessings to share.*

The dragon had abandoned his human form in favor of his natural one, which was now blocking the view of the musicians. Fortunately, the temple was spacious enough that people wouldn't struggle to get around him. Fern did prop her fists on her hips and glare at the tail sprawled through one of her flower arrangements.

More and more people did filter into the temple, some to approach Bhrava Saruth with awe, but most to head for the refreshments stand. The mead looked to be the preferred beverage, two to one over the wine.

"Is that dragon driving people to drink?" Lilah asked.

"I haven't noticed that people need reasons to enjoy free alcohol."

"This is true. Now I see why so many people wanted to come. It has nothing to do with my cousin's status as a legend."

Sardelle didn't comment on the ever so slight hint of irritation in Lilah's voice at the last sentence. It hadn't taken her long to realize that Lilah held a seed of bitterness for Ridge, for the fame he'd achieved through flying and shooting things. She'd always thought that she, with her fifty-odd academic papers published in respected journals, would be the first one in the family to make something of herself.

Actually, I believe they came for the dragon-shaped soaps, Jaxi said.

Hm?

The gift-basket giver hasn't made his way to you yet, but Fern has put together soap, candle, and weird scrubby bathing sponges for everyone.

Goodness, for everyone? Sardelle wondered if Bhrava Saruth's blessing had bestowed some extra vitality on the woman. She also wondered what Angulus would think about receiving a basket of bath products.

Well, presumably not you and Ridge.

There must be two hundred people filing off those ferries.

More. Some of the ferries are heading back to collect another batch of people. I believe a lot of the people who received invitations thought that meant they could bring their friends, families, and co-workers too.

"Ms. Terushan?" a man asked.

Sardelle turned and found a man she'd only met briefly standing before her in red and black robes, a priest of the Order of Nendear. He was the one who would bless the wedding and also officiate over it, recording the details of the marriage in the appropriate city logbooks. For some weddings, there were two different people for the job, but this priest could apparently do both. General Ort had recommended the man, who had overseen one of his daughter's marriages the year before.

"Yes, Priest Dimonon. It's good of you to come." Sardelle offered her hand.

He clasped it briefly, but his gaze drifted toward the columns and the high roof of the temple towering next to them. His expression was a touch dyspeptic. "I must admit I have a few reservations about this. When I originally agreed to officiate over your wedding, I was told it would be outdoors at a private residence, not at a… a temple to some fat faux god."

"If it helps, Ridge refers to it as the dragon's residence."

And Therrik calls it a dragon stable, Jaxi put in.

Sardelle assumed the irreverent thought was just for her, but the priest stumbled back and clutched his chest.

"Who was *that?*"

Jaxi! You don't speak to strangers unless it's an emergency.

It is *an emergency. This pompous priest is thinking of backing out. If he does, Bhrava Saruth will have to marry you, and I don't think that will count in the eyes of the country. I'll straighten this fellow out. Oh, wait. I have a better idea.*

"We all know he's not truly a god, Priest Dimonon," Sardelle said, hoping to sway the man on her own before Jaxi did anything… drastic.

"Nevertheless," the priest said, looking around nervously, "it's highly unorthodox and worse, I find it blasphemous. I—"

"Is there a problem over here?" Angulus asked in his deep authoritative voice as he walked up behind the man.

Not for long, Jaxi thought smugly, and Sardelle realized she must have asked Angulus to come over.

Sardelle was tempted to bury her face in her hand. Or maybe bury her whole body under that gift table. Too bad it would likely get her dress dirty.

The priest turned, a surly curl to his lip, and Sardelle thought he would argue with Angulus. But he must not have recognized the voice. His eyebrows flew up, and he dropped to his knee and bowed his head.

"Sire, I am your humble servant, most eager to serve the crown."

See? Jaxi thought.

"Then you'll certainly wish to preside over this wedding between an officer who's risked his life countless times to save Iskandia and a woman who has done the same on numerous occasions this past year. She is a friend to the country and to me."

The speech warmed Sardelle's heart, even if Jaxi had told him to come over and give it.

Actually, I told him to come over and wring the priest's neck until he agreed to do his job. He's extemporizing.

"Sire, I don't object to their union. I promise you. It's simply this unholy place. That *dragon*—" the priest flung his robed arm toward Bhrava Saruth, "—is a charlatan. Surely, you agree that he is not a god, not like Dlemnor or Nendear, whom I faithfully serve."

"I agree he's not a god." Angulus didn't mention what he thought of the other gods in the pantheon. "But he, too, has risked his life for Iskandia. We owe him much. Thus, we are humoring him."

Sardelle suspected those were royal *we's* and that the priest should feel himself included in them.

"But Sire, what will people think? It's been renamed Temple Island according to the newspapers. Some of the less educated of your subjects might be fooled and come out here to see him instead of going to a proper temple in town. Such as Mangrith Sanctuary." He touched his chest, making it clear that was his place of employment.

"That should be good for you," Ridge said, ambling up beside Angulus. He must have caught the gist of the conversation. "Less work. Shorter hours. Your life is about to get fantastic, Priest Dimonon." Ridge gave the man his best charming grin, even if the words themselves were sarcastic rather than charming.

Angulus gave him a flat you're-not-helping look.

"Sir," the priest said. "Sire. I'm happy to spend long hours at the temple to serve my flock. I—"

"If it helps," Ridge said, "we're not actually having the wedding *inside* the temple. The builders cleared a big flat lot in the back while they were working, and since it's sunny, my mother had the help set all the chairs up out there."

"Not inside the temple?" The priest peered through the massive open area, past the columns in the back, and toward the sunny area of raked gravel that was indeed full of rows of chairs.

"Nope. We'll be out there where Nendear can see us, and we'll pray He shines His divine light upon us. Come, let me show you the area." Ridge winked at Sardelle and draped an arm over the priest's shoulders. "Oh, and the mead station is on the way. Priests are allowed to drink mead, aren't they?"

"It's considered a holy beverage by four of the seven gods, yes. Because it comes from honey from bees, and bees are mentioned specifically in the scriptures as divine insects."

"Perfect. You must be parched after the long ride out here." Ridge guided the priest toward the beverage tables—tables set up inside the temple—but the man had lost his fight. If not forgotten about it. He and Ridge were still talking about how holy bees and mead were when they wandered out of earshot.

"Sardelle," Lilah said. "Is it just me, or does it look like my cousin is taking the priest who's going to officiate over your wedding off to get sloshed?"

It can only improve his personality, Jaxi said.

Lilah blinked, apparently hearing the comment, and Angulus did too. Then he snorted. Jaxi had communicated with him before. Sardelle couldn't remember if Lilah had experienced her telepathic wit yet.

"I'm trying to decide," Angulus said, "if I should take it as a slight to my manhood that Zirkander is better at convincing people to do things than I am."

"Definitely not, Sire," Lilah said. "It's not your fault he gets everyone around him drunk in order to convince them that he's charming."

"You heard about how the dragon temple came together, did you?" Sardelle smiled at her.

"It's a little alarming how much of my kingdom wants to drink with him," Angulus said. "I'm afraid that if I tried his tactic, I'd be disappointed to learn that people are less eager to imbibe in my presence."

"Only because they want you to think well of them, Sire," Lilah said. "They want to be buddies with Ridge."

Judging by the wry twist to Angulus's lips, Lilah wasn't doing a good job of bolstering him.

"Ah well," Angulus said. "There's no point in envying a man, right? The best thing for me to do would be to put his pilot charms to use for my own good."

"In what manner?" Sardelle worried that Angulus had some plan in mind that would involve Ridge being kept in the city for extra hours of work. He was already scarce at home, and Sardelle wanted to drag him off for a honeymoon for a few days, even if it only meant going to his little cabin on the lake.

"There's a hole in the wall of my office that I need repaired. At this point, I wouldn't even care if the people hammering the wood and laying the plaster were drunk." Angulus looked toward the stairs and caught sight of Tolemek and Cas heading toward the gift table, Tolemek in a sedate suit and Cas in her dress army uniform. "Dr. Targoson?"

Tolemek and Cas shifted their paths to join them, Cas saluting to Angulus and Tolemek bowing to him.

"Has your lab been sufficiently repaired?" Angulus asked.

"Repairs and cleaning are underway, Sire."

"How long before you can resume fulfilling orders?"

"Next week, most certainly."

"Excellent. I regret the loss of the dragon blood, but at least enemies shouldn't have any reason to target you going forward."

"Hm," Tolemek said. "Fewer reasons, perhaps."

Angulus snorted. "I'll give you that, but let us hope the rest of the year will be peaceful."

"I'm amenable to that, Sire."

"And about those malleable bombs you started working on. Were the prototypes lost or…" Angulus trailed off as he spotted Kaika approaching. "Are you coming to chastise me again for talking about work at a social event?" he asked her.

"No, because this isn't *boring* work." Kaika winked at Cas and nodded at Tolemek, Sardelle, and Lilah. "I want to hear about my prototype bombs."

"Perhaps I'll step away to get some of that mead," Lilah murmured.

"Me too," Cas said, drawing away from Tolemek as he launched into an explanation of the substances and materials he would need to recreate what he had been working on when he had been kidnapped.

Sardelle murmured a quiet parting and headed off with them.

"Ms. Sardelle," came a genteel call from the refreshment table. Lady Masonwood stood there with a stuffy-looking gentleman about her age on her arm, his gaze toward the high ceiling.

Sardelle hadn't noticed the gold dragon painted up there when she had been outside. He was standing on a snowy mountain peak, his wings spread wide, as he surveyed the timber and farmlands of Iskandia stretching out below him. She wondered if Bhrava Saruth had magically drawn that himself or if Ridge had brought in a drunken mural artist willing to work for free.

I think the whole temple was constructed for free, Jaxi thought as Sardelle walked toward Lady Masonwood, figuring she should thank her again for the deal on the dress. *Ridge convinced everyone to work for beer and godly love.*

For someone who complains about paperwork and any tasks that don't involve cockpits, he's actually quite efficient at getting things done, Sardelle thought.

Well, he was Bhrava Saruth's first worshipper in this time. It's good that he did a good job for his god.

"You look fabulous today, Ms. Sardelle," Lady Masonwood said, then smiled serenely. "I refer to all of you, not simply that wonderful garment. Or should I call you Mrs. Zirkander, now?"

"I believe we have about an hour until that's official." A flutter of anticipation teased Sardelle's belly as she imagined being called that from here on out.

"Ah, certainly. This is my gentleman friend, Lord Tibby Eagledraw."

Tibby? Jaxi snickered into Sardelle's mind. *Is that a popular name these days? I would have mocked a nobleman named that in my time.*

He met Sardelle's eyes and nodded, though it had a superior aloofness to it. "This is an interesting wedding venue," he said.

"It was suitably spacious for our needs, and history tells us that having your wedding overseen by a dragon ensures a lucky future. Assuming it's not an enemy dragon breathing fire on everyone."

Eagledraw blinked a few times, not seeming to know what to make of Sardelle's humor. Though it wasn't exactly humor. That bit about the desirability of dragons at weddings *was* in several history books, from back during the dragon-rider era when Iskandia had claimed numerous dragons as allies.

"Dragon fire would ruin your dress," Lady Masonwood said, "so you should avoid it."

"Exactly my thought."

"While my gentleman friend was admiring the artwork, I was trying to figure out who that person over there hiding in the rocks is." Masonwood pointed toward the grounds out front and past the corner of the temple.

Sardelle turned, her stomach clenching as she imagined some Cofah or Dakrovian spy here to report back on the wedding. Or worse, plant an explosive or some other sabotage.

She glimpsed a woman with dark hair, but the individual crouched out of sight behind a boulder before Sardelle could identify her or guess which nation she came from.

She's not Cofah, Jaxi said. *Or Dakrovian. I believe... Oh yes, that's why she's slightly familiar.*

Are you intentionally keeping me in suspense, Jaxi?

Sardelle reached out with her senses and could tell the woman hiding there hoped she hadn't been seen, but there was nothing familiar about her aura.

She's the journalist that was harassing Ridge and writing articles about you controlling him, Jaxi informed her. *I recognize her from Ridge's thoughts. Sadly, it looks like she was able to escape from the soldiers he requested hold her as a potential spy. I guess it should have been apparent that she was back at work when she penned that ode to Bhrava Saruth.*

It would be immature of me to do something mischievous to her, wouldn't it? Sardelle asked.

Yes, but I would delight in it. You aren't immature nearly often enough. You're not even a century old yet, Sardelle. Your maturity is terribly lamentable.

"Looks like a wedding crasher who doesn't have an invitation," Masonwood said. "Perhaps security should be alerted."

"Commoners don't *have* security men, dear," Eagledraw whispered. "Those are the king's guards that you've seen around."

"No security at all? How startling."

I can be security. Jaxi cackled a little. *Unless you have plans, Sardelle. I don't want to trample on your attempts at immaturity.*

Bhrava Saruth? Sardelle asked the dragon, who was lounging on his back with someone's children stroking his scales. Future worshippers, no doubt. *Are you aware that uninvited guests are spying on your temple?*

What?

Sardelle did the mental equivalent of pointing at the hiding woman. She must have guessed that she'd been spotted because she was keeping her head down and moving toward another clump of boulders.

Ah, that woman from the newspaper, yes? Bhrava Saruth asked. *Did you know that she was on the verge of releasing an article about how ridiculous it was that this temple was being built to honor me? That it was a waste of the king's land and resources, and that the people should revolt?*

Odd, that's not how the article read when we saw it.

No, of course not. I revised it before it went into that printing contraption. You do not think she found out, do you? Is she here to enact some inimical revenge?

Well, I'm sure she noticed the next morning that it wasn't quite what she wrote. Sardelle did not comment on the revenge plot. She suspected the journalist simply wanted juicy tidbits for the next day's newspaper.

I see in her mind that she wishes to write slanderous stories about my high priestess and *my temple. This cannot be permitted.*

A squawk came from the direction of the boulders. A few people heard and looked over in time to see the woman plucked from her hiding spot with a pen and journal clenched in her hand. She soon dropped the items. She was too busy flailing and screaming as she was hefted higher into the air.

Once she reached about thirty feet, a magical force levitated her out over the docks, where ferry boat captains and crew gaped up at her. Abruptly, her belt unbuckled and her trousers descended, showing bare white legs to the island—by now, everyone was staring at her.

Jaxi snickered into Sardelle's mind.

Once the journalist cleared the docks, the magic holding her aloft disappeared. Arms flailing anew, she plunged the thirty feet and landed in the water.

I take it from those snickers that you handled the clothing malfunction? Sardelle asked Jaxi.

Who, me?

I don't believe Bhrava Saruth realizes that a human lacking in clothing would be reason for embarrassment.

This is true. Given how many times we've had to remind him about clothes when he's shape-shifted.

Titters and speculation ran through the crowd. Nobody hurried down to help the woman out of the water, so maybe they guessed that she was an unwelcome guest. Indeed, as Ridge strolled toward Sardelle, several people hurried to pull out their invitations to display them.

"Was that the journalist from the *Observer*?" Ridge asked, quirking an eyebrow at Sardelle, then nodding at the two nobles.

"I believe so. She didn't have an invitation, I understand. Also, Bhrava Saruth sensed that she meant to write disparaging things about his temple." And his high priestess, but Sardelle didn't mention that. She was still trying to get the dragon to find another name for her. Sardelle, perhaps.

"So, he decided to drop her drawers?"

"No, he only removed her from his island. I imagine her trousers simply... fell."

Eyes twinkling, Ridge looked down at Jaxi's spot on Sardelle's waist. "Inconvenient when that happens in front of an audience."

"So I've heard."

Eagledraw snickered softly. "Sometimes, it's a delight to go to gatherings with commoners. Things get so delightfully raucous."

"You're not going to drag me to another of those sporting events, are you?" Masonwood selected a glass of mead and drew him toward a group of elegantly—and expensively—dressed people that Sardelle didn't recognize.

Ridge smiled and offered Sardelle his arm. "Shall we enjoy the refreshments and entertainment before the main event?"

She linked her arm with his. "I would like that."

* * *

Ridge's heart hammered in his chest as he and Sardelle stood, arm-in-arm, ready to walk up to the officiating priest. After what seemed days of eating, drinking, and socializing, the audience had finally settled into the seats set up in the empty lot behind the temple. Ridge knew about half of the people. He wondered if Sardelle knew the other half. He doubted it. With the possible exception of her hair cutter and that dress-hawking noblewoman, he was fairly certain they knew all the same people.

The priest looked imperiously back at them as "Heralding of the Wedding" played, building up to the point where Ridge and Sardelle would walk past the rows of onlookers to stand in front of him. The man didn't appear as inebriated as Ridge had hoped. So long as he didn't run out to the docks before completing the ceremony, making superstitious gestures at the columns of the temple.

If he does not wish to join you and my high priestess, I will be happy to do so, Bhrava Saruth announced from the shade of the temple, where he lounged in his full dragon form, a few plates of snacks on the floor around him, courtesy of the caterers. *Surely, the divine blessing of a god would mean more than one from some fictional entity that does not truly exist.*

Do me a favor, Bhrava Saruth, Ridge thought, *and don't share your opinions of our gods with the priest, eh?*

If he objects, I could drop him in the same spot where I deposited that newspaper woman.

Not necessary.

She was rescued by one of the ferry boat captains and is now watching from the deck. Her writing instruments were lost, alas. It is likely she now knows not to risk the ire of dragon gods.

Or dragons in general.

Indeed. But dragon gods especially.

"Are you ready?" Sardelle whispered, squeezing his arm. The music was almost to the right spot.

"Yes. Just discussing theology with a dragon."

"That *can't* be going well."

"You are perceptive as well as wise."

"If you heap compliments on me like that, I won't be able to wait until the cue to kiss you."

Ridge bit his lip to keep from grinning stupidly down at her, excited that the moment was finally here, even if he was nervous and feared he'd trip and fall on his face on the way down the aisle. Or that the priest would flee. Or that enemy dragons would soar into view and war would break out. Given the way the last few weeks had gone, he'd wondered a few times if they would actually reach this point, actually become man and wife.

"I'll assume from your goofy grin that you're amenable to that."

"I'm *always* amenable to being kissed." He thought he had been tamping down the goofy grin. Oh well. Surely, this was the right occasion. It pleased him that Sardelle also radiated a broad smile.

"By me or all people in general?"

"Mostly by you. Nobody else pokes me with a sentient sword hilt while we're kissing."

"Yes, I can see how disappointing it would be not to have that."

Ridge grinned wider and dug into his pocket. "Want to rub my dragon for luck?"

"Do you think we'll need it to get down the aisle?"

"Without tripping? It's possible." He rubbed the back of his wooden figurine, then held it out toward Sardelle.

"I'd like to think Jaxi would prevent that from happening, but it's possible she would watch and snicker. That's how it went with the journalist."

Pardon me, Jaxi said, *but the journalist deserved to be snickered at. And also to have her trousers removed.*

Sardelle patted the figurine. *Notice she didn't say anything about preventing us from tripping.*

I did notice that.

The music rose to a crescendo before segueing into the notes that would lead them up the aisle. Ridge pocketed his dragon—and his nerves—and he and Sardelle headed toward the priest, passing the rows of their seated friends.

He did his best to walk in step with her. And not to trip. Though he did almost stumble when he saw a silver-haired figure sitting in the back with Tylie. He hadn't expected Phelistoth to come, given the venue and Bhrava Saruth lounging in the back, presiding over all.

I convinced him that it is honorable to attend the wedding of one who provides your cheese and coffee supply, Wreltad spoke into Ridge's mind.

Tylie merely looked over at them and waved as they walked slowly past.

That was good of you, Wreltad, Ridge thought.

I would not have wished to miss the event and feared Tylie would not come if Phelistoth chose to be elsewhere.

Ridge thought Tylie would have come for Sardelle's sake, regardless, but he said, *I'm glad you made it.*

As am I. Though I am disappointed that you went into noble battle against Dakrovian shamans without me.

That battle was unplanned. And technically, I didn't do much.

You could have done much more had I been there.

I'll make sure to invite you to all festivals at the castle in the future, under the assumption that enemies will choose such moments to strike.

Excellent. I shall look forward to it.

Ridge and Sardelle reached the front of the audience and came to a stop before the priest. Fortunately, the man gazed at them without judgment, the holy book of the Order of Nendear resting in his hands.

"Kin watchers, come forth," the priest said in a ringing voice.

Lieutenant Ahn and Lilah walked up to stand next to the priest on Sardelle's side, Lilah in a blue dress that complemented Ahn's blue and gray dress uniform nicely. Ridge wondered if they had planned that. Coordinating outfits seemed like a thing women would do. Somehow, he doubted General Ort and King Angulus had chatted about matching their attire.

Angulus arrived first, four of his bodyguards coming up to stand at the end of the first row. He wore the full regalia that he donned for public speeches, including trousers and tunic trimmed with gold thread—or maybe real gold—and a cape lined with fur. A gold chain kept the cape around his shoulders, its huge links interspersed with squares stamped with the Iskandian seal. A ceremonial saber hung from his belt, similar to the one Ridge wore as part of his army uniform, but much more embellished. With gold, naturally. Ridge wondered if he should be honored the king had donned all of his royal clothing for the wedding, or if he should be worried Angulus would be mugged on the way home.

General Ort waited for Angulus to take his spot, then came to stand beside and slightly behind him, his dress uniform so starched it could have stood up in the shape of a man without him in it. He wore all his medals and awards on his breast, and Ridge realized for the first time that he had more than the older officer. His own jacket front bordered on the ridiculous thanks to all the awards he'd received over the years, one for almost every time he'd defeated a deadly enemy while nearly getting himself killed. Maybe he ought to donate some medals to Angulus, after all.

Sardelle nudged him with her elbow, and Ridge realized the priest was talking.

Am I supposed to be paying attention to that? he asked silently.

Just enough so you know when it's your turn to say something.

I think the kin watchers get to speak before we do. Even though Ridge couldn't say that he was a great fan of weddings, he had been to several over the years, so he mostly knew the script.

As soon as he said the words, the priest turned toward the men. He licked his lips, appearing a touch nervous at addressing Angulus. All the gold was intimidating.

"Sire, General, do you, being faithful and loyal friends of General Ridgewalker Meadowlark Zirkander—"

Someone in the audience snickered at the middle name. Ridge was fairly certain it was Duck.

"—affirm that you have researched the vitality and emotional stability of Sardelle Terushan and found her a suitable mate?"

Angulus stepped forward and faced Sardelle, giving her the cursory inspection that tradition required, then issued a prompt, "Yes."

He stepped back without further comment. General Ort followed his example precisely. Ridge decided he had been wise to select older and more mature kin watchers. Had he been in that position, he would have been tempted to give an irreverent response, and Sardelle deserved reverence.

If you say so, Jaxi spoke into his mind. *I believe she likes your irreverence. She finds it charming. She would be bored into a coma if she married someone like Ort.*

Are you sure that's Sardelle you're thinking of? And not yourself?

I am part of the package.

Ridge noticed his mother in the front row, a handkerchief clutched in her grasp, her eyes filmed with moisture as she watched the proceedings with obvious contentment. He decided that reverent kin watchers had been a good choice. It was too bad his father hadn't made it back in time for the wedding to sit next to Mom, but Ridge hadn't even known where he was in order to send an invitation.

The priest turned toward Ahn and Lilah and repeated the female version of the kin watcher question, wanting to know if Ridge was healthy and suitable to care for Sardelle.

After glancing at Lilah, Ahn stepped forward to face Ridge and look him up and down. He tried to keep his face solemn, as his weepy-eyed mother would no doubt prefer, but one of his eyebrows may have twitched upward of its own accord. It amused him to have one of his young officers being asked to vouch for him.

Ahn might have been more flustered than amused because her cheeks flushed as she uttered a quick, "Yes," and stepped back into place.

Lilah appeared far less daunted at vouching—or not—for Ridge. He trusted she wouldn't object with his mother sitting ten feet away, but he wouldn't be surprised if she offered something off the script.

"If he can keep from getting himself blown up by enemies, I suspect he'll prove suitable," Lilah said after her perusal. This time, she was the one to quirk an eyebrow as she looked frankly at him. There seemed to be a hint of a threat in that look, like he had better not get himself killed and leave Sardelle alone. Sardelle and the child—or children—they would have.

Ridge nodded solemnly. "I'll do my best to remain un-blown-up."

"What more could a bride ask?" the priest muttered under his breath.

Ridge glanced at him in surprise. He hadn't expected the priest officiating his wedding to be the sarcastic one. Maybe he shouldn't have foisted that second mug of mead on the man. Ah, well. He'd been certain there would be irreverence somewhere.

Angulus shot the man a narrow-eyed look, and the priest straightened.

"Have the bride and groom any oaths to offer each other?" he asked.

Ridge had told the man ahead of time that he wanted to do that. It was something that had fallen out of favor in Iskandian weddings of late, many preferring to say their oaths in private, without dozens—or hundreds—of people watching on, but Ridge was used to having an audience. He didn't mind.

"Yes." Sardelle turned to face Ridge and clasped his hands.

He hadn't realized she would want to say something, too, but he nodded for her to go first.

"I, Sardelle Jana Terushan, never knew I needed someone funny and fun in my life until I met you. I promise to support you, heal you, and love you, no matter how many times you try to get yourself blown up by enemies—" she smirked briefly at Lilah but promptly turned her gaze back on him, "—and no matter how many horrific pieces of furniture your officers give you and deliver to the house."

Titters went through the crowd, at least from those who had seen The Couch, and Ridge grinned broadly. He hadn't expected Sardelle to say anything irreverent or improper, but it was so much better when she did it, since she was so serene and mature the majority of the time. Or at least, she came across that way to most people. He knew better.

I've been a good influence on her, Jaxi said.

Ssh, Wreltad said. *Let them make their promises.*

Nobody asked for your opinion, Taddy.

And yet it is clearly needed.

After waiting to make sure Sardelle was finished, and that the swords were done with their commentary, Ridge spoke.

"I, Ridgewalker *Meadowlark*—" Ridge threw Duck a quick glare before turning his smile back on Sardelle, "—Zirkander, never thought someone so smart and classy would want to spend so much time with me and my recently acquired houseguests. I promise to love you, support you, polish your fuselage whenever you need it, and have your back in a fight."

His mother dabbed her eyes. Sardelle looked teary-eyed, too, and he wanted to kiss her, but supposed that had to wait until the priest said it was time.

Polish her what? Jaxi asked. *Was that dirty, Ridge? In front of all these people? And your* mother?

Of course not. You know how chaste and wholesome I am.

Please, I've yet to hear Captain Kaika make a joke that you didn't grasp fully and immediately.

Has she made any that you *didn't grasp?*

No, but only because I can read minds and am a sublime and worldly individual.

Ridge nodded to the priest to indicate he'd finished. He had originally written about three pages of things he wanted to say, but had decided that his memory wasn't that good, that his tongue would trip, and also that the part about love and support was the most important.

And polishing, apparently, Jaxi added.

Jaxi, shh. Sardelle added to both of them, *You're delaying important things.*

What? The kissing? You do that all *the time.*

I believe she's talking about the cake, Ridge thought, knowing his mother had stashed away the big multi-layered dessert somewhere that dragons wouldn't stumble across it. At least, he hoped that was the case. He'd promised cake to so many people that there might be a riot if they found only crumbs on the tray—and frosting smeared all over Bhrava Saruth's lips.

Technically, dragons don't have lips, Jaxi said.

I'm sure they have something to get frosting on.

Not privy to the debate, the priest lifted his hands and raised his voice toward the audience. "This union is blessed by the holiest and oldest of the gods, Nendear."

Even better, it is blessed by the god Bhrava Saruth, came the dragon's powerful telepathic words, echoing into everyone's minds. He strode out from under the shade of his temple in the back and rose on his powerful hind legs, stretching his wings wide so nobody could miss him. Further, he exuded that dragonly aura of his that compelled people to gaze at him in rapture and feel eager to do whatever he wished.

Ridge was about to drop his face in his hands when a golden glow wafted outward from the dragon, descending over the audience and over Ridge and Sardelle like a gentle mist. A warm tingle went through him, as it had before when the dragon had "blessed" him. Gasps came from the audience as people looked down at their hands, their skin glowing with magical power. Gradually, the glow faded, but if everyone felt like Ridge, they would be aware that something had happened, that they felt extra healthy and full of vitality.

"I can't believe I was upstaged by a scaled blasphemer," the priest growled under his breath, glancing at Angulus, as if the king should somehow make amends.

"When we get back from the honeymoon, I'll see to it that a donation is left in the box at your temple in town," Ridge said quietly, feeling he was the one who should make amends, or at least placate the man. After all, he hadn't originally planned on a dragon overseeing the wedding when he'd hired the priest.

"A sizable donation, I should hope." The priest sniffed. "And a jug of that mead would not go unappreciated."

"I'll keep that in mind," Ridge murmured, then took Sardelle's hands and pulled her close for the closing kiss.

Dozens of contented *awws* and *oohs* came from the crowd. His mother wept into her handkerchief.

As Sardelle slid her arms around his shoulders, Jaxi's hilt poked Ridge in the hip. "I do love a woman with a sword," he murmured against her lips.

Sardelle, busy returning the kiss, replied silently. *Your sword is poking me too. It seems fair.*

The ceremonial one, right?

I assume so, but I'm not looking down.

Ridge was vaguely aware of some people gasping in delight as fireworks went off over the temple and of others heading back to see if Bhrava Saruth had left any refreshments uneaten. He decided he would ignore the world for a while and stand there with his arms wrapped around Sardelle. Maybe until the honeymoon.

Epilogue

SARDELLE PADDED INTO THE LIVING room in slippers and her robe with two plates of griddle cakes in hand. She found Ridge sitting on the couch and contemplating an open box in his hand. The rest of the stack of still-wrapped gifts was piled in the corner between the window and fireplace.

"You started without me?" She nodded to the empty box, set his plate on the table in front of him, then sat in the comfortable chair adjacent to the hideous couch, folding up her legs.

He gave her a lopsided smile that might have been a commentary on the gift or a bemused acknowledgment that he'd come to accept that she would avoid sitting on that couch at all costs. He usually ended up joining her in one of the large chairs if he wanted to snuggle.

"I did not. This one had already been opened. In fact, several have." He gestured to a few more empty boxes at his feet. The table hid them, so she hadn't noticed them when she'd come in.

"Well, we were gone for three days on our honeymoon."

"And thus, it was acceptable for others to open presents addressed to us?" Ridge bent his head to sniff the empty box. "There are seeds in the bottom, and this smells like dried fruit. Like it *was* dried fruit."

"Three days is a long time for unopened gifts containing food to remain untouched in a house frequently visited by dragons."

"Hm."

Sardelle wished they'd had a week or two for their honeymoon, but she hadn't seen Ridge get a vacation or more than a day off since he'd become general, so she supposed she should be grateful that she'd been able to pry him away from the capital at all. She *had* been grateful for the upgrades he'd somehow found the time to have done to his lakeside cabin. She knew he hadn't been out there all summer, so she wasn't sure how he'd managed it. Offers of beer and camaraderie, no doubt.

Most of the cabin had been as she remembered, but a stylish addition had been built onto the back and housed an indoor toilet, a large tub for bathing, and a fancy sauna that they had put to good use for relaxing sore muscles after vigorous physical activities.

"You're smirking." Ridge looked over at her and lifted an eyebrow. He'd set the empty box aside and taken a few bites of his griddle cakes. "I do wish I had your mind-reading ability at times. Are you remembering our honeymoon? Our enjoyable evenings—and mornings—together? Or are you fantasizing about the upgraded lavatory?"

"All of those things." She grinned. "You know I'm going to want a sauna *here*, now, right? Especially when winter comes."

"That's probably doable." Ridge set his plate down and ambled to the unopened boxes. "Where shall we start? I'm going to assume that everything that's left isn't edible."

"You sound disappointed."

"I like dried fruit. And one of those other boxes smelled like cinnamon buns." His expression grew wistful.

Sardelle rested her own plate on the table and joined him, wrapping an arm around his waist. "The proper thing to do would be to send thank-you cards to everyone for these gifts." There was quite an impressive stack. Not every guest had brought one, but every guest who actually knew her or Ridge—and hadn't simply wanted to go to the social event of the year—had brought something, and some of his officers who hadn't been able to get away from work for the wedding had also sent gifts. "It'll be hard to do with the ones that have been eaten."

"Yes, we'll have to sniff the boxes thoroughly so we know what the people sent and can properly thank them. And then be vague with the wording. Dear Captain Davest, we're positive the dried fruit was enjoyed by the one who ate it."

"That one is from Colonel Quataldo." She pointed to a tidy green box and remembered the beautiful carved egg he had given them earlier that summer. "He was off on a mission and didn't make it to the wedding, isn't that right?" She hated to admit that so many people had been there that she could have missed seeing familiar faces. She had chatted to many people before the ceremony began, but after that, she had been too busy finding Ridge's goofy grins adorable to pay attention to much of anything else.

"Yes, perhaps spying on the very Dakrovian family that troubled us."

"He should be spying on the Cofah infiltrators who actually destroyed the blood. Or did we ever figure out who did that?" Sardelle assumed the Cofah had been responsible, but it could have been anyone who'd found the reward tempting. She wondered how much it had been.

"I haven't heard about it if we did. Maybe the gods didn't want us to tinker with dragon blood." Ridge grabbed Quataldo's box and gave it to her. "Hoping for another egg?" He glanced at the mantel where the first one was mounted on a wooden stand. "I'm surprised the first one hasn't been eaten."

She snorted. "He hollows them out. It's just the shell when he carves them."

"You say that as if Phelistoth wouldn't nosh on an egg shell while he enjoys his morning coffee."

Smiling, she unwrapped the box and opened it. A large ostrich egg lay nestled within, one side carved with the image of a flier and the other with a sword. A soulblade? She smiled, realizing the colonel must have chosen symbols to represent her and Ridge. What a thoughtful man. She wished Ridge had more interactions with him. And perhaps fewer with Colonel Therrik, though if Therrik and Lilah stayed together, that would be unlikely.

"That's pretty," Ridge said. "And doesn't look terribly edible. Is that Jaxi?"

"I believe so."

Not a bad rendition of me, Jaxi said from her rack on the wall. *Though I'm not sure how to feel about Ridge's flier being so much larger.*

Well, a flier is larger than a sword.

These are symbols, not physical things. Symbolically, a soulblade is much more important than a flier and thus, should be larger.

Such a fussy art critic.

"Who's next?" Ridge picked up a squishy package wrapped only in paper. "Captain Blazer?"

Sardelle wasn't sure whether to eye that one with wariness or not. Blazer definitely had an irreverent streak, but she wasn't quite as immature as Ridge's young lieutenants. At least from what Sardelle had seen.

"She knits, you know. And sews." Ridge handed her the package.

As Sardelle unwrapped it, she wondered if he was giving her the unwrapping duties because he thought she would enjoy it or because he was afraid of the gifts from his fellow officers. Maybe he wanted to experience them from a distance.

Sardelle withdrew an orange and brown knitted... item. She held it out and examined it from all directions. "I do like the autumn colors, but I'm not sure what it is. Some kind of covering for a box? A cylindrical box?"

Ridge plucked out a tiny card that Sardelle hadn't noticed. "Happy life together, you two. Hope this helps spruce up your lavatory for all your houseguests. Charlyn."

"Charlyn?"

"That's her first name. I think she prefers Blazer." Ridge poked the knitted cover. "The lavatory?"

"Hm, I think it may be a cover for an extra toilet paper roll. To keep it where you can find it without it being too obvious."

"What's wrong with obvious toilet paper?"

"Some people consider toiletry items on display to be uncouth."

"Are we those kinds of people?"

"We are now," Sardelle said and set the gift aside.

"Life sure gets weird after you're married."

If you don't want to use it for toilet paper, Jaxi said, *and Colonel Quataldo keeps giving you carved eggs, you could store them in there.*

Only one, Sardelle replied. *Those eggs are large.*

Maybe you can ask Blazer to make you more holders.

Sardelle imagined holders knitted from yarn and stuffed with eggs hanging all over the house and shook her head.

"Oh, this can't be good," Ridge said, distracting her. He lifted a large box. "This is the one that was ticking. That I had to come over and vouch for at the wedding."

"Ah yes. From the same minds that brought us that couch."

"Just one of them. It says it's just from Duck. I believe I heard that Pimples went in with a couple of others to get us a cheese club membership."

"That will be appreciated."

Ridge eyed the empty boxes on the floor. "Indeed." He held Duck's box up to his ear before opening it. "It's not ticking now. I don't know whether that's good or bad."

Sardelle resisted the urge to use her power to peek inside. She was afraid of what she might find.

"Perhaps we could open Lilah and Therrik's gift first," she suggested. "Or Lieutenant Ahn's. Or your mother's. I feel that the women in your life can be trusted to give us practical and thoughtful gifts."

Like egg holders, Jaxi said.

"You're including Therrik in with the women in my life?" Ridge asked.

"Well, I assume Lilah picked it out while Therrik stayed home and scowled."

"That does seem likely." Ridge poked around, found their gift, and handed it to Sardelle. "I've already sniffed the one Mom gave us to see if it smelled like soaps."

"Does it?" Sardelle was surprised by the heft of Lilah and Therrik's box.

"Surprisingly, no. Though it's in a rather large, flat box for soap. Maybe she ran out of ingredients after making all those baskets for the wedding guests. I was somewhat amused that she lifted her chin, strode up, and deposited one in front of Bhrava Saruth. What do you think a dragon will do with soap?"

"You don't think dragons need to scrub their armpits, the same as humans?"

"I assume they can handle bathing without manmade appurtenances." Sardelle slid the card out from under a leather band holding the lid of the gift box shut.

Ridge and Sardelle, the message read in Lilah's elegant penmanship, *I am pleased that you found each other—and that you, Sardelle, find Ridge as entertaining as he finds himself. I am honored you chose me to stand at your side at your wedding, and I'm glad I've gotten to know you this summer. Ridge, treat Sardelle well, and give her frequent foot rubs and massages. Women like these things. I hope this small gift will be useful in your household. Lilah.*

A postscript at the bottom was written in a heavier hand with far fewer embellishments in the penmanship. *Zirkander, don't screw things up. Her sword can fry a man's—* The words *cock and balls* had been crossed out, and Lilah had written *sexual reproductive organs* above them. Apparently, vulgarity wasn't allowed on gift cards. A simple signature of *Vann* finished off the message.

Ridge, reading over Sardelle's shoulder, grunted. "Nice correction, Lilah."

"You don't need to worry about that part. Just this line up here." Sardelle drew her finger under the bit about foot rubs and massages.

"I seem to remember there being some rubbing in the sauna."

"Foot rubs aren't the same thing as other types of rubbing."

"Maybe not, but I don't remember any objections at the time." He grinned and kissed her temple.

Sardelle opened the lid and found two gifts inside. One was a very military-looking cannon pencil sharpener that had to weigh five pounds. She handed it to Ridge, assuming that was Therrik's contribution and that it was for his desk.

"Heavy and dense," Ridge said. "Much like his head."

"What are you going to do if they get married, and he becomes your in-law?"

"Don't joke about that. You'll give me nightmares."

Sardelle withdrew Lilah's gift, a cookbook with some nicely carved wooden spoons and spatulas. "I mentioned to her that I was attempting to learn to cook," Sardelle said dryly. "I suppose this is more practical than the first edition paleontology book she asked if I was interested in."

"My cousin wants to encourage you to cook for me?" He raised his eyebrows, appearing surprised.

"Who said the cooking would be for you? We have many guests to feed."

"This is true. And then after dinner, they can go up and admire Blazer's gift."

Ridge started to set aside the cannon pencil sharpener, but noticed it had a few moving parts. He tugged at a pull chain in the back and something inside twanged. This sent him in search of a pencil. Once he found one, he stuck it in the barrel and pulled the chain. This time when the cannon twanged, it launched the pencil across the room. He grinned broadly.

"If I admitted that amused me greatly, would that be immature?" he asked.

"I think it would only be immature if you launched pencils at fellow officers entering your office."

"Hm."

"You'll have to let Therrik know you liked his gift. Here, might as well open Duck's while you're feeling immature."

"Do you know something I don't know?" Ridge accepted it, shaking it slightly. Something inside rattled.

"Let's just say that I know your men and have a hunch."

I have more than a hunch, Jaxi said. *It'll take a whole new level of immaturity to enjoy that gift. I feel you should demote Duck for having thought it would be appropriate.*

"That bad?" Ridge tugged open the metallic ribbon that had been tied in a messy knot.

He opened the lid and peered inside. Sardelle couldn't resist leaning close to look.

"A mechanical dog?" He withdrew it and examined the blocky construct from all sides. "It looks like it can move. Oh, there's a crank."

Jaxi sighed into their minds.

Ridge turned the crank and set the four-legged construct on the floor. The legs started moving and it ambled around in a circle. Ridge pulled something blue out of the box as the metal dog lifted a leg. It wasn't until Ridge lowered the additional piece—a miniature lamppost—that Sardelle understood what it was pretending to do. The "gift" was everything she had feared it would be, made worse by the fact that Ridge's grin was even broader than it had been for the cannon.

She dropped her face into her hand.

As the mature and put-upon housewife, you can demand that he not store it anywhere you'll ever see it, Jaxi suggested. *Or I could incinerate it the first time Ridge turns his back.*

Housewife? Is that what I am now? How odd. She thought of the child in her womb and wondered if her days of traveling the world and going on adventures were coming to a close.

You're still a teacher and healer, but you're now also a wife who resides in a house. And owns a cookbook.

So domestic.

You agreed to it. If it's any consolation, Ridge was amused by the cookbook. Though he appreciates that you've been letting his mother teach you how to make cookies and tarts, he's fairly certain you two will continue your tradition of dining on whatever takeout deli meals he picks up on his way out of the city after work.

I truly wouldn't mind learning to cook a few entrées... when I'm not busy tutoring my students.

Don't forget your duties as a dragon's high priestess. Business may pick up now that your god has a temple.

Oh dear.

Ridge cleared his throat and looked at her. "A totally impractical and goofy gift," he announced.

"You love it. I can tell."

"Er, yes, but I won't insist it be placed as prominently in the house as the couch."

"Good. Jaxi has already offered to incinerate it when you're not looking."

"But not if I store it in my duck blind retreat? Perhaps behind some books?"

"It might be safe then," Sardelle said. "Only Wreltad goes out there with you. Though he might feel compelled to incinerate it too."

It is loathsome, the heretofore silent soulblade announced from his rack. *I do, however, approve of the cannon pencil sharpener. Quite clever and amusing.*

"That's going in my office in the citadel," Ridge said. "But don't tell Therrik I like it."

"I wouldn't dream of it," Sardelle said.

"Here, maybe this is something that will make you feel better about our gifts." Ridge handed her the box from his mother.

Based on its size and shape, Sardelle guessed it had to be a painting, and she opened it without wariness. Ridge's mother didn't know *how* to be irreverent.

She withdrew a framed canvas featuring a beautiful gold dragon that she promptly recognized as Bhrava Saruth. She and Ridge stood side by side, leaning against the dragon's shoulder, she in her favorite green dress with Jaxi strapped at her waist, and Ridge in his uniform, both of them looking like they could leap onto Bhrava Saruth's back and fly into battle at any moment.

Her throat tightened, both at the beauty of the painting and at the realization of how Fern saw them. Maybe her finding out about Sardelle's magic—and the existence of dragons—hadn't been a bad thing after all. She was definitely relieved of the burden of having to hide everything from Fern.

"Huh," Ridge said. "Not bad, eh? Us, I mean. But I suppose if she had to put a dragon in it, that's the right one."

"I like the suggestion of it, that our adventures aren't over, even if we're married and expecting a baby."

"Oh, *I* could have told you that." Ridge wrapped an arm around her and wriggled his eyebrows. "Living with me will always be an adventure."

Sardelle eyed the dog, which was winding down with its perambulations, and also the pencil still lying on the floor. "I suspect you're right."

THE END

Bonus Short Story:

Crazy Canyon

"Potted plants?" General Ridgewalker Zirkander scratched his head. "You came to see me about potted plants?"

"Yes, sir." The young man from the king's castle—what was his title? Steward?—rolled out a blueprint of the courtyard. Or what the courtyard would look like *after* the construction finished. Thanks to dragons, demolitions, and a sorceress, the castle was still undergoing "renovations," as the newspapers called them. "We want to ensure the landing pad for the king's fliers meets the required specifications, but Lady Dilwandser—she's overseeing furnishing and decor, since the queen passed away—thought the pad would look too bare."

"It's supposed to be bare. So fliers can land on it and so the king, his entourage, and their supplies can be loaded."

"Lady Dilwandser wants to know if it's safe to place foliage *around* the pad. At the corners here and here. And then perhaps a hedge along this side."

"A hedge?"

"Yes, sir. Unlike the pots, it would be planted and immobile. We were worried about the heat from the thrusters wilting the plants. I brought you a sample of the shrub Lady Dilwandser suggested. It blooms in the spring, and the flowers are delicate." The man produced a leafy twig, or maybe that was a vine, and a dried red flower. "What do you think?" Very serious, earnest eyes regarded Ridge.

"I think I never imagined meetings like this when I accepted this promotion." Ridge glanced toward the window. All hint of daylight had disappeared outside, and he could no longer see the flier hangars perched on the bluff to the south of the harbor. To think, he'd believed he would make it home in time to join Sardelle for dinner. "General Ort didn't mention horticulture when I took over his position."

"Yes, sir. The foliage?"

"You've got Major Sanglor in charge of the king's personal fliers, don't you? What did he say?"

"He referred me to you."

"I may have to rethink my policy of being a lenient commander and not issuing demerits to lower-ranking officers."

The steward's brow furrowed.

Ridge sighed and rubbed the back of his neck. He had been at the citadel since before dawn. In meetings. His old squadron had been in the air all morning practicing maneuvers over the harbor. All he'd been able to do was gaze longingly out the window at them while he and the supply captain discussed lead time on ordering flier parts. Not to mention new casters for the rolling door in the hangar. Generals, apparently, had to be consulted on such important matters as casters. And hedges.

"Just plant and pot them outside of the pad," he said. "It was designed based on the operational guidelines and schematics of the existing two-man fliers. I'll be certain to let you know if the requirements change when the test models go into production."

"Excellent, sir." The man rolled up his schematics, tucked them under his arm, and headed for the door. "Shall I send in your next appointment?"

"There's a *next* appointment?" Ridge glanced at the clock. At this rate, Sardelle would be *sleeping* by the time he got home.

"There's a surly colonel who glowered at me when I said I had an appointment and pushed my way in first."

"A surly colonel?" Ridge groaned inwardly. It couldn't be *him*, could it? His unofficial but undeniable nemesis ought to have another six months, at least, left as the fort commander for the remote Magroth Crystal Mines.

"*Very* surly." The steward pursed his lips, shook his head, and walked out.

A second after he disappeared from sight, a large blunt-fingered hand thrust the door open. It was the kind of hand with the power to crack walnuts. Or skulls.

Colonel Vann Therrik strode inside, his customary glower in place. Even though the elite troops colonel had most recently been assigned to command a fort, a job that involved a lot of paperwork, Ridge had no doubt that Therrik and his overly muscled arms were still perfectly capable of killing people. He reminded himself that he outranked the man now and probably wasn't in danger of being maimed, mutilated, or murdered. Even so, his natural inclination was to keep the desk between them.

"You're not in my appointment book, Therrik," Ridge said, swiveling in his chair so he could lean his arm on the backrest. He refused to appear intimidated by the colonel, even if he did prefer it when Sardelle and her sentient—and powerful—sword Jaxi were nearby when he confronted him. "Did you perhaps come by to suggest we go out for beers?"

"No."

Ridge lifted his eyebrows, assuming Therrik would get right to the point. He did like points. The kinds on the ends of weapons, in particular.

Oddly, Therrik scowled, folded his arms over his chest, and glared... out the window. Ridge peeked in that direction, but all that was visible from the second-story office right now was the dark night sky.

"You didn't come to tell me the king accepted your application to become his new captain of the guard, did you?" Ridge asked, news he'd heard from his cousin Lilah, an incredibly smart and educated woman who was, against all logic, reason, and the understanding of the gods, *seeing* Therrik. In a romantic sense. Ridge's brain still hurt at the notion.

"No." Therrik's scowl deepened. "He said I was too *valuable* to the army. If that were true, he wouldn't have stuck me at Magroth."

"Unfortunate. I heard you were looking forward to being outside the military chain of command and thus able to frisk impertinent generals who visited the king."

Therrik's eyes narrowed to slits. "Lilah told you that?"

"Lilah told Sardelle, and Sardelle told me." Ridge had been moderately horrified at the idea of Therrik frisking *him*, likely with a hand around his throat. The best part of being promoted to general had been getting to the point where he outranked the man. But the king's guard was a unit outside of the military, and if they wanted to frisk suspicious visitors—and loyal pilots—they had that right. "They've become friends now, you know. If Lilah hadn't been living so far up the coast, I would have introduced them earlier. They have a lot of common interests. The academic ones, not the sorcerous ones, I gather." Ridge added the last since Therrik loathed everything related to magic.

Therrik grunted. Or maybe that was a growl. Some kind of vocal utterance that portrayed a belligerent lack of enthusiasm.

"The king is also concerned the Cofah will come sniffing around, or send their dragons sniffing around, for their emperor," Therrik said. "He wants me around in a military capacity in case I'm needed to defend the city or go on incursions."

Ridge suspected the king simply didn't want to see Therrik's scowling face in his castle halls every morning, but he decided not to share the thought.

"So you're stationed locally again?" Ridge told himself it shouldn't matter to him, since, as a general, it was unlikely he would be asked to ferry the elite troops around on missions anymore. He wouldn't need to worry about being stuck flying Therrik and his sunny disposition—and his airsickness-prone stomach—anywhere.

"Back with my old intelligence unit."

"Were they having trouble functioning without your keen contributions?" Every time Ridge saw Therrik, he resolved to stop goading the man. And every time, he failed. It was so hard to be a mature human being.

"I didn't come here to pound your face into a wall, Zirkander. Don't make me change my mind."

The words, "Just don't forget to call me sir while you do it," popped into Ridge's mind, but he managed to quash them before they came out. Score one point for maturity.

"What *did* bring you here?" he asked. "I can't imagine you wanted my advice on shrubbery."

Therrik took a deep breath, as if he were about to ask for

something deeply embarrassing. Or maybe the mere act of having to ask for anything embarrassed him.

"Can you give me the address of Lilah's mother in Portsnell?"

"Uh, what? Why?"

"I want to arrange for her to come to the capital to visit Lilah."

"Arrange?" Ridge imagined a team of elite troops planning a mission to abscond with Aunt Dotty before the more rational part of his brain decided that was unlikely.

"Buy her a train ticket so she can come visit us for a couple of weeks."

"*Us?*" Ridge heard the alarmed squeak in his voice, but it was too late to do anything about it. He'd known his cousin and Therrik had bonded on their adventure at Magroth and that they'd had a... dalliance, but he hadn't believed it would last. He certainly hadn't expected them to become an *us*. They weren't *living* together, were they?

"Yes, us. Could you act like a grown-up, Zirkander? Just give me—seven gods, you're not going to hyperventilate, are you?"

Ridge had no idea what expression was on his face, but he drew back and did his best to straighten it. "Of course not." Probably. "I just hadn't realized that you and she... ah. Never mind. Why can't Lilah give you her mother's address for this?"

"Because I'm not asking her for it. This is supposed to be a surprise. She's been talking about her mother being lonely, and I think *she's* lonely. She transferred to the university here, but classes haven't started for the year yet, so she hasn't met her new colleagues. I thought she might like her mother to visit before summer is over."

It took Ridge a moment to process Therrik's words, to realize he wanted to do something nice. Ridge wouldn't have guessed he had that in him, but he supposed women sometimes had the ability to bring out the best in men. Sardelle certainly did that for him. He wished she were here now for more reasons than one.

"The address?" Therrik asked.

"I don't know it," Ridge said.

Therrik's eyes narrowed.

Ridge spread his hands. "I know where she lives, but I haven't been up there for a few years, and I don't remember the house number or postal code."

Would he have given Therrik the address even if he had known it? He liked the thought of Lilah getting to spend time with her mother, but he loathed the idea that Therrik might be the one to give her that gift. Ridge didn't think they were a good match, and he hoped Lilah realized that as soon as possible. If Therrik did her *favors*, then how would she realize what an ass he was?

It was possible that he wasn't the ass to her that he was to Ridge, but it hurt Ridge's brain to imagine having to accept that.

"You don't have it written down?" Therrik stuck a fist on his hip. "What kind of man doesn't send his family members Solstice Fest cards?"

"The kind whose house was blown up last spring. My address book was inside at the time."

"Oh, hells." Therrik dropped his hand. He frowned at the window again, as if some other solution might appear in the night out there.

Ridge's mother might have the address, but the ride to her house was more than thirty miles round-trip. Besides, he didn't want to foist Therrik and his dubious charms on her without an introduction. Or *with* an introduction. Even if it would be amusing to see Therrik attacked by her legion of ham-hungry cats.

An idea popped into Ridge's mind, and he almost rejected it right away because it sounded like personal torture. Also, he didn't want to help Therrik. Or do anything to contribute to him and Lilah being a lasting *us*.

But... he didn't *not* want to help Lilah. She would enjoy having her mother come for a visit. And he imagined Aunt Dotty would enjoy visiting the capital and doing some of the historical tours with Lilah.

Ridge leaned his hands against his desk, thinking of the times he'd teased Lilah when they'd been kids. She had preferred reading books to playing with Ridge, her brothers, and their other cousins, which he'd found perplexing at the time. He hadn't been the sharpest sword in the rack.

"Never mind, then," Therrik said, turning for the door.

"Wait," Ridge said, wincing but forcing his offer out nevertheless. "It only takes two hours to fly up there. My last appointment is at four tomorrow. I can take you up there, and you can introduce yourself and ask her in person if she would like to come down."

The expression in Therrik's eyes might have been horror or distaste or nascent motion sickness. Ridge expected him to reject the offer outright, and that would be fine by him. He'd made the gesture. Another point for maturity.

"Can't you just draw me a map?" Therrik grumbled. "I'd rather take the five-hour train trip each way than climb into your back seat again."

"It would be a crappy map. Like I said, I haven't been up there for a while. I know I can find it in person, but…" Ridge shrugged. "You're more than welcome to take the train. It'll give you time to catch up on your reading. All those fascinating tomes about ancient weapons and killing people."

"You don't *read* about killing people, Zirkander. You just do it. It's much more satisfying."

Ridge suspected the man was fantasizing about killing him right now.

Shaking his head, Therrik turned for the door. Ridge scooted papers into a folder, cleaning up his desk so he could leave for the night.

But Therrik paused with his hand on the knob.

"Shit."

"Something else it's more satisfying to do than read about," Ridge offered.

The look Therrik launched over his shoulder was scathing. And definitely conveyed a desire for murder, or at least mutilation.

"I don't have any days off coming up for weeks," Therrik said. "I took leave between Magroth and starting up again with my unit here, so I could move my belongings into an apartment big enough for sharing."

"Unfortunate." Not wanting to hear about the details of why the man needed to share his apartment, Ridge grabbed his jacket off his chair, turned off the lantern on his desk, and waved his guest toward the door. He was surprised Therrik hadn't already left.

"So I don't have *time* to take an all-day train trip." Therrik's tone turned anguished. "Zirkander, I want to do this for Lilah. Before the school year starts back up and she's working all the time again. I…" The anguished tone turned into an anguished expression, as if he were wrestling with some terrible inner demon.

It slowly dawned on Ridge that Therrik was trying to make himself accept the offer. To ask for and accept a *favor*. From someone he would love to strangle.

Ridge leaned his hip against his desk and stuck a hand in his pocket, debating whether he wanted to stand there and wait for Therrik to ask, perhaps insisting he throw a *please* on the end. It would feel tremendously satisfying to have a small amount of power over him, if only for a few seconds. Since Therrik utterly ignored the fact that Ridge now outranked him, lording his generalness over him hadn't been as fun as he'd hoped.

However, he wanted to get home to Sardelle before midnight. And then there was that maturity thing he was trying to work on.

"Meet me at the hangar after final formation," Ridge said. "I can have you to Aunt Dotty's house in time for dinner."

"Fine," Therrik said, stalking out of the office.

"You're welcome," Ridge called after him.

***

Ridge couldn't help but smile as he left the tram car and walked across the bluff to the hangars. His butt hadn't been in a cockpit for more than two *weeks*. Oh, piloting Therrik would be a test of patience, and he'd probably have to clean the back seat of vomit afterward, but still, it was a chance to *fly*. To watch the sun over the mountains as he soared northward, the sea breeze rushing past, whipping his scarf about. He missed swooping and diving like an eagle, though he supposed he would have to limit that, and barrel rolls would be out of the question, no matter how fun they were. Therrik got sick just flying *straight*.

A few young Wolf and Tiger squadron pilots leaving for the day saluted him and one blurted, "General Zirkander, sir. Will you be joining us for the practice maneuvers tomorrow?"

"I have to make sure the new instructors at the flight academy get settled in tomorrow, but I'll try to come out and watch Wolf and Tiger for a while."

"Watch, sir? Won't you fly with us? I've heard about—I mean, I've never gotten to see." He glanced at his comrade. "You're a legend, sir!"

His buddy, Lieutenant Foam, elbowed him and gave Ridge an apologetic, "He's new, sir."

"Yes, I know. I approved his application into Tiger Squadron. If there's time, I would love to fly with you boys." Ridge patted the men on the shoulder before continuing on.

Seven gods, he would love to go up with them, but he doubted he would be able to slip away for long enough. This little jaunt up the coast would have to satisfy his flying itch, at least for now.

Their salutes and a "Yes, sir," and "Good evening, sir," trailed him as he headed for the hangar, but the respect ended after that.

As soon as he stepped inside, Therrik, already standing by Ridge's flier, growled, "You're late, Zirkander." He did not acknowledge in any way that he was pleased Ridge was doing him this favor.

"The castle steward returned with more shrubbery samples. Don't ever let them promote you to general, Therrik."

"I won't. I know I'd be crappy at it."

Ridge blinked, startled by the honesty. Or self-effacement. Whatever that had been. "Commanding Magroth didn't agree with you?"

"You *know* it didn't."

Yes, a few months earlier, when Ridge had flown up there to battle the dragon Morishtomaric, he'd arrived in the middle of a riot. The miner-prisoners the soldiers were stationed there to guard had been showing their displeasure at Therrik's draconian command style. With sledgehammers and pickaxes.

"Well, now that you're back here, maybe you'll be sent on some nice covert missions where you can ruthlessly slay enemies." Ridge didn't know which enemies those would be, since Iskandia had a ceasefire with the Cofah Empire right now, but surely some inspired intelligence officer could find someone for Therrik to slay.

A hint of hope entered Therrik's eyes, but then he shook his head. "Lilah tells me I shouldn't feel wistful about such things."

"Yeah." Ridge pulled himself into his cockpit to hide his grimace. It made him uncomfortable to hear his cousin's name—*first* name—on the rough colonel's tongue. He trusted that Lilah, who was in her late thirties and had been married before, wouldn't get involved with someone who didn't treat her well, but he did catch himself worrying about Therrik's explosive temper. If Ridge had his druthers, this wasn't a relationship that would be happening. But Lilah had told him—firmly—that she didn't care about his druthers.

Ridge double-checked to make sure the bag of apple pie taffy he'd purchased during his lunch break was safely in his jacket pocket. There was a woman in the capital that made all manner of flavors, and he recalled that Dotty enjoyed this one the best. He had no idea how well Therrik's offer—or Therrik himself—would be received. If nothing else, the taffy could be a consolation prize.

The flier creaked as Therrik settled into the back seat.

Ridge glanced back at the big man. "You didn't put on *more* muscle while you were in that frozen hole, did you?"

"What do you care?"

"I'm concerned the flier won't get off the ground with our combined weight. Especially your half—two-thirds—of it."

"I can't help you with your feelings of scrawny inadequacy. Just fly this boat, Zirkander. I want to get there before the woman goes to bed."

"Since you asked so nicely, I'll be happy to take off." Ridge shook his head, tugged his goggles on, and hit the ignition. The energy crystal that powered the craft flared to life, its soft yellow light illuminating the cockpit.

"No crazy flying on the way there."

"You're taking all the fun out of my escape from my office," Ridge said, though he didn't want to have to clean the back seat of the flier, so he hadn't planned any aerial antics. Alas.

He nudged the flight stick, and good old W-63 rolled toward the open hangar door. The sun was setting outside, but he'd flown up and down the coast a thousand times and would have no trouble landing in Portsnell in the dark.

The two-seater had thrusters, so he could have simply rolled out of the hangar and lifted off, but all the early fliers he'd trained on had required getting up to speed until the wheels left the ground, and he enjoyed the feel of the wind against his face, whipping his scarf about. He accelerated down the runway toward the edge of the bluff that dropped off into the harbor.

As he was about to tilt the wings for liftoff, a huge gold figure flew up from below and alighted on the bluff right in front of them.

"Shit!" Therrik swore.

Though startled, Ridge continued his takeoff, veering slightly to the left to avoid the dragon.

Greetings, human worshippers! Bhrava Saruth spoke into his mind—into *their* minds?

Ridge glanced back as the flier soared over the dragon's head. Therrik's eyes bulged, and his hands gripped either side of his seat well. One lurched toward the pistol at his waist.

Ridge made a cutting motion, hoping to stop Therrik's overtrained warrior instincts from shooting. It wasn't as if bullets did anything against a dragon, but Bhrava Saruth was one of only two winged allies that Iskandia claimed. And the only one who was *enthusiastic* about helping the country.

Good evening, Bhrava Saruth, Ridge thought, trusting the telepathic dragon would read his mind.

You are leaving? Behind them, Bhrava Saruth sprang into the air and flapped his wings to trail after the flier. *I just located you. You were not in your lair.*

My office in the citadel?

The place where you command the legions of my potential worshippers.

Ridge wondered what General Ort and all the high-ranking officers who worked in the citadel would think if he changed the sign out front to The Lair. The General's Lair. Alas, it sounded more like the name of a tavern in town.

"Zirkander," Therrik growled, "that dragon is following us."

"Yes, that's Bhrava Saruth, our ally."

"I know *that*."

With Therrik's head twisted to look back, Ridge barely heard him.

"It's why I haven't shot at it," Therrik added.

"So, you're just fondling your pistol for no reason?"

Therrik glowered at him. "There's a reason."

"We're not going to discuss killing again, are we?"

"Just do something about that dragon. I don't want it stalking us all the way up the coast. If I show up with a dragon at Lilah's mother's house... hells, what kind of impression would that be?"

"A memorable one, I'm certain."

Therrik's glower faded, and an expression Ridge wasn't familiar with took over his face. Concern?

It boggled Ridge's mind to imagine Therrik worried about making a good impression on... anyone. He was somewhat less of an ass around the king and superior officers who didn't irk him the way Ridge did, but Ridge couldn't imagine him having a vulnerable side under all that gruffness. Nor did he particularly want to imagine it.

I've come to discuss my temple, Bhrava Saruth announced, speeding up to fly beside them as they soared north, out of the city and along the coast.

"His what?" Therrik asked, and Ridge realized Bhrava Saruth was sharing his words with both of them.

Maybe he hoped that he would be more likely to get a temple if he talked to more people about it.

I have nineteen worshippers now, and I must have a place for them to come and receive my blessings and wisdom.

"It would be nice if that place didn't continue to be my house," Ridge said wistfully.

When he and Sardelle had chosen that quiet cottage on the dead-end lane outside of the city walls, he'd imagined it being private. Secluded. Definitely not a destination for mages in training or dragon devotees.

My high priestess has informed me that human money may be required in order to acquire land on which to build a suitable temple. As well as to hire construction crews for the building. Ridgewalker, finding human money would be a simple matter, but is this truly how temples for gods are built? Do not the worshippers simply come together and raise the structure themselves, thus to honor their divine lord?

A loud sigh, or maybe that was a moan, came from the back seat.

"You're not getting airsick already, are you?" Ridge asked over his shoulder. "I'm flying as straight as I can."

"For once, it's not you that's making me sick."

Therrik frowned over at the dragon.

Bhrava Saruth gazed back, his leathery wings flapping, easily matching the flier's pace. His golden scales gleamed beneath the light of the setting sun. He possessed deep green eyes full of power, and if one looked into them, one felt a pull to do everything the dragon wished, no matter how goofy.

"I think it might have happened like that in the old days, Bhrava Saruth," Ridge said, speaking aloud so Therrik wouldn't be confused—or miss any of the scintillating details. "But these days, you either have to have money or get the government to pay for it."

The government? This is your human king, yes? He will pay for my temple?

"Uhm."

Therrik snorted. "Why don't you fly that past him, Zirkander? You know you're one of Angulus's favorites."

Right. That hadn't been true even before Ridge had, against his will, flown an enemy sorceress that wanted to kill the king right to the castle.

"Bhrava Saruth, I think *you* should discuss this with the king. Since you helped defend the city from Cofah dragons, I wager he likes you a lot more than he likes me."

You will help me build my temple if your king pays for it, Ridgewalker? You were my first worshipper in this time, you know.

"Worshipper?" Therrik growled, half question, half exclamation of disgust.

"Yes, I haven't forgotten," Ridge said. "I'll find a way to help, and if you really need me to, I'll talk to the king. I'm sure he'll admit Iskandia owes you a few favors."

This is glorious news. I've been missing my old temple, where the clansmen—and clanswomen—brought me such fine offerings. And I blessed them and made them hale and fecund.

"I have no doubt."

I must hunt. Then I can muse upon how to recruit more worshippers to my imminent temple while savoring the succulent chops of a sheep.

Bhrava Saruth wheeled away from them, his body swaying and his tail swishing in something akin to a dance as he flew off.

Ridge looked toward the coastline, shadows darkening the nooks and cliffs as the sun dipped lower over the mountains. A couple more miles, and they would fly past Crazy Canyon. If Colonel Surly weren't in the back, Ridge would have swooped up the winding river and under the arches. Seven gods, he missed being in the air on a daily basis. He'd almost wished Angulus had demoted him after that castle-sorceress incident. Oh, to be a colonel again and leading one of the flier squadrons.

"Why can't a dragon build its *own* temple?" Therrik glared after Bhrava Saruth, who'd turned into a golden speck in the darkening sky as he flew inland. "Or magic one into existence?"

"I imagine he could if he wanted to." And if his ego allowed it. Ridge suspected the dragon believed one's worshippers should handle such prosaic work as building a temple to their god. "But I don't want to suggest it, only to have him plop a massive stone structure down atop the Grand Mason and Bell Hotel. Or any other buildings in the capital on the historic register. It's bad enough some of them were demolished in the various attacks on the city this year."

"Damn, Zirkander. You actually care about the city's architecture?"

Ridge couldn't tell if he was being mocked or if Therrik was genuinely curious. He suspected the former, but who knew? Therrik came out of the nobility. Maybe he had some notion of it being honorable to defend the country—and its architecture.

"Well, I care about the city," Ridge said. "And the people in it. I'd hate to see an innocent baker squashed by a dragon temple falling out of the sky."

Frowning ahead and to the right, Ridge didn't hear Therrik's response. The opening for Crazy Canyon had come into view, the striated rock walls rising more than a thousand feet from sea level. Something large, dark, and unfamiliar hulked in the water at the mouth of the river.

"Is that a ship?" he muttered.

"What?" Therrik yelled over the wind.

Ridge pointed and tilted the flier to offer a better view. They were flying closer to the top of the canyon walls than the sea and were about a mile out from land. But Ridge could tell that *was* a ship in the estuary, even though it lay deep in the shadows, and no lanterns burned on its deck or behind its portholes. Twilight's approach made it difficult to tell, but he thought it was all black, and it reminded him disturbingly of some of the original Cofah ironclads.

His first thought was that it was some old derelict that had floated to Iskandian shores, but it couldn't have floated *up* the river. Even though it was barely inland, it still would have had to go against the current to reach that spot. And for it to stay there, it had to be anchored.

"A Cofah Warstriker 87-C?" Therrik asked. "How in the hells did *that* get there? The last one was decommissioned more than twenty years ago."

Ridge wasn't surprised Therrik knew the exact model. Apparently, he was a student of military history, and some of his interests bisected with those of Professor Lilah, paleontologist and fan of time-traveling historical adventure novels. Ridge, however, liked to pretend they had nothing in common and would soon discover that.

"I'm going to take us closer for a better look." They had already flown past the canyon, with the ship almost hidden from view again, so Ridge nudged the flight stick to bank.

Therrik's hand clamped onto his shoulder.

"I promise not to do any loops or barrel rolls in the canyon," Ridge said. "Unless there are also enemy fliers in there, and we have to fight for our lives." Damn if his blood didn't charge up at the thought of that.

Was it possible that ship was part of some nefarious Cofah mission? Just because it was an old warship didn't mean it didn't have weapons and couldn't do damage. And this was the closest place to the capital one could feasibly dock without entering the harbor the city sprawled along.

What if the Cofah had deliberately chosen an old ironclad, believing Iskandia's magic-wielding allies—specifically, Bhrava Saruth and Sardelle—wouldn't sense the craft skulking about? The country had lighthouses and watchtowers all along its shores, but a ship running dark could conceivably make it to shore without being spotted. And the highway and train tracks crossed over Crazy Canyon nearly ten miles inland, where the terrain was less treacherous. Nobody would have seen this vessel from those bridges.

"Don't fly straight in." Therrik squeezed his shoulder. Hard. "If there are soldiers in that ship, they would see us coming and open fire. If it hasn't been modified, it has six Trokker guns with explosive shells, not to mention whatever rifles and other hand weapons the crew has."

"I don't object to being fired at."

"*I* do. Because you're incapable of dodging fire without twirling around like a damn ballerina in a tutu."

"It's hard for the enemy to target a flier in the middle of evasive maneuvers." Ridge did *not* twirl.

He considered shaking off that hand and taking them into the canyon anyway—he *was* the higher-ranking officer here—but maybe it would be easier to investigate the craft if they snuck up on the crew. Assuming there *was* a crew. Sneaking was hard to do in a flier with the propeller noise audible even over the roar of the ocean.

"Take a circuitous route, and park this thing on the floor of the canyon a couple miles up river. If your tender pilot's feet can't handle a march, I'll go in alone and scout, see if there's a problem."

"My tender feet don't object to marches, but I'm a lot deadlier in the air than on the ground." Ridge had his pistol and utility knife along, since they were part of the military uniform for anyone traveling out of the city, but the sidearm didn't pack nearly the punch of his flier's machine guns. And the knife... He mostly used that to cut cheese.

"You're not going to sink an ironclad with machine guns," Therrik said. "And if I kill the crew, there's no need to sink the ship."

"I thought Lilah spoke to you about not sounding so joyous about the prospect of killing people."

"It's different if they're Cofah scum," Therrik growled, releasing Ridge's shoulder, as if the matter was settled.

Ridge sighed. He hadn't finished his earlier banking maneuver and had flown them north along the coast while discussing the situation. If receiving orders from Therrik could be considered a "discussion."

Not that he had to obey them. He swung them inland, so they could circle back while he debated the options. Sending Therrik in wasn't a *bad* idea, whether to kill enemies or just to gather intel. Both were his job. But Ridge hated losing his offensive firepower. He was just another soldier when he was on the ground, and not one who specialized in making people dead.

Of course, if that was an abandoned derelict, it wouldn't matter. But he knew it wasn't. Logic—and his instincts—told him something fishy was going on down there.

Ridge tapped the communication crystal embedded in his flight stick. "This is General Zirkander. Who's at the desk?"

"Corporal Hannigot, sir," an enthusiastic young voice blurted. One of the new members of the ground crew. He sounded excited by this after-hours contact. Maybe he hadn't expected twelve hours of sheer boredom when he'd been assigned to the night shift.

"There any officers left in the hangar?"

"No, sir. Just me."

"All right. Get a report to..." Ridge snorted. Usually reports would go to *him*. Before he'd been promoted, they'd gone to General Ort, but Ort was the brigade commander now. Was this important enough to bug him about? "General Ort," he decided—it was early enough that nobody would be in bed yet. "I've spotted an old Cofah ironclad anchored in the mouth of Crazy Canyon. Haven't seen any sign of crew yet. No running lights. I'm going in to investigate. No request for backup at this time. I'll report in within two hours."

"Yes, sir. I'm writing it down." The kid sounded even more excited.

"Good. Zirkander, out."

Therrik slapped him on the back of the head.

Ridge scowled over his shoulder. "What was *that* for?"

"You didn't mention me. You didn't think that was important? *I'm* the one who's going to investigate while you stay by your flier and pick lint out of your pocket."

Ridge, somewhat annoyed that he was following—obeying—Therrik's demands already, said, "Colonels don't get to tell generals what to do with their pocket lint. I'm going in to take a look at that ship too."

Therrik's lip curled in distaste. "Can you even walk down a path without stepping on a twig?"

"In the dark? Probably not."

The lip curled further. Maybe that was disgust rather than distaste.

Ridge turned forward and decided he no longer cared about flying straight and keeping Therrik from getting airsick. He swooped low and tilted left and right as he soared above and around the rocky terrain, heading toward Crazy Canyon.

Something between a groan and an aborted upchuck noise came from the back. At least being airsick would shut Therrik up, if only until they landed.

***

Bhrava Saruth? Ridge asked silently, though he doubted the dragon was monitoring his thoughts. Too bad. It would have been nice if he could have gotten some intel from a magical creature that could sense life forms for fifty miles in all directions.

But he didn't receive an answer. Bhrava Saruth was probably still hunting. Or savoring sheep chops.

Ridge wished he had Sardelle along. He would have even settled for Jaxi. In addition to having magic of her own, the soulblade could have glowed softly, enough to illuminate the path he was following down the riverbank. Fortunately, the locals frequented the canyon often, leaving the trails wide and easy to follow. Also, the water flowed past nearby, and Ridge believed its noise would drown out the crunching of twigs, but who knew? Therrik had the ears of a starving hunting dog.

He had disappeared down the trail as soon as Ridge landed the flier on a rock ledge overlooking the water. Though large and hulking, Therrik could indeed sneak effectively. More than effectively. Large cottonwoods rose up from the riverbank, and he slipped through the shadows they provided like a ghost, rarely seen, never heard.

Ridge wondered if there was a point in trailing along. Had Therrik not been such a presumptuous ass, he probably would have decided that staying with the flier was a good idea. Especially since he'd lost fliers he'd parked in this canyon before. The group of witch-hating women who'd been responsible for the deed last time had dissolved, so he shouldn't have to worry about *them*, but what of the Cofah? Or whoever had brought that ironclad up the river?

He decided to turn back the next time he saw Therrik and had the chance to let him know. Not that Therrik would waste time worrying about him if he disappeared. They were only about twenty-five miles north of the city, so it wasn't as if he would be in major trouble if his pilot disappeared. Of course, if he still hoped to reach Dotty's house tonight, he would need Ridge.

"Zirkander," came Therrik's rough whisper from the brush ahead and to the side of the trail. "Get up here."

"I am working on that." Ridge kept his voice low, presuming there was a reason for Therrik's whisper. He thought they still had close to a mile before they reached the ship, but that didn't mean other threats couldn't lurk closer. "Though I was going to turn back. Do you need—"

"You to talk less on a stealth incursion? Yes."

A hand snaked out of the brush, gripped Ridge's arm, and pulled him off the trail.

Ridge's irritation with the man threatened to go from a simmer to a boil.

"I heard two men talking up ahead," Therrik whispered, "and went up to grab them and question them. But they were gone. Might have gone back up the trail to the ship, but it was more like they disappeared. Can you tell if there's any magic being used?"

"No. If you don't see a dragon, sorceress, or soulblade at my side, I've got no way to sense it any more than you do."

"Hells, you'd think sleeping with all those things would rub something off on you."

"I don't sleep with the *dragons*."

"Just the sorceress and the sword?" Therrik sounded amused. "What's she need with you if there's already a sword in bed?"

"You're not this much of an ass to Lilah, are you?" Ridge thought about pointing out that Therrik was chatting a lot for someone worried about silence on a "stealth incursion."

"*She* doesn't irritate me."

"Was that a yes? Or a no?"

"She *also* finds it annoying that our culture deems the antics of a pilot who twirls and flies upside down more newsworthy than discoveries made by historians and scientists or contributions made by teachers and *other* kinds of soldiers."

"Please tell me your mutual dislike of me isn't what drew you two together."

Ridge didn't think his cousin truly disliked him, but they didn't have any common interests, so they'd never had that much reason to get together as adults, at least until Lilah had moved down to the capital this summer, where she'd realized she *did* share interests with Sardelle. It hadn't occurred to Ridge that his cousin might resent his fame. He hadn't honestly considered that it might also be a reason for some of Therrik's resentment. He'd believed that all stemmed from Ridge's association, however inadvertently it had started, with magical beings, including Sardelle. Therrik made his hatred for magic—and those who could wield it—clear at every opportunity.

"It was a starting point," Therrik said.

"Then it sounds like you two owe your joint happiness to me."

Therrik glared at him. Ridge could tell, even in the dark. Ridge decided this wasn't the time to share his revelations, nor did he think Therrik would care about them.

"Also," Ridge said, "I shoot enemies while I twirl. *That's* why it's newsworthy. You got a write-up after slaying that sorceress, remember?"

"One paragraph buried in the middle of the paper. You were on the front page for twirling at a dragon."

"Twirling and *shooting*."

As he recalled, the soulblades Jaxi and Wreltad had helped a lot in that battle too, with fireballs and lightning strikes. He imagined that had made it memorable to any journalists hunkering in the city below and watching the sky. Not that Therrik would want to hear about that.

"Come on," Therrik said, stepping out of the brush. "You'd be more likely to recognize magic than I. Damn, I wish I'd brought Kasandral."

"You probably didn't think you'd need a dragon-slaying and magic-hating sword to visit your girlfriend's mother."

"I *should* have," Therrik said darkly. "I have in the past."

Ridge didn't know what to make of that statement. Judging by the uncharacteristic hunch to Therrik's shoulders, he didn't want to talk about whatever had prompted the comment.

Ridge looked back up the canyon in the direction he'd left his flier. Night had deepened, and he could no longer see it or the area where he'd landed it. He hoped he wasn't making a mistake in continuing after Therrik.

* * *

The hulking ironclad floated black and lifeless in the estuary, anchored out where the water was deep enough for its draw. Full darkness had fallen, and clouds had rolled in from the sea to blot out the stars, but Ridge could make out a rowboat that had been dragged onto the bank, as if to invite tourists to come visit the ironclad. Oh, he supposed the crew could have just left on their own mission, but he found it suspicious.

He and Therrik crouched, their backs against the canyon wall, as they studied the situation. Out on the ship, not a single light burned behind any of the portholes or on the deck, nor was there any sign of life.

After Therrik's warning, Ridge had been keeping an eye out for anything that hinted of magic, but he had never heard the voices. Had he been with some young private, he might have thought his colleague had imagined them, or mistaken the rustling grasses for people talking, but Therrik was far too experienced for that.

"It certainly appears abandoned," Ridge whispered.

"Someone anchored it there, and it couldn't have been that long ago."

"No," Ridge agreed. "Tiger Squadron ran a patrol up the coast north of the city yesterday. They would have noticed this."

The wind shifted, blowing in from the sea, and a faint clanking reached Ridge's ears, like someone rattling a chain. Or perhaps dragging it across a metal deck.

"You hear that?" Therrik asked.

"Yes."

A scrape punctuated the clanks. Definitely like something being dragged. Ridge imagined someone locked in a cell, walking around, ankles shackled and chained to an iron ball.

"*Someone* is on board," Therrik said.

"Or something."

"Let's take a look. Might be someone we can question." Therrik cracked his knuckles. His idea of questioning, no doubt, involved brute force.

"I'll stay here," Ridge said.

"To catalog your pocket lint?"

"In case you get in trouble and need to be rescued."

"You? Rescue me? Please." Therrik headed for the boat. "If you're afraid, just say so."

The way those chains kept clinking *was* eerie, but Ridge wanted to stay behind for the same reason he questioned leaving the flier. This could all be a trap.

"Afraid? I've survived half a dozen crashes, flown into hundreds of battles, and stared into the eyes of enemies firing machine guns at me. Some derelict ship that barely floats doesn't worry me."

"If you say so, Zirkander." Therrik picked up a couple of oars in the rowboat, but paused before stepping in, cocking his head to listen to something upriver.

The murmur of voices rose over the breeze, coming from the direction of the trail. It sounded like two men talking in loud whispers.

Therrik dropped the oars and sprinted past Ridge toward the noise. Ridge pulled out his pistol and followed more slowly. And warily. If there were only two men, Therrik could handle them without his help, but once again, his instincts twanged, and he worried they were being set up for something.

In the darkness, Ridge soon lost sight of Therrik. He walked to where he judged the voices had come from and squatted in the tall grass so he would be harder for someone to see. Then he listened, expecting to hear someone else rustling around nearby. At the least, he expected to hear Therrik, but the colonel must have shifted into stealth mode again.

Several minutes passed before a soft grumble came from behind him. "That you, Zirkander?"

Ridge stood, assuming the question meant Therrik hadn't found the men. "Yes. And stop using my name, will you?"

If there were Cofah infiltrators out here, Ridge didn't want them knowing who was wandering up and down the riverbank. The entire Cofah empire would celebrate his death, he had no doubt. Alas, there was little point in inviting Therrik to use his first name, as it was almost as well-known as his last. Why couldn't his father have named him something ordinary?

"What should I call you? General Fool? I seem to remember you suggesting that once."

"*Sir* would be appropriate."

"Far less appealing." Therrik stepped back out on the trail. "I didn't find anyone."

"You can't find any tracks?"

"In the dark? No."

They should have brought a lantern, but Ridge hadn't anticipated trouble on such a short flight, certainly not a stroll through a canyon on foot. Even if some mechanical failure had forced them to land, the flier's power crystal would have provided enough light to see while doing repairs.

"I'm going out to the ship to question whoever is clanking chains out there," Therrik growled and stomped back down the trail, making no move to be silent now. Maybe he hoped someone would leap out and challenge him.

But they made it back to the rowboat without seeing anyone. Therrik grabbed the oars again and shoved the boat into the water.

Ridge sighed and climbed in. Therrik's inability to find the source of those voices made him suspect that magic might indeed be involved. He was fairly sure Therrik taught wilderness survival and tracking classes to the infantry boys. Nobody should have eluded him, not by mundane means.

Even though Ridge wasn't an expert on magic, he knew more than Therrik. He might spot some being used on the ironclad.

"Are you feeling braver?" Therrik asked, shoving the boat away from the bank and jumping in. It rocked mightily before his bulk settled onto a seat. "Or were you afraid your throat would be slit if you stayed behind by yourself?"

"It's true. My knees started shaking when I contemplated

being away from your safe and protective presence." Ridge grabbed an oar. The faster they checked out the ironclad and got back to the flier, the better.

"Usually, only women say things like that to me."

"I'll bet a hundred nucros Lilah has never said anything like that to you."

"No, she can take care of herself."

Ridge ignored the implication that he couldn't and rowed. The clanking of chains drifted over the roar of the ocean again, and Therrik fell silent.

They reached the side of the ironclad and found a rope ladder dangling down to the surface. Therrik improvised a way to tie the rowboat to the end of it, then skimmed up the rungs without waiting to consult Ridge.

Ridge had come out in the hope of keeping Therrik from stepping on magical booby traps. Thus, he decided it would be immature of him to fantasize about that happening. And about Therrik being flung a hundred feet to land in one of those cottonwoods.

When Ridge reached the top of the ladder, he spotted Therrik disappearing into the wheelhouse on the upper deck in the bow of the vessel.

More soft clanks sounded, followed by the dragging noise. Ridge thought it came from below decks somewhere, not from the wheelhouse. Maybe Therrik was checking likely places to find crew members before looking for a way down.

Ridge walked toward midship where the dark opening of the ship's cargo hold yawned open. There should have been double doors covering it, but they appeared to have been removed. He crouched at the edge and peered inside, but didn't see or hear anything in the hold. But with the moon and stars behind the clouds, a platoon could have been crouching down there, and he wouldn't have spotted them.

"Hold empty?" Therrik asked, jogging up to look in.

"I think so."

"Nobody in navigation, and the clinks weren't coming from the stairs leading down to crew quarters." Therrik pointed aft. "The stairs to the boiler room and the brig will be back there."

Since Therrik had named the specific model of the vessel, Ridge wasn't surprised he knew the layout. They crossed the deck, and Therrik opened a rusty door that creaked when it moved. The clinking sounds grew louder, drifting up a stairwell from below. And had that been a faint moan? It was hard to tell over the omnipresent roar of the ocean.

Therrik headed straight down the steps. Ridge glanced toward the riverbank, thinking of those other voices and again feeling nervous about having left the flier behind. He wasn't even sure why he'd come out here. Yes, he knew more about magic, but so what? What did he care if Therrik got himself blown up in some magical booby trap? Other than it might upset Lilah. He didn't want to have to fly back to the city and explain to her that Therrik had died while with him.

Sighing again, Ridge followed him down the dark stairwell, feeling his way to the lower decks. The clinks grew louder as they descended and walked through a doorway, the heavy metal hatch standing open. Ridge had the sense of a cavernous space ahead of them. The boiler room? There were portholes on the starboard side of the hull, the blackness slightly less absolute beyond their glass.

Exploring down here without a lantern was ridiculous. Ridge wished he had thought to pry the communication crystal from his cockpit. When it was thumbed on, it provided a small amount of light.

Ridge stopped, listening to the clinks and dragging noises. They came from ahead and to the left. From one of the boilers? Or maybe the engine room was in that direction?

A soft thud came from ahead of him, from the same direction as the clinking. Ridge paused, his pistol in hand again.

"Crap," Therrik said.

"Not literal, I hope."

"I think I stepped on a—"

A squeal came from behind Ridge. He whirled, but too late to do anything. The heavy metal hatch clanged shut, and a thud followed, like a bar falling into place. It had an ominous finality to it.

"—trip wire," Therrik growled. "And what the hells is that?"

His voice was muted, as if he had gone behind something. Maybe one of the boilers.

More concerned about the hatch than whatever Therrik saw, Ridge ran back to it. He groped in the darkness, finding the latch and tugging.

"We're locked in," Ridge said.

A clang rang out from Therrik's direction.

"Are you fighting something?" Ridge turned, but he didn't dare aim his pistol in the dark.

"I kicked a boiler."

"Why?"

"Because I'm *pissed*, Zirkander." Therrik stomped into view, a soft yellow light in his hand illuminating his snarling face. He opened his palm, revealing a familiar glowing gem. "Is this one of your communication crystals?"

"Yes." Ridge stared at it, puzzled. He'd just been thinking of the one in his flier, but that had to be one from a different flier. What would it be doing here?

"Those clanks were coming from it. Whoever is on the other end is making the noise. And probably *listening* to us, damn it. How do I turn it off?"

Ridge mouthed an, "Oh," and came forward, realization sinking in. It *had* been a trap. Someone had been relying on their curiosity to draw them in. And was there also a communication crystal hidden in the grass somewhere on the riverbank? Maybe someone had put it in a pouch and thrown dirt over it so Therrik wouldn't see the light. He'd only heard voices and not guessed someone a mile away—or potentially *dozens* of miles away—was transmitting them.

Ridge took the crystal and tapped his thumb on the long, flat side. It went dark, working exactly like the communication crystals in the fliers. Because it *was* one. He rolled it around in his hand and contemplated how it could have gotten here. It wasn't as if the military sold them. Sardelle had been the one to make them several months ago, a few master controllers for the desks in the hangar offices around the country and one crystal for each flier in the various squadrons in the battalion. There weren't many extras floating around.

"The blown-up fliers," he said.

"What?" Therrik demanded.

"We lost a few fliers last spring when Angulus was kidnapped and *you* were in charge of the flier battalion. When my team got back from our mission in Cofahre, we landed in Crazy Canyon because we weren't sure what was going on in the city. And those fanatical women working with the queen blew them up. Later, we came back to salvage the parts, but the power crystals had been stolen. And, now that I think about it, I don't think the communication crystals were recovered, either." Ridge was surprised that whoever had set up this ruse had figured out how to switch them to the backup channel so the base and all the other fliers in the area wouldn't hear their transmissions. It wasn't as if the crystals had instructions printed on them.

"Nice story, Zirkander. Now move so I can get us out of here. Someone's probably stealing more of your magical flier crystals right now while we're trapped."

Therrik pushed past him and strode to the hatch.

"I knew I should have stayed back there," Ridge said, closing a fist around the crystal. "Someone could be stealing the entire *flier*."

Was that what all this had been? Some ruse to aid with theft?

Grunts and huffs of breath came from the hatch. Therrik using his big muscles to try to force it open.

Ridge doubted that would work. He ran toward one of the three portholes visible high on the hull, cursing when he banged against a crate or bin in the dark. His hand came down on the open top, on rocks inside. No, probably coal for the fire boxes. It felt damp, and he doubted it would burn. It had probably been there for years, if not decades.

As Ridge reached the first porthole, Therrik's grunts stopped. He must have decided the hatch wouldn't budge. The thuds of boots on the metal deck sounded as he searched for other exits.

The portholes all faced the side opposite of the rowboat and the bank where Ridge had landed the flier. Oh, well. He'd still go out that way if he could. Better than spending the night in a boiler room with Therrik.

Or *more* than the night. Who knew how long it would be until someone came looking for them? And how embarrassing would it be to have to be rescued by a couple of lieutenants from his own unit?

Ridge patted around the porthole, found the latch, and twisted it. He didn't know if Therrik could wedge his body through the opening, but he thought he could. Assuming he could get it open. The handle unfastened, but the porthole cover wouldn't open. A hardened lumpy substance covered the seam. He scraped at it with a nail, broke a tiny piece off, and brought it to his nose.

The resiny scent reminded him of pine pitch. Maybe it *was* pine pitch. With something added to harden it.

Ridge ran to the other portholes and found they'd been treated in a similar manner.

"The other two hatches are locked too," Therrik said. "They're solid iron, probably with bars across them on the other side."

"There's a bin of coal over there if you want to figure out a way to blow open a hatch."

Therrik grunted. "Coal is flammable, not explosive. Unless you're talking about coal dust. I could pulverize some coal, but we'd be more likely to blow ourselves up with dust floating in the air."

"I bet Captain Kaika would be able to find something to blow up in here."

"How about I blow up your head? Those portholes locked?"

"Yes." Ridge returned to the coal bin, debating if he could make a portable fire somehow, then take it over to melt the pitch.

The sound of glass shattering made him jump a few feet. He whirled as Therrik smashed a crowbar—or an improvised crowbar—against one of the portholes.

"Huh," Ridge said. "I always figured it would take a cannonball to break the glass in a porthole."

"You've got *me*. It's almost the same thing." Therrik slammed the end of his bar into the glass, shattering it further. He knocked pieces out of the frame, sending shards tinkling to the deck.

"I suppose those hulking muscles have to be good for something."

"I can't decide if your constant contemplation of my muscles means you're envious of me or attracted to me." Therrik smashed more glass free and dropped his crowbar.

"Which would you find more alarming?"

"The latter."

"So alarming that you would avoid me for the rest of your career?" Ridge probably shouldn't have sounded hopeful as he said that. "Because I might be able to rustle up an attraction if that was the result."

"I *try* to avoid you. Trust me."

Therrik tugged his shirt off, laid it over the frame, and tried to tug himself up and through. His head fit, but his shoulders were too broad, no matter how much he convoluted himself. "Damn it."

"Let me try. Pilots have to be lean and light, you know."

"Scrawny is the word the elite troops use for you people."

Therrik crouched, offering his cupped hands to give Ridge a boost. Only he would think nothing of helping a man and insulting him at the same time.

Ridge holstered his pistol, stepped in his grip, and pulled himself through the porthole. Tiny broken shards of glass still in the frame dug at him through his uniform, but he gritted his teeth. At least Therrik's shirt kept most of the prongs from stabbing him in the butt when he paused to consider his options. Unfortunately, there was only one option. The railing for the deck was too high to reach, and there was nothing on the hull to climb.

"I hadn't been planning to take a swim tonight," Ridge lamented.

Therrik shoved him the rest of the way out.

Ridge tumbled into the icy water with a squawk of alarm.

"Therrik!" he sputtered as soon as his head broke the surface. "You can't throw *generals* out the window."

"Yeah, you can. It's called defenestration. Now swim around, climb back up here, and let me out."

Ridge's next sputter involved a lot more cursing, but he did start swimming, more because he wanted to check on his flier than because he wanted to unlock Therrik. The bowels of an ironclad seemed like an excellent place for him to spend the night.

The current tugged at Ridge, threatening to sweep him out to sea. His uniform and boots weighed him down, making the swim even harder, especially when he paddled around the back end of the ironclad to swim toward the ladder on the far side. He thought he spotted a light upriver, on the side where he'd parked his flier. Was someone snooping around it even now? Whoever had set up this lovely trap?

Ridge was tempted to angle straight toward the bank, thinking he could come back once he had his flier—he could land it right on the deck—but he made himself head for the ladder. He doubted the bullets in his pistol would fire after being doused in the river, so he might need Therrik's help if he had to beat enemies into submission.

He flew up the rungs, racing across the deck and down to the boiler room. From the outside, the bar blocking the hatch was easy to lift. As soon as he shoved it up, Therrik thrust the door open, almost smashing Ridge against the wall. He wore his shirt again, not noticeably bothered by whatever glass shards stuck out of the fabric. He probably liked a daily dose of discomfort.

"Good work," Therrik said.

Ridge almost fell over. It wasn't exactly a thank-you, but it was more than he'd expected to get.

Not sure how to answer it, Ridge only said, "I saw a light up the river."

"Figures," Therrik grunted and charged up the stairs.

Instead of angling toward the ladder and the rowboat, he ran straight across the deck, jumped to the railing, and sprang off into the night. He landed halfway to the bank, swimming before he hit the water.

"That man is a loon," Ridge announced.

Unfortunately, he doubted the rowboat would be any faster, especially not with only him rowing. He ran for the railing and emulated Therrik's move. He was already wet, so it hardly mattered if he went for another swim.

"Hurry up, Zirkander," Therrik called back as soon as Ridge splashed down. "I saw the light too."

Hoping it wasn't already too late, Ridge swam as fast as he could, driven by the vision of standing in front of General Ort's desk and scuffing his soggy boots on the carpet as he explained how he'd managed to lose a flier—and one of the valuable power crystals—only twenty-five miles from the city. Ridge was used to being chewed out by superior officers, albeit less so now that he was a general, but not for ineptitude.

Not surprisingly, Therrik reached the bank first, but Ridge was right behind him. When he could touch the bottom, the silt threatened to tug his boots off, but he gritted his teeth and plowed through it.

As Ridge reached solid ground, his breaths coming in exhausted pants, a voice spoke into his mind.

Greetings, mate of my high priestess!

I don't have time to talk about temples right now, Bhrava Saruth, Ridge thought back.

Therrik had already taken off down the path. Ridge, his sodden uniform and flight jacket seeming to weigh twenty pounds as they clung to him, ran after him.

Did you know that strange men are examining your flying contraption? One is attempting to remove the light fixture.

The power crystal? Damn it. Are you there now? Can you stop them?

Of course I can stop them. I am the god, Bhrava Saruth!

Good. Please do so. Thank you!

Therrik outpaced Ridge, but Ridge knew from the startled exclamation of surprise when Therrik came upon the dragon. He just hoped the flier was still in one piece.

Vibrant yellow light grew visible through the leaves of the cottonwoods. Was all that from the power crystal? Those thieves hadn't succeeded in yanking it out, had they?

"Zirkander," came Therrik's growl. "What is this?"

Panting, Ridge ran out of the trees and onto the bare rocky spot where he'd landed. His flier was still there—thank the seven gods—and Bhrava Saruth's large scaled form dwarfed it. His wings were outstretched, his sword-like fangs bared, and for a moment, Ridge forgot this was the affable dragon that kept asking him for a temple.

Two men dangled in the air in front of Bhrava Saruth's reptilian snout, the yellow light showing the terror on their faces. One was blubbering—pleading for his life. The other simply swore and thrashed about in the air, as if he could escape if he could just find the right invisible opponent to punch.

The light was coming from the flier, the power crystal in the cockpit, but it glowed much more strongly than usual.

"Are you doing that, Bhrava Saruth?" Ridge asked as soon as he caught his breath. He waved toward the cockpit. "Or is something wrong?"

He imagined it somehow overloading and exploding.

I have merely amplified its light so these inferior beings can see their folly.

"Were you two dunderheads attempting to steal a military flier?" Therrik demanded, glowering up at the men dangling in midair.

"No," one blurted. "We were just looking!"

This human lies, Ridgewalker, Bhrava Saruth announced. *They are highwaymen who have concocted a most nefarious plan to lure sailing ships and travelers to investigate the derelict vessel they found and tugged into the estuary. When innocent people are examining the ship, these thieves circle back and steal their ships or steam carriages. Or in this case, they planned to take a valuable component in your flying machine.*

"Is he reading their minds?" Therrik asked Ridge. "Or was he watching?"

"Reading their minds, I think," Ridge said, though he could imagine the dragon atop one of the canyon's arches, snacking on sheep and watching everything play out below.

"I don't know if I should find that less alarming... or not."

"I don't either." Ridge rubbed his face.

How humbling to think that if not for Bhrava Saruth's help, he might have lost his flier, or at least the crystal. All because he'd let Therrik get to him. He never should have left the flier. So much for increasing his maturity level.

What shall I do with these humans? Bhrava Saruth asked, causing the men dangling in the air to float out over the river. *Since they attempted to steal from my high priestess's mate, they are not worthy to worship me.*

"Few are," Ridge said.

True, but a god does not demand perfection. I would accept wayward thieves as worshippers if they had brought me the appropriate offerings.

"I can bring offerings," one man blurted.

And hadn't plotted against my high priestess's mate.

The man's shoulders slumped, inasmuch as they could while he hung ten feet in the air. His buddy looked over at Ridge and Therrik, as if to ask which one of them held the lofty designation of high priestess's mate. Therrik promptly pointed at Ridge.

"Can you help us get them to Portsnell, Bhrava Saruth?" Ridge asked. "I have a feeling they may be part of a larger operation and also that they're known criminals that the police would like to get their hands on. Masterminds, no doubt."

Or so he would like to hope. Because it would be embarrassing if he and Therrik, military officers with more than forty years of experience between them, had been outsmarted by bumbling, neophyte thieves.

Ridge expected Therrik to grunt or snort and point out that the men didn't look like masterminds. But he only crossed his arms over his chest and glared. Maybe he also hoped they had been outsmarted by criminal geniuses.

I can transport them, Bhrava Saruth said, *while we discuss how you will approach the king to ask for money for the construction of my temple.*

"I guess I can't object to that," Ridge said.

I do look forward to having a meeting place where my worshippers can find me again.

"You ready to go, Therrik?"

"More than ready."

***

WANTED: HIGHWAY ROBBERS

Ridge considered the sign by the light of a lamppost while adjusting his damp clothes, trying to make them less uncomfortable. The wanted posters were nailed to a bulletin board on the way in to town, alongside a map and interesting historical facts about Portsnell. The faces drawn in black ink on the posters looked very familiar.

"I do believe that's you," Ridge said to the man Therrik gripped.

Ridge was leading the other man on a rope that Bhrava Saruth had magically woven from the tall roadside grass. Ridge had landed his flier half a mile outside the town walls, promising the dragon they could manage the prisoners that had been riding on his back, magically forced to stay there without falling—or leaping—the rest of the way without assistance. Ridge hadn't wanted Bhrava Saruth to fly close enough to be noticed by Portsnell's inhabitants. People living in the capital had grown somewhat accustomed to seeing a gold dragon soaring overhead, but he had no idea what the locals here would think of it.

"Prove it," the man said.

"I don't have to. We'll drop you off at the police office, which, if memory serves, is located right over there. *They* can prove it."

The man's mouth opened again, but Therrik shoved him, almost hard enough to knock him to his knees, and whatever insolence had been about to come out remained inside.

He and Ridge marched their prisoners to the police office, where a surprised young man on the night shift checked in the highway robbers and locked them in a cell for his superiors to question the next day.

"There's a five hundred nucro reward for those two, General Zirkander," the young officer informed them, recognizing Ridge without glancing at his nametag.

"That's not necessary," Therrik blurted before Ridge could open his mouth.

Ridge had intended to say something similar, however.

The officer looked at him curiously. "General?"

"There's a regulation specifically forbidding military officers from being compensated for doing their duty," Ridge said, patting the man on the shoulder. "If it'll save you some paperwork, you needn't even mention that we were the ones to bring in the thieves."

"Got that right," Therrik muttered and strode for the door, clearly not interested in receiving credit for their admittedly bumbling detainment of the criminals.

"If you say so, sirs." The officer scratched his head, but turned the gesture into an upraised hand. "Wait, let me at least reward you with something I can't enjoy while on duty."

Ridge arched his eyebrows.

The officer drew a stoneware bottle out from under the counter. "It's vodka infused with peaches. The captain's brother runs the local distillery, so we get free spirits for our after-hours office parties. We had a get-together earlier this evening."

Ridge accepted the bottle, swishing the liquid around. It was only about a fourth full, so he decided he could accept it as a gesture from one king's officer to another without feeling it was compensation. "Thank you."

"Least I could do for the man who keeps dragons, airship pirates, and Cofah invaders out of the sky."

Ridge glanced toward the door, certain Therrik would have a snide comment if he heard him getting praised, but he'd disappeared outside. Good. Ridge offered the officer a lazy salute and strolled out after him.

Therrik waited on the stoop. "You convince him not to record anything?"

"I believe so."

"Good. I'd rather there not be any record of our misadventure." Therrik closed the door firmly behind them. "Or the fact that we would have been walking back if your guard dragon hadn't been keeping an eye on the flier. I suppose *you'll* have to file a report, especially since you called back to the fort." From his tone, it was clear Therrik didn't want Ridge to file that report.

Ridge snorted, amused by his discomfort. Oh, he thought their detour was embarrassing, too, but he wasn't an elite troops soldier, so he didn't have to worry about living up to a reputation as a deadly killer who wasn't to be crossed. Not unless he was in the air.

"I'll need to file a report, yes," Ridge said, "but I don't think there's a need to mention anything other than that we found a derelict ship and apprehended a couple of thieves."

"You don't need to explain that your *dragon* helped?"

"There's not a field on the form for dragons."

Therrik stared at him. Ridge didn't truly think he would object—not when he was the one who wanted to save face. But he didn't expect what came next. Therrik threw back his head and laughed.

Ridge stepped away, more alarmed by the gesture than pleased by it. He'd never heard Therrik laugh, and he feared it was a sign of imminent insanity.

"Not a field for dragons," Therrik said, when he stopped laughing. "Some clerk was shortsighted in assembling those papers."

"I'm fairly certain Form DDIA-1079 came from a different time." Ridge doubted the report templates had been changed in a hundred years. Maybe longer. "A less dragon-filled time."

"The good old days."

"If not for a dragon, my flier would have been stolen, and we'd be walking back to the capital right now."

"Don't remind me." Therrik pointed to the bottle. "What's that?"

"Peach vodka, I'm told."

"Peach? Who would put fruit in a vodka? That's sissy."

"Someone who owns a distillery and likes to play around." Ridge unstoppered the bottle and sniffed. The aroma wasn't strong, but he found it pleasant. Curious, he took a sip. "It's actually good."

"Sissy."

Ridge didn't ask for clarification about whether that referred to the drink or to him. He didn't want to know. "Does that mean I can have it all?"

"Seven gods, no. You're flying me back tonight. It's bad enough riding with you when you're sober." Therrik snatched the bottle from him.

Ridge snorted. He hadn't planned to pour it all down his gullet before climbing back into his flier.

Therrik sniffed it dubiously, then took a swig.

"Not bad, right?"

"It's horrible." Therrik took another swig.

"Obviously."

"It's still mostly alcohol. It'll take the edge off."

"The edge off spending the evening with me?"

"That too." Therrik waved toward the street. "Which way to Dotty's house?"

"Follow me." As Ridge led the way, he realized Therrik must have been referring to meeting Lilah's mother. Was he actually nervous about that? Worried he wouldn't make a good impression?

Therrik grumbled something to himself, squeezed water out of the hem of his uniform jacket, and drank from the bottle again.

Ridge trusted he would only "take the edge off" and not drink enough to arrive on his Aunt Dotty's doorstep smashed.

He wondered if Dotty would even be awake when they arrived. When they turned down a new street and walked under a clocktower, he was surprised that it hadn't yet chimed eight. He could hardly believe their misadventure had only put them a little over an hour behind schedule.

"To answer your earlier question," Therrik said as they walked along, wet and chafing, "I am not an ass to Lilah."

Ridge glanced at Therrik, startled by the statement. Had he been thinking about that all night? Wanting to make sure to clear up any doubt? If so, Ridge was surprised Therrik cared enough about what he thought to bother. Maybe the alcohol was affecting him.

"Glad to hear it," Ridge said.

Therrik sipped from the bottle—he'd shifted from swigs to sips, perhaps also wanting to ensure he didn't arrive smashed.

"She makes me want to be a better man," he said quietly.

"Is it working?" Ridge asked.

As soon as the words came out, he realized Therrik would consider them flippant. Why couldn't he ever keep himself from goading the man?

Fortunately, the alcohol seemed to be mellowing Therrik, and he didn't respond with his typical glare. If Ridge had known vodka had that effect on him, he would have tried to get the colonel drunk every time they'd met.

"I didn't kill anybody tonight," Therrik said.

"Clear progress."

Therrik's grunt sounded agreeable.

They walked in silence through the residential neighborhood, and Ridge wondered if he should change his mind about Therrik's relationship with Lilah. At the least, he probably shouldn't try to stand in the way of it.

As they turned down the tree-lined street that Dotty lived on, Ridge dug into his pocket. Glad taffy was largely waterproof, he held the bag out toward Therrik.

"What's that?"

"Candy. I doubt offering Aunt Dotty alcohol will do anything to warm her up to you, but she adores taffy."

"You're saying I need to ply her with gifts to make her like me?"

"Hells, Therrik, you need to ply *everyone* with gifts if you want them to like you. You've got the charm of a scouring pad."

Therrik's eyes narrowed, but he took the bag of taffy and stuck it in his pocket. "You know people only like *you* because you twirl at dragons, right?"

"Because I twirl *and* shoot them."

"Damn coddled pilots," Therrik grumbled.

THE END

Printed in Poland
by Amazon Fulfillment
Poland Sp. z o.o., Wrocław